THE SOVIET CAGE

THE SOVIET CAGE

Anti-Semitism in Russia

WILLIAM KOREY

The Viking Press || *New York*

To Esther

Acknowledgment is made to Frederick A. Praeger
for portions of Chapters 2 and 3, which
originally appeared as
"The Legal Position of the Jewish Community of the Soviet Union,"
by William Korey, in *Ethnic Minorities in the Soviet Union,*
ed. Erich Goldhagen, © 1968
Frederick A. Praeger, Inc., New York.
Reprinted by permission.

Contents

Introduction

It was the night before Christmas, 1970, when a news flash from Leningrad was to stir the Western world, preparing for the holiday season of good will, into what was probably the most massive international demonstration against a court verdict since the twenties, when the Sacco–Vanzetti decision triggered a vast protest movement in the West.* The terse dispatch from Tass, the official Soviet news agency, announced that two Soviet Jews, Eduard Kuznetsov and Mark Dymshits, had been sentenced to death for preparing an airplane hijacking that was never consummated. Nine other members of the "criminal group" were to serve long prison terms.

A headline in the *Times* of London on December 28 summarized the mood of those days: "World Condemns Jews' Sentences." Giant crowds, Jews and non-Jews alike, crossing the lines of ideology, had taken to the streets in the capitals and major cities of Western Europe, Australia, North America, and South America in protest marches and demonstrations. Speaking on behalf of the American labor movement, George Meany appealed to the Nixon Administration to take "every diplomatic, political, and economic measure to have the Soviet Union rescind its savage verdict." The Communist-led General Confederation of Labor of France deplored "the conditions of the Leningrad trial sentence, whose gravity seems out of keeping with the grounds of the accusation." The general secretary of the British Labour Party warned the Soviet Government "not to make the trials of alleged hijackers the starting point for further acts of discrimination and repression against Soviet Jews." Symp-

* In the intervening years, only the public reaction to the verdict in the Rosenberg case of the early fifties may have approached the intensity of the Sacco–Vanzetti protest movement.

tomatic of labor's anger was the decision of the leftist dockworkers in Genoa, Italy, to hold a twenty-hour boycott of Soviet ships.

Christian religious bodies, stunned by the Leningrad court's verdict, delivered on the eve of Christmas, reacted with horror. Pope Paul VI, referring to "certain judicial proceedings" as well as to wars and unrest, commented to his weekly general audience at the Vatican: "This is not peace; this is not civilization; this is not Christianity." Responding to "numerous appeals some from highly qualified sources"—according to the Vatican newspaper, *L'Osservatore Romano*—the Pope appealed to Soviet authorities to halt the executions. Protestant leaders also asked for clemency. Characteristic was the action of the officers of the British Council of Churches, who cabled the head of the foreign relations department of the Russian Orthodox Church in Moscow asking him to intercede with the Kremlin on behalf of the convicted. A leading spokesman of American Protestantism, the Right Reverend J. Brooke Mosely, President of Union Theological Seminary, denounced the trial as "another expression of official anti-Semitism."

International organizations joined in the outcry. The International Commission of Jurists, based in Geneva, cabled the Supreme Soviet asking for clemency "in view of the tragic events suffered by Jewish people in our time." The Socialist International sent the following from its headquarters in London: "The death and heavy prison sentences in the trial of eleven citizens of the USSR have shocked the entire civilized world coming as they do at a time when the message of humanity is one of 'goodwill to all men, irrespective of creed, color or race.'" Intellectuals, writers, artists, professors, and scientists, including numerous Nobel Prize winners from various countries, added their voices to the chorus of protests. The telegraph offices in Moscow must have been swamped by the thousands of cables that poured in.

The principal Communist Parties in the West broke ranks with their Soviet colleagues and associated themselves with the vast protest movement. An Italian Party delegation, on the day the sentences were announced, lodged an official note of protest with the Soviet Embassy in Rome deploring the Leningrad verdict. The head of the Party fraction in the Italian Senate, Umberto Terracini, asked at a meeting of jurists in Rome: "Did the Leningrad trial correspond to Socialist, or even Soviet, legality? My answer is no. It represents a new, clamorous, and deplorable violation of Soviet legality." The headline in the Party organ, *L'Unità,* on December 27 said of the sentences: "An Incomprehensible Judgment."

The more docile French Communist Party spoke up vigorously through its organ, *L'Humanité*: ". . . we don't believe that an abortive attempt [at hijacking] should be penalized by a death sentence which we hope—and we say it again—will not be applied. It is almost unnecessary to say that French Communists, who respect a German Jew named Karl Marx, are resolutely against anti-Semitism, which is a stupidity and a degradation." The organ of the British Communist Party, the *Morning Star,* expressed "grave concern" about the trial and recommended that the death sentences be commuted. The American Communist Party took the same position, with its newspaper, the *Daily World,* commenting that "the interests of mankind will be served if . . . the Soviet authorities commute the two death sentences." The Marxist president of Chile, Dr. Salvador Allende Gossens, appealed to the Soviet Union to be lenient as a "highly humanitarian gesture."

Governments rarely intervene formally on human rights issues within the jurisdiction of other governments. But now, under the massive pressure of local public opinion and the exhortations of legislators, Western governments took the unique step of addressing appeals, directly or indirectly, to the Soviet authorities on the Leningrad case. The Belgian Government, intervening "as the interpreter of public opinion in Belgium," asked for commutation of the death sentence. The Danish and Norwegian prime ministers did the same. The Italian Government instructed its ambassador in Moscow to draw Soviet attention to the strength of Italian public feeling on the matter. The French Government, through its ambassador in the USSR, urged the Soviet authorities to grant clemency to the condemned. The president of Switzerland declared that the death sentences had "dismayed" the Swiss people and that his government "shares the dismay of our people and hopes that the appeals for clemency for the sentenced men and for the respect of human rights will be heard." The Australian prime minister called upon the UN secretary-general to use his influence with the Soviet Union, while other national leaders, including those in the United States, Canada, and the Federal Republic of Germany, made their appeals felt in a more discreet manner through diplomatic channels.

Editorials in the leading press organs of the West went beyond protest and appeals to examine the significance of the trial and its verdict. Universally, they found that the Leningrad case had marked a watershed in the evolution of official anti-Semitism in the USSR. The *New York Times,* on December 26, stated:

> This trial would not have received world attention nor would it have ended with death sentences if it were simply an ordinary criminal proceeding. On the contrary, this was one of the most important political trials held in the Soviet Union since World War II. The real defendants in the court were not the handful of accused, but the tens of thousands of Soviet Jews who have courageously demanded the right to emigrate to Israel. The real purposes of the death sentences is not to punish individual criminals, but to terrorize Soviet Jews.

Dagens Nyheter of Stockholm, on December 27, observed: "Anti-Semitism and anti-Zionism in an unholy alliance—that is the background of the verdicts in Leningrad." The *Times* of London, on December 28, commented that the character of the Soviet trial and verdict has stimulated "suspicions of anti-semitism," made ever more "ominous" by reports of planned trials of Jews to be held in Leningrad, Riga, and Kishinev. *Le Monde* of Paris, on December 30, noted: "What was until last week the 'Leningrad affair' is becoming a critical trial of Soviet anti-Semitism."

It was precisely because the Leningrad case was "one of the most important political trials" in the USSR since 1945 and was a "critical" measure of Soviet anti-Semitism that it warrants close study. Necessarily, such a study must include analysis of three subsequent trials of Soviet Jews, held in May and June, 1971, in Leningrad, Riga, and Kishinev, for they were, in purpose and character, intimately related to the Leningrad trial of December, 1970.

Analysis is inevitably limited by the virtually closed character of these trials. No Western observers or correspondents were allowed into the courtroom. And no official transcripts of the entire proceedings were published. Reportage of the trials was restricted to official Soviet handouts transmitted through the Tass and Novosti press agencies or printed in highly selective stories in a few Soviet newspapers. However, with the ending of each of the trials, a considerable amount of *samizdat* (i.e., underground, "self"-produced) material, based upon eyewitness accounts of the various proceedings, has become available in the West. Such material, together with the official reportage, as well as, in some cases, information obtained by Western correspondents in Moscow, enable the student to develop a fairly broad picture of what transpired in the courtrooms. Careful examination of these sources also provides insights into the purposes of the trials' architects.

No claim can, of course, be made for completeness or total accuracy of the analysis. Only when the full stenographic transcripts of the trials are made available—an inconceivable possibility in the foreseeable future—can a full and precise presentation be drawn. In the meantime, the historian of the trials must be guided by the discipline of his craft in attempting to provide as complete and truthful an account of them as possible under the circumstances. The results of the research on the trials are to be found in Chapters 11 through 13.

The anti-Semitic judicial processes of 1970–71 in the USSR can be understood only in the context of Soviet policy toward Jews. Jean-Paul Sartre underscored this point in an address on January 7, 1971, before 3,000 persons at the Mutualité in Paris. Remarking that the Leningrad trial "was openly anti-Semitic," the French philosopher emphasized that "it is imperative to understand" why the Soviet regime decided "to mount" the judicial processes against Jews. Sartre summed up an explanation in one sentence. "The basic reason is that the situation of the Jews in the Soviet Union is a major problem for Soviet society, one which the bureaucracy in power has no other way of resolving." If insightful, Sartre's explanation nonetheless leaves the evidence to be placed before the bar of history.

The author of this book has been accumulating data on the subject of the Soviet Jewish problem for over a decade. Papers based upon some of this data have been presented before several scholarly bodies, including the Brandeis University "Conference on the State of Ethnic Minorities in the Soviet Union" (October, 1965); the Far West Slavic Conference at the University of Southern California (May, 1970); the Second Conference of the Academic Committee for Soviet Jewry, held in Washington, D.C. (May, 1969); and the American Association for the Advancement of Slavic Studies at its meeting in Denver (March, 1971). Other studies have been prepared for the B'nai B'rith International Council, the Council of Jewish

Federations and Welfare Funds, and the World Conference of Jewish Communities (Brussels, February, 1971).

These papers and research studies, updated and considerably enlarged by further exploration of available resources, provide the core of the first ten chapters of the book. The purpose is self-evident: to provide a systematic analysis of the multifaceted character of Soviet anti-Semitism—its roots and origins; its striving to eliminate Jewish national consciousness; its patterns of discrimination; and its shrill anti-Zionist propaganda campaign, which but thinly masked an open bigotry. Analysis of Soviet anti-Semitism alone, however, could have proved insufficient to highlight the background of the trials. For the remarkable and courageous reaction of many Soviet Jews to official anti-Semitism is also an indispensable ingredient in the decision of the Kremlin to schedule the trials. Chapter 9 is devoted to this subject.

If the Leningrad trial and the succeeding judicial proceedings marked the apotheosis of Soviet anti-Semitism in its desperate effort to throttle the sudden renaissance of the Jewish spirit in the USSR, they also constituted a critical turning point in the Kremlin's policy toward Jews. For, instead of crushing the spiraling Jewish resistance movement, as the Soviet rulers had hoped, the trials galvanized three separate but intertwined forces: (1) The Jewish national movement was energized to an extent never contemplated, assuming forms of an escalating stubbornness and militancy that only a full-blown return to Stalinist terrorism—impossible under current Soviet circumstances—could have destroyed. (2) The humanistic Russian intelligentsia, in keeping with a century-old tradition, was spurred into playing the vigorous role of public defender of the Jewish activists, thereby challenging the claim of the Kremlin to be the authentic voice of Marxist ideology on the Jewish question. (3) International public opinion was prompted, by a profound and determined concern of world Jewry on behalf of its beleaguered brethren in the Soviet Union, to bring to bear on the Soviet authorities the weight of conscience, an intangible but by no means impotent factor. Conscience, finding expression in a never-ending stream of public demonstrations and denunciations, so embarrassed and stigmatized Soviet officialdom that it was transformed into an omnipresent irritant which hindered the course of Soviet diplomacy and severely marred its prestige. In Chapters 9, 10, and especially 14, these forces unleashed by the trial are explored.

Thus, the Leningrad trial, insofar as the intention of the Soviet rulers was concerned, proved to be a monumental blunder. What had been a minor, though thorny, internal problem—the plight of Soviet Jewry—became a major problem of Soviet society and a central human rights item on the agenda of the world conscience. In the end, the Soviet authorities beat a partial retreat and allowed thousands of Jews to leave. The heart of the problem, however, remained. The freedom to leave was encumbered by a host of arbitrarily imposed obstacles. And the critical factors which generated the desire to leave—discrimination and anti-Semitism—were by no means reduced.

If the trials merit study as a landmark in the Soviet treatment of its Jewish community, the reaction to them by Jews and by men of good will warrants the kind of commentary that Martin Luther King, Jr., so eloquently bequeathed to mankind. In the face of a ruthless juggernaut of power, men struggled to overcome. And did —to a considerable extent.

THE SOVIET CAGE

A free country cannot resemble a cage,
even if it is gilded and supplied with material things.

—Andrei D. Sakharov

Chapter 1
Popular Anti-Semitism in the Soviet Union

Soviet leaders, when speaking *ex cathedra* and in public, vehemently deny the existence of anti-Semitism in the Union of Soviet Socialist Republics. Premier Aleksei N. Kosygin, for example, has emphasized that "there has never been and there is no anti-Semitism in the Soviet Union."[1]* Such statements reflect an Alice-in-Wonderland world, as the satiric Soviet novelists of a generation ago, Ilya Ilf and Yevgeny Petrov, observed. In their classic novel *The Little Golden Calf* they expressed a wry sense of amusement about one of their characters who told an astonished foreign reporter that in the Soviet state "there are Jews but no Jewish problem."[2]

Scholarly inquiries into the character and extent of popular anti-Semitism are characteristic of the sociological field in many Western countries and, indeed, at UNESCO. In the USSR today, such studies, however fruitful they might prove to be, simply do not exist. When a prominent Western sociologist and philosopher, Professor Lewis Feuer, met in 1964 with officials of the Institute of Philosophy of the Soviet Academy of Sciences, he called attention to a massive study of anti-Semitic prejudice launched by the University of California at Berkeley, and urged a similar investigation by Soviet researchers.[3] The response was cold, if not vehemently hostile. It could hardly be otherwise, given the character of the authoritative

*Numbered reference notes begin on page 329.

position of the regime on the question. Why, indeed, conduct an investigation of anti-Semitic prejudice if it does not exist?

If sample scientific studies of current popular attitudes toward Jews in the USSR do not exist, there is, fortunately, available in the files of Harvard University's Russian Research Center a large mass of material obtained in interviews with Soviet refugees which throws a considerable amount of light on the strength and character of popular anti-Semitism in Soviet Russia. Indeed, it is probably the only systematic body of data which can provide significant insights into the subject. The interviews were accumulated in the so-called Harvard Project on the Soviet Social System, conducted in 1950–51.[4] The basic findings of the project were published in 1956, but the extensive interview material covering attitudes to Jews was not given attention in the published work.

The project interviews were of the "life-history" type: they covered a great variety of subjects and required from two to four days to administer. The total number of interviewees was 329, of whom 53 were interviewed in the United States and the balance in Germany and Austria. The sample was structured in such a way as to encompass as broad a cross-section of the Soviet European population as was reasonably possible under the circumstances. Thus, care was taken to include in appreciable numbers the various age groups of both sexes, the various class and status groups (except the very top elite), and the various national groups. In addition, the sample included both those who left the Soviet Union during World War II and those who left during the post-war period 1946–50 (approximately 25 per cent).

It would be an error to assume that as a group the refugee sample was made up of the disaffected or the misfits. Most of the respondents appear to have left the Soviet Union involuntarily—they were taken by the Germans as either war prisoners or forced laborers. From two-thirds to three-quarters of these, the Harvard researchers state, would have returned to their homeland had it not been for the fear that they might be mistreated upon returning. In addition, a very high proportion of the sample was made up of people who "were unusually successful in the [Soviet] system. . . ." Indeed, the proportion of respondents who admitted having been members of the Communist Party or the Young Communist League (Komsomol) was higher than the proportion of membership in the Soviet population as a whole.

What emerges clearly in a close study of the interviews is the high frequency of stereotyping of Jews.[5] Approximately three-quarters of the respondents characterized all Jews as having distinctive personal traits common to the group. The following constitute some of the major stereotypic images—both negative and positive—which were expressed:

1. Jews occupy a privileged and favored position in Soviet society.
2. Jews are business- and money-minded.
3. Jews are clannish and help each other.
4. Jews are aggressive and "pushy."
5. Jews are sly, calculating, and manipulative, and know how "to use a situation."
6. Jews are deceitful, dishonest, unprincipled, insolent, and impudent.
7. Jews don't like to work hard.
8. Jews are cowards and serve only in the rear of the armed forces.
9. Jews have a distinctive physiognomy and accent.
10. Jews don't drink and don't fight.
11. Jews are smart and intellectually oriented.
12. Jews are devoted to their families and take a special interest in their children.
13. Jews make good musicians and doctors.
14. Jews are religious (some called them religious "fanatics").

Such stereotypic images of the Jew are, of course, not restricted to the USSR. To some degree, they apply to various cultures in the West.

Of the total number of respondents, approximately 60 per cent held negative stereotypes of Jews, although a number of these, at the very same time, also held positive stereotypes. Approximately 10 per cent of the respondents expressed a violent hostility to Jews. A particularly extreme case was that of a thirty-seven-year-old Great Russian who had been both a fisherman and a machine shop worker, and had served in the army between 1941 and 1943: "Well, for example, [he said,] you take the Jews. You know at Easter they take the bread of Christ's body and they eat it and they dip it in blood and they will kill a child each Passover and they drink the blood at that time." When the shocked interviewer interrupted to ask: "Do you really believe that?" the respondent answered: "Oh yes, yes, I saw it with my own eyes and that is what they do."

Violent hostility was not restricted to the unsophisticated. A forty-nine-year-old Great Russian mechanical engineer who had held an important job in the Soviet military administration in Germany before he left for the West in 1946 stated: "I do not like these people [Jews] generally, this is my frank opinion." He went on to imply that he felt so strongly about Jews that he did not want to make further comments about them except to say: "They are the same all over." A thirty-seven-year-old Ukrainian who had been a controller and director of industry and had served, until 1948, as a chief of a secret financial section of the army staff, was vehement about Jews, charging them with virtual treachery during the war. In their haste to flee the German invaders, he said, they neglected to take with them important documents, thus leaving them for the Germans. He concluded: "There is a tradition that the Jews are always for the Jews and nobody else." A twenty-five-year-old Byelorussian farmer who had completed ten years of school (he fled in 1948) commented: "You know we had very bad relations with Jews. I don't know who you [the interviewer] are or what you are but I want to tell you the truth. We had very bad feelings against Jews. You can understand this. We used to see them eating white bread and their fathers had very good jobs. . . . Their only aim in life is to be in power and to draw their friends in with them."

In addition to those who expressed blatant anti-Semitic sentiments, approximately 25 per cent of the respondents revealed various shadings of strongly hostile attitudes toward Jews. Their characterization of Jews generally included a number of negative stereotypes. The most frequently expressed stereotype was that the Jews were the most privileged and favored group in Soviet society. Of the total number who expressed hostile attitudes, approximately 70 per cent stated that a characteristic feature of Soviet society was the "favored" position of Jews.

A Great Russian forty-six-year-old watchmaker who left in 1945 said that "Jews were more trusted" than any other group; ". . . if a Jew went to the NKVD and said he was Jewish, he would be treated better." A twenty-three-year-old Great Russian girl, student of the piano and ballet, who left in 1943, stated that Jews "live better" than others. She recalled how her father, who "wasn't anti-Semitic because he had many Jewish friends," used to tell her that Jews "have their hands in the best places and . . . they do whatever they want." A thirty-three-year-old Ukrainian doctor who left after the war in 1946 stated that the "Jews had it better"—they occupied the best positions in the army and in trade. Another Ukrainian, a thirty-seven-year-old tractor operator who was a lieutenant in the army until 1949 and then left, said that Jews occupied the "top positions" in the government. A thirty-two-year-old collective farmer from Byelorussia who left in 1946 stated that "Jews have more privileges than anyone else" and that "the power in Russia is composed mostly of Jews." A twenty-nine-year-old NKVD (secret police) employee with considerable university training who left in 1949 stated that the Russians "hate the Jews. That's because the Jews occupy the first place. There are some in the Kremlin and they help their own people."

The second most frequently expressed stereotype was that the Jews are business- and money-minded. A fifty-five-year-old Great Russian farmer taken to Germany in 1943 said: "If you listen to Jews talk, all you hear is making money. . . ." A thirty-nine-year-old Ukrainian engineer who left in 1947 said that Jews are "more busy with *geschaft* [business]." A thirty-year-old Great Russian veterinarian who left in 1948 stated that "one trait . . . is peculiar to all Jews. And that is business." A forty-three-year-old Great Russian movie cameraman who was captured by the Germans in 1943 stated that the Jews have "certain commercial traits. They are usually in trade, commerce." A thirty-nine-year-old Great Russian with many years of schooling who held a government position in political education said that "all the Jews in the world are characterized by the fact that they engage in trade and it is the same in the Soviet Union."

It is ironic that notwithstanding the Socialist character of Soviet society and the absence of private enterprise since 1926, a great number of European Russians evidently held to the ancient stereotype about Jews being engaged in commerce. More than one-half the total number of hostile respondents and a great number of others who held negative stereotypes believed that Jews were employed in commerce and trade (even if the stores were socialized) or were engaged in shady dealings.

Clannishness of Jews was the third most strongly held stereotype. Some 40 per cent of hostile respondents and a sizable number of others made comments about this presumed trait. A twenty-seven-year-old Great Russian with eleven years of schooling who had held an important post in the partisan movement (he fled in 1948) stated that Jews "like especially themselves and their own nation; they are also very close within their group." A thirty-eight-year-old Great Russian radio technician who fled in 1947 said that Jews were not liked because "they are more of a bloc, more united than the Russians." A thirty-nine-year-old Ukrainian engineer who left in 1947 said the Jews were not liked "because they help each other always." A forty-three-year-old Great Russian, an economist-engineer who left in 1944, noted that Jews "stick together and pull for each other." A thirty-six-year-old Great Russian, a full colonel in the Red Army with many years of schooling who was captured in 1942, stated: "The only thing that irritates people is that here and there you will see some 'Abram' who has managed to place all his relatives."

Many respondents had the feeling that once a Jew came to occupy an important position, he removed all his non-Jewish associates, replacing them with Jews. One respondent, a twenty-six-year-old Great Russian chauffeur who left in 1947 put it this way: "Nobody loves the Jews. . . . If a Jew gets a job in a store, then the next week there will be two Jews working there and the following week three Jews and before the end of the month there will be a revolution."

Some 20 per cent of the hostile respondents described Jews as a group that disliked and avoided physical labor. A thirty-nine-year-old Great Russian teacher and company commander who left with the Germans in 1941 said: "It is true that you do not often find Jews doing hard work. . . . If a Jew does happen to be a worker in a factory, the other Jews will laugh at him and say that he cannot be a real Jew. The people do not like the Jews." A fifty-eight-year-old Ukrainian woman, a factory worker who was taken by the Germans in 1943, said that Jews use their "cleverness" to avoid becoming "engaged in heavy labor."

The stereotype of Jews as aggressive and "pushy" was held by approximately 15 per cent of the hostile respondents. About twice that number held that Jews displayed the negative traits of dishonesty, impudence, insolence, and sycophancy. The stereotype of the Jew as a coward or as one who sought refuge in the rear of the army was held by about 13 per cent of the hostile respondents. Approximately 5 per cent of the same group had an image of the Jews as being distinguished by a certain often unpleasant physiognomy (e.g., "hook-nosed"), dress (unkempt), and speech (accented).

In some instances, an individual respondent tended to express all or virtually all of the negative stereotypes. Quotations from a few of their interviews may provide a flavor of the thinking of some of the European Soviet population. A well-educated forty-seven-year-old Great Russian who commanded a cavalry regiment until he was captured in 1943 said that Jews

> . . . have a tendency to commerce and to *geschaft*. . . . In order to attain their goal they are ready to look for all possible means. . . . They have an extremely developed sense of mutual help. . . . The personal interests in them are dominant over the other, over the interests of the service and duty. Also over the interests toward non-Jews. . . . They have an insufficient sense of honesty, by that I mean their tendency toward commercial deals. They are incapable for sacrifice in the name of say society or the State. . . . They are bad soldiers.

A forty-year-old Byelorussian factory worker who left in 1947 said that people ". . . hate the Jews because they are all in the power or in trade. They do not like to work with their hands and live by deceit and easy work. If a Jew has . . . a good position, he will immediately drag other Jews to fill the other positions in his organization. They like to deceive the people. In the army I never saw them in the front lines."

A fifty-eight-year-old Great Russian intellectual, a fine-arts teacher and painter who emphasized that Jews were his friends and that he lived at the time of the interview (July, 1951) with a Jewish couple in the United States, had this to say:

> I want to let you know how the people felt. . . . They were very negative to Jews because . . . Jews lived much better than did their neighbors. In the factories there were no Jewish workers; there were none in the *kolkhoz* [collective farm]. They helped each other, they were well organized. . . . During the post-war period, all the trade and most

of industry was in Jewish hands. In the Army, there were almost no Jewish soldiers. If they were in the Army, they were in the Quartermaster Corps. . . . There were many Jews in government circles and in the NKVD. . . . They knew how to get ahead. They were resourceful, unprincipled and did not mind walking on their hind legs before their superiors. The Jews had cars, luxurious apartments.

The "life-history" interviews also revealed that life in the Soviet Union was, at least in part, characterized by numerous anecdotes about Jews. A number of respondents—not all of whom were hostile—either referred to these anecdotes or themselves related some. A twenty-six-year-old university student who was taken as a forced laborer to Germany in 1943 recalled that "anecdotes about local affairs . . . usually concerned Jews."

A special unpublished study of attitudes of the Ukrainian refugee population suggests that hostility to Jews was particularly strong in this ethnic group.[6] In a variation of the Bogardus social distance scale (a device for measuring attitudes concerning acceptance of minorities), Sylvia Gilliam found that 47 per cent of the least-educated (of the Ukrainian refugee sample), 51 per cent of the middle-educated, and 36 per cent of the best-educated would exclude Jews from some social contact. The most frequently checked category (of contacts) was one which would exclude Jews from every contact. (The categories were: work situation, apartment house, friendship, marriage, or all of these.) She also found that Ukrainians perceived the Communist Party as composed in large part of Jews. She concluded that Ukrainian dislike of Jews was actually stronger than their dislike of Russians, and that the middle-educated respondent was "particularly anti-Semitic both in his perception of relations between his own national group and Jews, and in expressions of social exclusion he desired."

A noteworthy feature of the interviews was that approximately 8 per cent of the respondents believed that there was a law on the Soviet statute books which forbade anti-Semitism. Most of those who made reference to this ban, however, considered that it was a device which demonstrated that the Jews were favored by the regime. A typical comment came from a twenty-seven-year-old Great Russian tinsmith: "If you call a Jew a *zhid* [kike], he can go to the police and you will get a prison sentence. But if someone calls me a *katsak* [a term of similar opprobrium], I can do nothing. . . .

Each nationality has the right, except the Jews, to be treated alike. But the Jews have more rights. For example, a Jew could say 'He called me a *zhid*' and get a man in prison." In this connection it might be noted that 13 per cent of the hostile respondents thought that Jews either dominated or were influential in the secret police.

What implications can be drawn from the Harvard interviews so far as the broader Soviet European population is concerned? If caution in generalizing about the results is essential, there can be little doubt that the phenomenon of stereotyping of Jews was wide-spread. A detailed examination of the background information on those who registered hostile attitudes to Jews reveals that they were of various age, national, educational, and status groups, and that they left the USSR at different periods. Prejudice was not restricted to any specific age, national, educational, or status group, nor did any of these categories have an excessive representation of the hostile respondents. If the effects of Nazi propaganda upon those who were taken to Germany may have been a factor, it was partially counterbalanced by the knowledge that Jews were among the interviewers. This fact had filtered through the refugee community. Many of the respondents made efforts to show that they had friendly feelings about Jews. References to Jews as "my friends" or "my best friends" occurred not infrequently. Moreover, there does not appear to be a distinguishable difference of attitudes toward Jews between those who left with the Germans and those who fled during 1946–50.

In this connection, two further points made in the interviews ought to be noted. Approximately 10 per cent of the total respondents, including quite a few who registered no hostile attitudes, spoke freely of the widespread existence of anti-Semitism in the USSR. Secondly, the tiny number of Jews who were in the sample reported that anti-Semitism was strong. The comment of a twenty-five-year-old man whose father was Jewish but whose mother was not is of interest (a platoon officer with three decorations, he left in 1947): "I had been baptized but in school children would call me *zhid* and I used to fight them and tell them that my father was a Jew but I was not. It is even in my passport [that I am not]. . . . The Government did fight such things . . . but anti-Semitism continued exactly as before, in the army also. Russians are terrible anti-Semites."

Inevitably, however, analysis of the Harvard interviews is flawed by both the smallness of the sample and the fact that it was restricted to defectors. Only by comparing the interview material with available documentary evidence concerning the stereotyping of Jews in both Tsarist and Soviet Russia can its significance be more fully assessed.

Anti-Semitic folk imagery had been, of course, a distinctive feature of the social landscape of Tsarist Russia, especially in the Jewish Pale of Settlement, the area in western Russia where most Jews were compelled to reside. While there is no data available on the depth of pre-revolutionary anti-Jewish stereotyping, a clue to its pervasiveness and character can be obtained from an inquiry made by a special high commission appointed by Tsar Alexander III in 1883.[7] Chaired by Count K. I. Pahlen, a former minister of justice and a moderate, the commission labored for five years at the task of evaluating "wholly dispassionately and objectively" the various accusations directed against Jews by those seeking harsh restrictive measures. In 1888, it published its findings, which, in the context of the time, were quite moderate. The commission criticized burdensome restrictions upon Jews and endorsed a policy that would provide for considerable assimilation. Yet, at the same time, it found four stereotypes valid: "(1) Jewish isolation and exclusiveness; (2) a tendency to get control of the economic strength of the population; (3) a tendency to shirk State obligations . . .; (4) avoidance of physical, muscular labor." Even the liberally oriented commission could not but reflect pervasive folk attitudes. If it lauded, on the one hand, "the purity of their Jewish morals, their high respect for learning, their absolute sobriety," on the other hand, it found: "The passion for acquisition and money-grubbing is inherent in the Jew from the day of his birth; it is a characteristic of the Semitic race, manifest from almost the first pages of the Bible."

The stereotypes of the Jew presented in the Pahlen Commission found an echo in a completely opposite source—the revolutionaries who were seeking the overthrow of the Tsarist regime. The Narodnaia Volia (People's Will) organization, in seeking to win peasant support for its program, adopted the following proclamation justifying the pogroms of 1881: "People in the Ukraine suffer most of all from the kikes. Who has seized the land, the woodlands, the taverns? The kikes. Whom does the peasant beg with tears in his eyes to let him near his own land? The kikes. Wherever you look, whatever you touch, everywhere the kikes. The kike curses the peasant, cheats him, drinks his blood. The kike makes life unbearable."[8]

The folk anti-Semitic imagery was to find violent expression in the Ukraine during the Civil War period 1918–20. Responding to appeals calling for overthrowing the "yoke" of the Jews, the masses engaged in an escalating number of pogroms and lesser riots directed against Jews. During the three-year period, 857 pogroms and 335 assaults were inflicted upon Jews, leaving in their wake 30,000 Jews slain (and an additional 120,000 dead from wounds and disease), 28 per cent of Jewish homes destroyed, and widespread destruction of Jewish property.[9]

What is especially striking about the stereotyped attitudes reported by the Pahlen Commission is their remarkable similarity to the attitudes displayed by ex–Soviet citizens more than sixty years later, under totally different circumstances. The pre-revolutionary attitudes were to make themselves felt at various points in the immediate post-revolutionary period. A study of the Kronstadt uprising in March, 1921, for example, indicated that an ingredient of the populist uprising by sailors who but recently had been peasants was anti-Semitism, the "cursed domination" of Jews.[10] Throughout the twenties, the Soviet press carried extensive evidence of widespread anti-Jewish stereotyping as well as of "hooliganism" directed against Jews. In the book *Against Anti-Semitism,* published in 1928, Mikhail Gorev revealed that the articles attacking anti-Semitism he had written for *Komsomolskaia pravda* had touched "a sore and vital point."[11] The newspaper had received "dozens of letters" daily which disclosed "what many comrades had been worrying about." In November, 1926, the chairman of the Central Executive Committee of the Soviet regime, and titular head of the state, made a frank, if startling, admission: ". . . the Russian intelligentsia perhaps [is] more anti-Semitic today than it was under Tsarism."[12] By intelligentsia, he meant the stratum of white collar workers.

Presaging the Harvard interview revelations were the disclosures of a "seminar on anti-Semitism" held in August, 1928, at the headquarters of a Communist Party unit in Moscow.[13] Gathered together were several score of the better-educated and politically advanced workers who were also either Komsomol or Party members. Many of the questions asked in the seminar revealed a distinctive set of negative stereotypes similar to the ones Harvard respondents offered twenty years later. The following are examples:

(1) How is it that Jews always manage to get good positions?

(2) Why is it that Jews don't want to do heavy work?

(3) Why are there so many Jews in the universities? Isn't it because they forge their papers?

(4) Won't the Jews be traitors in war? Aren't they dodging military service?

(5) Should not the cause of anti-Semitism be looked for in the [Jewish] people itself, in its ethical and psychological upbringing?

A "survey of anti-Semitism among trade union members" conducted in Moscow during February, 1929, concluded:

> Anti-Semitic feeling among workers is spreading chiefly in the backward section of the working class that has close ties with the peasantry and among women. . . . Many facts reveal the presence of Komsomol and Party members among the anti-Semites.
>
> Talk of Jewish domination is especially widespread. The offensive taunting, aping and ridiculing of working Jews are frequent occurrences. The telling of jokes about Jews is common.[14]

Pravda, in February, 1929, found the frequent reports of anti-Semitic manifestations disturbing. It condemned the "connivance of the local Party, trade union and Komsomol organizations" which "makes it possible" for the anti-Semitic stereotyping to continue unhindered "for months and years."[15] In at least one place—Dagestan—in the twenties, the ancient accusation that the Jews use the blood of children (in this case, Moslem children) for ritual purposes became a matter of public investigation after it had led to a pogrom.[16] (In 1960, a similar incident would occur in the same place—Dagestan.)

The late Professor Merle Fainsod of Harvard University, who had closely examined the Smolensk archives, noted that they yielded considerable evidence of the pervasive character of popular anti-Semitism in the twenties.[17] A report on one factory divided the workers at a discussion into three groups: "(1) those strongly contaminated with anti-Semitic prejudice. This is an active group—they asked questions, objected, made speeches, wisecracked, etc. (2) The bulk of the audience, who tacitly agreed with the arguments and speeches of the former. (3) A tiny minority who timidly tried to reason with the first group." Fainsod observed that "many similar experiences" are to be found in the archives, indeed "a whole folder which contains nothing else."

During World War II, the negative imagery concerning Jews, probably reinforced to some extent by Nazi propaganda, found numerous expressions. They are noted in Anatoly Kuznetsov's *Babi Yar*, in Ilya Ehrenburg's memoirs, and most notably in accounts of Soviet partisan units.[18] Jews as privileged, Jews as money-minded, Jews as army shirkers were the themes that, in macabre fashion, ran parallel with the enormous tragedy of the Holocaust itself. Even after the war, returning Jewish army veterans and refugees found popular attitudes, in many places, distinctly hostile.[19] Such attitudes were profoundly intensified by the official anti-cosmopolitan campaign which from 1949 on was directed against Jews.

In 1953 the latent popular sentiment was brought to a ferocious level by the Doctors' Plot. A group of doctors, mainly Jews, were accused of poisoning or killing prominent Soviet leaders and planning to murder the current Party leaders. They were charged with being agents of Zionism. Ehrenburg, consistently an apologist for the Soviet state, was stunned by the spewing of anti-Jewish hate on street corners; later he commented that although "our people had matured spiritually," nonetheless, events of 1953 show that "the 'thinking reed' stops thinking at times."[20] He acknowledged that he had been in error in supposing that anti-Semitism, an "ugly survival" of the past, would disappear with the advent of socialism. "I now know . . . that to cleanse minds of age-old prejudice is going to take a very long time."

A perceptive Western correspondent who visited Moscow in April, 1953 (shortly after Stalin's death, when the "plot" was revealed to be a hoax fabricated by the secret police), was provided insights into the depth of anti-Jewish feelings that had burst forth during January–March of that year.[21] He was told that "everyone in those days could tell you of a drugstore which they knew had been padlocked because the authorities discovered the Jewish pharmacist secretly mixing poisons in the medicine." And "everyone had a father or a brother or a cousin who had died because a Jewish doctor deliberately bungled an operation or gave a wrong diagnosis." The correspondent concluded that the Russian people have a "terrible, terrible need . . . for a scapegoat, for someone . . . on whom to pile the blame and the guilt for the horrors of the Stalin epoch."

The explosive character of popular emotions during the period was particularly illuminated by the correspondent's taxi driver, who expressed regret on the day that the Soviet press revealed the "plot" to be a fraud: "Those *svoloch* [rascals]. They got away this time. But their day will come. We will get those yids!" A leading authority on the Stalin era, Isaac Deutscher, was convinced that had Stalin not died and had the trial of the doctors been held, it would have had "only one sequel: a nation-wide pogrom."[22]

That the pervasive negative stereotyping of Jews which was uncovered in the Harvard interviews and which surfaced in especially flagrant forms during the Doctors' Plot has persisted until the present can scarcely be doubted. In 1956, Nikita Khrushchev admitted to a group of French Socialist parliamentarians that "anti-Semitic sentiments still exist here," and his remarks were repeated by Politburo member Anastas Mikoyan.[23] Shortly afterwards, Sally Belfrage, a young woman who can hardly be said to have been hostile to the USSR, wrote of her experiences during a half-year stay in that country.[24] She commented that "as bad as anti-Semitic attitudes can be elsewhere, they seemed to me often worse in Russia." She went on: "I could almost never hear a Jew described except with the apologetic preface 'He's a Jew, but. . . .' (He's very nice, he's very intelligent.) And frequent anti-Semitic jokes, Rabinovich this, Rabinovich that (always Rabinovich). Some Russians spend a great deal of their verbal energy on attacking anything and everything Jewish."

Yevgeny Yevtushenko was to address himself to the question of the persistence of anti-Semitism in his poem "Babi Yar," published in *Literaturnaia gazeta* on September 19, 1961. The poem recalled the pogroms and the activities of the reactionary Black Hundreds during the Tsarist era. It then proceeded to imply, clearly, the continued existence of anti-Jewish feelings:

> Oh, Russian people mine!
> I know
> That you are at heart internationalist
> But often those whose hands were unclean
> Brandished your purest of names.

The Communist theme song, "The International," he wrote, can "thunder forth" only when anti-Semitism is "buried for good." When the poem was first read to twelve hundred students at the Polytechnical Museum in Moscow, three days before its publication, Yevtushenko defined the pervasive, if latent, character of anti-Semitism more sharply. He declaimed that anti-Semitic sentiments among Russians "still arise on the vapors of alcohol and in conversations after drinking."[25] The lines were excised in the published poem.

In December of the following year, the rebellious poet was to challenge the Soviet premier and Party boss on the subject. At a Moscow meeting of several hundred intellectuals called by the Party leadership on December 17, he recited the verse dealing with "The International."[26] Khrushchev was angered: "Comrade Yevtushenko, this poem has no place here," he warned. The poet was not to be silenced. He read "Babi Yar" because "the problem of anti-Semitism" continued to have "a negative consequence" which has "not yet been resolved." When Khrushchev insisted that it was "not a problem," Yevtushenko retorted: "It is a problem, Nikita Sergeievich. It cannot be denied and it cannot be suppressed. It is necessary to come to grips with it time and again. It has a place. I myself was a witness to such things. . . .We cannot go forward to Communism with such a heavy load as Judophobia."

Even *Pravda* found it expedient to recognize that anti-Semitic prejudices were deep-rooted. In a rare editorial that appeared on September 5, 1965, it recalled that Lenin had "wrathfully assailed any manifestations of nationalism whatsoever, and in particular demanded an unceasing 'struggle against anti-Semitism, that malicious exaggeration of . . . national enmity.' " The Party organ could scarcely have made such a comment were the issue at the moment not a pressing one.[27] Lenin's remarks on one or another subject are resurrected to fit a specific, relevant concern.

The clearest indication that at least some Soviet social scientists are acutely aware of the depth and character of the problem of anti-Jewish stereotyping came in an article entitled "The Psychology of Prejudice," written by sociologist I. Kon. Published in *Novyi mir* in September, 1966, the article explored the "social-psychological roots of ethnic preconceptions" in the United States.[28] But, at the end, the author offered some pertinent remarks unrelated to the immediate subject matter. He cautioned Communists—the reference was clearly to the USSR—that they "must not follow the modes and mistakes of the masses such as . . . anti-Semitism. . . ." The sociologist went on to say that it would be an error to assume that racial and ethnic prejudices have "entirely disappeared." "On the contrary," he emphasized, such prejudices exist and, "when particular difficulties arise, they again make themselves felt, influencing backward sections of the population."

The "difficulties" were to "make themselves felt" following the Six-Day War in June, 1967, when the Soviet authorities unleashed a violent anti-Israel and anti-Zionist campaign in the mass media which was to be climaxed by trials of Jews during 1970–71. *Samizdat* literature and petitions of Jews addressed to Soviet leaders as well as to various international bodies and personalities are replete with examples of anti-Semitic prejudice. One of the first petitions, written on February 15, 1968, and addressed to A. Snietskus, first secretary of the Central Committee of the Lithuanian Communist Party, is illustrative.[29] Written by twenty-six Lithuanian Jewish intellectuals, some of whom were Party members, the petition notes that the press campaign and, particularly, the use of cartoons depicting Jews in an unfavorable light "have revived anti-Semitic passions in a certain part of the Lithuanian (and not only Lithuanian) people." In other *samizdat* literature, remarks of an anti-Semitic character, such as the use of the term *zhid* (kike, or dirty Jew), are described as widespread. Thus, one important document declares that all public life in the USSR is "infected" with anti-Semitism: "Every Jew living in the USSR could tell of humiliations personally suffered in diverse circumstances—in communal housing or on the street, on public transport, in shop queues, in the army barracks or the municipal hospital."[30] The *Chronicle of Current Events,* a *samizdat* publication appearing regularly, has reported numerous instances of harassment of Jews, especially in areas where trials have taken place. Descriptions of the trials frequently make note of the atmosphere in the courtroom: vulgar anti-Semitic verbalisms appear to be characteristic.

Academician Andrei D. Sakharov, the distinguished Soviet physicist and co-inventor of the hydrogen bomb, in 1968 used the phrase "zoological kind of anti-Semitism" to characterize the thinking of Stalinist bureaucrats.[31] It suggests an especially primitive and virulent form of Jew-baiting that the noted physicist maintains has by no means been dispelled. How far beyond the "highest bureaucratic elite"—the phrase is Sakharov's—this "zoological" anti-Semitism extends is not known. Certainly, as the Harvard interviews suggest, virulent Judophobia, while reflecting the attitudes of a small minority, would appear to be a matter of concern. Far more widespread are stereotypic attitudes of a generally anti-Jewish nature. Running deep in the Russian past, they persist today as a factor which cannot be discounted. Andrei Amalrik, the brilliant historian whose iconoclastic activities have resulted in his incarceration, has called attention to a feature of current thought that expresses "extreme scorn and hostility toward everything non-Russian." Integral elements of that pattern of thinking are "national enemies," of which Amalrik lists two—the Chinese and the Jews.[32]

Albert Einstein once observed that "a people, a nation, is like a tree which is born with its own shadow."[33] After noting that the "shadow" of the ancient Romans was fame and domination of foreign lands, he turned to the Russians. Their "shadow," he said, is anti-Semitism.

Chapter 2
Forcible Assimilation as Policy

As social-psychological analysts have amply demonstrated, anti-Semitic attitudes or even anti-Semitic remarks need not necessarily find expression in formal discriminatory acts against Jews. A predisposition for creating patterns of discrimination or erecting barriers to participation and advancement of Jews may exist but, without authoritative sanction, it will remain nothing more than a predisposition. Sanction by governments, whether formally or informally, is central to the question of overt anti-Semitic acts.

Under Tsarism, little distinction could be drawn between the two: pervasive anti-Semitic folk imagery, especially in the areas of the Jewish Pale of Settlement, was accompanied by and probably helped sustain a government policy which placed burdensome restrictions upon Jews in residence, employment, and education. From time to time, open violence against the Jews, in the form of pogroms, was organized by state officials.[1] If the object was scapegoating, it was made possible, if not respectable, by the folk stereotypes of the Jew. In the same way, Tsarist attempts, in the early twentieth century, to make anti-Semitism an official state ideology that "would make possible a comprehensive attitude . . . toward history and society" drew upon popular myths about Jews.[2] The incredible Beiliss case, based upon the blood libel myth, can be understood, Professor Hans Rogger of the University of California at Los Angeles has noted, as a search by the authorities "for a common belief which would rally and bind" the forces supporting Tsarism.[3]

Bolsheviks in Russia drew their inspiration from a completely different source: Marxism. Classical Marxism's view of anti-Semitism was perhaps best summarized in the brief but withering characterization by August Bebel, the German Social-Democratic Party leader: anti-Semitism is the "socialism of fools." If many of the theorists of utopian socialism (including the Narodnaia Volia), anarchism, and syndicalism revealed a deep respect for anti-Semitism, Marxists held it in sharp contempt.[4] Contempt was transformed by V. I. Lenin's vitriolic pen into angry denunciation. In a speech delivered in March, 1919, he cried: "Shame on accursed Tsarism which tortured and persecuted the Jews. Shame on those who foment hatred towards the Jews. . . ."[5] As early as March, 1914, Lenin drafted model legislation which provided for "the repeal of all restrictions upon the rights of Jews"; four years later he would play a key role in the enactment of a historic decree banning anti-Semitism in the new Soviet state.[6]

What kind of policy would be adopted by the Soviet government in keeping with Lenin's formulations? The treatment accorded the Jewish community must be examined in the context of a society embracing 108 nationalities and 22 lesser ethnic groups. In Soviet society, nationality is a fundamental component of citizenship carrying vital psychological, cultural, and even political ramifications. On the occasion of the fiftieth anniversary of the October Revolution, for example, major stress was placed on the multinational character of the regime. The Tsarist program of oppression of its numerous nationalities had been replaced—the Party Central Committee said on June 21, 1967—by a "Leninist programme for the solution of the national question" through the "socialist fraternity of the peoples of our country."[7] The Bolshevik Revolution had "created conditions for the burgeoning and mutual enrichment of national culture"; and the Soviet Government has been oriented to "preserving and furthering" the "best national traits and traditions" of each nationality. The then titular head of the Soviet state, Anastas Mikoyan, added that the Communist Party would "continue to attend the interests and national peculiarities of each of the peoples [of the USSR]."

From the very inception of the Soviet state, the Jewish community has been accorded the legal status of a nationality. Even if Bolshevik ideologists, prior to the October Revolution, were to deny that the Jewish community had those specific characteristics which they considered essential for nationhood—most notably a continuous territory and an agricultural base—nonetheless, they recognized, Jews have a "common 'national character.' "[8]

In March, 1914, Lenin drafted a bill on nationality which clearly defined the future legal status of the Jewish community in the state as a distinct national entity. The bill was to provide for "the repeal of all restrictions upon the rights of Jews, and, in general, of all restrictions based on a person's descent or nationality." After noting that the "citizens of all nationalities of Russia" were to be equal before the law, Lenin's draft went on to specify the removal of barriers against Jews.[9] Five years later, after the Bolsheviks had seized power, Lenin once again juxtaposed Jews and the nationality question when he called for "particular carefulness in regard to the national feelings of nations that were oppressed (for example, on the part of the Great Russians, Ukrainians and Poles toward Jews, on the part of Tatars toward Bashkirs, etc.); support not only for real equality in rights, but also for the development of the language, the literature of the toiling masses of the formerly oppressed nations." Significantly, a Communist Party resolution, adopted at its Tenth Congress in 1921, after referring to the "equality of nationalities" and "the right of national minorities to free national development," specifically mentioned Jews among a very small list of examples.[10]

Formal political expression was given to the acknowledged legal status of a Jewish nationality in January, 1918, when a Commissariat for Jewish National Affairs was established as a special section of the Peoples' Commissariat for National Affairs. The Peoples' Commissariat, or Narkomnats, was established, with Josef Stalin at its head, only one day after the Bolshevik seizure of power. Its function, the official text stated, was that of being "the initiator of the entire Soviet legislation on the national question . . . measures regarding the economic and cultural uplifting of the nationalities, etc."[11] But the principal task of the Commissariat for Jewish National Affairs became the establishment of "the dictatorship of the proletariat in the Jewish street"—the spreading of the ideas of the Bolshevik Revolution among the Jewish masses. In this capacity, it sought—as reported in *Izvestiia* in June, 1919—the abolition of the existing autonomous institutions of the Jewish community and the transfer of their funds and property to itself.[12] A formal decree of August 5 accomplished the task.

Alongside the Jewish Commissariat (and its provincial sub-bodies) the Communist Party in 1918 created Jewish Sections (Yevsektsii) whose task it was to carry out Communist Party policy and propaganda among Jewish workers in the Yiddish language and "to see to it that the Jewish masses have a chance to satisfy all their intellectual needs in that language. . . ."[13] While the Jewish Commissariat passed out of existence in early 1924 (along with the Peoples' Commissariat itself), the Jewish Sections continued a checkered existence until January, 1930, when they, too, were liquidated. But the category of a Jewish nationality remained and finds expression today in all official publications that deal with nationalities or that indicate nationality categories.

The reference to language in the functions of the Jewish Sections specified above reflected the fact that Yiddish was formally recognized as integral to the legal identity of the Jewish nationality. Indeed, the Byelorussian Republic—wherein existed the largest number of compact Jewish communities and where 90.7 per cent of the Jews expressly stated, in the 1926 census, that Yiddish was their mother tongue—decreed in law that Yiddish was among the four official languages of the government. (The 1897 census had indicated that 97 per cent of the Jewish population of Tsarist Russia identified Yiddish as their "mother tongue," and the 1926 census showed that, notwithstanding the assimilatory process of the intervening decades, 70.4 per cent of the "Jewish nationality" declared Yiddish to be their mother tongue.)

If the Jewish community, as a nationality, has a fixed legal status so, too, does the individual born of Jewish parents. A Jew is not someone who desires to be identified as a Jew or chooses to identify himself as such; he is a juridically defined person who inescapably is a part of the Jewish nationality. The determining legal factor in fixing the designation is not the distinctive attributes, whether supposed or real, of the ethnic group; rather, it is the simple biological fact of being born of Jewish parents.

The establishment of a legal category that permanently fixed the identity of a person born of Jewish parents as being a Jew by nationality did not come until late 1932. Ironically, it appeared under circumstances that bore no direct relationship to the national question. On December 27, 1932, a decree was adopted by the Central Executive Committee and the Council of Peoples' Commissars that created the "single passport system" for the USSR[14]—a system that still exists. The decree stipulated that the passports, to be issued in 1933, were to contain the "nationality" of the bearer. Urban residents sixteen years of age and over were to acquire the passports.

The principal reason for the introduction of the passport was the severe housing shortage in the major urban areas, a consequence of the enormous influx of new workers into cities resulting from the intensified industrialization effort of the Five-Year Plan. The passport became the basic means of regulating the distribution of apartments. As the decree noted, the objective was "an improved registration of the population of the cities, of workers from villages and new factories, and the combing out from living quarters those persons not connected with production or labor in institutions and schools, and not engaged in socially useful labor . . . and also with the purpose of removing from these living quarters concealed kulaks, criminals, and anti-social elements. . . ." At first, the passport system was to be introduced in the major cities—Moscow, Leningrad, Kharkov, Kiev, Odessa, Minsk, Rostov-on-Don, and Vladivostok—but the decree also specified that the system was to be extended to all the remaining localities in the USSR.

Nationality ranked high among the items which the decree listed for specification in the passport. Thus, it was listed immediately after name, date, and place of birth, and before social position, permanent residence, and place of work. The decree noted further that the passport would include a listing of documents providing proof of nationality as well as of the other categories. The types of documents were to be spelled out in "instructions." While such "instructions" were not published, it is known that among the documents required was the birth certificate, which carried, among other types of "proof," the nationality of the person involved.

The listing of the nationality of the registering sixteen-year-old is a virtually automatic process. He is required to produce papers which specify the nationality of each of his parents. If both are of the same nationality—which has been the typical situation—then that nationality is the one inserted in Point 5 of the passport. No voluntary choice is permitted: if both parents are Jewish, the youngster is listed as *yevrei*—Jewish. An option exists for the sixteen-year-old only when the parents are of different nationalities. In that case, he selects one of the two nationalities as his own.

Since the passport is the principal means of identification in the USSR, not merely in obtaining housing, but in making application for jobs and, indeed, in dealing with all governmental institutions, it becomes a potentially powerful means for either discrimination or favoritism on nationality grounds. It is for this reason that some leading intellectual dissenters have advocated the removal of Point 5 from the passport.[15]

The fixed personal legal category has particular significance for the Jews since, unlike most other nationalities, they lack a distinct geographical national base. There is, of course, the Jewish Autonomous Region of Birobidzhan, established by decree of the Presidium of the Central Executive Committee of the USSR on May 7, 1934. But, despite government pronouncements in the mid-thirties which recommended Birobidzhan as a "homeland" for Soviet Jews, the area, lacking any historical sentiment, attracted relatively few Jews as permanent residents, so that, according to the 1959 census, only 8.8 per cent of the region's population—14,270 persons—are of the Jewish nationality.[16] While precise figures are lacking in the 1970 census, there is little doubt that the percentage of Jews has declined even further. Of the region's five representatives in the Soviet of Nationalities of the Supreme Soviet, one is identified as a Jew. The name of the region, as Jewish, is thus an anomaly, and the applicability to it of Article 110 of the Soviet Constitution, stipulating that "judicial proceedings" are to be "conducted in the language" of the region, becomes meaningless.

Numbering 2,150,000, according to the census of 1970, the Jews are dispersed throughout all of the fifteen union republics: 38 per cent in the Russian Republic; 36 per cent in the Ukraine; 7 per cent in Byelorussia; another 15 per cent in Uzbekistan, Georgia, Lithuania, Moldavia, Latvia, and Estonia; and the balance of 4 per cent in the remaining six republics.[17] Everywhere they are a small minority; the highest percentage of Jews in a union republic population is in Moldavia, where they are a little over 2 per cent. On a national level, Jews constitute a little less than 1 per cent of the total population. The small percentage of Jews in the total population does not, however, reflect their relative weight in the nationality pattern. Actually, among 108 principal nationalities, they rank twelfth in numbers. Nonetheless, they are a minority everywhere and, therefore, more vulnerable to the misuse of the passport system.

The dispersal of Jews, together with the fact that they are one of the most highly urbanized nationalities in the USSR (96 per cent of the Jews live in urban areas), has no doubt accelerated the normal trend to linguistic assimilation. This is reflected in the 1959 census figures on how many Jews use their "mother tongue." In contrast to the census figures of 1926, when over 70 per cent of the Jews indicated Yiddish as their native language, in the 1959 census approximately 18 per cent, or a little more than 400,000, did so. (The figure of 21.5 per cent, or 488,000 persons, often cited by both Western and Soviet analysts, is an error resulting from a misreading of the data. The data were broken down to indicate whether the respondents declared their native language was that of their nationality or whether it was Russian or another language other than that of their nationality. While 21.5 per cent of the Jews were reported as saying that their native language was that of their nationality, the "native language" or "mother tongue"—rodnoi yazik—of the Jews of Georgia, Bokhara, and Dagestan is not Yiddish. The figures concerning the language declaration of these groups of Jews have erroneously been added to that of the other Soviet Jews to produce a mistaken total.) The 1970 census showed a further drop; 17.7 per cent—380,000—stated that their "mother tongue" was a Jewish language.[18] The percentage of Jews who consider specifically Yiddish their "mother tongue" would be less.

In the 1959 census, Jews ranked far and away the lowest among the nationalities in declaring that their native language was the language of the nationality to which they belonged. But, as one Yiddish specialist in the USSR, Yakov Kantor, has indicated, the structuring of the census questionnaire in 1959 distorted and exaggerated the extent of linguistic assimilation.[19] In an analysis published by the Warsaw Jewish Historical Institute, Kantor noted that since the census instructions did not define "native language" many Jews thought it meant "language spoken." In consequence, "many people who speak and read Yiddish, enjoy Yiddish books and appreciate Yiddish plays nevertheless gave Russian as their language because they speak Russian at work, in the street, and even to an extent at home." Kantor's argument would apply to the 1970 census as well.

Besides, the overall percentage obscures the fact that, in the territories incorporated into the Soviet state in 1939–41, the percentage of Jews specifying Yiddish as their native tongue is fairly high—over 60 per cent in Lithuania, over 40 per cent in Latvia, and close to 50 per cent in Moldavia.[20] A Soviet linguistic scholar at the University of Leningrad, M. Friedberg, several years ago criticized as "wholly incorrect" the assertion in the *Large Soviet Encyclopedia* that the Soviet Jewish community is on the road to "complete linguistic assimilation."[21] He noted the extensive use of Yiddish in areas in the Ukraine and Byelorussia where compact Jewish populations exist.

The distinctiveness of the Jewish community as a nationality having a dispersed character is further complicated by the legal status accorded to the Jewish religious community. A governmental decree of June, 1944, which formally established the Council for the Affairs of Religious Cults specifically mentioned the Jewish religious community among the approximately dozen non–Russian Orthodox faiths which were granted formal status.[22] (A separate Council for the Affairs of the Russian Orthodox Church was established in 1943.) The Council for the Affairs of Religious Cults, according to the decree, was directly responsible to the USSR Council of Ministers and was assigned the task of maintaining liaison between the government and the recognized religious communities.

As distinct from the category of the Jewish nationality, participating in the Jewish religious community is, from a legal viewpoint, exclusively a voluntary act, with the Jew (or any citizen) given the right "freely to choose his religion" or "to profess no religion at all. . . ."[23] An official government report to the United Nations states that "the laws in force in the Soviet Union on religious matters bar any state registration of citizens of the Soviet Union according to religion. . . ." In consequence, "no indication of religious affiliation is given in State documents such as passports or in State censuses," and, indeed, "no statistics or numerical records concerning religious affiliation are kept. . . ."

The last statement obviously refers to official records and not to records that individual religious bodies may keep. Figures on the number affiliated with the Jewish religious community are unknown, although a member of the Council for the Affairs of Religious Cults, in 1960, offered an estimate—undoubtedly inflated—of five hundred thousand "practicing" Jews.[24] The chief rabbi of Moscow, in 1963, stated that there were ninety-six synagogues in the country (the Novosti press agency gave the number as ninety-seven). In addition, there are an unknown number of *minyanim,* private prayer groups of ten or more having no legal status. (To acquire status a group of "not less than twenty citizens" who combine "to form a religious association" must register and be approved by the local authorities.)

Notwithstanding the voluntary character of membership in the Jewish religious community, use of the same root term for both the nationality and the religion—*Jew* or *Jewish*—makes the complete separation of the two in the public mind difficult. The intertwining of nationality and religion becomes particularly apparent in the atheist propaganda campaign directed by the Party. The Jewish religion is frequently attacked on the grounds that it either stimulates *nationalist* feelings or expresses "national exclusiveness." Lenin himself contributed to the confusion by stating in 1913 that Jewish "national culture" was a "slogan" of the rabbis.[25] Thus, the "voluntary" character of adherence to the Jewish religion may appear to be less voluntary than the law would require. In the minds of readers of atheist propaganda, the Jew can take on the character of an objective category in which both nationality and religion are conjoined.

The juxtaposition of religion and nationality together with the dispersion of the Jewish nationality may have contributed to the popular anecdote related by Maurice Hindus and reflecting the uncertainty about Jewish identity: "Why is the sputnik a Jew? Because it wanders around the earth and has no place to stop."[26] Nonetheless, the laws on the status of the Jew are clear. Those laws entitle him to a set of constitutionally prescribed rights embracing the areas of nationality, religion, and civil law. Lenin once said that "a constitution is a fiction when law and reality part, not a fiction when they meet."[27] Do "law and reality part" in the treatment of the Jewish community?

As a distinctive *nationality* in the USSR, the Jewish community was and is entitled to enjoy a host of national rights, inscribed in law, that stretch back to the early days of the Soviet regime. Only a week after the seizure of power, on November 15, 1917, the government issued a formal Declaration of Rights of Peoples which proclaimed the "free development of national minorities and ethnic groups inhabiting Russian territory."

In keeping with this principle, the first Soviet Constitution (1918) stipulated, in Article 22, that "to oppress national minorities or impose any limitations whatsoever on their rights" is "contrary to the fundamental laws" of the regime. Following the formation of the USSR in 1922 and the enactment of the new federal Constitution in 1924, the principle of equality of rights for nationalities was restated in the constitutions of the individual republics. Thus, the 1925 Constitution of the Russian Soviet Federated Socialist Republic (RSFSR) declared in Article 13 that "oppression of national minorities in whatsoever form [and] any restriction of their rights . . . are wholly incompatible with the fundamental laws of the Republic."

The same article filled the general principle of equality with linguistic content by stipulating that RSFSR citizens "have the right to use their native language freely in meetings, in the courts, in administrative bodies and in public affairs." It further specified that the national minorities "have the right to receive education in their native tongue." The "native tongue" of the Jews, it should be emphasized, was not considered to be Hebrew. That language was regarded as an instrument of Zionism and, like the latter, was banned in the early twenties.

In both the Ukraine and Byelorussia,[28] where sizable compact Jewish communities existed, statutes were enacted to give expression to linguistic rights. The Ukrainian Code of Criminal Procedure of 1922 permitted court proceedings "in the language of the majority of the population concerned." A Ukrainian decree of August 1, 1923, "concerning measures to ensure the legal equality of languages" provided that in localities where one of the minority nationalities was in the majority, the authorities were to use the language of that nationality. A subsequent decree in July, 1927, restated this right and specified the teaching of the native language together with both Russian and Ukrainian in minority schools.

In Byelorussia, the Declaration of Independence of August 1,

1920, recognized Yiddish as being one of the four "legal" languages enjoying "equality" with Byelorussian, Russian, and Polish. This principle was reiterated in a formal act of the Byelorussian Central Executive Committee in February, 1921, and by a decree of July 15, 1924, "concerning practical measures to implement the policy on nationalities." That decree guaranteed both native schools and the use of the "mother tongue in dealing with any kind of organ and institution of the Republic." The Byelorussian Constitution of 1927 again recognized Yiddish as an official republic language.

The decrees in the Ukraine and Byelorussia led in the twenties to the establishment of a complex of Jewish administrative and judicial institutions in areas where the Jews constituted a sizable and compact group. With, however, the stepped-up industrialization campaign of the thirties, in consequence of which the compactness of old Jewish communities broke up and a dispersion of their population to new industrial areas followed, the complex of institutions disintegrated. Administrative pressures and voluntary actions by assimilationists contributed to this disintegration. Nevertheless, the school apparatus remained. By the end of 1940, according to the Yiddish researcher, Jacob Lestchinsky, there were some eighty-five thousand to ninety thousand Jewish children—about 20 per cent of the Jewish student population—studying in schools where Yiddish was the language of instruction.[29]

The 1936 Constitution of the USSR no longer made reference to the right of use of the native language in meetings, courts, and administrative bodies. However, it reaffirmed, in Article 121, the right of "instruction in schools . . . in the native language." Similar provisions exist in the constitutions of all the union and autonomous republics.

In August, 1962, the USSR ratified the UNESCO Convention Against Discrimination in Education, which obligated it, according to Article 5 (1c) "to recognize the right of members of national minorities to carry on their own educational activities, including the maintenance of schools and . . . the use of the teaching of their own language. . . ." Ratification of the UNESCO Convention was reflected, earlier, in a law adopted on April 16, 1959, in the Russian Republic, "Concerning the Strengthening of the Connection of the Schools with Life and the Furthest Development of the System of

People's Education in the RSFSR."[30] Article 15 declared: ". . . the education in schools will be conducted in the native language of the students. The right is given to parents to decide with what language in schools to register their children." A 1956 letter from the deputy minister of education of the Russian Republic, A. Arsenyev, stated that Soviet law requires that, in the event that 10 parents request that their children receive an education in their mother tongue, "the organization of such a class [in the "mother tongue"] in any school" will be arranged.[31]

The Party Program adopted by the Twenty-second Congress in 1961 underscored the Soviet commitment to the teaching of the native language. The Party guarantees "the complete freedom of each citizen of the USSR to speak and to rear and educate his children in any language, ruling out all privileges, restriction, and compulsion in the use of this or that language."[32]

Today, notwithstanding the numerous laws and decrees governing education in the native tongue, nowhere in the entire length and breadth of the USSR is there a single Yiddish school or a Yiddish class. The Jewish schools in the Ukraine and Byelorussia that were destroyed by the Nazis were not reopened by the Soviets. Efforts to reestablish a Yiddish school system in Lithuania, once this republic had been freed of the Nazi invaders, came to naught. And, by 1946, the few Jewish schools in the Birobidzhan were closed.

Two types of arguments have been advanced by Soviet authorities to explain the absence of Jewish schools. One is based upon the burdensome costs involved in establishing schools for a widely dispersed nationality. Khrushchev told Professor Jerome Davis, an American pacifist leader, that since "Jews are dispersed, . . . to set up separate schools all over Russia would be expensive."[33] In contrast, dispersed Hungarians in the USSR have 99 schools for a population numbering 149,000. There are also Polish schools for Poles living in Lithuania and Byelorussia. The validity of Khrushchev's argument is made especially suspect by Soviet school policy affecting another dispersed Soviet nationality—the Germans.

Numbering over 1,800,000 persons (according to the 1970 census) and dispersed, since an August 28, 1941, decree, over a wide area embracing eastern parts of the RSFSR and almost a dozen other union republics, the former Volga German inhabitants were fully restored to their national rights by a 1964 decree of the Presidium of the USSR Supreme Soviet. The decree revealed that "in districts of a number of provinces, territories and republics that have a German population, there are secondary and elementary schools where teaching is conducted in German or German is taught to children of school age. . . ."[34]

In March, 1964, the Soviet teachers' journal offered some details concerning the extent of the rehabilitation of the linguistic school rights of the Germans in the RSFSR. Under the headline "Two Native Languages," the article observed that "at present there exist hundreds of schools in the RSFSR where from the second grade the German language as the mother tongue is used as the basis for teaching."[35] Thirteen textbooks on the teaching of German as a mother tongue have been published and republished in 431 editions. Teachers were being trained in four pedagogical institutes for higher grades and in three seminars for lower grades.

The Soviet German weekly on January 20, 1965, carried an article which complained that in one village where the Germans number one-third of the local population, the teaching of German as a "native language" had been introduced only in the lower classes of the schools.[36] A week later, the newspaper published an article by a Kirghiz school official who disclosed that five thousand German pupils in thirty-three schools of various regions in Kirghizia were learning their "native language," and that, in 1960, the Council of Ministers of that republic had promulgated a decree that all schools with classes containing ten or more German pupils must, if their parents so request, introduce the teaching of German as a "native language."[37]

The second argument that is offered for the absence of a Jewish school system is the extent of assimilation of Jews. A parliamentary delegation of French Socialists was told by Khrushchev in 1956 that assimilation is so advanced that "even if Jewish schools were established very few would attend them voluntarily."[38] He added that "if the Jews were compelled to attend Jewish schools there would certainly be a revolt. It would be considered some kind of ghetto." This type of argument raises more questions than it answers. Assuming there are insufficient numbers to build a Jewish school, why are there no special Jewish classes? If all that is required is the request of ten parents to provide such classes, is it conceivable that in areas of large Yiddish-speaking populations (as in Vilnius, Kovno, Riga, and elsewhere in the Western Ukraine, Western Byelorussia, and Moldavia), no such request would be forthcoming?

Simply to put these questions is to suggest the determination of school administrators to discourage these requests, or to avoid informing parents of their right to make such requests. The article in the Soviet German weekly had criticized a high school principal in one village where there is a sizable German minority for his failure to inform German parents of their legal rights to request teaching in the "native language." Are Jewish parents similarly not informed of their rights with respect to instruction in their "native language"? The external stimulation from on high of a popular desire or request is a frequently used device of Soviet policy-makers to arouse support for one or another position. In contrast to the press stimulation of German parents, there has not appeared a single article in the press to stimulate such interest on the part of Jewish parents.

But perhaps a more fundamental question would be the following: Is not the assimilation of Jews a product, at least in part, of the absence of specific Jewish institutions to perpetuate their language and culture, rather than the converse? Yakov Kantor, a Soviet Jewish researcher who wrote, in the thirties, an authoritative work on Jewish institutions, observed several years ago:

> Such things as schools of all kinds, museums, theatres, libraries, even sections of academies and so on, all work toward the consolidation, the support, and the strengthening of minority cultures.
>
> Unhappily, the Jews belong to that group of national minorities where such supporting and strengthening factors for their culture do not exist. They have not existed for a number of years, since the time of the reinforced cult of the personality.[39]

The value judgment implied in the word *unhappily* reflects the strength of the author's conviction that the absence of schools and other cultural institutions is the decisive factor in causing assimilation, and is not a reflex of it. It is significant that the author's penetrating analysis was published in Warsaw, Poland, and not in the Soviet Union, where he had lived until his death in September, 1964.

There is now little doubt that, in the late thirties, the regime initiated a determined effort to bring about the forcible assimilation of the Jewish community. While the Great Purge struck in numerous directions, it struck an almost mortal blow at the Jewish community.[40] Virtually the entire Jewish cadre responsible for Jewish affairs was liquidated. This included the former leadership of the Jewish Sections and the dominant figures in Jewish affairs in Moscow and Birobidzhan. Of even greater significance was the decimation of a large number of Jewish communal institutions, the ethnic-cultural infrastructure that is essential to the preservation of Jewish identity.

A partial restoration of the infrastructure took place during World War II, especially with the establishment of the Jewish Anti-Fascist Committee. After the war, it served as the Jewish "address," with a large, bustling staff engaged in a variety of activities and contemplating a host of imaginative programs for the future.[41] The Yiddish publishing firm Emes issued a tri-weekly newspaper in Moscow, *Aynikayt,* and produced 110 works during the period 1946–48. But in the late fall of 1948, the blow that literally pulverized Jewish communal life was struck. The Jewish Anti-Fascist Committee was dissolved and almost all of its members arrested (and later killed); Emes was padlocked and its newspaper shut down; and in 1949, the famed Jewish State Theater in Moscow was closed, its leading actor, Shlomo Mikhoels (who had been chairman of the Jewish Anti-Fascist Committee), having been murdered by the secret police a year earlier. Performances at all other Jewish professional theaters—in Kiev, Minsk, Odessa, Kharkov, Chernovtsy, and Birobidzhan—were halted. The Department of Jewish Culture of the Ukraine Academy of Sciences in Kiev was shut. Jewish communal structures in Birobidzhan (except for a small newspaper) were made barren. Nothing now remained of Jewish institutional life.

Equally devastating was the deliberate effort to decapitate the Jewish leadership of the country. Between 1949 and 1953, hundreds of prominent Jewish activists and literary figures were arrested, were killed, or disappeared.[42] The climax of the drive was the trial of twenty-five key Jewish personages, principally in the literary world, on July 11–18, 1952. They were charged with plotting to sever the Crimea from the USSR and establish there a Zionist-bourgeois republic. Twenty-four were executed on August 12, and one, a woman, received life imprisonment. The elite who had borne the challenge of Jewish ethnic survival was liquidated with one stroke.

For eleven years the Jewish national scene in the USSR was a cultural desert—no theater, no books, no publications (except for the *Birobidzhaner Shtern,* a small tri-weekly, now daily, with a circulation of one thousand, produced locally in Birobidzhan). Only the popular Yiddish concerts performed by troupes of traveling singers provided some linguistic sustenance. Beginning in 1959 a small trickle of publications began to water the parched Yiddish-reading population. A book of stories by Sholem Aleichem appeared that year, followed during the next three years by four other Yiddish books written by deceased Jewish authors. Then between 1962 and 1964 no books were published. Since 1965, in response to a growing outcry in the Western world, about two dozen additional books have been published. All told, thirty-two Yiddish books were published between 1948 and 1970.[43]

The most important development was the establishment in August, 1961, of a bi-monthly Yiddish literary review, *Sovietish Heimland,* with a press run of twenty-five thousand.[44] The likelihood is that the journal, like the few Yiddish books, would never have appeared except for the outside pressures challenging the discriminatory policy toward Yiddish culture. The Soviet minister of culture, Yekaterina Furtseva, in 1961 told André Blumel, vice-chairman of the Franco-Soviet Friendship Society, that if the Soviet Union "did anything at all" for Yiddish culture "it would not be for domestic reasons but to please our friends abroad."[45] General David Dragunsky, a Jew, who was often used as an unofficial Soviet spokesman on Jewish matters, said some months later: "Frankly speaking, they [Yiddish books] are being published more for political reasons than in answer to a real need."[46]

Sovietish Heimland, which, in January, 1965, was turned into a monthly with a larger number of pages per issue, has become a focal point of the very limited Jewish activity. Besides publishing the writings of over one hundred Jewish authors, it has organized a number of literary conferences some of which have been attended by audiences running into the hundreds. The Yiddish theater, however, has not been restored. Instead, in 1962, a touring Yiddish repertory company was launched under Veniamin Schwartser, a former member of the Moscow Jewish State Theater.

But the Jewish community still remains without an "address." As compared with the situation that prevailed in 1945–48—let alone in the twenties and thirties—Jewish institutional and cultural life is severely impoverished. Yet the brisk sale of the few Yiddish books and of *Sovietish Heimland,* the sizable attendance at literary conferences, at performances of Schwartser's company, and particularly at Yiddish concerts—a semi-official estimate once placed it at one-half million per year—testify to the continuing vitality of the *Yiddish vort.* The response tendered foreigners who sing in Yiddish is also indicative. Thunderous ovations greeted Jan Peerce, the Metropolitan Opera tenor, when he sang Yiddish songs at sell-out houses in the USSR in May, 1963.

There exist no laws or statutes in the USSR which—in contrast to the school question—undergird the cultural rights of minorities. These rights, however, have been implicit in the Party policy on the nationality problem enunciated in the twenties. As early as March, 1921, the Tenth Party Congress resolved to assist the nationalities "to set up a press, schools, theatres, community centers and cultural and educational institutions generally, using the native language."[47] Stalin, in his famous speech at the Communist University of the Toilers of the East in May, 1925, provided an elaborate dialectical rationale for party support of "national culture." National cultures, he said, "must be given an opportunity to develop, expand, and reveal all their potentialities in order to establish the conditions for their fusion into a single common culture with a single common language."[48]

The early years of the post-war period were marked by a decisive reversal of this policy so far as the Jewish national culture was concerned. And arbitrary administrative actions gave effect to forcible assimilation. The new policy can hardly be said to have been discontinued by Stalin's successors even with the changes introduced in 1959. The refusal to permit Jewish schools is especially glaring. Current and future developments involving the Jews can properly be understood in the context of Party decisions taken at its Congress in 1961. The ultimate objective of a "single common culture," as expressed by Stalin, was given a greater degree of urgency and immediacy by the Party, which, in its new Program, called for "the effacement of national distinctions ... including language distinctions." Khrushchev, while heaping ridicule on those "who complain about the effacement of national distinctions," told the Party that "Communists are not going to freeze and perpetuate national distinctions."[49] The implication of an activist program dedicated to achieving the "voluntary" adoption of Russian as "the common medium of intercourse and cooperation"—in the language of the Program—is clear. Also clear was the determination to accelerate the process of assimilation, of the "drawing even closer together" of the nationalities of the USSR.

A leading Soviet analyst of the national question, M. S. Dzhunusov, has stressed the "drawing closer" process by citing statistics on the changing ethnic composition of the union republics (particularly the greater number of Russians and Ukrainians in the various non-Slavic republics), the more extensive use of the Russian language by non-Russian nationalities (over thirteen million, according to the 1970 census), and the frequency of intermarriage. (According to a 1963 Soviet report to the UN, there are in urban areas 151 mixed families per 1,000 families in the USSR as a whole, 108 in the RSFSR, 263 in the Ukraine, and 237 in Byelorussia.)[50]

At the Party Congress, it was also emphasized, however, that besides the "drawing together" of nationalities, there was simultaneously taking place a contrary development of "tempestuous all-round [national] development." For a number of nationalities this is clearly the case. Professor Richard Pipes of Harvard University has shown that major Soviet national groups, in areas where they enjoy a numerical and administrative preponderance, are acquiring a "linguistic hegemony," counterposed to the Russian hegemony elsewhere, and that such hegemony is an indicator of their "national viability."[51] Yakov Kantor also took note of the two opposing tendencies, that of assimilation and that of the strengthening of minority cultures and languages. But he underscored the fact that the decisive factor is the presence or absence of vital institutions among the minority nationalities. It is precisely because of the dismantling of such institutions of the Jewish nationality, in violation of rights inscribed in Soviet law and expressed in Party policy, that the victory of the first tendency has been and is being facilitated.

Implicit in the policy of forcible assimilation is the severance of connections with Jewish communities abroad. Such links had been recognized and formalized by the USSR especially during the twenties (through, for example, arrangements with the American Jewish

Joint Distribution Committee) and even to some extent during the thirties. World War II marked a high point in such arrangements, with officials of the Jewish Anti-Fascist Committee permitted, indeed encouraged, by the Soviet state to maintain contacts with Jewish organizations.

But a key article in *Pravda* in September, 1948, written by Ilya Ehrenburg at the instance of the Party organ's editors, established a new line which rejected the contention that a "bond exists between Jews of the whole world."[52] The official position of the regime was made clear in the second edition of the *Large Soviet Encyclopedia,* published in 1952. Jews do not constitute a "compact ethnic entity"; on the contrary, in the different countries, they differ in "language, culture, and way of life," thus making them "ethnographically closer to the countries in which they are living" than to Jews elsewhere.[53]

A debate at a United Nations seminar held in Yugoslavia in 1965 throws light on the resistance of Soviet authorities to formal ties between Soviet Jews and Jews abroad.[54] The seminar, which dealt with multinational societies, had on its agenda the item: "measures which should be taken to ensure the realization by ethnic, religious, linguistic or national groups of the special rights necessary to preserve their traditions, characteristics or national consciousness. . . ." Included was a discussion of the right of members of ethnic and religious groups to associate across national boundaries. When the issue was posed in terms of the special responsibility of one-party states to permit association across national borders, the Soviet response was violently negative. The Soviet spokesman vehemently argued that individuals have no standing in international law and, therefore, could not be granted rights of association. The right of association existed only for organizations. A participant described how the Jewish issue became central to the discussion: "By this point everyone in the conference was aware that Russian Jews are not permitted to have any national organization. What therefore was the value to them of a right for national organizations to associate with international ones?" Significantly, in 1963, there had been established a Soviet Committee for Cultural Ties with Compatriots Abroad, the purpose of which, according to *Izvestiia,* was to initiate contacts with "Russians, Ukrainians, Byelorussians, Latvians, Estonians, Lithuanians, and Armenians" who "have turned up in distant countries," and who "burn with the desire to know as much as possible about their homeland. . . ."[55] The absence of Jews from the list is notable.

Forcible assimilation carried a further implication, far more devastating in its psychological ramifications: consciousness of a distinctive Jewish past and Jewish identity and, therefore, consciousness of a heritage, was to be obliterated. Jews were to be transformed into non-persons with a past that was—in the words of George Orwell—to be plunged down the "memory hole" of history. Later chapters will delineate the contours of this tragedy.

The official treatment of Judaism, as distinct from the treatment meted out to the Jewish ethnic community, can fruitfully be examined in the context of Soviet policy toward religion generally. The distinction between religion and the secular culture of ethnic groups was, indeed, a fundamental one in early Bolshevik thinking and in the normative judgment of Party officials. Dedicated to "scientific materialism" and to the conviction that religion is the "opiate of the masses," the Soviet Communist Party conducts an unceasing, vigorous campaign against all religions. At the same time, the Soviet state distinguishes between its conduct toward religion and that of the Party: "There are fundamental differences between the two [State and Party]. In its legislation on religion, the Soviet State . . . accords completely unrestricted freedom of worship to citizens of the Soviet Union who are believers."[56] The above assertion was placed on record at the United Nations. The Soviet Government went on to say that while the state, "taking into account the fact that parts of the population have not yet abandoned their religious outlook, guarantees them the right . . . to worship freely," the Communist Party, "on the other hand, on the basis of the law on freedom of conscience, carries on a scientific atheist propaganda among the population."

The reference to the legal basis for Party propaganda work against religion is of interest. The earlier RSFSR Constitutions of 1918 (Article 13) and of 1925, as part of their "Bill of Rights," provided for both "freedom of religious and anti-religious propaganda." However, a law of April, 1929, that regulated the activities of religious organizations in the Soviet Union deprived religious bodies of the right of religious propaganda. The 1936 Constitution took account of this change by deleting the reference to "religious propaganda." Only "anti-religious" propaganda is permitted, although "freedom of religious worship" is legally assured. Article 124 reads: "In order to ensure freedom of conscience, the church in the USSR is separated from the State, and the school from the church. Freedom of religious worship and freedom of anti-religious propaganda is recognized for citizens." There were some who had proposed that Article 124 prohibit "religious rites" along with religious propaganda. But this proposal was rejected after Stalin described it as "running counter to the spirit of our Constitution."[57]

The rights guaranteed to the recognized religions are also spelled out in the still-valid decree of the Council of Peoples' Commissars on January 23, 1918, the Order of the All-Union Central Executive Committee and the Council of Peoples' Commissars of the RSFSR on April 8, 1929, and in the various criminal codes. The Soviet Government has provided the United Nations with a detailed listing of and commentary upon these rights in two major documents that are available in *Study of Discrimination in the Matter of Religious Rights and Practices, Conference Room Paper* no. 35, and *Manifestations of Racial Prejudice and Religious Intolerance* —Doc. A/5473/Add. 1.

At the very heart of the decree of July, 1918, is the equality of all religions. Abolishing the domination that had been enjoyed by Russian Orthodoxy under the Tsars, Article 2 of the decree prohibited governmental actions that would "establish any kind of privileges or advantages on the grounds of religious affiliation of citizens." The Soviet Government, in commenting upon the provision, stressed that the legislation is designed in part to respect "scrupulously" the "equality of faiths," and, therefore, the state "accords to no one religion any special privileges over any other."

In a number of vital respects, the principle of equality of religious rights is observed in the breach insofar as Judaism is concerned. This became apparent in the immediate post-war period, when, according to one authority, Professor John Curtiss of Duke University, "favorable treatment" by the state was given to Russian Orthodoxy, Islam, and other religions while Judaism was held in "disfavor."[58] Another close student of the Soviet religious scene, Walter Kolarz, concluded that "Stalin anticipated that religious Judaism would disappear much more quickly than other religions . . . and he was determined to hasten this natural process as effectively as possible."[59] The concessions granted other religions after 1945 were withheld from Judaism.

The critical area concerns the right to organize a central or federative body. The order of April 8, 1929, permits

> . . . religious communities of the same denomination . . . [to] form religious associations which may or may not coincide geographically with the administrative subdivisions of the Union of Soviet Socialist Republics . . . and may set up *religious centres*. . . . These *religious centres,* which are governed by their own rules and regulations, may hold republic or All-Union congresses, church councils, and other conferences on matters related to the administration of church affairs. . . . [Emphasis added.]

The order further noted that the "religious centres" may publish "periodicals and the necessary devotional literature." Unlike the other recognized religious bodies, Judaism has not had any semblance of a central or coordinating structure since 1926. In August, 1919, the Soviet Government banned the previously existing central Jewish body, the Central Board of Jewish Communities. No central body has been permitted to be established to replace it. A Conference of Rabbis of the Soviet Union met for the last time in 1926.[60] The meeting place was Korosten, with twenty-five rabbis as delegates—principally from the local and nearby areas—and ninety other rabbis as guests.

The absence of a central or federative structure for Judaism results in fragmentation of religious life and limits effective resistance to the Party's anti-religious campaign. It also makes the enjoyment of specified as well as unspecified rights difficult if not impossible. Thus, while the "religious centres" of the other faiths are in a position to publish periodicals and devotional literature, Judaism finds this task virtually prohibited. Unlike other religions, it publishes no periodical. More important, it has not published a Hebrew Bible since the late twenties, while the Russian Orthodox Church in 1957 printed fifty thousand copies of a 1926 edition of the Bible, the Baptists in 1958 printed ten thousand copies of the Bible, and the Moslems in 1958 printed nine thousand copies of the Koran. (Another edition of the Koran was published in 1962 by the Moslem Board of Central Asia.)

Jewish prayer books in the USSR are scarce. If the state has assured those faiths having no "religious centres" a supply of the "necessary paper and the use of printing plants," it is apparent that this privilege has been extended to Judaism in a most restrained manner. In 1957, for the first time since the twenties, an edition of the *siddur* (prayer book) was permitted, but of only three thousand copies. Another edition of five thousand copies appeared in 1968. It is apparent that the number published is scarcely adequate to the need.

Without a "religious centre," too, Judaism has been deprived of the opportunity to produce such essential devotional articles as the *talith* (prayer shawl) or the *tfilin* (phylacteries). The Soviet Government says that it extends to "religious organizations" the right "to set up undertakings, such as candle factories and ikon painting studios, for the manufacture of the requisite articles for religious worship." The right becomes meaningless without a "religious centre."

Of even greater significance is the fact that the existence of "religious centres" enables the religions of the USSR to have formal and official contacts with their respective co-religionists abroad. A lengthy report on this subject by the Soviet Government to the UN in 1963 shows indirectly how Judaism is deleteriously affected. The report merits quoting:

> Religious centres in the USSR maintain extensive communications with kindred international ecclesiastical organizations and take part in international ecclesiastical congresses, councils and conferences. . . .
> The Russian and Georgian Orthodox churches, the Lutheran Church of Estonia and Latvia, the Armenian Church and the Church of Evangelical Christian Baptists are members of the World Council of Churches. The Christian Churches of the USSR—Orthodox, Armenian, Lutheran, Old Believer, Reformed and Evangelical Christian Baptist—are members of the International Association of Christian Churches called the "Prague Christian Movement for Peace." . . .
> The All-Union Council of Evangelical Christian Baptists are members of the World Union of Baptists and the European Baptist Federation. The Buddhist Central Religious Authority in the USSR is part of the World Brotherhood of Buddhists. The Mohammedan Ecclesiastical authorities in the USSR take an active part in the Islamic Congress. The Catholic Church in the USSR participated in the first session of the Second Vatican Congress.[61]

The lack of reference to Jews reflects the stark reality of a religious community which is permitted no formal affiliations with an external body of its co-religionists. The UN seminar in Yugoslavia in the summer of 1965 highlighted the issue. The Soviet representative at the seminar insisted that individual persons have no status in international law and that, consequently, members of an ethnic or religious group cannot be accorded the right of association with international bodies of the same ethnic or religious affiliation. Only organizations have such status, he argued. The fact that Judaism has no "religious centre" in the USSR precludes its right to have an "association" with co-religionists abroad.

Besides permitting formal contacts between religious organizations, the Soviet Government allows theological students of many of its faiths to journey abroad and study at foreign seminaries or religious educational institutions. Judaism is an exception, as this report from the Soviet Government to the UN indicates:

> . . . The Soviet Government does not impede the training of ministers at theological institutions abroad. In the last five years students from religious groups in the USSR have studied at the following educational establishments abroad: The Moslem Theological Academy in Cairo, Baptist colleges in the United Kingdom, the Theological faculty of Oxford University, the Lateran University of the Vatican, Göttingen University (Federal Republic of Germany), Bethel Theological Seminary, McMaster University (Canada) and the Moslem University of Syria.[62]

During 1971 there was talk of the Soviet Union's permitting young Jews seeking rabbinical training to go to Hungary, where appropriate training facilities are plentiful. These hopes have yet to be fulfilled.

With reference to the training of theological students, Judaism operates under a heavy burden. Only one Yeshiva had been allowed to operate. Permission for its opening in Moscow was finally granted in 1957, while the Russian Orthodox, for example, were permitted to establish a number of seminaries immediately after the war. Since its opening it has ordained but two students. Of the thirteen students who were at the Yeshiva in April, 1962—eleven of whom were over forty years of age—nine students from communities in Georgia and Dagestan were prevented by Soviet authorities from coming to Moscow on grounds of a housing shortage. Between 1965 and 1972 no students were reported to be in attendance at the Yeshiva. Only in March, 1972, were its doors opened to permit six students—none of them rabbinic students—to study there.

Lack of a Yeshiva seriously affects the future course of Judaism. Without replacements for a fast-aging rabbinate (the average age is close to seventy years) numbering approximately a dozen persons, Judaism may soon be without spiritual leadership. In this connection, it is to be noted that all religions are affected by a state law that forbids "any teaching of a religious belief to children or persons under age, done in governmental or private teaching establishments or schools."[63] Only in a family setting is such teaching allowed. The chairman of the USSR Supreme Court's Collegium for Criminal Cases has emphasized that "the raising of children in a religious spirit when carried out by parents and other relatives does not constitute a crime. . . ."

Synagogues themselves, virtually the only remaining Jewish institutions in the USSR, were the target of particularly severe administrative measures during the 1959–62 drive against houses of worship.[64] The massive closures that occurred assumed the following pattern: first, letters and articles appeared in the press citing alleged illegal activities or pro-Israel propaganda in the synagogue; then, requests from readers, including "religious believers," asking for the liquidation of the "nest of corruption" and the "nest of anti-Soviet propaganda" would be published; finally, local authorities would "bow to the ardent wishes of the community" and padlock the synagogue doors.

By the time the campaign ended, the number of synagogues in the USSR was drastically reduced. An official report to the UN in 1956 referred to 450 synagogues. By 1961, it was down to 100. Nine years later, only 62 synagogues remained (by July, 1972, the total dropped to 58); 13 functioned in Georgia and 17 in the northern Caucasus and the Central Asian republics. The latter are areas inhabited by Oriental (Sephardic) Jews, who number approximately one hundred thousand. The balance of 32 synagogues was expected to serve the two million European (Ashkenazic) Jews. A specialist on Judaism in the USSR, Joshua Rothenberg of Brandeis University, provides the following comparative data to demonstrate the unequal treatment rendered the Jewish religion: Russian Orthodoxy—one church for 2,000 faithful; Islam—one house of prayer for 10,000 worshippers; Latvian Lutheranism—one church for 1,740 worshippers; Judaism—one synagogue for 23,400 worshippers.[65] Another authoritative account sums up the findings of specialists on the various religions of the USSR: "All experts agree that the Jewish religious group is even less equipped with rights and opportunities to perform the traditional functions than the Christian sects or the Moslems."[66]

What is especially striking is the extent and character of the propaganda attack upon Judaism. A bibliographical study reveals that between 1958 and 1967 the number of published books and pamphlets attacking Judaism constituted 9 per cent of all works attacking various religions.[67] The Jews then numbered but 1 per cent of the total population. And the number of copies of books attacking Judaism was seven times as great as the number of copies attacking Islam and twice as great as the number of copies attacking Christianity.

Many of the broadsides directed at Judaism suggest that it is regarded as even more harmful and reactionary than the other recognized religions in the USSR.[68] A Soviet "authority" writing in the leading newspaper of Byelorussia declared that "there is no crime that has not been justified by the Holy Book of the Israelites." The introduction to a book published by the Ukrainian Academy of Sciences states: "Judaism . . . has incorporated and condensed everything that is most reactionary and most anti-humane in the writings of contemporary religions." A prominent book on Judaism published in Moldavia—*Contemporary Judaism and Zionism*—was so hostile that *L'Unità,* the organ of the Italian Communist Party, denounced it for proclaiming Judaism as "the worst of all religions."

Why is Judaism subjected to special disabilities and why has it been the target of an especially vicious propaganda campaign? An "old Bolshevik," speaking to an American visitor in the offices of *Pravda,* summed up the answer neatly: "Synagogues are in themselves of no consequence. But they serve as the last assembly for our Jews, often for those who are no longer religious. They help maintain cohesion, to nurture the feeling of belonging to a distinctive Jewish entity. And this is exactly what we are trying to prevent."[69] If Judaism is sharply attacked it is "not so much because it is a religion as because of its effect in unifying the Jews." Clearly, the enemy is not Judaism per se, a force which the Soviets correctly assess as weakening under the impact of secularization; rather, the target is the Jewish community as a distinctive ethnic group. To the extent that it is impregnated with cultural traditions which carry religious underpinnings or overtones, these traditions must be totally uprooted. To the extent that the synagogue remains the only institutional form, however weak, providing a certain unity and cohesiveness to *national* Jewish existence, it must not be permitted to stand unchallenged.

Significantly, the two Jewish religious rites which have been subjected to the strongest administrative pressures and propaganda are those which have a distinctive *national* character: the Passover service and circumcision. Passover is, in many ways, a national holiday recalling the historical experience of the liberation of the Jewish people from Egyptian bondage. It is at least minimally commemorated, if not *religiously* observed, by secular-minded and atheist-oriented Jews wherever they might be. Central to its observance is the dietary article *matzoth* (unleavened bread), and how the USSR has handled the baking and sale of this article is a measure of its extraordinary concern about the holiday. In a report to the UN in 1956, the Soviet Government said that "on days preceding particularly important holidays" such as "Passover in the case of the Jews" the stores of "the State trading organizations sell . . . matzoth (unleavened bread) for Orthodox Jews . . . to enable worshippers to perform the appropriate ritual."[70]

But as early as 1957, restrictions on the public baking and sale of matzoth began to appear, first in Kharkov. In succeeding years, the ban spread to other cities, and, by 1962, it virtually blanketed the entire country. On March 16, 1963, Rabbi Yehuda Levin, the chief rabbi of Moscow, formally announced that the authorities had banned entirely the public baking and sale of matzoth. He advised his congregants to bake the unleavened bread at home. Three months later, on July 16, 1963, four elderly Jews were convicted of "illegal profiteering" in the sale of matzoth—the first trial of its kind in forty-five years, according to the chief rabbi. The arguments made by the defense attorney are interesting in pointing up the disabilities under which Judaism operates in contrast to Russian Orthodoxy: ". . . All churches sell candles and wafers at high prices and nobody holds them for criminal responsibility. . . . Those accused did it not for profit but for their religious beliefs; they used no hired labor, they distributed the production which they didn't use themselves."[71]

In 1964, while the public baking and sale of matzoth remained forbidden, the Moscow Jewish community was suddenly permitted, prior to the Passover, to rent a small bakery for production of the dietary article. Since only a limited amount could be produced, the chief rabbi granted a special dispensation to religious Jews to eat beans and peas instead. The outcry from abroad, in 1965, was accompanied by a loosening of previous restrictions. In a few of the major communities, synagogues were given the right to bake matzoth for the Passover, and the chief rabbi told an American delegation in that year that the authorities had assured him adequate supplies of flour for the baking of matzoth in the future. But that assurance did not extend to the rest of the country.

The concession did not affect the propaganda campaign. Agitation in the press directed against Passover continues to be vindictive, with the ancient and traditional phrase of the Haggadah—"Next Year in Jerusalem"—singled out for the sharpest condemnation. The reason is obvious. It is less the seemingly Zionist flavor which it imparts as the implication that Jews as a group everywhere subscribe to a historic loyalty enshrined in a symbol that memorializes the ancient struggle for freedom and group integrity.

The rite of circumcision is even more characteristic of the Jew, whether religious or atheist. Circumcision has been throughout time a distinguishing mark of the Jewish male. Indeed, in many parts of the world today it is practiced upon great masses of non-Jewish male infants because of health considerations.[72] Medical specialists have found that the incidence of carcinoma of the genito-urinary organs among both males and females is reduced by circumcision. Yet, Soviet authorities consider ritual circumcision a barbaric practice which is injurious to health. Even medical circumcision, in contrast to ritual circumcision performed by a *mohel,* is frowned upon. The Soviet medical encyclopedia carries no entry on the subject, and the relationship between carcinoma of the genito-urinary organs and circumcision has never been discussed in the principal Soviet journal on the subject (*Voprosy onkologii*).

Soviet law does not specifically prohibit circumcision, probably because the regime is reluctant to antagonize its twenty-five million

Moslem citizens, a majority of whom still faithfully observe the rite. Indeed, Moslems are not criticized for practicing the rite even though it is performed openly by them in the Central Asian republics and in the Caucasus, sometimes by Party members. Oriental Jews living in these areas benefit from the leniency shown Moslems.

Non-Oriental Jews in the USSR, however, face the harshest social consequences should they have their newborn sons circumcised. Party members are expelled and non–Party members may be demoted in their jobs, lose opportunities for advancement, kept from acquiring a new apartment or in winning a resort vacation, and face a social ostracism for themselves and their families. The *mohel* is subject to strong pressures unless he is among the fortunate few in large towns who are granted official permits. He may be punished for performing surgery without a license or for functioning as a clergyman without registering. In one "public trial" in Moldavia, widely covered in the Soviet press, the *mohel,* after imprisonment and interrogation, told the audience that he had come to understand that his occupation was repulsive and "contrary to the requirements of advanced Soviet medicine." He called upon the young parents in the audience not to entrust their male infants to the "filthy hands of the *mohelim.*"

Soviet authorities, it is clear, are determined to eradicate not only every institutional form by which Jewish identity can be preserved, but even those traditional practices by which a certain minimal awareness of that identity is maintained.

Chapter 3
Patterns of
Anti-Jewish Discrimination:
Civil Rights, Soviet Style

Charges of discrimination against the Soviet Jewish community, as an ethnic community, frequently evoke from Soviet authorities a response that shifts the question to a fundamentally different level. They point to a mass of statistical data demonstrating the extraordinary participation of Jews in numerous occupations and in various aspects of life. Thus stress is placed upon the rights of Jews *as individuals,* not Jewish communal rights. The issue is transformed into what is known in the West as civil rights. But do law and reality coincide in regard to civil rights? Or is the constitution here, too, a fiction?

Under the Tsars, there had existed a host of severe limitations upon the civil rights of Jews—residence, education, military service, participation in government and in elections. The very first decree of the Provisional Government that took power following the overthrow of the Tsar in March, 1917, abolished all restrictions upon the individual based upon ethnic, religious, or social discrimination.[1] Two weeks later, the Ministry of Defense removed all discrimination against Jews in the army (where they had been permitted to serve only as soldiers, not as officers) and in the navy (where they could not serve at all). And on April 5, the Provisional Government issued a number of decrees that specified the areas in which restrictions on the rights of citizens on grounds of race or creed were to be eradicated: residence and movement, ownership and use of property, employment, and schooling.

The Bolshevik seizure of power in November, 1917, was accompanied almost immediately by assurances concerning hard-won civil rights. On November 15, 1917, the new regime issued a Declaration of Rights, signed jointly by Lenin as head of government and by Stalin as commissar of nationalities, which formally abolished "all national and national-religious privileges and restrictions."[2]

The first Soviet Constitution reaffirmed the Declaration of Rights, at least as far as non-discrimination on ethnic grounds was concerned. The anti-religious campaign already launched by the Bolsheviks precluded guarantees of non-discrimination on creedal grounds. Article 22 of the 1918 Constitution of the RSFSR recognized "that all citizens enjoy equal rights without distinction of race or nationality [and] ... it is contrary to the fundamental laws of the Republic to grant or tolerate any privileges or advantages based on race or nationality. . . ." Similar civil rights provisions were inserted in the constitutions of other Soviet republics—Article 15 of the Byelorussian Constitution (1919), Article 32 of the Ukrainian Constitution (1919), Article 13 of the Azerbaidzhan Constitution (1921), and Article 7 of the Georgian Constitution (1922).

Following the formation of the USSR in 1924, the new republic constitutions repeated with slight variations the earlier formulations on civil rights. Thus, the Constitution of the RSFSR adopted in 1925 stated in Article 13 that "the principle of the equality of rights of all citizens without distinction of race or nationality" is fundamental, and that "any restriction" of these rights and, "still more, the granting or toleration of any national privileges whatsoever, whether direct or indirect, are wholly incompatible with the fundamental laws. . . ."

The 1936 Constitution of the USSR gives expression to the historic emphasis upon civil rights of all Soviet citizens and spells out the areas to be covered. Article 123 reads:

Equality of rights of citizens of the USSR, irrespective of their nationality or race, in all spheres of economic, government, cultural, political and other public activity, is an indefeasible law.

Any direct or indirect restriction of the rights of, or conversely, the establishment of any direct or indirect privileges for citizens on account of their race or nationality . . . is punishable by law.

Article 135 applies the guarantees on civil rights to all Soviet elections. Soviet citizens, "irrespective of race or nationality" are eligible to vote and to be elected. In the constitutions of each of the fifteen Soviet republics there are to be found formulations similar to those of Article 123 and Article 135.

Constitutional provisions on civil rights are undergirded by the provisions of the various criminal codes. Article 8 of the law on the Fundamentals of Criminal Jurisprudence of the USSR and the Union Republics emphasizes that all citizens are equal in the eyes of the law and the courts. The latest Criminal Code of the RSFSR (January 1, 1961) is especially pointed in its treatment. Its Article 74, which is entitled "Infringement of National and Racial Equal Rights," specifies that "any direct or indirect limitation of rights or the establishment of direct or indirect privileges" on grounds of race or nationality will be punished by a deprivation of freedom for a period of from six months to three years or by exile for from two to five years.[3]

In a number of areas, Jews enjoy the civil rights spelled out in the legal statutes. Residential restrictions are non-existent, and there are no barriers to participation in various aspects of social life— trade unions, army, the social services, clubs. Employment opportunities in a number of fields—particularly science, medicine, law, and the arts—are widespread, as available data indicate. As of 1967–68, there were 497,100 Jewish technical specialists working in the economy—327,800 with a higher education, the balance with a secondary or technical school education.[4] In the category of "specialists," Jews outnumber all nationalities except Russians and Ukrainians. In the sciences and arts, they rank especially high. Among "scientific and academic workers," Jews number 58,952, constituting 7.65 per cent of the total. At the level of the prestigious Academy of Sciences, the percentage is even higher (Minister of Culture Yekaterina Furtseva stated that it was 10 per cent). They also rank high among Lenin Prize winners in science and technology. In 1963, the Soviet press agency Novosti stated that Jews constituted 14.7 per cent of all doctors; 10.4 per cent of lawyers; 8 per cent of writers and journalists; and 7 per cent of actors, sculptors, musicians, and other artists. (The percentage of Jewish doctors has dropped since then. Data published in a Soviet health journal in 1970 show a sharp decline between 1958 and 1965 in the percentage of Jewish doctors in the largest union republic—the Russian Republic—from 14.3 per cent to 10.3 per cent.[5] A comparative decline must have occurred in the USSR as a whole.)

However, there is also considerable evidence that, notwithstanding the numerous constitutional provisions and criminal statutes, discrimination against Jews in a number of vital and decision-making fields exists. Indeed, there is evidence that unpublished governmental regulations have been issued, whether in written or oral form, which call for quotas limiting the number of Jews in specific areas. One prominent Soviet historian, in a *samizdat* document, states that the usual form is oral.[6] There is no evidence that the criminal codes have been used against anyone for discrimination against Jews on racial or national grounds.

Quotas or patterns of discrimination in governmental employment were certainly not the case during the early years of the Revolution or during the twenties. In December, 1927, at the Fifteenth Congress of the Communist Party, S. Ordzhonikidze, a high Soviet official, reported that Jews (who then constituted 1.8 per cent of the population) held 10.3 per cent of the administrative offices in Moscow, 22.6 per cent of the civil service posts in the Ukraine (Jews numbered 5.4 per cent of the Ukraine population), and 30.6 per cent of the posts in Byelorussia (Jews here were 8.2 per cent of the population).[7] The late thirties and forties were characterized by a sharp drop in these percentages. Three interviews in 1956 with top Soviet officials made it apparent that the central government had consciously established quota systems to restrict Jewish employment, and that even more rigid quotas were installed in the governments of the various union republics.

The first interview was conducted with Khrushchev and other officials by a visiting parliamentary delegation of the French Socialist Party. At the third meeting of the delegation with the Russians, held on May 12, Khrushchev said:

Our heterogeneous populations have their republics . . . Each of them has an autonomous government. Formerly backward and illiterate, these peoples now have their engineers and professionals. . . .

Anti-Semitic sentiments still exist there. They are remnants of a reactionary past. This is a complicated problem because of the position of the Jews and their relations with the other peoples. At the outset of the Revolution, we had many Jews in the leadership of the Party and State. They were more educated, maybe more revolutionary than the average Russian. In due course we have created new cadres. . . .[8]

At this point, Khrushchev was interrupted by Mikhail Pervukhin, a high Party official, who attempted to clarify Khrushchev's term "new cadres." Pervukhin explained: "Our own intelligentsia." The "we" and "they" type of bigotry was clear. Khrushchev continued, driving home the rationalization for a set of quota devices in a particularly vulgar fashion:

Should the Jews want to occupy the foremost positions in our republics now, it would naturally be taken amiss by the indigenous inhabitants. The latter would ill-receive these pretensions, especially as they do not consider themselves less intelligent nor less capable than the Jews. Or, for instance, when a Jew in the Ukraine is appointed to an important post and he surrounds himself with Jewish collaborators, it is understandable that this should create jealousy and hostility toward Jews.

In a second interview, the following month, the minister of culture, Yekaterina Furtseva, told a correspondent of the *National Guardian*: "The Government has found in some of its departments a heavy concentration of Jewish people, upwards of 50 per cent of the staff. Steps were taken to transfer them to other enterprises, giving them equally good positions and without jeopardizing their rights."[9]

The third interview was one conducted in August by J. B. Salsberg, a former Canadian Communist leader, with a number of key Soviet officials.[10] One of them corroborated Furtseva's statement: "He tried terribly hard to prove to me [Salsberg] with examples that the transfer or dismissal of Jewish employees in once-backward republics, that now have 'their own' intelligentsia and professional people capable of occupying posts previously held by Jews or Russians, has nothing to do with anti-Semitism." Six years later, Khrushchev was to return to the same theme in an unpublished speech to a meeting of artists held on December 17, 1962. He told the audience that were Jews to occupy too many top positions it would tend to create anti-Semitism.[11]

If the interviews and the Khrushchev speech were hidden from the Russian public and appeared only in the Western press, the facts about restrictions and the use of the quotas were nonetheless known to many in the Soviet population. In March, 1962, at a meeting of the Central Committee, Academician Konstantin Skriabin, speaking on the importance of appointing competent cadres in the scientific field, critically commented, in an indirect manner, upon the misuse of the passport. "From my point of view, a scientist should not be evaluated by his passport but by his head, from the point of view of his ability and social usefulness."[12] Another oblique disclosure of the preferential uses of the quota was made in the Party theoretical journal, *Kommunist,* in June, 1963: "The less developed nations of the USSR were granted various privileges and advantages . . . in the preparation of cadres. Only under these circumstances could the actual equality of nations be achieved."[13]

Membership in the All-Union Supreme Soviet and in the union republic supreme soviets is a critical indicator of official policy toward Jews in the political area. For the election of delegates is a Party-dictated choice with only one name appearing on the ballot. As early as 1938, only two Jews were elected to the Ukraine Supreme Soviet, which had a total membership of 304.[14] Jewish deputies thus constituted but 0.7 per cent of the total, while the Jewish population in that republic then constituted 5 per cent of the total population. Since, in most other union republics, the percentage of Jews elected to supreme soviets was far higher than their ratio in the respective populations, the Ukrainian experience can be understood only as a state decision to appease popular anti-Semitism in the Ukraine.

Comparative data concerning the All-Union Supreme Soviet is even more revealing.[15] In the last election of the Supreme Soviet prior to the war, held in December, 1937, 47 Jews were chosen (of 1,143 members)—4.1 per cent of the total. Jews numbered 32 of 569 members, or 5.6 percent, in the Soviet of the Union, and 15 of 574, or 2.6 per cent, in the Soviet of Nationalities. In the first election of a Supreme Soviet after the war, January, 1946, the drop in Jewish membership was catastrophic and hardly explicable in terms of even the sizable Jewish population losses due to the Nazi

Holocaust. Only 5 Jewish names were to be found among 601 members of the Soviet of the Union, or less than 1 per cent. The number of Jews "elected" to the Soviet of Nationalities is not known. However, the official rapporteur of this body ranked them twenty-sixth among ethnic group deputies. In 1937, they ranked eleventh.

The process of anti-Jewish discrimination in the political area unfolded steadily during the fifties and sixties.[16] In 1950, 2 Jews were elected to the 678-member Soviet of the Union and 3 to the 638-member Soviet of Nationalities. The 1958 Supreme Soviet had but 3 Jews among 1,364 members of both houses. In 1962, only 5 Jews were selected by the Party leaders to be "elected" to the 1,443-member Supreme Soviet. The percentage was 0.35 per cent, far below the percentage of Jews in the population as a whole. (Jews then constituted 1.09 per cent of the total.) The percentage declined further to 0.3 in 1966, when the new membership of the Supreme Soviet increased to 1,517, but the Jewish representation remained at 5. There was not a single Jewish deputy to be found among those chosen to represent Moscow or Leningrad, both containing large Jewish populations. Nor was there a Jewish deputy for any constituency in the Ukraine, Byelorussia, Lithuania, or Moldavia.

Even more pronounced was the pattern of discrimination in the selection of deputies to the union republic supreme soviets.[17] Of the 5,312 deputies elected to these bodies in 1959, only 14 were Jewish—0.26 per cent. Only one Jewish deputy was to be found among the 835 deputies in the Russian Republic; a single Jew among the 457 deputies in the Ukraine (0.22 per cent of a Jewish population constituting 2 per cent of the total population); and but 2 Jews among the 407 deputies in Byelorussia (0.45 per cent of a Jewish population constituting 1.9 per cent of the total). Similar percentages were to be found in various non-Slavic republics. For example, of the 281 deputies in Moldavia, where the Jews numbered 3.3 per cent of the population, there was not a single Jew; of the 200 deputies in Latvia, where Jews constituted 1.7 per cent of the population, no Jew was chosen. Lithuania was an exception: Jewish representation in its Supreme Soviet paralleled the percentage of the Jews in the population, with 3 of 209 deputies—1.44 per cent.

The composition of local soviets reflects approximately the same disparate proportions as are to be found in the higher bodies. Although the Novosti press agency has trumpeted abroad the figure of 7,623 Jews elected to local bodies in 1961, it has failed to note that a total of 1,822,049 deputies were elected to local soviets that year, thus making Jewish representation only 0.4 per cent.[18]

Of far greater significance was the drastic drop in membership of Jews in the elite Central Committee of the Communist Party. At the beginning of the twenties, one-quarter of the Central Committee were Jews.[19] (At the Fourteenth Party Congress in November, 1927, 10 per cent of all the delegates were Jewish.) In 1939, of 139 members of this body, 15 were Jewish.[20] The percentage then was 10.8, greater than that of Ukrainians and Byelorussians combined. The percentage had dropped to 3 in 1952, then to 2 in 1956. In 1961, it had declined to a mere 0.3 per cent. Today there is one token Jew, V. Dymshits, on the Central Committee. An analyst of the Soviet elite concluded: "The Jews are the only nationality whose relative weight and absolute numbers in elite representation declined consistently in both the Stalinist and post-Stalin eras."[21] An earlier study of the Party elite in the Ukraine pointed in the same direction. After noting that the proportion of Jews among delegates to the Ukrainian Party Congress declined from 4.1 per cent in 1940 to 2.6 per cent in 1956, the author concluded: "It would seem that Jews were deliberately restricted to a lower proportion of the higher and more conspicuous levels of Party leadership."[22]

There are no Jews today in the top Party organ, the Politburo; and, with one exception, there do not appear to be any Jews among lists of key figures either in the central Party apparatus or among first secretaries of provincial and district Party organizations.[23] The exception is the very recent appointment of one, Lev Shapiro, as first secretary of the Party organization in Birobidzhan.[24] Even in the selection of ordinary Party membership, there appears to be a clear, if still very limited, discriminatory pattern emerging. A 1970 study of Party membership reveals that "the party saturation of the Soviet Jewish community fell from about 300 per cent of the national average . . . in 1940 to about 140–180 per cent of the national average in 1965."[25] The author of the study speculated that this decline may be "due to official discrimination" as well as to the great expansion in recent years of membership recruitment, especially among workers and peasants. Nonetheless, the Jews continue to be the most Party-saturated nationality in the USSR, with eighty out of every thousand Jews estimated as belonging to the Party in 1965 as compared with fifty-one per thousand for the Soviet population as a whole. This is hardly surprising, since most Party members have been recruited from urban areas and Jews are overwhelmingly an urban community. Leadership in the Party, of course, is of a completely different order of importance than membership.

The Soviet diplomatic corps appears to be virtually *judenrein*—in striking contrast to the situation that prevailed in the twenties and thirties. A former UNRRA official in the Soviet Union, writing shortly after World War II, noted that "in recent years Jews have been barred from recruitment into the Soviet foreign service. . . ."[26] At about the same time, a *New York Times* correspondent reported that "Jews were no longer being accepted by the Foreign Office in the diplomatic training course."[27] Examination of a 1962 list of 475 top Soviet officials in the Ministry of Foreign Affairs and in high diplomatic posts abroad showed that only five had names which might be considered as characteristically Jewish.[28] A similar pattern emerged in lists of officials in the Ministry of Defense and the Ministry of Foreign Trade.

That anti-Semitism motivates the selection of personnel in the entire political-security complex, whether on the national or the republic level, is clear and unmistakable. Andrei Sakharov, writing in 1968, observed that "after the nineteen thirties," the "appointments policy" made by the "highest bureaucratic elite of our government" was consistently affected by anti-Semitic considerations.[29] Writing two years later, in May, 1970, another prominent dissenter, Roy Medvedev, stated: ". . . access to work in the higher Party apparatus, in the provincial and regional branches of the Party, in various kinds of central ideological institutions, in the higher organs of the military leadership, in the diplomatic service and in the organs of the KGB and procuratorship [i.e., the equivalent of the U.S. attorney-general's office] were in practise closed to individuals of Jewish descent. . . ."[30] Medvedev went on to say that "there were several exceptions in this regard, but they only confirmed the general rule." The "exceptions" were required, he noted, "to prove the absence" of anti-Jewish discrimination.

Recent petitions of Soviet Jews frequently report various instances of discrimination, but the most revealing documentation is offered by a petition of twenty-six Lithuanian Jewish intellectuals on February 15, 1968, sent to the top Lithuanian Party official (a copy of which was smuggled out to the West).[31] Although Jews totaled 10 per cent of the population of Vilnius, the capital of Lithuania, "not a single Jew" has been elected either chairman, deputy chairman, or secretary of the city's four regional soviet executive committees. Jews have not been chosen as secretary of the Party, of the city committee, or of the regional committee. Jews have not been appointed as heads of any departments, or elected judges of the peoples' courts, or chosen to high positions in the trade unions. "During the entire post-war era, not a single representative of the Jewish youth has risen to a leading position in the state, party or trade union activity," according to the petition. The authors of the petition relate that when the deputy minister of trade was reproached for not selecting cadres on a non-discriminatory basis, he replied: "To be a Lithuanian in Soviet Lithuania is a political qualification." The president of the Pedagogical Institute in Vilnius was reported to have bluntly told a Jewish instructor: "It matters little that today you excel others in the German or English languages, in physics or mathematics, chemistry or music. We will develop our own cadres so that tomorrow Lithuanians will be more qualified than you."

The quota system in admission practices of universities, which is the key to advancement in Soviet society, is perhaps the most disturbing aspect of the discriminatory patterns. In 1959, the minister of higher education, V. P. Yeliutin, vehemently denied the existence of quotas directed against Jews.[32] And, three years later, the USSR ratified the UNESCO Convention Against Discrimination in Education, which obligates contracting states "to abrogate statutory provisions and any administrative practices which involve discrimination in education."[33]

In 1963, both *Kommunist*, by implication, and the *Bulletin of Higher Education* explicitly acknowledged the existence of "annually planned preferential admission quotas."[34] N. DeWitt, an American specialist on Soviet education, has explained that the quota system operates "to the particularly severe disadvantage of the Jewish population."[35] Noting that the quota system operates on the principle of "equivalent-balance" (i.e., "the representation of any national or ethnic grouping in over-all higher education enrollment should be as the relation of the size of that group to total USSR population"), DeWitt offered data showing that, between 1935 and 1958, "the index of representation rose for most nationalities, but fell for Georgians and all national minorities, with a drastic decline for the Jews." The quota system varies from place to place. Thus, according to Maurice Hindus, the University of Moscow has a particularly restrictive admissions policy for Jewish applicants, the University of Leningrad has less rigid restrictions, while admission to various universities in Siberia is apparently without racial bars.[36]

Roy Medvedev provides additional information validating Hindus' findings. In Kiev, he asserts, the quota on Jews is smaller than it is in Moscow, whose quota, in turn, is smaller than in Odessa. Even within Moscow, the pattern differs: the quota for Jews is less at Moscow State University than at Moscow State Polytechnical Institute. As described by Medvedev, the quota system "varies from city to city and university to university." In military academies and diplomatic schools, however, the quota system works "in all practicality," to exclude Jewish youth entirely. He goes on to note that a specific quota exists on the appointment of Jews to leading offices in universities and institutes of scientific research. The process is described in the following manner: "And, if in some institute, there is one Jew among nine or ten department chairmen or professors, then a second will not be appointed; and if one is appointed, then this must be compensated for at the expense of some other institute."

Soviet data released in 1961 showed that the number of Jewish students in higher education at the end of 1960 was 77,177, which constituted 3.2 per cent of the total number of university enrollments.[37] (Yeliutin had contended that it was 10 per cent.) On a percentage population basis, Jewish enrollment ranked highest among all nationality groups. It probably still does. The most recent statistics indicate that there are 110,000 Jews in higher education, their percentage of total enrollment being 2.55.[38] Yet, the percentage marks a sharp drop from the percentage of 1935, when Jewish enrollment was 13 per cent. Furthermore, when note is taken of the high proportion of Jews in urban areas (96 per cent), the statistics suggest "that in those republics where Jews constitute an above-average proportion of the urban populations, their representation among university students is well below the rate of the general population's access to higher education."[39] This is especially true in Lithuania and Moldavia. The Jewish petition from Lithuania throws some light on this point. It reports that "during the entire post-war period, not a single Jewish student living in Lithuania (except for a few children of privileged persons) was given a state scholarship to continue his studies at institutions of higher learning in Moscow or Leningrad." No Jew from Lithuania was selected to take post-graduate courses in the institutes of Moscow or Leningrad. And, with one exception, not a single Jewish Communist Party member has been allowed to attend either the Academy of Social Sciences or the Party university run by the Central Committee.

The quota device in education may be one explanation for the sharp percentage decline of Jews in scientific and academic fields.[40] While the figures show an absolute increase in the number of Jews in these fields from 24,400 in 1947 to 36,200 in 1961, the percentage of Jews among total scientific personnel dropped from 16.8 in 1947 to 8.8. By 1967–68, the percentage declined to 7.65 (even as the absolute numbers of Jews increased to almost 59,000). In medicine, the quota system appears to have had a more direct effect. Both absolutely and percentage-wise the number of Jewish doctors, as indicated earlier, has significantly declined.

But probably a more important reason for the percentage decline of Jews among the scientific cadres in the USSR is the widespread character of education generally, which has generated a significant increase in the number of trained scientific and technical personnel among numerous ethnic groups. The continuing absolute increase in the number of Jews employed as specialists (approximately 25 per cent of the total Jewish community are specialists or are training to be specialists) suggests that opportunities for Jews in the USSR are still great.[41]

Moreover, the Soviet Union, in its striving to maintain and increase its technological level, is most unlikely to block the acquisition of skills essential to an age of computers and electronics. To do so would imperil its striving to reach, let alone surpass, the productivity of the West. The Soviet Union's scarcest commodity remains highly skilled professional manpower. With Jews comprising somewhere between 5 and 10 per cent of that manpower, the regime could ill afford to dispense with such an invaluable resource.[42] No doubt it is this decisive consideration that played a key role in explaining a rare editorial that appeared on the front page of *Pravda* on September 5, 1965. The editorial reminded its readers that Lenin had demanded an unceasing "struggle against anti-Semitism, that malicious exaggeration of racial separateness and national enmity."

Not since 1929 had *Pravda* editorialized against anti-Semitism. That the authorities regarded the subject as vital is indicated by the fact that the editorial was reproduced in the provincial press throughout the USSR. A close and critical examination of its contents, however, indicates that its purpose was not a broad-ranging attack upon anti-Semitic stereotypes or upon anti-Semitism as a social evil. Rather, the principal purpose of the editorial was the narrow one of limiting discrimination against Jews in the field of production, especially in the non-Russian union republics. The key sentences read: "It is necessary to remember that the *growing scale of Communist construction* requires a constant exchange of cadres among the peoples. Therefore, any manifestations of national separateness in the *training and employment* of personnel of various nationalities in the Soviet *Republics* are intolerable." (Emphasis added.) No doubt the main targets of the editorial were bureaucrats in the various non-Russian republics—as in Lithuania—who, in response to the obvious long-standing anti-Semitic cues of the Party leadership at the top, and popular national pressures and prejudices from below, went beyond acceptable forms of discrimination and threatened to jeopardize local productivity plans by exclusion or limitation upon employment of Jewish technical cadres.

The editorial served a secondary purpose as well. Constantly sensitive to criticism in the Western world about its patterns of anti-Jewish discrimination, the regime was clearly determined to avoid too broad an exclusionary policy. A passage in the editorial emphasized that "we must keep in mind" in "conducting our ideological work" the "imperialists" who "slander" the USSR.

Local bureaucrats must of necessity be constantly impaled on the horns of a dilemma. In responding both to popular attitudes (which they themselves often share) and to definitive cues from the Party leadership, they are apt to be sufficiently inflexible as to erect barriers to the employment of highly skilled Jewish professionals at the peril of the economy as a whole. From time to time, the issue must be clarified for the local bureaucrat. The September, 1965, editorial was one form of clarification. A more recent example was a lengthy article in *Pravda* on July 16, 1971. Referring to the area of production, it warned provincial officials that "it is impermissible for us to oppose [the hiring of] some peoples or some individuals because of their nationality."[43] The article took note of the need for further training of native cadres in the economic system, but it emphasized that "the Party demands strict adherence to the selection of cadres according to . . . working qualities." Although no reference to anti-Semitism was made in the *Pravda* article, there can be little doubt that, at least in part, the Party had again become concerned with the effect of employment discrimination on the economy. A foreign correspondent, commenting on the report, stated that some union republics—Lithuania, Latvia, and Georgia were specifically mentioned—resented "outsiders."[44]

Yet, the difficulties in applying the Party line on Jews will remain. Some members of the Soviet intelligentsia who are anxious to maximize Soviet productivity have advanced the notion of eliminating the reference to nationality on the internal passport. Thus, on March 19, 1971, two physicists—Andrei Sakharov and V. F. Turchin—and the historian and educator Roy Medvedev sent a long memorandum to Party Secretary Leonid Brezhnev, Premier Kosygin, and President Nikolai Podgorny with proposals aimed at ending "threatening signs of dislocation and stagnation" in the national economy.[45] Pointing to the need to improve "the decisive factor" of labor productivity in order to catch up with "the scientific and technological activity" of the West, the letter called for, among other measures, the "abolition of registration of nationality in passports and questionnaires." It is clear from the context of their long memorandum that it was discrimination against Jews which was on the minds of the three prominent Soviet intellectuals.

But their proposal, if simple and logical, would create even greater difficulties for the Party leadership, for it clashes with another Party aim, that of keeping Jews away from decision-making positions and under continuous surveillance as a potential security risk. A keen student of minority problems in the USSR effectively summed up the issue in the following way:

> In all these [highly skilled] occupations Jews are (with rare exceptions) excluded from key decision-making positions, but they receive

many material perquisites. To put it another way, the regime has a very definite though declining interest in holding the Jews as captive labor, performing pleasant and highly remunerative tasks, but captives nonetheless in the sense that they must serve the system without participating in its decisions.[46]

In highly sensitive defense work, this type of labor may already be dispensable. A *samizdat* document, apparently written in May, 1970, and only recently revealed to have been drafted by Professor Mikhail Zand, stated: "A circular has become known concerning the undesirability of employment at responsible levels in institutions connected with defense, rocket, atomic and other secret work of persons belonging to a nationality the state organization of which pursues an unfriendly policy in relation to the USSR. It is evident that this means Jews."[47] Roy Medvedev appears to have seen the text of the circular to which Zand refers, for he places the key section of the circular in quotes: "And, thus, we see, as the replacement of the previous formulas about the 'non-indigenous population,' which served as a basis for discrimination against Jews . . . there are new formulas regarding 'persons belonging to a nationality the state organization of which pursues an unfriendly policy in relation to the USSR.' "[48]

The Zand document indicates, however, that this new pattern of discrimination applies to "responsible levels." Below those levels, the need for highly skilled "captive labor" remains. An important consequence of that need, inevitably, is an unsympathetic official attitude to applications for exit visas made by Jews with extensive technological abilities. Of course, once the Jews cease to be as occupationally productive as they now are, such an attitude may change. For the present and the immediate future, this can hardly be expected. On the other hand, the very nature of patterns of discrimination and the limitations placed upon advancement within the system—however satisfactory the remuneration may be for "captive labor"—cannot but generate among some Jews, especially the young, both a resistance to forcible assimilation and a desire to emigrate.

Chapter 4
The Origin and Persistence of Soviet Anti-Semitism

On the eve of the February Revolution, Lenin delivered a public lecture in Geneva, Switzerland, in which he went out of his way to laud the role of Jews in the revolutionary movement. "It should be said to their credit," he observed, "that today the Jews provide a relatively high percentage of representatives of internationalism compared with other nations."[1] Maxim Gorky has related a conversation with Lenin that displays the latter's philo-Semitism even more sharply. He quotes Lenin as saying: "There are few intelligent people among us. We are, generally speaking, a gifted people but intellectually lazy. An intelligent Russian is almost always a Jew or a man with Jewish blood."[2] The founder of the Soviet state not only denounced anti-Semitism; he refused to bow, in his own political appointments, to popular sentiments about Jews however expedient such compromises might have proved. When Trotsky demurred about taking the position of commissar of home affairs proffered by Lenin lest it stimulate or reinforce popular anti-Semitism, Lenin found the argument irrelevant.[3] Opportunism with respect to public attitudes would simply not be countenanced.

At what point—and why—in Soviet history was Lenin's uncompromising policy on anti-Semitism fundamentally altered? When and for what reason did the Soviet regime not only begin to give appropriate recognition and even obeisance to popular imagery about the Jews but, in fact, to absorb it in such a way as to make anti-Semitism an official policy? This policy would eventually extend beyond discriminatory practices to propaganda campaigns laced with sometimes subtle, sometimes overt forms of virulent anti-Semitism.

The young Soviet state vigorously combatted popular forms of anti-Semitism during the period of civil war (1918–20), when large-scale violence against Jews was supported and stimulated by various White military forces. As early as July 27, 1918, the Council of Peoples' Commissars issued a decree aimed at destroying the "anti-Semitic movement at its roots."[4] Lenin inserted the key phrase in the decree which ordered that "pogromists and persons inciting to pogroms be outlawed." The edict was a clear reflection of the determination of the state to uproot ideas and practices which, in fact, were considered as threatening Bolshevik rule.

During the twenties and especially in the latter part of that decade, the regime continued to make strong efforts to contain the virus of anti-Jewish bigotry. The RSFSR Criminal Code of 1922 provided a minimum of one year's solitary confinement (and death in time of war) for "agitation and propaganda arousing national enmities and dissensions."[5] The Criminal Code of 1927 was even more encompassing.[6] It provided for loss of freedom of "no less than two years" for "propaganda and agitation aimed at arousing national and religious enmities and dissensions." Even the mere possession of hate literature was subject to the above penalties. If the appropriate section of the criminal codes was infrequently invoked and if severe sentences for anti-Semitic offenses were rare, nonetheless educational campaigns were energetically conducted by Party organs, and various pedagogical efforts were undertaken.[7] Close to a hundred books and brochures—an extraordinary number—dealing with anti-Semitism were published by state organs.[8] On at least one occasion, *Pravda* sharply attacked "the connivance of the local Party, trade union and Komsomol organizations" in various "manifestations of anti-Semitism."[9] The editorial emphasized that the "connivance makes it possible for the anti-Semitic campaign of persecution to go on unpunished for months and years."

Yet, even during the twenties, the record was not unblemished. In early 1926, during the bitter intra-Party warfare, N. Uglanov, a

Stalin aide who was in charge of the Moscow Party organization, sent out agitators to Party cells to incite workers against both the Zinoviev opposition and the Trotsky opposition.[10] The agitators hinted at the Jewish origin of the leaders of the two oppositions and suggested that the struggle was between native Russian socialism and "aliens" who sought to pervert it. Trotsky wrote to Nikolai Bukharin on March 4 expressing shock that "anti-Semitic agitation should be carried on with impunity."

While only an isolated development, the episode indicated that Stalin would hardly be fastidious as to the choice of means in his political maneuvers. It was, indeed, a harbinger of things to come. For the time being, however, and until the Great Purge in the later thirties, Party and state leadership avoided all uses of political anti-Semitism. Stalin told the Jewish Telegraphic Agency in January, 1931, that anti-Semitism was "a phenomenon profoundly hostile to the Soviet regime and is sternly repressed in the USSR."[11] He called it "a survival of the barbarous practices of the cannibalistic period."

The interview was not, at the time, published in the Soviet press, but almost six years later Premier V. M. Molotov read it out to the Eighth Soviet Congress, and he himself went on to characterize anti-Semitism as "bestiality."[12] At the same time, Molotov called attention to Marx's Jewish origin and pointed out that "the Jewish people" gave "many heroes to the revolutionary struggle" and "continue to produce more and more fine and gifted leaders and organizers" in the Soviet Union. There can be little question that the publication in 1936 of Stalin's earlier interview and the additional comments of Molotov were designed to fit a Soviet foreign policy aimed at solidifying its links with the West in the face of the growing Nazi threat.

During the Great Purge, a notable change in Party policy on anti-Semitism became apparent, although not in a sharply pronounced form. Leon Trotsky detected anti-Semitic undertones in the Moscow trials of the Old Guard,[13] and, at least in the questioning of the physician Dr. L. G. Levin, a clear note of bigotry was sounded. "Perhaps you belonged to some national party, Jewish, for example?" he was asked by his "defense attorney."[14] The proportion of Jews in the Old Guard was far higher than in the Party as a whole, and, as Svetlana Alliluyeva later observed, "with the expulsion of Trotsky, and the extermination during the years of 'purges' of old

Party members, many of whom were Jews, anti-Semitism was reborn on new grounds and first of all in the Party itself."[15] A Soviet Jewish researcher, writing in 1963 about the Great Purge, called attention to the "spy mania" that accompanied it and emphasized how the "mania" particularly affected Party attitudes toward Jews.[16] He stated that suspicion fell upon all minorities who were believed to have ties with the West, an observation that especially fit Soviet Jewry. Yet most overt expressions of anti-Semitism were muted. Some foreign Party circles, especially in Canada, were, however, sufficiently concerned about the uses of political anti-Semitism by Soviet authorities as to raise the issue, in 1939, with the Comintern chief, Georgy Dimitrov. A proposal was even advanced that a study commission be created by the Comintern to look into the question.[17] It was overtaken by events leading up to World War II.

The end of the thirties marked a watershed in the history of anti-Semitism in the Soviet Union. The timing is crucial for an understanding of the origin of official anti-Semitism. All too often, Soviet anti-Semitism is linked to the establishment of Israel in May, 1948. This is completely erroneous. From the late thirties and early forties on, if slowly and unevenly, anti-Jewish discrimination became an integral part of official state policy. Andrei Sakharov has given emphasis to this time demarcation, noting that anti-Semitism entered into the policy of the "highest bureaucratic elite . . . after the nineteen-thirties."[18] He emphasized that an "unenlightened zoological kind of anti-Semitism was characteristic of the Stalinist bureaucracy. . . ." Svetlana Alliluyeva has made a similar observation.[19]

According to Hitler, Stalin told Nazi Foreign Minister Joachim von Ribbentrop in the fall of 1939 that he would oust Soviet Jews from leading positions the moment he had a sufficient number of qualified non-Jews with whom to replace them.[20] Stalin's commitment was more than a mere diplomatic gesture to placate the new racist ally. If Sakharov's assertion is somewhat vague, Professor John Armstrong states categorically that in 1942, one year after the Nazi invasion of Russia, the Soviet authorities handed down a secret order establishing quotas for Jews in particularly prominent posts.[21] And, according to Ilya Ehrenburg, during the summer of 1943, Aleksander Shcherbakov, head of the army's Political Commissariat and a close associate of Stalin, instructed him to play down the exploits of Jews in the Red Army.[22]

Igor Gouzenko, a former Soviet diplomatic official in Canada who later defected, related that he was told in 1939 that a "confidential" decree of the Party Central Committee had been sent to all directors of educational institutions ordering them to establish quotas of admissions for Jews.[23] Gouzenko also said that in the summer of 1945 he was informed by the chief of the secret division of Soviet intelligence that the Central Committee had sent "confidential" instructions to directors of all factories to remove Jews from responsible positions. According to Milovan Djilas, Stalin in 1946 boasted to him that "in our Central Committee there are no Jews!"[24] Stalin's daughter revealed that after the war "in the enrollment at the university and in all types of employment, preference was given to Russians. For the Jews, a percentage quota was, in essence, reinstated."[25] Armstrong estimated the quota at the time to be 10 per cent.[26]

The emergence of anti-Jewish discrimination as state policy in the late thirties and early forties certainly cannot be considered a function of the foreign policy of the USSR. That policy had swung wildly from a pro-West position ("collective security") to a pro-Nazi position (the Nazi-Soviet Non-Aggression Pact) and then back to a pro-West position (the Grand Alliance). Anti-Jewish discrimination, with an important exception, developed along a single line with little fluctuation. The exception involved the area of group rights, as distinct from individual or civil rights. The Jewish Anti-Fascist Committee was created in 1942; together with the publication establishment Emes, it was to constitute, until November, 1948, the Jewish "address" in the USSR. The formation of the committee was designed to win strong Jewish sympathy in the Western world for the Soviet cause. Mention, too, might be made of the lifting of the earlier severe restrictions upon Judaism as a concomitant of a general easing of pressures upon the recognized religions in the Soviet Union. In any case, the concessions did not affect the application of anti-Jewish restrictions in employment, cadre appointments, and education.

Official anti-Semitism (from which the Jewish community, as a community enjoying certain ethnic and cultural rights, was now excepted) must clearly be seen as a function of internal developments beginning in the late thirties and continuing into the forties. Two of these internal developments stand out.

A deepening Russian nationalism, bordering on xenophobia, was a dominant characteristic of the struggle against the "internationalism" of the Old Guard. Suspicion fell equally upon those suspected of harboring sympathies with various non-Russian nationalities of the USSR and those linked, in one way or another, with the West. If nationalism was inherent in the Stalinist doctrine of "socialism in one country," its edge was sharpened through fears engendered by the growing external threat to the regime in the late thirties. World War II would but aid and abet the process, with Stalin, at the war's end, according it the strongest, if scarcely a Leninist, endorsement. At a Kremlin banquet, he declared the "Russian people" to be the "most outstanding of all nations of the Soviet Union."[27] Many years earlier, in 1907, in joking about the struggle between the Mensheviks and Bolsheviks at the 1903 London Congress of the Russian Social-Democratic Workers' Party, he had warmly contrasted the alleged predominance of Great Russians in the Bolshevik leadership with the predominance of Jews in the Menshevik leadership.[28] Svetlana Alliluyeva disclosed that Stalin "never liked Jews";[29] yet this bias would not find a systematic expression until circumstances warranted.

A concomitant of Russian chauvinism, as it had indeed been during the Tsarist era, at least since the reign of Nicholas I, was anti-Semitism. Certainly it was not accidental that official anti-Semitism made its first, if then only momentary, appearance at the time, in 1926, when Stalinist forces were attempting to inculcate a national pride in the doctrine of "socialism in one country." Chauvinism catered to and fed upon popular prejudices. The war years were replete with examples of an unleashed bigotry linked to nationalist fervor. Many of the partisan units, for example, were riddled with anti-Semitism. Khrushchev in 1956 acknowledged to a visiting French Socialist delegation that popular prejudice toward Jews did play a role in affecting the state discriminatory policy. He explained that were Jews to continue to hold high positions, in the Ukraine, for example, it would "create jealousy and hostility toward Jews."[30] In December, 1962, he told a Party-organized meeting of artists and intellectuals that were Jews to occupy top posts, it would tend to create anti-Semitism.[31]

The second development was the erection of a totalitarian structure, the levers of which were geared to the mobilization of total mass energies for purposes determined by the Party. Totalitarianism could of course tolerate no genuinely autonomous or corporate social units independent of the central manipulators of power. For those ethnic groups with a territorial base, the dismantling of autonomous communal structures or their penetration involved a fairly lengthy process and could not easily be completed. All the more so if the sheer weight of demography (as in the case of the Ukrainians) was added to that of geography. But with the Jewish community the task was simplified. A dispersed people, the Jews would find that their communal establishment could literally be pulverized, as happened first in the late thirties, then again in 1948–49. The Jews were particularly suspect in a totalitarian structure impregnated with a distinct chauvinist character because they, indeed, were a unique minority which history provided with an international tradition and which drew upon the sources of an ancient world-wide religion. For Jews everywhere there were cultural, emotional, and even family ties that transcended national boundaries.

But there was yet another feature of totalitarianism which could and would have a distinctive relationship to anti-Semitism. Hannah Arendt has noted that totalitarianism requires an "objective enemy" who, like the "carrier of a disease" is the "carrier" of subversive "tendencies."[32] The very nature of a system which claims both a monopoly on truth and the control of the "commanding heights" by which the preordained may be reached precludes human error or inadequacy. Only plots and conspiracies by hidden forces could interrupt, hinder, or defeat "scientifically" planned programs.[33] Stalin even considered his daughter's marriage to a Jew a "Zionist plot."[34] Other Soviet leaders may not necessarily have perceived the Jew as a "plotter," but, cynically, accepted the functional usefulness of such a perception. Such cynicism would enable the Jew to be cast in the role of scapegoat upon whom blame could be heaped for failures or difficulties in the regime's internal and foreign policies.

If both chauvinism and totalitarianism lent themselves to the absorption of popular anti-Semitism, the character of the Party leadership since the late thirties helps explain the transmission and persistence of folk imagery about the Jew. A close study of the top 306 Party executives on both national and regional levels (in 1958 and 1962) shows that almost one-half of them have peasant fathers.[35] Only 6 per cent have white-collar origins, while a little more than a quarter have proletarian origins. The transmission of negative stereotypes about Jews from the folk level is thus fairly direct. Moreover, the nature of the schooling of Soviet leaders was hardly of a kind to overcome characteristic popular stereotyping. It was both limited and narrow (with respect to the type of specialization). Almost 40 per cent of Party leaders either acquired no education beyond secondary school or attended only a Party school. Of those who completed a college education, 40 per cent studied engineering and 30 per cent agronomy—"narrowly specialized and highly applied skills." Training in the broad humanistic disciplines was negligible.

The training experience of the Party leaders was also not particularly conducive to broadening their horizons. About a third of the leaders studied specialized skills in farming, a third in industry, and a third in ideology. Most conjoined their specialized experience with work in the organizational apparatus before reaching their top posts. The difference between the training and experience of the top Party leaders before and after the Great Purge is enormous. The wide cultural and intellectual horizons which characterized the pre-Purge Party leaders have turned into horizons that are provincial and cramped. In the narrow range of outlook, the traditional conception of the Jew, imbibed, as it were, from the environment, emerges as an accepted and acceptable model. The ethnic composition of the Party leadership contributes, indirectly, to the reinforcement of anti-Semitic attitudes. Ninety-two per cent of all top Party posts on the USSR level are held by Russians. If this figure clearly bares the post-war trend toward Great Russian chauvinism, it just as clearly reflects one of the principal tendencies inherent in such chauvinism —anti-Semitism.

The character of a leader's origin and training is significant in another respect. Given the totalitarian indoctrination to which he is subject from the time he has embarked upon a course destined to enable him to perform the function of a high Party *apparatchik*, whether in the central secretariat or in the provinces, the personality that emerges from both his milieu and his upbringing would probably take on the classic features of the authoritarian.[36] It is precisely this type of "personality" which is especially prone to anti-Semitism. Rigidity, discipline, and obedience would combine with adoration of the symbol of one's own nationality and suspicion of the alien and outsider to make the Jew, especially the "cosmopolitan" and "international Zionist" Jew, the embodiment of the evil fantasies conjured up to explain the plots and conspiracies which may arise to threaten the Socialist "fatherland."

The absorption and assimilation among the Party elite of popular stereotypes about the Jew are vividly illustrated in the assertions of the voluble Khrushchev. In August, 1956, he told a leftist delegation from Canada that among the "negative qualities" of Jews was a determination to avoid manual labor.[37] He cited a supposed instance: After the Red Army had captured Chernovtsy from the Romanians during World War II, it found the streets full of debris which the Jews had refused to clean up, arguing that this type of manual labor was usually done by non-Jews. A second "negative" trait, Khrushchev told the Canadians, was the Jew's inclination, whenever he "settles in a place," to "immediately" begin building a synagogue.

The former Soviet Party boss, in an interview with a French Socialist delegation in May, 1956, described another "negative" trait of Jews—clannishness.[38] He referred to the example of a Jew who "is appointed to an important post" and then "surrounds himself with Jewish collaborators." Two years later, in April, 1968, while being interviewed by the editor of Le Figaro, Serge Groussard, Khrushchev pointed to yet a fourth "negative" trait—individualism: "The Jews have always preferred artisans' trade; they are tailors, they work with glass or precious stones, they are tradesmen, druggists and carpenters. But if you take, for instance, construction and metallurgy where people work as a team you would not find a single Jew to my knowledge. They do not like collective work, or group discipline. They have always preferred to be dispersed. They are individualists."[39]

Such stereotypic images of the Jews are remarkably similar to the imagery which emerged during the Harvard interviews and which, earlier, were reported upon by Larin (and later found in the Smolensk archives). Far more serious was the image of the Jew as a potentially disloyal member of Soviet society. For it is precisely such an image which lends itself to viewing the Jew as both a "cosmopolitan" and an "alien." Khrushchev unburdened himself on this point when a member of the Canadian delegation asked him about Stalin's reported refusal to allow Jews, after World War II, to resettle in the Crimea. Khrushchev's reply was forthright, if distressing to the Canadians: he was "in full agreement" with Stalin because he also feared "that in case of another war the Crimea might become a landing place and the enemies' bridgehead against the Soviet Union."[40]

A Communist member of the Canadian delegation later commented that he was "greatly disturbed by Khrushchev's views because they express old prejudices towards the Jews as a people," and because they reflect the "Great Russian chauvinism which Lenin fought against all his life." It was these "old prejudices" that led Khrushchev seven years later to accept as truth an extraordinary fabrication about a Jew who was supposed to have actually worked as translator for Nazi Field Marshal Friedrich von Paulus at Stalingrad. This episode will be examined in detail in the discussion on Babi Yar (Chapter 6).

The onset of the Cold War deepened both the chauvinist and totalitarian tendencies in Soviet life. The impact upon the Jewish community was to prove devastating. At the end of 1948 and in early 1949, all specifically Jewish cultural institutions, including those that remained after the Great Purge and the few that had been established during the war, were obliterated. Certain patterns of anti-Jewish discrimination were already apparent prior to and during World War II. The Cold War aroused morbid suspicions about imperialist plots supposedly emanating from the West. Earlier suspicions about Jews and Jewish institutions now inevitably sharpened.

It would be a mistake to view the destruction of Jewish institutional life as a reflex of Soviet policy to Israel. The contrary is true. Even as Soviet authorities were preparing the ground for liquidating Jewish communal structures, its relations with Israel were cordial. The brutal murder of Shlomo Mikhoels, the chairman of the Jewish Anti-Fascist Committee and, therefore, the veritable leader of the Soviet Jewish community, was carried out by the KGB with Stalin's personal endorsement as early as January, 1948.[41] In May, 1948, the USSR played a leading role at the UN in creating the State of Israel and was the first to extend it formal recognition. In the Arab-Israeli War that followed and that lasted until early 1949, the Soviet state was both a harsh critic of the Arab side and a vigorous supporter of Israel, enabling the latter to obtain great quantities of military supplies from Communist-dominated Czecho-slovakia. Not until 1950 did the Soviet Government switch to a policy of overt antagonism toward Israel.

Much has been made of the appearance in Moscow's main syna-gogue in October, 1948—the occasion of the Jewish New Year—of Israel's first ambassador to the USSR, Golda Meir (then known as Meyerson). The fervent emotion which her presence stirred among Moscow's Jews was, indeed, powerful and overt, and it could scarcely have gone unnoticed in Kremlin circles. Yet, eight months before her entrance upon the scene, the crucial decision to murder the leader of the Soviet Jewish community had been taken. And, one month before her synagogue visit, Ilya Ehrenburg, at the "request" of the editor of *Pravda*, had written an authoritative four-column article that provided the ideological rationale for a virulent hostility to Zionism.[42]

The Ehrenburg article merits closer examination than it has here-tofore been given. While he attacked Israel as a "laughable dwarf capitalist state," the principal thrust of Ehrenburg's article was against the concept of the unity of the Jewish people. Only "obscur-antists pretend," he stated, "that some mystical bond exists between the Jews of the whole world." In fact, he insisted, "little in common exists between a Tunisian Jew and a Jew from Chicago who speaks and thinks American."

What concerned Ehrenburg (and the editors of *Pravda*) was the need to isolate Soviet Jews from the outside world. Soviet Jews are "citizens to a socialist society" and therefore are united by a "com-radeship-in-arms" with all Soviet peoples. They have no ties with Jews who "bear the yoke of capitalist exploitation." It was less the links with Israel that aroused anxiety among Soviet leaders than links with the large and important American Jewish community. If Israel was criticized, it was because it was shaped by the "intrusion of Anglo-American capital."

Clearly, an anti-Semitism that now found its reflection in the eradication of Jewish communal institutions was an outgrowth of a powerful chauvinist drive which, in turn, was a response to the deepening East-West conflict. But that drive was to transcend the purely secular. Once unleashed, the chauvinism was to take on, during 1949–53, a distinctive racist quality. Intellectuals of Jewish origin, who, in most instances, had become completely assimilated, were now dubbed "cosmopolitan," "rootless," and "passportless." Ehrenburg himself was identified, at one public rally, as "Cosmopolitan Number One."[43]

A recent study of anti-Jewish bigotry defines "political anti-Semitism" as "an attempt to establish the corporate Jew as a general and public menace, the implication being that some official public remedy is called for."[44] If, until 1949, official anti-Semitism lacked an ideological rationalization and, indeed, was shielded from public view, the campaign against "cosmopolitanism" clearly identified the "corporate Jew" as the enemy.[45] To make the identification even clearer, editors listed in parentheses the original, Jewish-sounding names of "cosmopolitans" after their adopted Russian names. That chauvinism was the principal source of the new political anti-Semitism was evidenced by the terms of abuse that were hurled at the "corporate Jew"—"cosmopolitan," "rootless," and "passportless." They suggested the un-Russian character of the "corporate Jew."

The purge of the "cosmopolitans" affected the livelihood of thousands of the most highly assimilated Jews, those who were totally divorced from Jewish communal and religious life and who had involved themselves completely in Party affairs. Yehoshua Gilboa, in a careful study, listed the following occupations and fields in which Jews were either excluded or sharply limited: the diplomatic corps; foreign trade institutes and colleges; the Red Army; the Party leadership and staff; the Komsomol leadership and staff; the legislative institutions; the leadership in planning, economic, and industrial agencies; teaching and research staffs of universities; journalism (especially editorial staffs); the trade union leadership; the judiciary and legal profession; certain specific industrial branches and science institutes labeled "sensitive areas"; and the humanistic fields of philosophy, historiography, and pedagogy. Only in literature and the arts, and in the scientific and technological fields, did Jews manage to escape the hatchet that was ceaselessly wielded by the regime. Every area touched by political or security considerations to which Jews had contributed enormously since the Revolution was now to be virtually taboo for them. To have been born a Jew, to carry the identification of *Jew* in the internal passport was sufficient to endow an individual—however assimilated he was—with the corporate quality of "cosmopolitanism."

But a more insidious identification emerged in January, 1953, with the fabrication of the Doctors' Plot. The "corporate Jew" in Soviet society was not merely alien to that society; he was an instrument of the "international corporate Jew" or rather of "international Zionism." "Murderers in white aprons"—as the doctors, mainly Jewish, were called—were accused of working in behalf of the "international Jewish bourgeois national organization," the Joint Distribution Committee, which had given them orders to "wipe out the leading cadres of the Soviet Union."[46] That exactly fifty years after the infamous forgery *The Protocols of the Elders of Zion* had made its appearance in Russia a similar crude concoction should be introduced testifies to the vigor and virulence of the strain of popular anti-Semitism. Yevgeny Yevtushenko relates in his *Precocious Autobiography* that "the general public . . . by and large had believed in their [the doctors'] guilt."[47] State authorities could easily transmute popular belief into official policy when it would serve their interests.

Those interests in 1953 could hardly be said to be determined by external considerations. If the Soviet Union had broken relations with Israel in February, 1953, it was due far less to foreign policy considerations than to the need to justify an internal policy which required Israel, in the guise of Zionism, to be portrayed as an enemy. The corporate Jew, defined earlier as "cosmopolitanism," was now redefined as "Zionism." It must be emphasized, in this connection, that the beginning of a pro-Arab policy on the part of the USSR did not emerge until 1954.

The propaganda spewed forth by the state organs, in providing an ideological rationale for anti-Semitism, took on a deliberately poisonous character with the use of an imagery borrowed from the traditional Jew-baiter and pogromist. Thus the doctors were said to have been trained by "the hypocrite Mikhoels" who "for thirty pieces of silver" sold himself to the United States.[48] They, "loyal adherents of the Zionist kehillah," are the "personification of baselessness and abomination, the same kind as that of Judas Iscariot." The medieval formulation was stunning, made all the more provocative by a cartoon showing a predatory face with stereotypic Jewish features. Another example of the venomous hate propaganda was the following (from the supposedly sophisticated humor journal *Krokodil*): "Weeping was heard by the rivers of Babylon, the most important of which is the Hudson. The Joint [Distribution Committee]—the carrion vulture wrapping itself in the feathers of a dove of loving-kindness and philanthropy—was plucked."[49] The leaders of "Zionist organizations" from "Jerusalem to London" were the culprits who were "embarrassed" by the disclosures of the Doctors' Plot.

The ideology, in addition to justifying the expulsion of thousands of Jewish medical specialists from hospitals, laboratories, institutes, and medical faculties, portended a far-reaching development. As described by Roy Medvedev:

> . . . the organs of the NKVD hastily prepared for a massive expulsion of the Jews from the main cities. . . . In several districts of Kazakhstan, barracks for Jews were urgently erected. A text of an appeal to the Jewish people, which several distinguished scientists and cultural leaders of Jewish nationality had to sign "requesting" resettlement, was prepared; several large-scale factories passed resolutions about the eviction of Jews; . . .[50]

It could have been the Soviet version of "the final solution of the Jewish question."

The ideological rationalization of anti-Semitism was dropped with Stalin's death and the emergence of the Thaw. But in the public exposure of the Doctors' Plot as a gigantic hoax, nowhere was it made clear that political anti-Semitism was at its root. *Pravda* gingerly hinted at this: "Despicable adventurers of the type of Riumin [a high secret-police official who played a key role in the fabrication of the Doctors' Plot] have tried to arouse in Soviet society . . . feelings of national enmity that are completely alien to socialist ideology. In their provocative intent, they did not shrink from a shameless slander of reputable Soviet men."[51] But even this hint is missing from Khrushchev's secret speech at the Twentieth Party Congress. Indeed, seven years later, in 1963, the Soviet premier told Bertrand Russell that "there never has been . . . any policy of anti-Semitism in the Soviet Union since the very nature of our multinational socialist state precludes the possibility of such a policy."[52] Instead of denouncing the openly anti-Semitic ideology that characterized the Black Years, Soviet authorities for the time being simply shelved it. But the ideology would be removed from the political shelf and refurbished later when an opportune occasion again required its use.

If, for the next fourteen years, an anti-Semitic ideology was absent, anti-Semitism remained as state policy, whether in the form of civil discrimination in the political-security area, in administrative and cadre appointments, or in quota systems in universities.)

Sometimes, during the fourteen-year period between 1953 and 1967, especially in the early sixties, anti-Semitism went beyond the discriminatory patterns and became an integral part of campaigns directed against what the regime considered a particular social ill. In the context of these campaigns, anti-Semitism no doubt reflected popular stereotypes of the Jew held by various Party officials. At the same time, the injection of anti-Semitism helped ease public tensions generated by the campaigns themselves; in this sense, the Jews performed the classical role of scapegoat, channeling off resentment that might have been directed against the regime itself.

The campaign against economic crimes during 1961–64 is a case in point. Soviet authorities were deeply concerned about the extent of black market activities, bribery, currency speculation, and stealing of public property, which outside observers found well-nigh universal in an economic system then characterized by a relative shortage of consumer goods. The Presidium of the Supreme Soviet, in May, 1961, adopted a decree extending earlier laws covering misappropriation of state property and illicit trading to embrace a host of so-called "economic offences."[53] At the same time, the Presidium reintroduced the death penalty for such offenses—a punishment that had been banned in 1947. The campaign was conducted on both the juridical level and, more important, on the propaganda level, with a furious intensity.

A careful investigation in 1964 by the respected and responsible International Commission of Jurists demonstrated that anti-Semitism was closely intertwined with the campaign.[54] For one thing, the commission found, the number of Jews executed or sentenced to heavy terms of imprisonment was "greatly disproportionate to their number as a minority group." Of the nearly 250 persons known to have been executed for economic crimes during 1961–64, more than 50 per cent were Jews. In the Ukraine, a stronghold of popular anti-Semitism, the percentage of Jews among those executed was 80 per cent (in that union republic, Jews constituted 2 per cent of the population).

Even more disturbing, the commission concluded, was "an

insidious and sometimes subtle propaganda campaign" against Jews that accompanied and highlighted the press reportage of the economic offenses. A practice that had characterized the "anti-cosmo-politan" campaign of 1948–52—printing the clearly Jewish patronymic in parentheses after a typically Russian name—was restored. In addition, the Jewish offender was highlighted by a description of the site wherein the economic offenses were plotted: all too often, it was the synagogue. Thus, in a Vilnius case involving eight persons which was widely commented upon in the national as well as the local press, the culprits were described as having engaged in foreign currency deals in the synagogue, with the rabbi acting as the "arbitrator" of their disputes.[55] The Lvov case in March, 1962, was even more illuminating. The local press entitled the case "Prayer and Speculation" and went on to describe how "crooks and speculators of all types gather in the synagogue where they strike up acquaintances and conclude all sorts of transactions."[56] If a widely held stereotype of the Jew, as the Harvard interviews suggest, is that he is given to *geschaft*—asocial business dealings—the propaganda campaign drove home the point with a vengeance. The age-old symbol of the Jewish people—the synagogue—was the very locus of the *geschaft*.

The campaign reached a particularly provocative level in October, 1963, when an *Izvestiia* editor went out of his way to emphasize the Jewish origin of two of the accused economic criminals. He wrote in a long story about one of the trials that he was deliberately mentioning the "Jewish family names of the accused—Roifman and Shakerman—because we pay no attention to the malicious slander . . . in the Western press."[57] It was no less a figure than Bertrand Russell, a frequent supporter of Soviet aims, who had given expression to the strong criticism in the West of the manner in which the economic crimes campaign was being conducted in the USSR. The official Soviet response to Russell took the form of a letter by Khrushchev published in *Pravda* in February, 1963. Charges of anti-Semitism, it read, were "a crude concoction, a vicious slander on the Soviet people, on our country."[58] How could it be otherwise when the Soviet Ukraine told the United Nations a little later that year, in a formal report, that in that union republic "there are no instances of racial prejudice or of national and religious intolerance either *de jure* or *de facto*"?[59]

The comment of the Ukrainian government has a special, if ironic, pertinence in that shortly afterwards, in October, 1963, the Ukrainian Academy of Sciences in Kiev published one of the crudest canards about Jews since the heyday of Nazism. Entitled *Judaism Without Embellishment* and written by Trofim K. Kichko, the so-called "scientific" work, carrying the stamp of one of the more prestigious bodies in the USSR, depicted Judaism as a belief which promotes hypocrisy, bribery, greed, and usury. The stereotype of the Jew as a man of *geschaft* is underscored: "What is the secular God [of the Jews]? Money. Money, that is the jealous God of Israel." Judaism was linked with Zionism, Jewish bankers, and Western capitalists in a great conspiracy. A distinguishing feature of the work was the incorporation into it of a series of illustrative cartoons showing Jews with hooked noses, and similar vulgar stereotypes. It reminds one of Julius Streicher's *Der Stürmer* in the halcyon days of Hitler.

The Kichko book was by no means an accident. For, in addition to the campaign against economic crimes, the Soviet authorities had since 1959 been pursuing a vigorous anti-religious propaganda campaign. The attacks upon Judaism had a peculiarly sharper edge which could not but reinforce anti-Semitic stereotypes. Synagogue leaders were depicted as money-worshippers who use the religious service, kosher slaughtering, religious burial, matzoth-baking, and other ritual practices in order to exploit a duped congregation. A typical example was the following from a newspaper in Minsk, the capital of Byelorussia, in 1961: "Money! That is the God of the Minsk Jewish religious community and their aides."[60] A top American Communist theoretician, following the Kichko episode, was to comment appropriately that "historically the maligning of the Jewish faith has been an intrinsic part of anti-Semitism."[61] He cautioned the Soviet authorities that "it is necessary to be extremely sensitive to such things, otherwise anti-religious propaganda can all too easily degenerate into anti-Semitism and encourage such expression of it as the Kichko book."

A massive chorus of criticism in the West greeted the Kichko book when its contents were divulged prior to a session of the United Nations Commission on Human Rights in the spring of 1964. Major foreign Communist parties were among the most vociferous in the widespread condemnation of the officially authorized publication.

At first, Soviet organs avoided any positive response to the public revelations and criticisms, contenting themselves with the observation that Kichko was merely engaged in anti-religious propaganda, which, they emphasized, was guaranteed by the Soviet Constitution. The crescendo of angry voices throughout the world proved too insistent. Concerned about the image of the Soviet Union, the Ideological Commission of the Party Central Committee finally issued a statement on April 4, 1964, which criticized the Kichko work for containing "erroneous statements and illustrations likely to offend believers."[62] The Ideological Commission continued with a curiously cautious remark. It stated that the book "might be interpreted in a spirit of anti-Semitism."

The word *might* was as indicative of Party thought as the word *interpreted*, if not more so. *Judaism Without Embellishment* was not on its face anti-Semitic; nor could one unquestionably "interpret" it as being anti-Semitic. It only *"might* be interpreted" in this way. The Party's caution was understandable. In the same statement, the Ideological Commission recommended as a "useful publication" the book *Catechism Without Embellishment*, also published in 1963, by a colleague of Kichko, A. Osipov, which contained the following: "Where Jews are concerned, the principal bloodsucker turns out to be God himself. . . . The first thing we come across is the preaching of 'intolerance,' the bloody extermination of people of other faiths. . . . God recommends real racial discrimination to Jews."[63] Shortly after the Party criticism, the Soviet authorities in Moldavia published a work by F. S. Mayatsky—*Contemporary Judaism and Zionism*—which used as sources material prepared during the discredited Doctors' Plot to illustrate a presumed conspiracy between Zionism, Jewish bankers, and Western intelligence agencies.

Much of the extensive literature attacking Judaism that has been published in the Ukraine and Moldavia, it can be argued, may be considered as anti-Semitic on its face. Were the propaganda tracts written in Russian or Yiddish, it might be said that they were designed to foster atheism among Jews. But they were published in the native languages of Ukrainian and Moldavian, which were regarded by only 3 per cent of Ukrainian Jews and 1 per cent of Moldavian Jews as their native tongue.[64] The propaganda clearly was aimed at the general populations of these two republics, and can only stimulate or reinforce strong traditional currents of anti-Semitism.

Soviet law, to be sure, has continued to ban anti-Semitism. Under the current Criminal Code of the Russian Republic, based upon Article 11 of the Fundamentals of Criminal Jurisprudence of the USSR enacted by the Supreme Soviet in December, 1958, "propaganda or agitation aimed at inciting racial or national enmity or discord . . . is punishable by loss of personal freedom for a period of six months to three years, or exile from two to five years." (Article 74 of the Russian Republic's Criminal Code. Similar articles are to be found in the criminal codes of the other union republics.) The 1961 Criminal Code deleted the reference to propaganda inciting religious intolerance which had appeared in the 1927 code. Soviet legal analysts contend, however, that religious intolerance can be considered a veiled form of nationality incitement and, therefore, is punishable under Article 74.[65] But the fact remains that the article is a dead letter. There is no known case on record of its having been applied. Even a blatant example of anti-Semitism was treated as a mild, if irrelevant, political deviation. Thus when a local newspaper, *Kommunist*, in Buinaksk, Dagestan, on August 9, 1960, carried the ancient libel that Jews mixed Moslem blood with water for ritual purposes, the provincial authorities, after a world outcry, dismissed the newspaper piece, two days later, as a mere "political error."[66] (As the Harvard interviews record, the belief in the blood libel still exists. Strikingly, Dagestan was the site of a vicious blood libel campaign in the late twenties. At that time, the authorities acted more forcefully.) As with other statutory forms that apply to Jews, provisions of the Criminal Code dealing with racial incitement are, to use Lenin's term, a "fiction," with law and reality moving in completely different directions. The gap was to become a yawning chasm in the summer of 1967, when a massive campaign against Zionism would be launched.

Chapter 5
Jews as Non-Persons;
The Holocaust as a Non-Happening

On January 13, 1970, there appeared in *Pravda* one of those officially sponsored letters by a Soviet Jew designed to provide a moral buttress to the state's policy on Jews. It was published as part of a massive Soviet propaganda campaign against Zionism designed to squelch the aspirations of nationally-conscious Jews who were seeking exit visas for Israel. The letter was instructive: "I don't know what has remained in me of Jewishness, perhaps only the nationality paragraph in my passport. . . ." What may have escaped the attention of the *Pravda* editors was the curious coincidence of the date of its publication. It was on January 13, 1948, that the Stalin regime had murdered the leader of the Jewish community, Shlomo Mikhoels, an act that would trigger the destruction of the Soviet Jewish communal structure. And on January 13, 1953, *Pravda* had unveiled the Doctors' Plot. If the calendrical coincidence was not immediately apparent, the significance of the letter's wording was not lost upon the editors. It, indeed, reflected a state policy purposefully oriented to the elimination of Jewish consciousness.

Not only had all Jewish cultural institutions been closed; equally important, the entire cultural leadership of the Jewish community had been liquidated at one blow on August 12, 1952. The Jewish Communist newspaper of Warsaw, Poland, in November, 1956, summarized the significance of these developments: "The fact that other nationalities suffered, especially in the years 1949 to 1953, does not refute the inescapable fact that not only were the leading Jewish writers and cultural leaders imprisoned and murdered, but the entire Jewish social and cultural life in the Soviet Union was liquidated. And this, to our deep regret, is not a fantasy, but the horrifying truth."[1] Opportunities for writing on Jewish themes are now severely curtailed. A distinguished Soviet Jewish poet, Josef Kerler, clarified the problem in a letter on November 18, 1969: "I am a Jewish poet and, as such, I am utterly superfluous in the Soviet Union. Surely no one can any longer deny that because of certain historical developments there is absolutely no future for Jewish culture here. Without Jewish educational and cultural institutions, without a press, a theatre and, above all, without a mass Jewish readership—what is there for a Jewish writer to do here?"[2]

The writing of Jewish history is all but taboo. A letter sent by an elderly Moscow Jewish woman, Elizaveta Kapshitser, on September 24, 1969, to the United Nations General Assembly is especially poignant in highlighting the problem.[3] "In 1966," she wrote, "my son decided to write a book dealing with the history of the Jewish people so as to attain mutual understanding between peoples and nations. He was, however, denied the possibility of carrying out this work." She pleaded for UN intervention to enable her son to emigrate to Israel. If during the twelve-year period 1918–30 a total of approximately sixty works on Jewish history written in the Russian language had been published, during the next thirty-seven years a total of only twenty-four works were published.[4]

An episode related by the Pulitzer Prize–winning American dramatist Arthur Miller, after he returned from a lengthy trip to the USSR in 1967, offers a remarkable insight into the official attempt to black out the Jewish past.[5] A prominent Soviet author had written a children's book titled *The Story of the Bible*. The editors, though enthusiastic about the book, were unhappy with the author's treatment of certain concepts, such as "God" and "Jewish People." As the editors put it, "God is a mythological construction, and in any strict sense mentioning God is really unnecessary." But what disturbed the editors even more than this reference to an important contribution of the ancient Israelites to world history and world literature was the repeated reference in the work to "the Jewish People." "Why is that necessary?" the editors asked. When the author began to answer that "the Bible, you see is . . . ," he was cut off with the following: "Why not simply call them 'the People'? After all, it comes to the same thing, and in fact it generalizes and enhances the significance of the whole story. Call them 'the People.' " Not only was the title changed to read *Myths of the People,* but the Jews suddenly, as if by magic, disappeared as a historical entity. They had been plunged down the "memory hole" of history.

This episode was no isolated incident. A close study of the history textbooks used in Soviet elementary and secondary schools reveals that Jews are virtually invisible whether in Russian history or in world history.[6] Not only are Jews rarely referred to; Jewish culture is never treated, and the contribution of Jews to civilization is completely neglected. Both ancient and present-day Israel, if mentioned at all, are discussed in a highly critical and condescending manner. As disturbing as the neglect of Jews and Jewish culture as positive phenomena is the almost complete indifference to anti-Semitism as a negative factor in Russian and world history. Even the anti-Semitic racism of the Nazi epoch is understated.

Fifteen textbooks used in the elementary and secondary schools of the largest and most important republic of the Soviet Union, the Russian Republic, were closely examined. These are the officially prescribed texts (and have been translated into the languages of other Soviet republics, where they are used in the corresponding class levels). Since the educational system of each Soviet republic is highly centralized, with a single curriculum for each elementary and secondary school, the fifteen texts constitute the sum total of required history textbooks in the Russian Republic. To the extent that they are used, in translation, in other Soviet republics, they have an almost nation-wide character and provide the Soviet elementary and secondary school student with his principal source of information on the historical past.

The texts studied are of the most recent vintage, all having been published since 1966. They cover each of the history courses beginning with the fourth (elementary school) grade and ending with the final (tenth) grade of secondary school. In addition to these basic textbooks, a two-volume textbook for history students in state universities was also examined. Finally, a sampling was made of other history textbooks written in the native language and used in the Soviet republics of the Ukraine, Latvia, Estonia, and Lithuania.

History, as a separate subject in the Russian Republic, begins in the fourth grade, when the child is eleven years of age. The fourth-grade text by T. S. Golubeva and L. S. Gellerstein[7] focuses on Russian history and doesn't mention the Jews at all, although a number of Soviet minorities are discussed. Official anti-Semitism, whether of the Tsars or of the Nazi occupiers, is not mentioned.

In the fifth grade, the Soviet student studies ancient history. The textbook of F. P. Korovkin[8] does not examine the history of the early Israelites even though it contains chapters on Babylonia, Assyria, Egypt, Greece, and Rome. If the origins of Christianity are discussed, the influence of Judaism and Jewish personalities is completely neglected.

During the sixth grade, the history textbook by Y. V. Agibalova and T. M. Donskoi covers the Middle Ages.[9] Jews are not mentioned, and the anti-Semitism of the Crusades or in England and Spain, which led to mass expulsions of Jews, is entirely ignored. The anti-Jewish character of the Inquisition is not noted. A special history textbook designed for evening schools by E. M. Golin, V. R. Kuzmenko, and M. I. Lorberg also ignores both Jews and anti-Semitism.[10]

When the Russian youngster reaches the age of fourteen and enters the seventh grade, he begins studying the history of his own country in some detail. The two textbooks used are by M. B. Nechkina and P. S. Leibengrub,[11] and by P. P. Yepifanov,[12] and they cover the ancient period through the eighteenth century. Neither book mentions Jews, though Jews had lived in Russia from the very earliest times and great numbers entered Tsarist society during the incorporation of the Ukraine in the seventeenth century and through the three partitions of Poland in the eighteenth century. Anti-Semitism is not mentioned either.

In the eighth grade, the student works from both a text by I. A. Fedosov[13] and a manual by A. A. Vagin and T. S. Shabolina.[14] They deal with Russia of the nineteenth century and make no reference to either Jews or the rich Jewish culture. Significantly, several chapters in these works are devoted to the cultures of a large number of ethnic groups and highlight the roles of important literary figures of these groups. But Sholem Aleichem is not mentioned. Another striking feature of these texts is the absence of any reference to either anti-Jewish repressive legislation or pogroms, even though the reactionary character of Tsarism is otherwise fully delineated. If the books also describe the rise of the revolutionary movement in Russia, they neglect both Jewish personalities and the Jewish Bund (a Socialist organization which played an important role in Tsarist Russia in the early part of the twentieth century).

The textbook and manual for the ninth grade, both written by I. A. Fedosov,[15] are designed to embrace Russian history of the twentieth century. Nowhere is there a treatment of the Jews or of Jewish culture. The Jewish Bund is finally mentioned, only to be dismissed as "opportunistic" and given only to "nationalist positions." For the first time, the student learns of anti-Semitism during the late Tsarist period, but the subject is treated briefly and cursorily.

In the Russian Republic there is a two-part general history textbook for secondary schools. The first, written by A. V. Yefimov,[16] covers European and American history from the seventeenth century through the first half of the nineteenth century. Neither Jews nor anti-Semitism appear in it. Even a biographical sketch of Karl Marx fails to mention his Jewish origin. The works of Heinrich Heine are hailed as having later "aroused the hatred of the Fascist barbarians," but the key factor of his being Jewish is not noted. The second part, edited by V. M. Khvostov,[17] deals with the period from the second half of the nineteenth century to the 1917 revolution and embraces Europe, North America, Latin America, Asia, and Africa. Again, the role of Jews and anti-Semitism is disregarded. A description of Benjamin Disraeli neglects his Jewish origin. A chapter on France carries no discussion of the infamous Dreyfus case.

Completing the two-part general text for secondary schools is a separate textbook, written by I. M. Krivoguz, D. P. Pritsker, and S. M. Stetskovich,[18] which brings the history of the world up to World War II. The character of Nazism is given considerable analysis, except that its anti-Semitism is almost completely neglected. There is only a brief indication that Nazism was directed against Jews (among numerous other ethnic groups). The Nazi concentration camps, one is surprised to learn, were created to house only Communists.

A special history manual edited by P. M. Kuzmichev and V. A.

Orlov,[19] for the final grade of secondary school, covers both the war and the post-war world. The Holocaust is not mentioned at all. There is not even a hint that the Nazis' machinery of death was designed to annihilate the Jews. Besides the neglect of the Holocaust, the textbook ignores the establishment of the State of Israel. A table listing all the new states of the world formed since 1946 does not include Israel. Though Egypt and Algeria are treated at length, the Jewish state is but mentioned in passing as an "aggressor" in the 1956 war.

Nor does the learning situation in the universities of the USSR appear much different. A two-volume required history work on the Middle Ages used in the state universities carries only passing references to Jews and anti-Semitism.[20] But it is in the elementary and high schools that the neglect of Jewish history and cultures is particularly egregious. Aside from the Russian Republic, the other Soviet republics follow the same technique of excising Jews from history. A characteristic Ukrainian textbook by V. Diadichenko and R. Los'[21] used in the seventh and eighth grades and chronicling the history of the Ukraine until the end of the nineteenth century nowhere notes the presence of Jews or Jewish culture. The Ukrainian textbook covering the twentieth century and designed for the ninth and tenth grades, written by F. Los' and V. I. Spytskii,[22] also deletes the Jews, except for a passing reference to the anti-Jewish pogroms following the 1905 revolution.

A Latvian history textbook by V. Kanale and M. Stepermanis[23] has but one reference to Jews, when it describes the Nazi occupation policies. The book notes that thirty-two thousand Jews of Riga were put in a ghetto and later shot in the Rumbula forest. An Estonian history text by J. Kahk, H. Palamets, and S. Vehtre[24] makes no mention of Jews or anti-Semitism. A required Lithuanian history textbook by J. Z. Pilkauskas[25] briefly mentions Jews among revolutionary workers and bourgeoisie, but does not deal with anti-Semitism in Lithuania.

The invisibility of Jews and Jewish culture in current Soviet textbooks is consistent with the manner in which the *Large Soviet Encyclopedia* treats the subject. In contrast to the first (1932) edition of the encyclopedia, which dealt with Jewish history and culture in 117 pages, the second edition, published in 1952, has 2 pages devoted to Jews. Virtually all Jewish history is deleted. Instead the entry argues that Jews are not a nation, as defined by Stalin, since they presumably lack a common language, territory, culture, and economic life. Zionism is condemned as "a reactionary bourgeois nationalistic movement which . . . denies the class struggle and strives to isolate the Jewish working masses from the general struggle of the proletariat." Oppression of the Jews under the Tsars and later in Nazi Germany is briefly treated, and is followed by the assertion that the Jewish question no longer exists in the Soviet Union. The same edition of the encyclopedia devotes eight pages (four times as much as to Jews) to the Yakuts, a very small nationality.

In the initial preparation of the second edition of the encyclopedia, a plan was advanced for incorporating in it a glossary covering all of Jewish literature. The authors of the proposal were promptly condemned in February, 1949, as "cosmopolitans without a Homeland."[26] Two reasons were given: (1) the authors had allegedly planned to allot as much space to contemporary Jewish literature as that allotted to Uzbek, Kazakh, and Georgian literature combined; and (2) the authors had dared to have their glossary embrace "the entire Jewish literature," thereby placing themselves "on the same level as confirmed present-day businessmen in America, Palestine and other countries" in subscribing to the belief in an "alleged existence of an all-world Jewish literature."

Especially glaring in the fifty-volume encyclopedia is the absence of entries on most of the very prominent Russian Jewish writers.[27] No Soviet Yiddish writer is mentioned at all, while such names as Sholem Asch, S. Ansky, Ahad Ha-am, Y. L. Gordon, Jacob Gordin, Saul Tchernikhovsky, and even Yitzhak Leib Peretz were passed over in silence (although the last was finally added in a supplemental fifty-first volume published in 1958). Excluded, too, were the great Jewish historians Shimon Dubnow and H. Graetz; the famous Moscow-founded Hebrew theater, Habimah; the father of political Zionism, Theodore Herzl; and numerous Jewish scholars and artists. Distinguished Jews who were included were treated with contempt: the famed Hebrew poet Chaim Bialik was described as "a bourgeois nationalist and cosmopolite," while the Russian-born first president of Israel, Chaim Weizmann, was characterized as an agent operating "on the instructions of the imperialists" in order to suppress "the Jewish toiling masses and the Arab national minority."

Significant, too, is the practice in the encyclopedia of avoiding, except on rare occasions, mentioning the Jewish origin of many prominent Soviet scientists and artists. If references are made, for example, to a "Soviet Ukrainian inventor," or "Soviet Georgian composer," or "Soviet Russian mathematician," celebrated Jews are typically referred to as a "Soviet physicist" or "Soviet meteorologist."

It was insufficient to blot out the Jewish past from history textbooks and encyclopedias. Pressing deeply upon the memory of every Jewish family was the trauma of the Nazi Holocaust, the greatest tragedy ever inflicted upon the Jewish people throughout its long history. Moreover, there was hardly a Jewish family in Soviet Russia that was spared the consequences of Hitler's genocidal plans. Expunging the Holocaust from the record of the past was hardly a simple matter, but unless it were done the profound anguish of the memory was certain to stir a throbbing national consciousness. Martyrdom, after all, is a powerful stimulus to a group's sense of its own identity.

Prior to the curtain descending upon Jewish communal life in 1948, Soviet authorities did permit the publication in Russian of two books dealing with the Holocaust: one dealt with Jewish resistance in the Minsk ghetto and the other concerned Jewish partisans. The Jewish Anti-Fascist Committee had planned to publish, in 1948, *The Black Book,* which was to include memorials and documents on the destruction of Soviet Jewry.[28] Its type, which had already been set up, was deliberately smashed when the committee was liquidated, and a blanket of silence enveloped the Jewish community. Except for the Russian translation of *The Diary of Anne Frank* and a similar story by a girl who lived in the Vilnius ghetto, no work on the Holocaust has been published.[29] Symptomatic of the neglect of the Holocaust was the manner in which the USSR handled the twentieth anniversary of the Warsaw Ghetto uprising. If in the mass media of many countries the occasion was commemorated in 1963 by a spate of editorials and essays, in the USSR only one article appeared—in *Izvestiia*—and that was given over to an attack upon the rulers of the Federal Republic of Germany.[30]

Particularly illuminating was the manner in which the Adolf Eichmann capture and trial was treated in the Soviet mass media.

Eichmann was a symbol of the Nazi murder machine, and his appre-
hension by the Israelis in the spring of 1960, after fifteen years of
hiding, principally in Argentina, brought forth an extraordinary
amount of world attention. A close study of the Soviet press and
radio coverage offers an unusual insight into the policy of Soviet
leaders on the Jewish question.[31] Prior to the opening of the trial
on April 11, 1961, Soviet coverage of the case was marked by (1)
relative paucity; (2) an emphasis upon an alleged relationship
between Eichmann's crimes and the then rulers of West Germany;
and (3) a general minimization of Eichmann's crimes against Jews
as compared with his crimes against people generally. While these
features continued after the trial began, a further one was added
which carried sinister overtones: a charge that Israel had made a
"deal" with Bonn to suppress embarrassing revelations.

On May 25, 1960—the day after the announcement of the capture of Eichmann—the Soviet journal *Sovietskaia Rossiia* carried
a brief news item on the event. Then, for a period of an entire
week, while the Eichmann case was the principal topic of discussion
in the international press, Soviet newspapers maintained a blackout
of news on the matter. The silence was finally broken on June 1 by
Pravda with a short news dispatch from Athens quoting sources in
Bonn to the effect that the West German Government was worried
that Israel's determination to try Eichmann would increase anti-
German feelings and that Chancellor Konrad Adenauer had written
to Premier David Ben-Gurion requesting him not to give wide publicity to the case. The *Pravda* article established the official Soviet
line on the Eichmann case.

Six days later, the Moscow evening newspaper, *Vechernaia
Moskva*, published the first substantial Soviet account on Eichmann.
A lengthy description of Eichmann as "one of the most blood-
thirsty hangmen of fascist Germany" was accompanied by an accusation that Adenauer was sympathetic to Nazism and permitted
"yesterday's assistants of Hitler, Himmler and Kaltenbrunner" to
occupy leading posts in the government, army, and judiciary of
West Germany. On June 14, a long article in *Literaturnaia gazeta*
used the Eichmann case to attack West Germany as a place where
"quite a number of war criminals are hiding" and where "the ruling
circles of the Western Powers" were "encouraging" fascist political
activity. The article charged that West Germany was fearful of the

revelations that might flow from the Eichmann trial and that
Adenauer had sought to obtain Eichmann's extradition both by
appealing to Ben-Gurion and by seeking intervention in Washington.

In none of the above accounts was there more than passing
reference to Eichmann's crimes against Jews specifically. In the
lengthy *Vechernaia Moskva* article, for example, no mention was
made of Jews. Instead it spoke of "six million shot, burned in gas
chambers." A brief spurt of press attention to the Eichmann case
came in the latter part of June, 1960, during the course of the
United Nations Security Council discussions of the Argentine complaint against Israel. *Pravda* on June 24 and *Trud* on June 25 gave
prominence to the speeches of both the Soviet delegate to the
Security Council and Golda Meir, Israel's foreign minister. The
press made it clear that the Soviet Union was in favor of the right
of Israel to try Eichmann and criticized Argentina for failing to
arrest and extradite war criminals.

In August, 1960, one Soviet organ appeared to depart to some
extent from the previous line insofar as references to Jews were
concerned. *New Times*, a semi-official foreign affairs publication,
carried a lengthy story on Eichmann describing in some detail his
"butchery" of Jews. While genocide of Jews was the major object
of description and criticism, and Israel's capture of Eichmann was
sympathetically portrayed, the article also took the occasion to
attack West Germany. It expressed the view that the trial "could
bring disclosures that would compromise many big-wigs in Bonn"
and that, for that reason, West Germany's politicians were "very
much perturbed by it." *New Times* is, however, not a mass-circulation journal and its article did not signal a new approach to the
Eichmann case. Earlier issues of *New Times* had suggested that
Israeli authorities, under the pressure of West Germany and the
United States, were attempting "to go easy" and "to play down"
the Eichmann trial. West Germany—it was argued—was fearful of
incriminating evidence against some of its leading politicians, and
the United States was fearful of the same thing, as well as concerned that revelations about Eichmann's passport would hurt
the Vatican. After the summer of 1960, references to the Eichmann
case did not appear in the Soviet press.

Two weeks prior to the opening of the Eichmann trial *Pravda* reported upon the publication in Russia of a new seven-volume edition of the Nuremberg trials which the reviewer described as revealing the "ghastly, unheard-of, thoroughly planned and meticulously executed felonies aimed at the enslavement and extermination of peoples. . . ." Those who may have regarded the publication of the massive work on Nuremberg as an indication of a fulsome treatment of the Eichmann case were to be sadly disappointed. The political line of the Soviet Government, to play down Jewish martyrdom and to play up West German Fascism, was dominant.

In keeping with this objective, *Pravda* on April 8—three days before the opening of the trial—used the Eichmann case as a peg for a wide-ranging attack upon West German's leaders and particularly the newly appointed inspector-general of the army, Friedrich Förtsch, whom *Pravda* called a "war criminal." From the point of view of the Communist organ, some Bonn leaders were "feeling a chill" because "maybe Eichmann will say too much." It went on: "After all, there is abundant evidence indicating a direct connection between Eichmann's past actions and the occupations of Hans Globke, the Federal Chancellor's present State Secretary. . . . Eichmann probably could tell something as well about other Nazis for whom Bonn has found comfortable jobs." In the course of this lengthy article, not once did the word *Jew* appear. Eichmann was identified as the "killer of millions" or as one "who exterminated millions of men, women and children in the furnaces of . . . Hitlerite death camps."

The opening of the Eichmann trial in Jerusalem on April 11 was marked in the Soviet press by a blackout of news. Neither *Pravda* nor *Izvestiia* on that day carried any reference to the historic occasion. (The day before, *Pravda* had carried a short item from Tel Aviv reporting that a group of "fighters against Fascism" in Israel had demanded that the "Eichmann trial must become a trial of Nazism" and that the group had carried placards reading: "Bring to trial the collaborators of Eichmann—Globke and Oberländer.") On April 12, *Izvestiia* had an item, almost completely buried, announcing that the trial had begun.

If the press was silent, Radio Moscow began developing a new line, the basic elements of which had been only hinted at earlier. The line suggested that a conspiracy existed to prevent disclosure of the true facts about Nazism in West Germany. In a broadcast on

April 11, Radio Moscow noted the presence at the trial of a large West German press and observer delegation. It also noted that Eichmann's defense attorney was Robert Servatius, whose "political complexion" is shown by his zealous defense at Nuremberg of Fritz Sauckel, "the chief of Nazi concentration camps." The broadcast stated that Servatius and the Bonn delegation were in Jerusalem "to fulfill the assignment of the West German Government; to prevent the Eichmann trial from turning into a trial of Nazism and to prevent the publication of testimony on the past of a number of Nazi criminals, such as Globke, who now hold high government posts in the Bonn Republic." A radio commentator darkly hinted that there existed some kind of "secret understanding" between Bonn and Tel Aviv, the precise nature of which was not disclosed.

During the next two and one-half weeks, *Pravda* carried no references to the Eichmann trial, while *Izvestiia* had one short item quoting an Italian newspaper reference to a "deal" between Bonn and Israel. No doubt Soviet leaders were waiting to see whether the Israeli prosecutors would provide the hoped-for disclosures of connections between Eichmann and Bonn leaders. When none appeared, the press was prepared to reveal the details of the "secret understanding." On April 28, *Pravda* charged that "the Israeli Government, to satisfy West Germany's ruling circles, has made a deal with the revanchist circles of the F.G.R. and is trying to protect other Hitlerite criminals from exposure." *Pravda* contended that as far back as July, 1960, Ben-Gurion, after meeting with a representative of the Bonn Government in Brussels, "issued a directive to abridge the publication of the investigative materials in the Eichmann case and to acquaint the F.G.R. Government ahead of time with these materials." *Pravda* criticized Israel for making possible the appointment as defense attorney of Servatius, who is "virtually an official representative of numerous fascists" living in West Germany. According to *Pravda*, Servatius was being used by "the ruling circles of Bonn . . . to exert pressure simultaneously on Eichmann himself and on the court agencies of Israel . . . to conceal instances of criminal activity by former Nazis." The Communist organ reproached the Israel prosecution for the "noticeable silence . . . about the past and present" of Eichmann's "partners in crime"— Oberländer, Schröder (minister of interior in the Bonn Government),

Förtsch, General Hans Speidel, and even Defense Minister Franz Josef Strauss. But although *Pravda* expressed "concern" about the "marked tendency on the part of Israel's ruling circles" to avoid a "genuine exposure of the bloody crimes of the Hitlerite butchers," the Party organ expressed the hope that the masses within and without Israel would compel the prosecution to make "a proper exposure of all those Nazi war criminals" so that the trial does not become "a simple farce in the interest of the dark forces of revanchism."

Following the *Pravda* blast, the major Soviet mass media organs retreated to the blackout technique. Except for one brief item in *Izvestiia* in early May, the Eichmann trial did not command further attention until May 15, when Radio Moscow, taking note of the fact that Globke's name had finally been mentioned in the trial (on May 12) as one who had been present at an inter-ministerial meeting in 1941 that decided upon the revocation of the citizenship of German Jews, contended that his name was disclosed only because of "public pressure." The radio commentator continued to insist that "behind-the-scene deals . . . between certain representatives of Bonn and Tel Aviv . . . are striving to prevent the Jerusalem trial from becoming a forum for the exposure of former Nazis now in power. . . ." The commentator demanded that the names of other Eichmann associates—who have "found refuge and protection" in West Germany—should be disclosed.

Three days later, *Izvestiia* summed up the Soviet attitude with a front-page cartoon that depicted Israeli justice in the form of a judge shielding with his long black robe Globke and other unnamed Nazi generals and politicians. The caption read: "Hitlerites under protection in Jerusalem and Bonn."

After another month of silence, *Pravda* again returned to the attack on June 23. Israeli leaders were charged with being "accomplices of the Bonn revanchists" by suppressing revelations about "Eichmann's accomplices who hold high posts in the state apparatus of West Germany." Though the terms *Jews* was rarely used in the Soviet press treatment of the Eichmann case, this time it did appear once, and in a most unusual manner. *Pravda* declared that it was "receiving many letters from citizens of all nationalities, including Jews who . . . furiously condemn the governmental and political figures of the West who covertly or overtly have entered into criminal collusion with the descendants of the Hitlerite butchers and have extended protection to the Nazi criminal Eichmann and his West German accomplices. . . ."

Eichmann's testimony in the late stages of the trial pointing to Globke as responsible for an increase in the authority and activity of Eichmann's Gestapo bureau evidently pleased Soviet authorities. On June 28, *Izvestiia* noted that the "trial is revealing more and more about the criminal character of many high Bonn officials. . . ." It cited approvingly a Budapest dispatch that stated: ". . . during the Eichmann trial . . . the criminal face of the Bonn Minister Globke has become more and more exposed."

But Kremlin officials were not sufficiently satisfied to give the Eichmann trial more detailed attention. After June 28 and until the trial's end on August 14, neither *Pravda* nor *Izvestiia* (nor Radio Moscow) carried a single reference to the trial. If Israelis could derive some satisfaction from the fact that they were no longer criticized for the conduct of the trial, they must have been aware that they had not been particularly successful in impressing upon the Soviet public their reasons for trying Eichmann. The extent and character of Jewish martyrdom were neither defined nor described in the Soviet press. And anti-Semitism as the source of genocide was not touched upon. A *New Times* article on July 29 emphasized that the accusers of Eichmann were not the Jews, but rather mankind. And, it argued, Eichmann was not guilty merely of the mass murder of Jews; he (and Fascism) were guilty of threatening "all mankind." The "historic justice" of the trial—as the Israelis had envisaged it—was to a great extent lost upon the Russians.

In striking contrast to the Soviet mass media were the extent and character of the coverage of the Eichmann case in the mass media of Poland, Hungary, and Czechoslovakia.[32] As in the West, the press of these Communist countries provided frequent and extensive coverage of both the capture and the trial, with an extraordinary amount of background reporting added. Feature articles and editorials accompanied the newspaper stories. Significantly, the mass media of both Poland and Hungary gave emphasis to the theme of Jewish martyrdom, describing in considerable detail the travail which the Jews had experienced through Eichmann's efficient organization of deportation and extermination. Even when note was taken of the Nazi butchery of non-Jews, and even when criticism was directed against the West German Government, stress was repeatedly placed on the Jewish Holocaust.

The Soviet attempt to obliterate the Holocaust in the memories of Jews, as well as non-Jews, becomes especially pronounced in the method chosen to erase from the historical record Babi Yar, the site and symbol of Soviet Jewry's greatest single tragedy during the Nazi era.

Chapter 6
No Monument Over Babi Yar

Courtroom 214 in the district court building of the West German city of Darmstadt, in Hesse, is small and dingy, an unlikely setting for rendering justice in one of the twentieth century's greatest crimes.[1] But every Monday and Tuesday for fourteen months, beginning on October 2, 1967, three judges sat here and listened to 175 witnesses give testimony concerning eleven (later, after the death of one, ten) defendants implicated in the massacre of Jews at Babi Yar. The defendants were also charged with mass killings in other parts of the Ukraine—Kharkov, Zhitomir, Lutsk, Radomysl, and Belaya Tserkov. But Babi Yar was the central focus of the trial.

Chief Judge Vinzenz Paquet made it clear that "this is not a show trial . . . not an attempt to master the German past." But, he added with emphasis, "there is a historical background," involving, at the onset of the Nazi invasion of Soviet Russia, preparations for mass killing. That "historical background" was to be starkly illuminated by the court proceedings. Together with other documentation it forms an objective record of what transpired at the death ravine of Babi Yar, on the outskirts of Kiev.

Those tried at Darmstadt were members of Einsatzgruppe C, Sonderkommando 4A, which had been assigned a special function in the Kiev area. This unit, numbering some 150 men, with the assistance of several hundred men from two police regiments, was responsible for the shooting of 33,771 Jews during a 36-hour period on September 29–30, 1941. The gas chambers of Auschwitz at the peak of their effort could not duplicate this feat. During the next two years, tens of thousands more Jews, Russians, and Ukrainians were to be put to death at the same site.

Einsatzgruppe C was one of four "special task forces" organized in May, 1941, by Reinhard Heydrich, chief of the Security Police and Security Service, under a directive of Adolf Hitler and Heinrich Himmler.[2] Numbering approximately three thousand men (drawn from SS, SD, and Gestapo forces, as well as from various police units), the Einsatzgruppen were to be the principal instruments of terror in the Nazi war machine. Each Einsatzgruppe was divided · into special commando groups (Sonderkommandos or Einsatzkommandos).

A confidential Fuehrer Order was given to the assembled leaders of the Einsatzgruppen and Sonderkommandos at top secret meetings held in Pretzsch, Saxony, in May, 1941. The order was not written; it was transmitted orally by Major General Streckenbach, chief of personnel of the Reich Security Main Office, in the presence of Heydrich. Under the guise of insuring the political security of the conquered Russian territories, the Einsatzgruppen were to liquidate all opposition to the Germans.

First listed for extermination were all Jews. Then came the following categories—gypsies, the insane, "Asiatic inferiors," "asocial people, politically tainted persons, and racially and mentally inferior elements," and, finally, Communist functionaries. The imprecision of the last two categories made curbs on the homicidal operations of the Einsatzgruppen difficult, if not impossible.

An intimate relationship between the army high command and the Einsatzgruppen was worked out in written form at the end of May, 1941. Each of the Einsatzgruppen was attached to a major army group ("C" was detailed to Army Group South), and extermination orders required the express approval or tacit consent of the appropriate commanding general. Indeed, the mass shootings were regarded by high military officials as a kind of Roman spectacle to relieve boredom. As the Darmstadt trial made clear, many officials watched the executions from a nearby hill with fascination.

The hunt for Jews was the first task of the Einsatzgruppen. It is significant to note that the Fuehrer Order with respect to Jews came six months before the infamous decision taken at Wannsee (January, 1942) to bring about "the final solution of the Jewish question." As a high official of the Einsatzgruppen explained at

Nuremberg, "Jews were to be killed . . . for the reason that they were considered carriers of Bolshevism and, therefore, endangering the security of the German Reich."

The mass carnage that was to befall Kiev was illustrative of this objective. Two of the defendants at Darmstadt, August Haefner and Adolf Janssen, headed a fifty-man advance party of Sonderkommando 4A which entered the city on September 19, the day Army Group South began to sweep into the area. Two days later, the chief of the Sonderkommando, Colonel Paul Blobel, arrived, and on the twenty-fifth the rest of the unit marched in. Final preparations were made for a decisive action "carried out exclusively against Jews with their entire families," as a top secret Einsatzgruppen report revealed.

On September 28, some two thousand notices were posted throughout the city:

> All Jews of the city of Kiev and its environs must appear on the corner of Melnikov and Dokhturov Streets (beside the cemetery) at 8 A.M. on September 29, 1941. They must bring their documents, money, valuables, warm clothing, etc.
> Jews who fail to obey this order and are found elsewhere will be shot.
> All who enter the apartments left by Jews and take their property will be shot.[3]

These notices were printed in Russian, Ukrainian, and German. (But the usually punctilious Germans had incorrectly designated the streets. There was neither a Melnikov Street nor a Dokhturov Street in Kiev. There were, however, a Melnik Street and a Degtyarev Street, the intersection of which was near the Lukyanovka cemetery. Thus the designation was clear, notwithstanding the printing error evidently resulting from the use of incompetent translators.)

The notices were accompanied by a word-of-mouth rumor, a deliberate falsehood spread by the Kommandos, that the Jews were to be evacuated and resettled elsewhere. Since the designated intersection site bordered on a railway station, the rumor seemed to have a plausible foundation. A secret official report spoke of the "extremely clever organization" utilized to overcome "the difficulties resulting from such a large-scale action."

The Kommando group did not expect the majority of the Jews to show up immediately. At the most, they expected some six thousand. But Kiev's Jews, unaware of the Nazi extermination campaign, believing apparently that they would really be resettled elsewhere, and fearful of the death threat for disobedience, assembled by the thousands—"more than thirty thousand," said the official report. It must be remembered in this connection that the Nazi-Soviet Non-Aggression Pact was accompanied by a blackout of news in the Soviet press concerning Nazi atrocities against Jews in Poland. And the implementation of the Wannsee decision lay in the future.

The Jews who gathered on the streets of Kiev on September 29 were mothers, children, the elderly, and the sick. The youth had left the city with the retreating Red Army. Ilya Ehrenburg described, in a moving section of his memoirs, how "a procession of the doomed marched along endless Lvovskaya [a thoroughfare leading to the intersection]; the mothers carrying their babies; the paralyzed pulled along on hand carts."[4]

The unexpected size of the crowd made for a slow procession through the principal streets. It was not until late morning or early afternoon that most of the victims reached the cemetery. At that point the street was blocked with a barrier of barbed wire and anti-tank obstructions. A passage had been left through the middle, guarded on both sides by Kommandos assisted by Ukrainian *Polizei*. The victims were ordered to remove their clothing. An eyewitness, Sergei Ivanovich Lutzenko, the warden of Lukyanovka cemetery, related, in an official Soviet account, the grim finale of the march: "They were ordered to deposit on the ground in a neat pile all the belongings they brought with them and then, in tight columns of one hundred each, were marched to the adjoining Babi Yar. . . . I could see well how at the ravine's edge the columns were stopped, how everyone was stripped naked, their clothes piled in orderly bundles."[5] Before the shooting began, the Jews were required to run a gauntlet of rubber truncheons or big sticks as they entered the long passage. The Ukrainian *Polizei* were especially brutal with those who dallied. As Soviet novelist Anatoly Kuznetsov described it in his novel *Babi Yar*, they were "kicked, beaten with brass knuckles and clubs . . . with drunken viciousness and in a strange sadistic frenzy."

Kuznetsov observed that, judging from their accents, the *Polizei* came from the Western Ukraine, which had been under Polish rule, and in which anti-Semitism was rampant. An Einsatzgruppen secret report suggests that the Ukrainian population was sympathetic to the German objective: ". . . the embitterment of the Ukrainian population against the Jews is extremely great because they are thought responsible for the explosion in Kiev [which, on September 24, had wrecked the headquarters of the Rear Army Command of the Sixth Army]. They are also regarded as informers and agents of the NKVD. . . . The population hardly knew that the Jews were liquidated, but recent experience suggests that they would not have objected." A witness at Darmstadt, Karl Henneke, who had served with the task force, testified that the Ukrainian population was simply indifferent to what had happened to their Jewish neighbors.

The initial executions were described in an early Soviet note dated January 6, 1942: "The first persons selected for shooting were forced to lie face down at the bottom of the ravine and were shot with automatic rifles. Then the Germans shoveled a little earth over their bodies. The next group of people awaiting execution was forced to lie on top of them and was shot in the same way. . . ."[6] Evidence at the Darmstadt trial confirmed the description. Later the procedure was altered. According to the Lutzenko account, the victims were "put in a row at the very edge of the ravine and shot in the neck by machine guns; children were thrown alive into the ravine." A Darmstadt defendant recalled how he would then enter into the "glutinous mass" of bodies to shoot at those which seemed still alive. Shovelfuls of sand covered the bodies. Then the machine guns would again stutter, and another group plunged downward. The sole known survivor of the Babi Yar mass murder, Dina Mironovna Pronicheva, now with the Kiev Puppet Theater, came from the Soviet Union to provide the court with the harrowing details that verified the technique of slaughter.

Colonel Blobel later testified that his unit had been divided into squads of thirty men each; a squad would shoot for an hour and would then be replaced by a second squad. The shooting continued until night, when the Germans retired to their quarters, herding the remaining Jews into empty garages. Early in the morning the massacre was resumed. That evening, an eyewitness reported, "the ravine was dynamited so as to cover with earth both the dead and those still alive." Illustrative of the mentality of the Einsatzgruppen was the testimony of one of them at Darmstadt. Following the massacre, he presented himself to an officer (also a defendant at Darmstadt) and asked: "Lieutenant Colonel, don't you have anything more for me to shoot?"

An official Einsatzgruppen comment expressed pride in the operation: "The transaction was carried out without friction. No incidents occurred." At the end of the thirty-six hours, the precise calculations of the Germans showed 33,771 dead. What percentage of the total Kiev Jewish population this was cannot be precisely ascertained. The total pre-war Jewish population of Kiev numbered approximately 180,000, out of a total population of 846,000. After the war began, the total population was reduced by evacuation to 304,500. If the Jewish population was reduced at the same rate, then approximately 65,000 Jews remained.[7] Thus it can be estimated that at least one-half of the Jewish population was liquidated in two days. (However, Kuznetsov, basing himself upon Soviet figures, estimates the number of Jews shot during September 29–30 at 70,000.) If this is correct, the number of remaining Jews was 30,000. The remainder must have scattered, seeking hiding places in the city or in nearby areas. The Einsatzgruppen continued to hunt them down to feed their unsatiated machine gunners at the ravine.

During the subsequent two years of German occupation, the death roll of Babi Yar victims continued to mount, with executions of Soviet prisoners of war, partisans, and Communist activists. Though the extraordinary pace set by the September 29–30 massacre was not duplicated, the rain of bullets never ceased. A report of the Einsatzgruppen stressed that even "the immediate hundred per cent exclusion of Jewry . . . would not remove the political source of danger." The "main task," the report went on, was "the destruction of the communistic machine" and this purpose could not be replaced "in favor of the practically easier task of the exclusion of the Jews." A post-war report of a USSR Special Commission chaired by Nikita Khrushchev estimated that over 100,000 men, women, and children were liquidated at Babi Yar. (A total of 195,000 are said to have been executed in the general area of Kiev.) Tens of thousands of Russians and Ukrainians lay buried in a common grave with Jews.

But the uniquely Jewish feature of the extermination procedure remained. Characteristic was the selection process by which Soviet prisoners of war were chosen for execution at Babi Yar. An Einsatzgruppen directive specified that "the racial origin has to be taken into consideration." Thus, a report of executions by Sonderkommando 4A in November, 1941, noted: ". . . the larger part were again Jews, and a considerable part of these were again Jewish prisoners of war who had been handed over by the Wehrmacht."

For the Einsatzgruppen killers, Babi Yar represented an apotheosis of their anti-Jewish objective. In March, 1942, Colonel Blobel was driving in the vicinity with Gestapo agent Albert Hartel when the latter noticed that the surface was agitated by pressures from below—the spring thaw having released gases from decaying corpses. Blobel proudly explained: "Here my Jews are buried."

But the SS colonel had not finished his task, for the dead were not to be permitted even their rest. As German defeat neared and they feared that the butchery might come to the attention of the world, the SS ordered Blobel to erase all traces of the Babi Yar mass burial. In August, 1943, he supervised the digging-up of the area; each corpse was examined for rings, earrings, and gold teeth. Huge, crude crematoria were built; the bodies were stacked alternately with logs, and doused with gasoline. Each pyre took two nights and one day to burn. The bones that did not respond to incineration were crushed, mixed with earth, and scattered over the area. The fires lasted almost six weeks, the stench suffocating the entire Lukyanovka district.

The evidence could not, however, be suppressed. Disclosures of a hidden eyewitness, revelations of a survivor of the shooting, captured Einsatzgruppen records, reports of escaped slaves who had participated in the 1943 excavation, and charred pieces of bone which even today are dug up at the site—all brought to the world details of what had happened.

Some details were made public at the Nuremberg trials of 1947–48, which concluded with the death sentence imposed upon Blobel and other Einsatzgruppen leaders. The Darmstadt trial provided the final chapter in the documentation process. Long prison terms were meted out to the ten defendants.

The trial received almost no coverage in the Soviet Union. This was hardly surprising, since Babi Yar constituted the most poignant example of Jewish martyrdom on Soviet soil. Soviet authorities have from the very beginning attempted to blur this aspect of its character. The official government report on the massacre, published some six months after Kiev's liberation, spoke of Nazi crimes at Babi Yar against Soviet citizens generally rather than against its Jewish community specifically.[8] Apparently the local authorities were anxious to remove all traces of Babi Yar, for they planned to build a modern market on the site. Ehrenburg, at the time, asked the Ukrainian premier, Nikita Khrushchev, to intervene, and was promptly advised by the premier "not to interfere in matters that do not concern you."[9]

But in the immediate post-war years, the Soviet regime was not yet overtly hostile to its Jewish community, and the Soviet public was able to learn of the distinctly anti-Jewish aspects of what had happened at Babi Yar. Much became known through Ehrenburg's novel *The Storm,* published in 1947, which won the Stalin prize. The massacre of Jews at Babi Yar also was sympathetically treated in poetry, such as the poem composed by the Ukrainian-Jewish writer Savva Golovanivsky, and in recorded songs of the Yiddish singer Nekhama Lifschitz (one of which told of the grief of a Jewish mother unable to find the remains of her children who perished at Babi Yar). Indeed, official plans were advanced for a public monument at Babi Yar. A prominent architect, A. V. Vlasov, prepared the design of a memorial, "strict, simple, in the form of a prism," and the artist B. Ovchinnikov worked out the appropriate sketches "dedicated to Babi Yar."[10]

But the anti-Semitic campaign which burst forth in late 1948 required that Babi Yar be plunged into the "memory hole" of history. Golovanivsky's poem was singled out for attack in March, 1949, because he had dared to suggest that Ukrainians and Russians "had turned their back on an old Jew, Abraham, whom in 1941 the Germans had marched through the streets of Kiev to be shot."[11] The poet was charged with "nationalist slander" and "defamation of the Soviet nation." Another Ukrainian-Jewish poet, Leonid Pervomaisky, was also denounced for "repeating Golovanivsky's defamation of the Soviet people." The theme of Babi Yar was no longer countenanced in literature, and the plans for the memorial were quietly shelved.

So complete was the blackout that Soviet citizens were never informed that in June, 1951, one of the principal architects of the

Babi Yar holocaust, Colonel Blobel, was executed in Nuremberg for his crimes. And even such a knowledgeable Soviet writer as Anatoly Kuznetsov, the author of a documentary novel on Babi Yar, stated that ". . . not a single Nazi has been tried or punished specifically for Babi Yar."[12]

The death of Stalin and the beginning of the Thaw did not bring any immediate change in the official attitude on Babi Yar. It was not until 1959, following the consolidation of Khrushchev's authority, that the search for coexistence with America coupled with the growing awareness of the need for widespread reforms in various parts of Soviet social life enabled Soviet policy-makers to loosen some inhibiting restraints. The three years that followed saw a veritable renaissance in Soviet literature. Even Jewish communal life was tendered a few concessions.

The moment was opportune for sensitive Soviet intellectuals, brooding over the double tragedy of Babi Yar—first the holocaust there and then suppression of any reference to it—to voice concern. It was not long in coming. The distinguished Soviet writer Viktor Nekrasov, upon learning that the Architectural Office of the Kiev Town Council planned to flood Babi Yar, fill it, and "turn the site into a park, to build a stadium there," wrote a long letter to *Literaturnaia gazeta* which appeared on October 10, 1959:

> Is this possible? Who could have thought of such a thing? To fill a . . . deep ravine and on the site of such a colossal tragedy to make merry and play football?
> No, this must not be allowed!

Nekrasov noted that other sites of Nazi atrocities had been turned into memorials, and "lest people ever forget what happened," he boldly demanded similar "tributes of respect" for the Kiev citizens who had been shot in Babi Yar.

Two months later (December 22, 1959), the same journal carried a letter signed by a number of inhabitants of the district near Babi Yar in which they supported the recommendation to erect a monument on the "murder site." They observed that Nekrasov's article "concerning the tragically famous Babi Yar attracted the particular attention of the Kiev inhabitants" but, at the same time, they welcomed the idea that "a park be first planted in Babi Yar," and then "a monument erected in its center." What made the letter particularly significant was the lack of a single reference to Jews. It signaled an eventual half-way response of the authorities to the outraged conscience of the intellectuals: a monument should indeed be built, but one not specifically commemorating the martyred Jews. A further small item in the literary newspaper on March 3, 1960, pointed in the same direction. The editors noted that the deputy chairman of the Kiev Town Council Executive Committee had replied to the Nekrasov article with an explanation that the monument had not yet been erected because of "lack of reclamation of the region." The deputy chairman went on to promise that once the afforestation of the slopes of the ravine was completed, and a public park planted there, then "an obelisk with a memorial plaque to *Soviet citizens* exterminated by the Nazis will be erected in its center." (Emphasis added.) The special martyrdom of Jews was not mentioned. The deputy chairman's reply is interesting for another reason. He pointed out that his commitment to build a memorial was a consequence of "a resolution adopted by the Ukraine Government in December 1959," three months *after* Nekrasov had raised the issue. It was clear that Nekrasov had pricked the conscience of the Kiev community.

A much larger community, extending far beyond even Soviet borders, was to be stirred by Yevgeny Yevtushenko in September, 1961, almost twenty years to the day after the Babi Yar tragedy. In an autobiographical sketch published later in *L'Express*, Yevtushenko explained how he had come to write his courageous and moving "Babi Yar."[13] He had waited for a long time, he said, to publish a poem on anti-Semitism, but an appropriate form had not presented itself until after he had visited Babi Yar in the fall of 1961 to see and sense the Holocaust. Upon his return to Moscow he wrote the poem in "a couple of hours." In it he identified himself with "each man they shot here," "every child they shot here," and, in his profound mourning, he was transformed into "one vast and soundless howl."

On September 16, Yevtushenko recited "Babi Yar" to twelve hundred students at the Moscow Polytechnical Museum. He afterward recalled being "so agitated" that he kept the text in front of him. The reaction was overpowering: "When I had finished there was dead silence. I stood fidgeting with the paper, afraid to look up. When I did, I saw the entire audience had risen to their feet. Then the applause exploded and went on for a good ten minutes. People leaped onto the stage and embraced me. My eyes were full of tears." He was uncertain whether the poem would be published, but the then forthright editor of *Literaturnaia gazeta* gave the go-ahead signal, not without a last-minute warning to Yevtushenko: "Of course, anything may happen. I hope you're prepared." To which the poet replied, "I am." The poem was published on September 19 and immediately became an international sensation.

The poem began with a reminder that "No monument stands over Babi Yar." Only a "steep precipice," remains as an "epitaph." Yet the memory cannot be erased:

> There is a rustling of wild grass over Babi Yar.
> The trees look fearsome, like judges.
> Everything here screams in silence.

The poem was more than a reminder of tragedy; it probed the roots of popular anti-Semitism, and what made it particularly unusual was that Yevtushenko did not hesitate to indict historic anti-Semitism in Russia. On an official level, it is taboo to suggest that popular anti-Semitism persists to any significant extent. Yevtushenko dared to suggest that it does.

More remarkable even than the attack on anti-Semitism was the poet's characterization of Jews throughout the world as a people with a long, common history and a unifying tradition that made them a distinct entity. In a striking section of his poem he linked together the ancient Israelites, Christ, and Dreyfus, and, significantly, defined this unity as a distinct and separate "Jewish people." This conception not only does violence to the analysis prescribed by Soviet ideologists; it flies in the face of the accepted doctrine that Soviet Jews have little, if anything, in common with Jews elsewhere in time or space.

The storm of criticism that followed the poem's appearance was not unexpected. Five days after "Babi Yar" was published, *Literatura i zhizn'*, the journal of the Writers' Union of the Russian Federated Republic, carried a response in the form of a poem by another Soviet writer, Aleksei Markov. Yevtushenko's patriotism was questioned—"What sort of real Russian are you . . . ?" By referring to Jewish martyrdom at Babi Yar and to Russian anti-Semitism, Yevtushenko had attempted to defile (with a "pygmy's spittle") "Russian crew-cut lads" who fell in battle against the Nazis. In a concluding line, Markov flung at Yevtushenko the accusation "cosmopolitan," which, in the Soviet lexicon of previous years, was an epithet that carried the implication of treason.

A less crudely violent if sharper attack appeared in the same journal three days later. Written by a well-known Soviet critic, Dmitry Starikov, the article by implication denied that anti-Semitism existed in the USSR. "The friendship of our people," Starikov wrote, "is now stronger and more monolithic than ever," and to suggest that anti-Semitism among Russians still exists is nothing less than a "provocation," as well as a "monstrous" insult to those "who have entrusted him [Yevtushenko] with their word. . . ." Yevtushenko's conception of the Jews as a people was vehemently denounced on the usual grounds of being "supra-class, petty bourgeois illusions" which nurture "chauvinism." For Starikov, the poet's conception was but "reverse racism" for there are no "real historical links" between the ancient Hebrews and modern Russian Jews, and to speak of a "Jewish people," as such, is "illiterate." Yevtushenko, Starikov observed, had fanned "the dying flames of nationalist attitudes" and he warned him—using quotations from the authoritative Draft Program of the Soviet Communist Party—against taking any further steps into this "foul, swampy quagmire. . . ."

Finally, in typical post-war Soviet fashion, Starikov challenged the view that Babi Yar represented the martyrdom of Jewry. The "destinies of the persons who died there cry out" against the notion that Babi Yar was "one of history's examples of anti-Semitism." For, he went on, "the anti-Semitism of the Fascists is only part of their misanthropic policy of genocide . . . the destruction of 'the lower races' including the Slavs." To underscore his argument, Starikov appealed to the authority of one of the Soviet Union's leading literary figures (and a Jew as well), Ilya Ehrenburg. Quoting arbitrarily from various wartime articles, including one on Babi Yar, Starikov contended that Ehrenburg "did not stress the fact that it was Jews who were killed there." Ehrenburg came to the defense of the embattled Yevtushenko. He wrote a short note to *Literaturnaia gazeta* on October 3 (published on October 14) in which he sharply disassociated himself from the Starikov article, observing that the selected quotations in fact "contradicted" Ehrenburg's own views.

But Starikov had not limited his criticism to Yevtushenko. In a scarcely veiled threat, he wondered aloud why the editors of *Literaturnaia gazeta* permitted the poet "to insult the triumph of the Leninist national policy" with "provocations." At the Twenty-second Party Congress, the powerful chief editor of the journal *Sovietskii soiuz*, Nikolai Gribachev, charged *Literaturnaia gazeta* with "irresponsibility" in "systematically publishing cheap sensations."

Yevtushenko won the hearts of young people throughout the USSR. Every copy of the *Literaturnaia gazeta* issue in which his poem appeared was "sold out in a matter of minutes," he later reported. He was flooded with letters and telegrams—approximately twenty thousand of them. Only thirty or forty were abusive, and these, he said, "were all unsigned and in obviously disguised handwriting." Everywhere he went in Russia, his audience wanted to hear him read "Babi Yar." Patricia Blake, a close observer of the Soviet literary scene who attended a number of Yevtushenko's readings, reported: "When he had finished, the crowd began pounding on the floor with their feet. 'Again, at once!' He read it again, and later in the evening, when the audience would not relent, read it once more. When this happened for the fourth time, Yevtushenko shouted for silence and said, 'Comrades, you and I have been in this hall for six hours, and I should think you would be as tired of hearing it as I am of reciting it.' But again they pounded and once again he complied."[14]

Yevtushenko and the support he received not merely stung the doctrinaire apologists into action; the highest Party authorities became concerned. Khrushchev was later to reveal that the "Party Central Committee had been receiving letters expressing anxiety that in some works the position of Jews in our country has been depicted in a distorted way."[15] He referred specifically to Yevtushenko's poem. At a Moscow meeting of several hundred intellectuals called by the Party leadership on December 17, 1962, the poem became a key issue. When Yevtushenko recited the last two lines of his poem to the audience, Khrushchev interjected: "Comrade Yevtushenko, this poem has no place here."[16]

It was time for the "appropriate" discipline to be applied and for the customary public denunciations to be made. Besides, by the end of December, 1962, the Party leadership had become convinced that the liberalism of the previous three-year period had gone too far in various art forms—in literature, painting, sculpture, cinema-tography. Lest the trend of critical examination of the past be extended to embrace the hallowed institutions of public life, brakes had to be applied. A Kremlin conference of writers and artists on March 7–8, covered in detail in the public press, provided the set-ting for the disciplinary action. And none other than the Party boss and premier, Nikita Khrushchev, was designated to administer it.[17] While condemnation of liberating trends extended to all spheres of the arts and to numerous individuals, "Babi Yar" was the focus of the attack. Two types of criticism were leveled at Yevtushenko. The first was a rehash of the principal argument used by Markov and Starikov: "Events are depicted in the poem as if only the Jewish population fell victim to the Fascist crime, while at the hands of the Hitlerite butchers there perished not a few Russians, Ukrainians, and other Soviet people of other nationalities."

The second criticism was more serious, and Khrushchev felt obliged to wander into a forest of questionable data to buttress it. The clearly implied reference in the poem, that anti-Semitism con-tinued to exist in the Soviet Union, revealed that the author lacked "political maturity" and displayed "ignorance of the historical facts." Sharply the premier demanded, "For whom and why was it necessary to present the matter as if the population of the Jewish nationality in our country was being harmed?" The charge is "not true," for, since the very early days of the October Revolution, Soviet Jews have been treated "on an equal basis in every way" with all other national groups. A bludgeoning suggestion that Yev-tushenko had permitted himself to be used by alien and foreign sources followed: "With us there is no Jewish question, and those who devise one are singing to somebody else's tune."

Khrushchev then proceeded to a characteristic Soviet class analy-sis of anti-Semitism: it is typical of capitalist society and is alien to socialism. Jews do not constitute a single undifferentiated whole. Properly, they are to be broken down into social classes: bourgeois Jews are like the bourgeoisie everywhere; proletarian Jews are like the oppressed proletariat everywhere. "People's deeds," Khrushchev emphasized, are to be "measured not from a national, but from a class point of view."

To illustrate his theme, the premier pointed to a particular in-stance of alleged treachery to the Soviet state by a Jew during World

War II. A certain Kogan who had been an instructor at the Kiev Komsomol City Committee, he said, was found to be a translator at Nazi Field Marshal Friedrich von Paulus' headquarters. Khrushchev related that after von Paulus had been captured, a Soviet general called him to report the presence of Kogan. This exchange was then alleged to have taken place:

> Khrushchev: "How did he get here? You haven't made a mistake?"
> The Soviet general: "No, there is no mistake."

Khrushchev contrasted the alleged conduct of Kogan with that of a Jew named Vinokur, who was political commissar of a mechanized brigade that participated in the capture of von Paulus and his entourage. The point was then driven home: "That was how it was, one Jew served as a translator at Paulus' headquarters, and another, as a member of our forces, took part in the capture of Paulus and his translator."

The illustration went beyond the argument about anti-Semitism and raised the earlier issue of the specific martyrdom of Jews. For if the Nazis' program was not designed to effect the wholesale liquidation of all Jews, if some Jews had been permitted to escape genocide and even to serve in a fairly responsible post in the Nazi war machine, then the idea of a specific martyrdom of the Jewish nationality was placed in question. This was clearly Khrushchev's intention.

Curiosity was aroused by the story. Could von Paulus have employed a Jew? Only one other reference to a "Kogan" such as described by Khrushchev had appeared. In the very same year that the Kremlin conference of intellectuals was held, the Soviet youth publishing house, Molodaia Gvardiia, issued a novel by P. Gavrutto entitled *Clouds Over the City* which made reference to a certain Kogan as a traitor. The reference was greatly amplified in a revised edition of the book which appeared in 1965. Kogan was charged with having committed the "foul crime" of singlehandedly betraying the anti-German underground to the Gestapo and then becoming von Paulus' interpreter.

Not until August 9, 1966, was the Kogan story revealed to be fallacious. On that day, *Literaturnaia gazeta* published a long letter by Ariadna Gromova, a literary critic, which sharply attacked the Gavrutto novel for its treatment of Kogan. Entitled "In the Interest of Truth," her letter emphasized that the names of the traitors to the underground were known, and that Kogan was not among them. Moreover, the name of von Paulus' interpreter was known, and it was not Kogan. Indeed, Kogan, she observed, had never seen von Paulus, having left Kiev with the Soviet forces before the city was occupied. The letter noted that the false charges about Kogan had ruined his life.

One can only speculate as to how many other lives had been affected by the Khrushchev tale about Kogan. The year 1963 marked a high point in the Soviet campaign against economic crimes, which had pronounced anti-Semitic overtones in a number of areas. Were prosecutors and newspaper editors in these areas encouraged by the Kogan hoax to give vent to a personal bias against Jews or to exploit local anti-Semitic sentiments? No one can ever be sure. What is clear is that the Gromova criticism, even if it made no specific reference to Khrushchev and his tale (it focused only upon the Gavrutto story), shattered a malicious libel.

The pressures exerted upon Yevtushenko's "Babi Yar" in December, 1962, and even more strongly in the following March, had the required result. It was first made apparent not in the literary field, but rather in the musical field. By December, one of the USSR's most prestigious cultural figures, Dmitry Shostakovich, had completed his Thirteenth Symphony, a musical and choral setting of five poems by Yevtushenko, including "Babi Yar." The work received its first performance in Moscow on December 18, 1962, and was accorded a tumultuous reception. But no review appeared in the major press organs. The official reaction to the Shostakovich symphony was hardly surprising. Just the day before its public debut, at a specially called meeting held in Moscow between top Party leaders and leading Soviet intellectuals, the Party's then principal ideologist, Leonid Ilyichev, criticized Shostakovich for choosing an undesirable theme for his symphony and therewith failing to serve the true interest of the people. Public performances temporarily ceased.

To meet the powerful Party thrusts, Yevtushenko made two additions to the text. At one point, the following line was added: "Here together with Russians and Ukrainians lie Jews." A second insertion read: "I am proud of the Russia which stood in the path of the bandits." Yevtushenko vehemently denied in a Paris interview in

February, 1963, that he had capitulated to Party pressures. "I am not a man to take orders," he observed. All that he had done, he said, was to make a slight addition without changing a word of the poem. He further commented that the addition was merely a result of a letter he had received, after the poem's publication, which described how a Russian woman had saved the life of a Jewish child threatened by the SS.

The fact is, however, that the first addition does violate, to some extent, the spirit and intent of the poem, which had treated Babi Yar as a distinctive Jewish episode of martyrdom. Still, the character of the poem had not been basically altered, and a public airing of the symphony could be assured. After Shostakovich incorporated the revisions in the symphony, performances were renewed and *Pravda*, on February 10, 1963, observed that it was a truly "Russian" work.* But sharply critical voices continued to be heard on the subject of the theme of the symphony. On April 2, the Minsk newspaper *Sovietskaia Byelorossiia* asked: Why did Shostakovich "look only here," at Babi Yar, for "material revealing the bestiality of Fascism? . . ." "Why was Fascism terrible only and first of all because of anti-Semitism?" The critic chastised those who would "elevate a petty incident to the rank almost of national tragedy."

The toll had been taken. Discussion about Babi Yar disappeared from the public arena, not to reemerge until the summer of 1966. The intervening period was marked by increasing pressures upon the literary intelligentsia, culminating in the Sinyavsky-Daniel trial in January, 1966. The first secretary of the Komsomol, S. P. Pavlov, typified the official attitude when, in an article in *Pravda* on August 29, 1965, he sharply criticized those writers who engendered among young people "a certain skepticism toward everything bright, advanced, and progressive that comprises the essence of our society." But the intellectuals refused to capitulate. In March, 1966, a sizable number of them petitioned the Presidium of the Twenty-third Congress of the Party, then meeting in Moscow, concerning the Sinyavsky-Daniel case, charging that it "creates an extremely dangerous precedent." Their criticism and the strongly critical reaction emanating from Communists abroad may have encouraged the authorities to relax the pressures. In the momentarily changed

* In late 1972 a recording of the Shostakovich work performed by the Moscow Symphony Orchestra became available in the West.

atmosphere, it could be anticipated that the Babi Yar issue would once again take on a public character.

In August, *Yunost'*, a liberal literary monthly, initiated a three-part serialization of a powerful documentary novel, *Babi Yar*, by Anatoly Kuznetsov. The young writer had accompanied Yevtu-shenko on the latter's inspirational visit to Babi Yar in the fall of 1961. The impression which the visit made on both of them was described by Kuznetsov in the Soviet journal *Sputnik* (April, 1967):

> One day we both walked to Babi Yar; we forced our way through the dense undergrowth, and stood on the edge of the ravine. The sun was shining, everything was so peaceful, so quiet.
>
> We were standing where hundreds of thousands of people had once writhed and screamed in the throes of death. Almost all the victims had screamed horribly.

In fact, Kuznetsov, who had experienced Nazi rule in Kiev while a child of twelve, had been accumulating a thick notebook on Babi Yar filled with clippings, documents, and personal notes for some eighteen years. Just prior to the Yevtushenko trip, Kuznetsov had returned to Kiev to visit his mother. Deciding to take another look at a favorite childhood haunt, he climbed to the top of Babi Yar "and suddenly I caught my breath and I realized that the time had come to start writing my book." With painstaking detail, graphically presented in a compelling literary format, Kuznetsov catalogued the overpowering events of Babi Yar. For the first time since the war the Soviet public would learn the full dimension of the Nazi massacre.

Included in that dimension was the genocide of Kiev's Jewish population on September 29–30, 1941, described in all its gruesome detail. In painting the panoramic death scene, Kuznetsov had the benefit of drawing upon the personal experience of Dina Mironovna Pronicheva, the survivor of the Babi Yar carnage. Accidental circumstances plus quick thinking and enormous courage enabled her to escape.

Kuznetsov does not hesitate to define the initial Nazi objective as being aimed exclusively against Jews. One of his characters, the grandfather, bursts into the household on September 28, 1941, to report the German plans: "Here's news! Not a Jew will be left in Kiev by tomorrow." If a few non-Jews were killed during those two days it was because they accidentally had appeared in the line of march or at the ravine. Approximately fifty had been sorted out and sent to a nearby hillock. (Pronicheva was among them, for she had claimed to the Ukrainian *Polizei* assisting the Nazis that her name and face marked her as typically Ukrainian; in fact, she was a Jew married to a Ukrainian.) But then a Nazi officer had driven up demanding to know who the non-Jews were. This exchange followed.

"These are our people," replied the *Polizei*. "We weren't sure whether to release them."

"Shoot them! Shoot them right away!" stormed the officer. "If just one gets away and spreads the story, not a Jew will come here tomorrow."

The author's candor further required him to take the difficult step of showing that some Ukrainians welcomed the conquering Nazis, that others actually collaborated in the mass killings, and that many passively accepted German rule, striving in every way possible to survive.

Kuznetsov's story is not limited to the two-day episode; rather it embraces the 778 horrifying days of Nazi rule of Kiev. During that period, tens of thousands more—Russians and Ukrainians, in addition to Jews—were to be brutally murdered at Babi Yar. The victims included Communist activists, partisans or suspected partisans, suspected saboteurs, war prisoners, violators of Nazi regulations, or sometimes just plain bystanders arbitrarily selected in a purely irrational manner. The machine guns chattered at the ravine daily and endlessly.

But even after the genocidal episode of September 29–30, Babi Yar was to continue to be the execution point for *all* Jews who might be apprehended by the Nazis. This, too, is documented by Kuznetsov. Thus, in describing the selection process for Babi Yar in a nearby camp holding war prisoners, he reported: "The quickest to die were the Jews and half-Jews. . . . But the other prisoners clung to life with all their might, fighting for food and clothing."

By extending the story to the entire period of Nazi rule, during which thousands of others would fall under the Nazi guns, Kuznetsov may have hoped to blunt the kind of criticism that had been leveled at Yevtushenko. In his *Sputnik* article, he noted that the latter's poem had "provoked some serious criticism because he had devoted it to only one aspect of the problem and only to the very first few days of Babi Yar when the Germans were shooting the Jewish population of Kiev." Still, Kuznetsov refused to suppress the distinctive Jewish martyrdom that Babi Yar symbolized. In a personal foreword to the novel, he recounts how, as a youngster, he and a friend shortly after the war went to the general site of the ravine to explore the precise point at which the mass murders took place. Seeing an old man crossing the ravine, the young Anatoly shouted: "Hey uncle! Was it here that they shot the Jews or farther on?" The response was typical of those who had criticized Yevtushenko. "And how many Russians were killed here, and Ukrainians and other nationalities?" After following the stream in the ravine until washed-up pieces of burnt bone appeared, they were able to define the approximate point of the killings. "From this we concluded that they had shot the Jews, Russians, Ukrainians and other nationalities higher upstream." Even after the old man's comment, Babi Yar would continue to be associated in his mind first with Jews.

Following his defection from the USSR in July, 1969, Kuznetsov revealed in the *London Daily Telegraph* that at the time of his book's publication, a hornet's nest had been stirred up: "I had my own troubles. There was an unpublicized row over *Babi Yar*. They suddenly decided that it ought not to have been published. At *Yunost'* they told me that it was practically an accident that it had ever appeared at all *and that a month later its publication would have been out of the question. In any case they forbade the reprinting of it."* (Emphasis added.) A recently published disclosure appears to validate Kuznetsov's observations. An underground newsletter of Soviet dissenters—made public only in August, 1971— reported that in October, 1966, at a closed meeting of ideologists, several speakers called for a new (and favorable) look at Stalinism.[18] Seventy per cent of the ideologists responded warmly. The speakers at the meeting singled out for criticism *Yunost'* as well as *Novyi mir,* with General Aleksei Yepishev, chief political commissar of the armed forces, noting that military men were forbidden to subscribe to the two publications.

Even when Kuznetsov's work was published a considerable amount of his original draft had been edited out. The excised portions, significantly, provided much anecdotal material concerning anti-Semitism among Ukrainians.

Public reaction to the appearance of the Kuznetsov book was

slow in coming. The first comment appeared on November 18 in *Literaturnaia Rossiia.* The reviewer, Georgy Radov, described the book as "genuine art" embracing the "richest prose." Then on November 22, the journal that had first printed the Yevtushenko poem, *Literaturnaia gazeta,* carried a powerful endorsement of the book by the liberal literary and film critic Aleksander Borshchagovsky. Its "destiny," he wrote, is "beyond doubt." Terming the book "a marvel of art," Borshchagovsky went on to say that "Soviet literature has gained a passionate and talented work."

The critic did not hesitate to challenge the literary Establishment for avoiding the Babi Yar theme: "Our writers have hardly touched on the tragic theme of Babi Yar; they have treated it with caution that does not promise discoveries." He gave emphasis to the overwhelming fact of Jewish martyrdom: ". . . the first act of the [Babi Yar] tragedy [was] when the Jewish population of Kiev was murdered, wiped out and cast into the ravine in the course of a few days." This "massive 'total' massacre was unprecedented" in history. Borshchagovsky then went on to note that Babi Yar became, after September, 1941, "a commonplace of terrible everyday reality" with "victims of every nationality" sacrificed there by the tens of thousands.

While Borshchagovsky spoke for the liberals, official comment from the principal authoritative sources was far slower and, when it appeared, much more restrained in its praise. On January 22, 1967, *Izvestiia* finally carried a review, by P. Troitsky. He found "contrivance" in the book's structure, an artificiality that was "at variance with the seriousness" of the author's purpose. Nor did he think that Kuznetsov had revealed a world of unexplored facts. The Babi Yar atrocities, the *Izvestiia* reviewer contended, had "already cut deeply into our consciousness." But, if they did, the reviewer himself was reluctant to give expression to their principal feature. The words *Jew* and *Jewish* are strikingly absent from the fairly lengthy commentary.

Yet, the *Izvestiia* review seemed to place a stamp of approval upon the work: ". . . the author evidently has been able to relate known facts in such a way that we feel we are coming upon much afresh." The portrayal of the leading character was "scrupulously" presented, said the reviewer, and the emotion of hatred for the Nazi ideology effectively developed. The fact that the book was reviewed at all in this central Soviet organ, and in a not unfavorable manner, indicated that doctrinairism was, for the moment, not completely in the ascendant.

Notwithstanding official rejection of Jewish martyrology, the editors of *Literaturnaia gazeta* would not be held back from underlining the specifically Jewish character of Babi Yar. On February 22, they ran another piece on the Kuznetsov book, this time a portion of a letter written by Dina Mironovna Pronicheva, the survivor of the Babi Yar massacre of September 29–30. The letter, in part, read:

> After the massacre of the Jews, the Germans combed apartments and houses; if they found children of a Jewish mother they killed them, even when, as in our case, the father was Russian. The *Polizei* seized my son, who was two years and three months old then, and took him to the courtyard to shoot him. My husband begged them not to kill the child, saying that I would return that evening and they would then be able to seize mother and child together. They left the child until evening. As soon as the *Polizei* went off, my husband wrapped Vovochka [her child] in paper, tied him with a string like a large parcel and carried him to me in Darnitsa. I hid in an attic together with the child for four months.

In the same month, another strongly favorable review appeared in the liberal *Novyi mir*. The author was Ariadna Gromova, who had, a half-year earlier, exploded the anti-Semitic myth fostered by Khrushchev that some Jews had served the Nazi cause. Her review, entitled "Truth, Only Truth," stated that the Kuznetsov Babi Yar story is "vitally necessary both here and abroad." The specific Jewish martyrdom of Babi Yar was briefly but emphatically alluded to: "The remembrances of Tolia Semerik [the young woman in the novel] deal chiefly with precisely those [Russian and Ukrainian] people whom the Hitlerites did not specially hunt down. . . ." In a parenthetical remark that followed, she observed that the killing of Jews and prisoners of war are related in chapters which constitute the remembrances of others.

The preparation, publication, and open discussion of Kuznetsov's *Babi Yar* was accompanied by related developments which suggested that strong pressures from the liberal intelligentsia for a memorial to the victims of Babi Yar were having some impact upon the political authorities. The outcry of Nekrasov in 1959 and the poetic appeal of Yevtushenko seemed in 1966 to find the appropriate milieu for fulfillment. The first hint that consideration was being given to the victims of Babi Yar came in April, 1965.[19] The president of the France-USSR Association, André Blumel, who was touring the Soviet Union with forty prominent Paris lawyers, was told by Mikhail Burka, the mayor of Kiev (as reported in the *London Jewish Chronicle*, May 14, 1965), that plans were being laid for building a memorial at the Babi Yar site to the victims of Nazi persecution. The mayor acknowledged that a housing development had been initiated at the site in 1963 but said that he had halted it when great numbers of human bones were found in the foundation. Projection of a memorial was now in process, he told Blumel, but he carefully explained that it would carry no specific reference to Jews.

Early in 1966, Novosti, the Soviet press agency, publicly announced that the Ukrainian Architects' Club in Kiev had placed on exhibit over two hundred projects and some thirty large-scale detailed plans for a memorial at Babi Yar.[20] Visitors to the exhibition were invited to express their views. The announcement further stated that after the exhibition the entries would be judged by a special tribunal consisting of representatives of municipal and governmental authorities as well as representatives from the Academy of Sciences and other cultural institutions.

Significantly, the inscriptions on the submitted projects avoided reference to the particular character of Babi Yar as a symbol of Jewish martyrdom. Instead, the inscriptions note that "in this place," over one hundred thousand "Soviet citizens, Russians, Ukrainians and Jews were murdered" in 1941 by the Fascists. One architect of Jewish origin, Abraham Miletsky, was rumored to have submitted a plan bearing an inscription in Yiddish, but he was requested to withdraw it and to submit another without the inscription.

Those who might be disappointed with the projected character of the memorial could still take heart from the fact that the idea for a memorial was alive. Further verification came on April 29, 1966, when the *London Daily Telegraph* correspondent in the Soviet Union, John Miller, cabled his newspaper that he was "emphatically" assured by Ukrainian writers that "Babi Yar would have its monument in time for next year's 50th anniversary of the Revolution. Some proposed models of a monument had been examined by a commission and the final choice would be announced soon." Miller reported that the Ukrainian intelligentsia were "highly sensitive" to charges of "deliberate neglect" of the memory of the victims of Babi Yar. They offered the explanation that Russia had to rebuild its factories and homes before it could erect monuments to the past. The explanation did not take account of the fact that in various parts of the country Soviet authorities had already built monuments to victims of Nazi persecution.

Final assurances about the memorial appeared during the publication by *Yunost'* of the Kuznetsov novel. On September 9, 1966, Peter Tempest, the Soviet correspondent of the British Communist daily, the *Morning Star*, cabled from Kiev: "The memorial at Babi Yar to 200,000 people, mostly Jews, massacred here during the war will definitely be erected next year, I was told today." It is significant that Tempest had included in his cable the point that the Babi Yar victims were "mostly Jews." Soviet authorities, needless to say, rejected this view. More pertinent was the timetable which Tempest reported. Like Miller, he was assured by Kiev authorities that the monument would be in place *before* the fiftieth anniversary of the Russian Revolution. Tempest went on to say that a group of sculptors and architects were currently working on the final design of the monument, which would be inscribed simply "to the victims of Fascism."

So heady was the atmosphere that, on September 29, the twenty-fifth anniversary of Babi Yar, many Kiev citizens spontaneously assembled at the site in what has been described as "a very impressive scene."[21] Dina Pronicheva, Viktor Nekrasov, and the Ukrainian liberal writer Ivan Dzyuba addressed the audience. Dzyuba's remarks have been preserved in the "Chornovil Papers," and they are remarkable for their courage.[22] He demanded from the authorities that they "let the Jews know Jewish history, the Jewish culture and the Yiddish language and be proud of them." The character of the event prompted some cameramen from the Kiev news-film studio to rush down and film it. According to Kuznetsov, this act resulted in "a great row in the studio," followed by the dismissal of the director and the confiscation of the film by the secret police.

The authorities, however, were sufficiently alarmed to arrange, a few days later, to place at the site a granite plaque on which was written the commitment that a monument would be erected there to the memory of the victims of Fascism. But the celebrations of the fiftieth anniversary produced no memorial at Babi Yar. The year 1967 was to be marked by one long paean to the October Revolution, with unpleasant reminders of the past fifty years muted and critical observations censured. The blow to Soviet pride flowing from the overwhelming defeat of the Arab armies—both militarily supplied and diplomatically supported by the Soviet Government— in the Six-Day War intensified a burgeoning nationalism.

The super-patriots struck back. It was hardly unexpected that the first and principal criticism of the Kuznetsov book would appear in a journal of the military—always the repository of correct national pride—or that its date of publication would be August, 1967, following the setback to Soviet Middle East diplomacy in the United Nations General Assembly. The rhetorical title of the review in *Sovietskii voin*—"To a full extent?"—set its tone. The reviewer, Aleksei Yegorov, answered quite simply and dogmatically that Kuznetsov's portrait of Babi Yar was limited, restricted, and therefore distorted. Equally unobjective, Yegorov noted, were such reviews as those by Borshchagovsky (who gave "free rein to his [own] imagination") and by Gromova (who had the gall to suggest that the book is "vitally necessary for readers both here and abroad.").

What Yegorov found particularly distasteful was Kuznetsov's description of those Russians and Ukrainians who had been "Fascist lackeys and obeyed their criminal orders." References to Russian and Cossack collaborators, Ukrainian pro-Nazi policemen, Soviet black marketeers who pandered to the Germans, ordinary citizens who cooperated with occupation authorities (some by turning over their Jewish wives or informing on other Jews)—from Yegorov's viewpoint— are nothing short of "offensive" and hardly appropriate for a "historical work."

Not much better was Kuznetsov's characterization of the category of the martyred. In a sarcastic introductory remark, Yegorov reminded his audience that Kuznetsov is "not the first artist who chose the tragedy of Babi Yar as a topic"; Yevtushenko had "touched upon it and, as is known, twisted historical facts." The same type of "twisting," although not to the same extent, was characteristic of the Kuznetsov book, the critic thought. He recalled the exchange in the foreword of the novel between fifteen-year-old Anatoly

Kuznetsov and the old man. Anatoly's question as to where the Jews had been shot was intolerably irritating ("Hey uncle! Was it here that they shot the Jews or farther on?"). Yegorov preferred the response of the old man: Russians, Ukrainians, and other nationalities were the Nazi victims.

But even Kuznetsov's treatment of Babi Yar as a "multinational tragedy"—the words are Yegorov's—was inadequate. Kuznetsov is to be faulted for being "brief" and "perfunctory" about the martyrdom of "Soviet citizens." His emphasis should have been: "In Babi Yar there lie buried many Russians, Ukrainians, and other nations. Here were shot the sailors of the Dnieper flotilla; the railway workers of the Kiev region; workers and employees of Kiev; Red Army soldiers and commanders who were taken prisoner."

However Soviet ideologists may attempt to distort the reality of Babi Yar, they cannot make its significance compatible with their own prescribed historical view. Embarrassment emerges each time the symbol is resurrected by one or another writer determined to confront Soviet society with the truth about Jewish martyrdom. For such confrontation would inevitably place on society's agenda the question of Jewish national consciousness and the problem of anti-Semitism, both currently among the unmentionables. The more comforting posture is therefore suppression of the symbol of Babi Yar or of reference to it, rather than mere distortion. Thus, the promise of 1966 that a memorial would be built at the site must remain unfulfilled while the architectural designs for the memorial accumulate dust on the shelves of government agencies in Kiev or Moscow. Thus, too, Shostakovich's Thirteenth Symphony must forego being performed in the USSR. Finally, the trial of the Babi Yar killers in West Germany had to go almost unnoticed in the Soviet press.

And Soviet Jews must not publicly declare that Babi Yar symbolized the Holocaust. On May 13, 1969, a young Jewish radio engineer of Kiev, Boris Kochubiyevsky, was placed on trial[23] and charged, among other things, with saying at a Babi Yar memorial service the previous September 29: "Here lies part of the Jewish people." He had evidently also asserted that anti-Semitism exists in the USSR, and he had criticized at a factory meeting the Soviet Government's position that Israel had committed aggression in June, 1967. But the basic point in the prosecution's case was that

Kochubiyevsky had asserted that the victims of Babi Yar were not merely victims of Fascism; rather, they were fundamentally victims of genocide against Jews. *Samizdat* material records the following exchange between the defendant and the judge after the former began making reference to the fact that Yevtushenko's "Babi Yar" was published in the USSR:

> Judge: Accused, keep to the subject of the charges.
> Kochubiyevsky: The poem "Babi Yar" . . .
> Judge: Accused, you have been given the chance to make a final statement in your defense, not to make excursions into history and literature.
> Kochubiyevsky: I ask that it be placed on record that I have been admonished for mentioning Yevtushenko's poem, "Babi Yar." . . . Very well, I omit this part of my final statement. All my statements at Babi Yar fully coincided with the sense and spirit of this poem.[24]

In a four-day trial that presaged the big trials of 1970–71, Kochubiyevsky was accused of having "during 1968, systematically disseminated by word of mouth slanderous fabrications, defaming the State and the social system of the USSR. . . ." The trial—held, ironically, in the same courthouse in which Beiliss had been tried in 1912–13—was replete, according to *samizdat* accounts, with numerous instances of anti-Semitism emanating from the bench, the prosecution, the guards, and the persons permitted by the authorities to attend. For not keeping silent about Babi Yar, Kochubiyevsky was sentenced, under Article 187 of the Ukrainian Criminal Code, covering "slander," to a term of three years in corrective labor camps.

But the silence can never be total. Yevtushenko, describing the deathly-still ravine of Babi Yar, commented: "Everything here screams in silence." If today the ravine is filled in and a highway runs through it, if housing construction proceeds on both sides of the highway, Babi Yar as memory and martyrology cannot be erased. In the final chapter of Kuznetsov's book, he underlined a fundamental truth: "History will not be cheated, and nothing can be hidden forever."

Chapter 7
Cacophony of Hate:
Israel as "Nazi"

The Six-Day War fanned the flickering national consciousness of Jews perhaps because it brought to the surface suppressed memories of the Holocaust. The pronouncements of Egypt's President Gamal Abdel Nasser and of Ahmad Shukairy, the head of the Palestine Liberation Organization, on the eve of the war, could not but stir an anxiety for the remnant of those in Israel who had survived the Nazi gas chambers. For they spoke of "liquidation" of Israel, of "driving the Jews into the sea." Anxiety was transformed into relief, then pride, by the victories of the Israelis. The *samizdat* poetry and songs of Soviet Jews testify to the emergence and growth of pride and self-respect. Even Ehrenburg, of whose assimilation and anti-Israel credentials there can be no doubt, was strongly affected. He told Alexander Werth:

> Well, it's just as well they didn't allow themselves to be exterminated by the Arabs, as they were in the Hitler days. Although there were plenty of excellent Jewish soldiers in the Red Army, and many of them were even made Heroes of the Soviet Union, there is still this unpleasant feeling that it's "natural" for Jews to be massacred. If, following in Hitler's footsteps, the Arabs had started massacring all the Jews in Israel, the infection would have spread: We would have had here a wave of anti-Semitism. Now, for once, the Jews have shown that *they* can also kick you hard in the teeth; so there is now a certain respect

for the Jews as soldiers. . . . And, in Russia, we always have a great respect for highly efficient soldiers and airmen, which the Jews—sorry, I mean the Israelis—certainly proved to be. . . .[1]

Having taken, over the years, the most intense measures to obliterate Jewish consciousness, Soviet authorities could not and would not tolerate its revival. Israel's image had to be blackened. A vituperative propaganda campaign of unprecedented proportions against the Jewish state was unleashed. Israeli leaders were depicted as "Nazis," no different at all from the Brownshirts of Hitler.[2] Like the Nazi aggressors, they were accused of planning an "empire from the Nile to the Euphrates" in which Israelis would be the *Herrenvolk*. Israelis were charged with engaging in the most brutal forms of persecution, including genocide, against the Arabs. *Izvestiia*, on June 15, 1967, for example, stated that the Israeli "invaders are killing prisoners of war and defenseless peasants, driving the inhabitants from their homes and publicly executing men, women, and children." Such "crimes" were similar to "those the Nazis perpetrated in the occupied countries during World War II." On July 5, 1967, Leonid Brezhnev, addressing the graduates of the military academies in the Kremlin, stated: "The Israeli aggressors are behaving like the worst of bandits. In their atrocities against the Arab population it seems they want to copy the crimes of the Hitler invaders."[3] The target of the campaign, it is clear, was not only Soviet Jewry but the entire Soviet public, whose enthusiasm for the Arab cause may have left something to be desired.

To reinforce the desired impact of the press campaign, newspaper and magazine cartoonists were set to work to portray in the most vivid manner possible the Nazi-type ugliness of Israel.[4] Not since the Kichko caricatures of 1963 had such anti-Jewish features appeared, the one difference being the size of the reading audience, which now reached into the millions. One typical cartoon portrayed an Israeli as a slithering animal with a long nose, holding a smoking revolver and sticking Stars of David on the graves of his victims. Another showed General Moshe Dayan with a skull covering his right eye, beneath which was the legend "Moshe Adolfovich Dayan." (The "Adolfovich" was designed to suggest that he was the son of Adolf Hitler.)

The violent verbal hostility to Israel was accompanied by a step which is almost unique in the history of Soviet diplomacy. The regime deliberately broke relations with the Jewish state. (It wasn't the first time; in February, 1953, the USSR had pursued the same course vis-à-vis Israel.) Even with its most dangerous and avowed enemies, the USSR was careful to maintain diplomatic relations. The list is impressive: Pilsudski's Poland, Mussolini's Italy, Hitler's Germany, Tito's Yugoslavia in 1949, the United States during the Cold War, anti-Communist Indonesia after 1965, and Mao's China in the sixties and early seventies. Only with Albania in 1961 did the Soviet Union sever relations, and that under extreme provocation. Even so, the break was only *de facto*, not *de jure*. The Jewish state was obviously considered to be in a distinctive category. The unrelenting hatred directed at it and expressed in diplomatic terms cannot be explained on rational grounds. The component of irrational anti-Semitic prejudice clearly entered into the decision of Soviet policy-makers.

The campaign was brought by the USSR to the United Nations. There was a certain irony in this development. For the late secretary-general, Dag Hammarskjöld, the work of the United Nations, however frustrating, brought the world ever closer to the spirit of brotherhood. It was for that reason that he asked that Beethoven's Ninth Symphony be played at all UN ceremonial occasions. Its mighty chorale, suffused with the theme of brotherhood, was for him the symbol of the world organization. To have had this powerful theme drowned out by a cacophony of hate propaganda would have appalled him. Yet this is what happened at the emergency special session of the General Assembly in the summer of 1967.[5] A massive propaganda campaign, unleashed by the Soviet Union and its Arab allies and aimed at reversing, diplomatically, the decisive military victories of Israel, was replete with appeals to bigotry.

Only once in the history of the United Nations had such a virulent hate effort been attempted—but it was isolated and quickly rebuffed. In December, 1962, Ahmad Shukairy, at that time the Saudi Arabia representative, delivered himself of a four-hour diatribe against Zionism which was climaxed by an open endorsement of anti-Jewish tactics. Terming Zionism "a blend of colonialism and imperialism in their ugliest forms," Shukairy had recommended that the UN "exterminate" the Zionist movement by formally "adopting" the Argentine Tacuara, a notorious anti-Semitic group. UN delegates, at the time, were quick to denounce the Shukairy vitriol. The Argentine representative asked that his country be lauded for its respect for human rights and not because of the genocidal aims of "some" Argentine Nazis for which "the representative of Saudi Arabia has seen fit to congratulate my country." The Chilean delegate pointedly told Shukairy: "Do not wish upon us those diseases which mankind is trying to wipe out. We cannot accept these sinister and ominous hopes." Similarly incensed remarks came publicly from the Danish and New Zealand delegations, and privately from numerous others.

The character of the Soviet attack upon Israel in the General Assembly was first suggested by the Soviet Union's chief delegate, Nikolai Fedorenko, in remarks made to the Security Council on June 9.[6] He then had denounced Israel's advance into Syria as following in "the bloody footsteps of Hitler's executioners." A few days earlier, in speaking to a journalist, he gave expression to the familiar, clichéd disclaimer: "Some of my best friends and closest companions are Jews."[7]

It was, however, Premier Aleksei N. Kosygin who developed the theme of the relationship between Israel and Nazism to the fullest extent. He arrived in New York to open the fifth day of the debate, on June 19, with an hour-long presentation read in a hasty, perfunctory, and pedestrian manner.[8] But the words contrasted sharply with the delivery. The incendiary charge was made that the Israelis were perpetrating "heinous crimes" similar to those committed "by the Fascists during the Second World War." Kosygin went on:

> In the same way *as Hitler's Germany* used to appoint *gauleiters* in the occupied regions, the Israeli Government is establishing an occupation administration on the territories it has seized and is appointing military governors there. Israeli troops are burning villages and destroying hospitals and schools. The civilian population is deprived of food and water and of all means of subsistence. There have been facts of prisoners of war and even women and children being shot and of ambulances carrying the wounded being burned. [Emphasis added.]

It was the first time that a Soviet prime minister had ever identified Israeli policy with Hitlerism. Aside from the distortions which supported the charge, the very nature of the identification—given the horrifying experience with Nazism suffered by the Russians and other European peoples—could not but contribute to inciting a strong hostility against Israel and, beyond Israel, against Jews, who might be linked in the minds of various peoples with Israel.

Premier Kosygin further stoked the fires of hatred by a deliberate attempt to link Israel with the Federal Republic of Germany, the fear of which continued to linger, especially in East Europe. Thus, he said: "In the Federal Republic of Germany, in particular, it was announced that discriminatory financial measures against the Arab States had been introduced. Recruitment of so-called volunteers for Israel started in several West German cities." He neglected to observe that volunteers came from a great number of Western European countries and from North America.

Significantly, and notwithstanding the probable urgings of the Soviet Union, not a single other Communist country in the UN General Assembly debate juxtaposed Israel with Nazism. Each, of course, bitterly criticized the Israeli military action, but each took obvious care to avoid the deadly comparison. Even the Albanian delegate, whose oratorical vehemence left little to the imagination, did not link Israel with Hitlerism. Two of the Communist representatives—those of Bulgaria and Poland—appeared to go out of their way to express their sympathy with Jews.

On June 20, the chairman of the Bulgarian Council of Ministers, G. Zhivkov, told the General Assembly that the Bulgarian people, during the last war, had rendered active assistance against Hitler's Fascism. He then went on: "The Bulgarian people have never been and will never be against the Jewish people. . . ." Premier Zhivkov may have been trying to live down the vituperation of his delegate to the Security Council, Ambassador Milko Tarabanov, who on June 9 had followed the lead of Fedorenko by accusing Israelis of having learned "many lessons from the Nazis." The chairman of Poland's Council of Ministers, Jozef Cyrankiewicz, also took note of "the solidarity and compassion" of world public opinion "for the Jewish martyrology." However, he made a bow to the Soviet line by characterizing the Israeli campaign as a "blitzkrieg." "For us in Poland," he said, "a blitzkrieg is tantamount to the Hitler aggression against Poland, to the terrible Nazi occupation. . . ." The note of sympathy was nonetheless still there. But it remained for the chairman of the Romanian Council of Ministers, Ion Gheorghe Maurer, to electrify the Assembly not only by avoiding criticism of Israel, but by openly advocating direct negotiations between the Arabs and

Israel as a precondition of peace in the Middle East. Ironically, the only Communist power that came close to the Soviet position was Yugoslavia, which, until then, had been the most independent in its foreign policy. The president of Yugoslavia's Federal Executive Council, Mika Spiljak, on June 21 told the Assembly: "In accomplishing his aims, the aggressor has resorted to ruthless violence against the Arab populations, a violence *having the character of genocide*, thus making his international responsibility even graver." (Emphasis added.) The accusation of genocide was, no doubt, a consequence of the profound concern felt by Marshal Tito on seeing his erstwhile ally among the non-aligned rulers, Gamal Abdel Nasser, so thoroughly beaten on the battlefield.

But Premier Kosygin's was not the only voice that utilized the Nazi or Hitler comparison. For the Soviet Union, at the General Assembly, speaks with three voices—its own and those of Byelorussia and the Ukraine. The premier of Byelorussia, Tikhon Kiselev, based his line on the relationship between Israel and the Federal Republic of Germany: "Bonn has in fact supported the Israeli aggression against the Arab States. And this is by no means surprising, for the ruling circles of both West Germany and Israel are seeking to expand their frontiers at the expense of other nations." The comments of the Ukrainian premier, Vladimir Shcherbitsky, not unexpectedly, were sharper, more virulent and provocatory:

The Ukrainians hold particularly dear to their hearts the sufferings of the Arab workers. The passage of years has not and, indeed, can never erase from our peoples' memory the hard times suffered when Hitler's invaders occupied Ukrainian territory and brought ruin and death to millions of people, expelled them from their cities and villages, imprisoned them in concentration camps, carried out mass executions, looted and carried away valuable goods, and doomed women, children and old people to starvation.

Why do not the Israeli leaders stop and think how indignant are the peoples because of the arbitrary actions committed by Israeli militarists in the occupied Arab territories? Why do they not think about what millions of victims of the Second World War, citizens of various countries and nationalities, would think if they should hear the truth about the Israeli invaders, whose actions and arguments *remind us so much of the black days of Hitler's aggression?* [Emphasis added.]

The accusations were reiterated by the foreign minister of the

USSR before the General Assembly's final voting on July 4. Andrei Gromyko, who in May, 1947, had delivered a compassionate address to the Assembly that urged the establishment of a Jewish state, now charged that "the propagandists from Tel Aviv . . . sing . . . old Goebbels songs. . . ." His Ukrainian colleague, Dmitri Belokolos, told the Assembly that the "perfidy" of Israel's rulers "is comparable to [that of] the rulers of Hitler's Germany." The Byelorussian, this time, was silent concerning the comparison.

While the noxious Hitler imagery was found to be unpalatable even in the ranks of the Communist powers, the same could not be said for the Arab powers. For some of them, the verbiage fell on fertile ground. On June 10, the day after Fedorenko had inaugurated the comparison, the Jordanian representative, Mohammed El-Farra, declared that the Israelis "are using the same tactics as those used by the Nazis. . . ." His Egyptian colleague, Ambassador El-Kony, joined in the analogy: "The Israelis are equally repeating the same policy which they learned from the Nazis. . . ." Not to be outdone, the Syrian representative, George Tomeh, spoke of "the criminal, neurotic, Zionist-Nazi complex." He added his own vindictive touch by describing Israeli policy as aimed at "the final solution of the Arab problem"—"to deport, expel and expropriate, kill and annihilate."

Other Moslem countries, principally in Africa, also repeated the Soviet comparison of Hitlerism with Israel. The Mauritanian minister of foreign affairs, Mamadon Birane Wane, on June 22 declared that "the creation of a Zionist State" was "as tragic and abominable a crime as that committed by German Nazism against the Jewish communities of Europe." He went on to state that the conduct of Israeli troops is "strangely reminiscent of that of the soldiers of Hitler in the countries occupied by the Nazis during the Second World War." The foreign minister of Mali, Ousman Ba, used the same words, contending that Israel's military administration "is strongly reminiscent of brutal Hitlerian methods of occupation. . . ." Guinea's foreign minister, Lansana Beavogui, repeated the imagery and then attempted a new, psychoanalytic interpretation of Israeli "bellicosity"! "Extremist Zionist circles" in Tel Aviv and "in other capitals of the Western world" were "contaminated by the brutal methods of force used by the Nazis against the Jewish people. . . ." Thus the Zionists took on the character of their tormentors. Iraq's

foreign minister, Adnan Pachachi, welcomed the Guinean interpretation. He observed that the persecutions of centuries culminating in
the Hitler holocaust left "a deep scar in the spiritual make-up of the
European Jews who today guide the destinies of Israel." The frus-
trations and hatreds of the past, he continued, found "an outlet in
the unparalleled savagery" against the Arabs. The Algerian foreign
minister, Abdelaziz Bouteflika, added further "insight" of a pseudo-
sophisticated kind into the causes of Israeli behavior: "Then came
Israel. German theoreticians of Zionism and activists in Central
Europe with German culture, forged themselves a predominant
place in the political leadership of the usurped [i.e., Israel]
country."

Once unleashed by the Soviets, the cacophony of hate took a
depressing turn. Jamil Baroody of Saudi Arabia gave expression to
the thinking that emerged in some quarters. In lengthy speeches to
the General Assembly, he declared that the Israelis were bearers of
commercialization, computers, and a "decadent culture," who will
make of Jerusalem a "fun city," a "Coney Island" with "topless
bikinis." Beyond that, they will "bring homosexuality . . . incestuous
films of which *My Sister, My Love* is only a mild example, and
synthetic narcotics, such as LSD. . . ." Baroody offered additional
insights that sounded as if they had been drawn from the writings of
a cross-section of world hate-peddlers, past and present. A few of
them follow:

1. The Romans "brought down" the Temple of Jerusalem because Jews "went to excess in their demands." "That beautiful
Temple of Solomon was wrecked by the Romans because of the
excesses and the incessant demands of the leaders of those days."

2. Western Jews are descendants of the Khazars.

3. The Zionists "promised" to push "the United States into the
First World War in 1917" as "the price of the Balfour Declaration."

4. The "wealthy Zionists" of Germany collaborated with Hitler
in the "asphyxiation" of "poor" Jews. The latter were the "victims"
of those who "were frenzied by the dream of carving for themselves
a home in the Holy Land."

5. The Zionists are for pushing the United States "into a war"
for "the sake of Israel." The Zionists "would have plunged the West
into a Third World War everywhere."

Not only were the formulations of the Soviet Union on Israel carefully avoided by the other Communist powers at the UN; they were avoided at home as well.[9] In this sense, they recall the wide differences in treatment of the Eichmann case in the mass media of the various Communist countries. Beyond this difference, there is considerable evidence of internal Party debates during May–July, 1967, in which significant forces, varying from country to country, opposed the Soviet line. Among Communist Parties in the West similar debates and opposition arose.

Of necessity, whether explicitly or implicitly, the internal Party debate was cast in traditional Marxist-Leninist terminology. The Soviet Union portrayed the Arab world as one engaged in a "progressive" national-liberation struggle against imperialist forces. Israel, on the other hand, was presented as a capitalist state under the domination of imperialist powers who aspired to cripple the national-liberation struggle. In this simplistic formulation the various aggressive Arab actions leading up to the June war emerged as but expressions of "progressive" Arab nationalism, not threats to the existence of Israel. Israel's military response, therefore, constituted unjust aggression. Since the Arabs were not bent upon aggression there was no need to have direct negotiations concerning secure borders or open waterways; Israel must withdraw unconditionally from the territories she occupied.

Other Communists rejected the assumption that all the Arab states were "progressive" and engaged in no activity of a provocative and aggressive nature. Some went so far as to depict the Arab movement as "chauvinism" against which Israel had to take defensive action. Thus the war for Israel was a just one, fought for her national survival; she was not acting as an instrument of foreign imperialism. And if peace was to be achieved in the Middle East, direct negotiations were required to bring about security and a diminution of hostility.

The split in the Communist world first came into wide public view when Romania, despite strong pressures, refused on June 9 to sign a joint statement of the European Communist countries which branded Israel the aggressor, and then rejected the proposal to break relations with her. Instead the Party in Bucharest issued a declaration which called for direct negotiations between the belligerents—a course violently opposed by the USSR. On June 12, the Romanian foreign minister told the Egyptian ambassador that he rejected any steps which could lead to the reopening of hostilities, and again he recommended direct negotiations.

On June 23, Romania's premier, Ion Gheorghe Maurer, delivered a key address at the UN General Assembly in which he suggested that the refusal of the Arabs to recognize Israel was an important factor which had prevented a stable solution to the Middle East problem: "One should respect the basic interests of every one of the nations in the Middle East, having fair regard for their independent standing and existence as sovereign states." It was a stunning rebuke to the Soviet position, made even sharper when Maurer demanded the removal of "all foreign interference in the countries of the area." Once again urging direct negotiations, Maurer emphasized that nothing "could replace a real settlement accepted by the Middle Eastern countries themselves." In the voting on the Yugoslav resolution for unconditional withdrawal by Israel, Romania pointedly abstained.

A second Communist regime which avoided a break with Israel was Cuba. Indeed, some Israeli technical personnel were working in that country, and Fidel Castro specifically noted that "Cuba will not take the initiative in breaking off relations with Israel." But here the parallel with Romania ends. Cuba's mass media carried on a shrill pro-Arab campaign, accompanied by characteristic anti-Israel diatribes. Yet, Castro made it publicly clear, in an interview with K. S. Karol of the *New Statesman*, that he refused to accept the USSR's conception of the Arabs as purely progressive democrats, innocent of aggression: "I was shocked during the period prior to the Six-Day War at the Arab propaganda which revealed a lack of revolutionary principles. *After all, true revolutionaries never threaten an entire country with destruction.* We have spoken out clearly against Israel's policy, but we do not deny its right to exist."[10] (Emphasis added.) The departure from the vulgarity of the Soviet press campaign was illustrated by the following incident. When a Cuban radio commentator, Captain Jorge Enrique Mendoza, on June 7 drew upon the Soviet theme of equating Israelis with Nazis ("Israel's army is trained by the USA and by West Germany with Nazi officers. . . . Israel's strategy is a typical Nazi strategy"), his view was firmly disclaimed two days later. The director of Cuban

National Television News announced that Mendoza spoke neither "in the name of the Revolutionary Government, nor of any other state agency. . . ."

In Warsaw, the Soviet line was the order of the day, with Party boss Wladyslaw Gomulka advising "Polish citizens of Jewish nationality" against holding any enthusiasm about Israel's victory. In an ominous warning which carried a veiled anti-Semitic threat, he declared on June 19 that "we cannot remain indifferent towards people . . . who come out in favor of the aggressor. . . ." But at the UN, Poland avoided the excesses of the Soviet representatives. Important sectors of Polish public opinion refused to bow to the general line of the Party, as an article ("Neither Race Nor Cash") in *Zycie Literackie* admitted on June 18. No doubt due to this resistance, high officials in the press and the armed forces who would not bend to the official view were dismissed. On February 18, 1968, the *New York Times* correspondent in Warsaw reported that "a number of leading Polish intellectuals, many of them Jews, have resigned from the Communist Party since the Middle East conflict last June. . . ."

The Hungarian Party leadership was far less vituperative than that in Poland. Soviet charges and analogies were avoided even if the Hungarian radio on June 20 broadcast an appeal to avoid appraising the Israeli-Arab situation on a "sentimental" basis. The official government organ, *Magyar Nemzet*, on June 12 departed from the Soviet line by urging "sober and wise negotiations"— almost an echo of the Romanian position—that would include "such questions as the future of the Gulf of Aqaba." Unlike Gomulka, Hungarian leaders went out of their way to condemn anti-Semitic incitement. Gyula Kálay, speaker of the Parliament, severely reproached "certain people who try to exploit the Arab-Israeli conflict for anti-Semitic incitement." A Politburo member, Zoltán Komotsy, appeared on television to declare: "We must not confuse our opposition to the extreme elements in the Israeli Government with the people of Israel. We disassociate ourselves from any sympton of anti-Semitism in our country and shall, as always, fight against it with all our might."

While Czechoslovak Party leaders parroted the general Soviet line, the prominent Czech novelist Ladislav Mniachko asserted that the "general mood" in that country was one of sympathy for Israel.

In a press conference in Israel, the non-Jewish writer and Communist Party member said: "I could not concur with a policy which was likely to assist in the extermination of a people and the liquidation of its state. Between such a policy and communist ideas . . . there is nothing in common." So widespread was the opposition in Czechoslovakia that the press launched a campaign aimed at rebutting it. One can infer the extent and character of popular sentiment by the following comment in the official Party organ, *Rude Pravo*: "There are people whose reasoning is rather simple even on complicated matters: since Czechoslovakia is a small country and Israel is also a small country, shouldn't our sympathy be with Israel and not with the Arabs?" The article went on to note that some people compared Israel's position with that of Czechoslovakia in 1938 when Hitler was shouting for its destruction.

If Tito's Yugoslavia was at the forefront, along with the USSR, in condemning Israel at the UN, not all of its leaders found the policy satisfactory. One Central Committee member, Saifulla, stated that "it should be clear that we, as Marxists, must recognize the historical fact of Israel and should strive to have relations with Israel and the Arab states established in a positive manner." Another Central Committee member, Svetozar Vachmanovic, offered a trenchant Marxist argument that would be echoed by Marxists in the democratic West: "Why should we support the Arabs who have declared a 'Holy War' on Israel and are ruled by feudal rulers . . .?" The argument was further developed in a most revealing article in the Yugoslav journal *Ekonomika Politika* on July 10:

> The rulers of Rijadh and Amman incite to a holy war against Israel. They elevate religious fanaticism to the level of a political theory. . . . The Jewish people was the first victim of German Nazism. Five million Jews were annihilated in the gas chambers. This explains the sympathies of all progressive and humane popular circles. There are two and one-half millions in Israel and there are twenty times that many Arabs! The royalist and feudal rulers of Islam and of the Arab states have declared a holy war against Israel and to our deep regret the progressive circles in the Arab world have never opposed the warmongering.

The most critical comments on Soviet policy came from various Western Communist Parties. *De Waarheid*, central organ of the Dutch Communist Party, on July 28 challenged the Soviet charac-

terization of the Arab movement as a "progressive" national-
liberation struggle. On the contrary, the Dutch Party organ said,
"when all is said and done," the Arab countries "are capitalist and
in part feudal." Calling attention to the appeals of Egypt and Syria
for the "extermination of Israel," the Party organ sarcastically noted
that such appeals which "strengthen anti-Semitic feelings" did not
"at all stop the material help of the Soviet Union." It then went on:
"The whitewashing, the presentation of the matter as if Israel were
not a 'Jewish state,' but a 'capitalist state' makes no difference. Could
the fact of Holland being a capitalist state justify a declaration about
'exterminating Holland'?" *De Waarheid* also took to task the
Soviet Government's tolerance of the Arab refusal to recognize
Israel. This Soviet attitude is a "bad sign" since persistent non-
recognition excites Arab "chauvinistic and racist feelings." Finally,
the Party newspaper called for a halt to armament shipments to the
Middle East, including "weapons from the Soviet Union."

Even more vigorous chastisement of the USSR came from the
Central Committee of MAKI, the wing of the Israeli Communist
Party headed by Shmuel Mikunis and Moshe Sneh. (The other
wing, RAKAKH, largely composed of Arabs, followed the Soviet
line.) MAKI denounced the Soviet description of the war, insisting
that it was "a defense war of the Jewish people for its physical
existence . . . against a scheme of liquidation and extermination by
the chauvinistic Pan Arab front." Its policy statement on August 10
read:

> The Central Committee of the Israeli Communist Party once again ex-
> presses its regret about the one-sided and distorted attitude by Soviet
> policy in the Israeli-Arab conflict . . . disregarding the threats and
> belligerent actions of the rulers in the Arab countries. . . . The MAKI
> Central Committee demands a revision by the Soviet Union Commun-
> ist Party which should be . . . in favor of negotiations [between the
> Arab states and Israel] . . . as it has acted in the past on similar
> occasions.

The Soviet press campaign against Israel was labeled by Sneh as
"atrocity propaganda that has gone beyond all limits."

The Swiss Communists sent a letter to MAKI endorsing its stand,
as did the Norwegian Communist Youth Club. In July, the secretary of MAKI, E. Vilenska, visited with the secretary-general of the

Swedish Communist Party, who expressed sympathy with MAKI's position and urged a just peace agreement between Israel and the Arab states. A similar view was voiced to her by high officials of the Norwegian Communist Party, including the chief editor of the Party's weekly journal.

Another Communist Party supporting the Israeli stand was Austria's. One of its leaders, Dr. Schoschbinsky, who was also chairman of the organization of Nazi ex-prisoners, reminded listeners of a long history of Arab aggressive plots. Noting the Arab slogan of "throw the Jews into the sea," he warned that hostility to Israel breeds anti-Semitism "in all countries." The Party's theoretical journal, *Weg und Ziel,* in November, 1967, carried a host of articles calling attention to the feudal and reactionary character of some Arab states and to the Arabs' chauvinist appeals for the extermination of Israel. One veteran Communist writer, Bruno Frey, observed that the Soviet Union failed to follow the principles it had advocated in Tashkent when India and Pakistan were brought together under its aegis. Recommendation that the Russians return to this policy in dealing with the Arab-Israel conflict was implicit.

The two big Western European parties—the Italian and the French—publicly endorsed the Soviet position, but not without a broad-based opposition in each Party. This was especially the case in Italy, where Israel was generally popular and where, during the height of the pre-war tension (May 26), Umberto Terracini, the chairman of the Party fraction in the Italian Senate, had taken this stance: "It is my view that the right of the State of Israel to independent and sovereign existence, a right which the Arabs are denying with great fanaticism, must be asserted definitely. . . ."

The principal Party organ, *L'Unità,* in supporting the Russians, avoided the usual harangues about Israeli atrocities and eschewed analogies with Nazism. The top Party leader, Luigi Longo, was quoted as advocating "negotiation" between Israel and the Arab states and insisting upon "the right of every nation to independence and security." Significantly, he criticized "certain trends of exaggerated nationalism which have manifested themselves in certain Arab quarters." The more independent Party organ *Paese Sera* reportedly set up a front-page headline denouncing Egyptian aggression (on May 29) but, after violent debate, was required to withdraw it. It was nonetheless widely recognized that the paper's editor, Dr. Fausto Coen, was sympathetic to Israel's position. And, indeed, so were many of the leftist intellectuals who appealed for direct negotiations both in *L'Unità* and in the Party's theoretical organ, *Rinascita*. The latter's October 6 issue went so far as to carry a long letter by Luciano Ascoli, a leading Marxist intellectual, which defended Zionism as a positive "historical creation" by which a section of Jewry is striving for "recognition as a people."

The French Party, historically known for its subordination to Moscow, was more rigid than the Italian Party in its treatment of the Middle East. Nonetheless, it was aware that, as one public opinion poll showed, 37 per cent of Party members were favorably disposed toward Israel, while only 15 per cent were inclined toward the Arab view. In consequence, the Party opened its organ, *L'Humanité*, to the publication of letters often sharply critical of the Soviet position. Such important Communist officials as Roland Leroy, a member of Parliament, called for "negotiations . . . on the basis of respecting Israel's right to exist," and recommended the Soviet Union's "Tashkent" policy as a model approach. French leftist intellectuals, many of them close to the Party, others active members of it, used the pages of such journals as *Presse Nouvelle* to air their criticism of the Soviet's pro-Arab bias. As early as May 30, Jean-Paul Sartre, Pablo Picasso, Simone de Beauvoir, and almost fifty other intellectuals issued a public statement calling upon France to back Israel's right to exist, freedom of navigation in international waterways, and "direct negotiations."

The smaller Communist Parties in the United Kingdom and the United States followed the Soviet line, but without the latter's vituperation. Even so, the letters-to-the-editor column of both Party organs (the *Morning Star* in Britain and the *Worker* in the U.S.) showed that much dissent existed. Among such leftist organs in the U.S. as *Jewish Currents* and the Yiddish *Morning Freiheit*, vigorous opposition to the Soviet position was consistently expressed.

The fact that not a single Communist regime or Party, aside from the Soviet Union and the Soviet Party,[11] utilized and elaborated upon the Hitler-Israel equation is indicative of how little Soviet policy on Israel, at least in its formulations, is rooted in Communist ideology, and how much of it—again in terms of formulations—springs from traditional Russian sources of which anti-Semitism is a component. Significantly, among the Soviet intelligentsia not only was the equation eschewed; the regime's policy toward Israel was seriously questioned.

Thus, Andrei Sakharov, whose views were "formed in the milieu of the scientific and scientific-technological intelligentsia," set forth in his 1968 memorandum *Progress, Coexistence, and Intellectual Freedom* that "if direct responsibility" for the war in Vietnam "rests with the United States," in the Middle East "direct responsibility . . . rests with the Soviet Union. . . ."[12] The USSR, he wrote, engaged in "irresponsible encouragement" of the Arab powers which "in no way" can be said to be "socialist"; rather they were "purely nationalist and anti-Israel." The Six-Day War was described by Sakharov as a "preventive war," undertaken by Israel "in the face of threats of destruction by merciless, numerically vastly superior forces of the Arab coalition. . . ." If Israel is to be faulted for a variety of reasons including "cruelty to refugees and prisoners of war," nonetheless the Soviet act of breaking relations "appears a mistake, complicating a peaceful settlement in this [Middle East] region. . . ."

Roy Medvedev took a somewhat similar approach.[13] While he considered the Six-Day War an "act of aggression" by Israel, that "aggression," he said, was "provoked" by "extreme Arab nationalists." He pointed to statements made by Arab leaders "that the time had come to annihilate the State of Israel," to the demand by Nasser for the removal of UN troops from the cease-fire line, and to the blockade of the Gulf of Aqaba. Noting that the Israeli action was supported by "the majority of European public opinion," including all the Socialist parties, Medvedev observed that "even Communist parties were not, as is known, in agreement in their appraisal of the events in the Near East."

The prominent dissenter was especially critical of the Soviet state's unqualified support of Egypt and failure to note the "totalitarian" features which emerged within it, the "extraordinary growth of corruption" in its army and state apparatus, its ruthless persecution of Communists, and the former ties of some of its leaders with Hitlerites during World War II. If Medvedev found Soviet policy in the Middle East to be "in its main features, undoubtedly correct," at the same time, he insisted, "we have not exerted our influence to weaken Arab extremism."

A more detailed critique was advanced in *Politicheskii dnevnik,* an underground newsletter of Soviet intellectual dissenters printed monthly since 1964, parts of which were published in the *New York Times* on August 22, 1971. An unsigned article written after the Six-Day War stated that "a significant part of the population of our country, and especially the intelligentsia, has taken a position quite different from the official view." The position was described as "more a pro-Israeli than a pro-Arab" one, and resulted from the fact that Nasser had embarked upon a course of aggression in May, 1967, with the hope of winning a "victory over Israel" in order "to achieve his hegemony in the Arab world."

The views of the Soviet dissenters had no influence upon the regime's policy-makers. Still less did they affect the manner in which Soviet policy was formulated and expressed for popular consumption. The invectives hurled against Israel were and continued to be unrestrained. However, in the restricted and limited attack upon Israel specifically, the impact upon Soviet Jewry and the population as a whole was probably far less than the impact which would be caused by an even bigger campaign upon a much broader target— "World Zionism." This campaign would emerge several months after the Six-Day War.

Chapter 8
Myths, Fantasies, and Show Trials: Echoes of the Past

Early in the twentieth century there appeared a crude anti-Semitic work in Tsarist Russia which purported to be the *Protocols of the Elders of Zion*. It described the hidden and sinister plans of the all-powerful "Elders of Zion" to establish control over the world by fostering discontent within each state, then by discrediting governmental authorities, and, finally, by exacerbating relations between states. A patent forgery composed of absurd allegations, the *Protocols* nonetheless took on a life of its own, was accepted in certain fashionable circles both in Russia and elsewhere, and eventually became what one scholar has called a "warrant for genocide."[1]

Exactly a half-century after the first edition of the *Protocols* was printed, a similar hoax was fabricated on the same soil but under a different regime. The Doctors' Plot had conjured up an elaborate conspiracy of "Zionists" who planned the destruction of the Soviet state by the murder of its leaders. The principal mechanism of the Zionist plot was identified as the American Jewish Joint Distribution Committee—known generally as the "Joint"—a Jewish social relief and rehabilitation agency. Several months before the Doctors' Plot was unveiled to the Soviet public, a rehearsal of the conspiracy theme was held in Prague under instructions of the Soviet secret police.[2] Rudolf Slansky, the Czech Party secretary-general, and his associates were charged with being agents of the "Joint" and part of the world Zionist underground.

Later, after Stalin's death, the Doctors' Plot would be presented to the public as an aberration, a product of the dead dictator's paranoia. (His daughter, Svetlana Alliluyeva, many years later revealed that Stalin's hysterical suspicion about Zionism led him to warn her that her first husband, a Jew, had been insidiously "thrown your way by the Zionists.") But recent developments in the field of Soviet propaganda suggest that the fantasy conceptions concerning a Zionist conspiracy may be a reflection less of an individual's whim than of something endemic to reactionary Russian tradition. Fifteen years after the Doctors' Plot and sixty-five years after the *Protocols* appeared, the Soviet press and radio shaped the contours of a newly discovered Zionist plot that is disturbingly familiar.

A new dimension, however, has been added. If previous conceptions of the Zionist conspiracy were principally geared to domestic considerations, i.e., the need for a scapegoat upon which the ills of society can be heaped, the recent conception was linked to a foreign policy consideration: rationalization of the invasion of Czechoslovakia. Cloaking military intervention with some ideological justification is an inevitable function of the propaganda machinery of an aggressor state. What is extraordinary about the Soviet rationalization (as well as that of Poland and East Germany) is not so much the application of the concept of the "socialist commonwealth," the roots of which can be traced back to the early years of the Communist International, but rather the utilization of a myth that has a distinctively anti-Semitic character.

Sometime during late July, 1967, a high-level decision was taken in Moscow to launch a massive internal and external propaganda campaign depicting Zionism as a major threat to the Communist world, the newly independent states, and the national-liberation movements. In the first week of August, 1967, an article entitled "What Is Zionism?" appeared simultaneously in the principal provincial organs of the USSR.[3] Its opening paragraph struck the dominant note of the campaign: "A wide network of Zionist organizations with a common center, a common program, and funds exceeding by far the funds of the Mafia 'Cosa Nostra' is active behind the scenes of the international theater."

Stereotypic images of the Jew abound in the paranoid portrait sketched by the author. The global "Zionist Corporation" is composed of "smart dealers in politics and finance, religion and trade" whose "well-camouflaged aim" is the "enrichment by any means of the "international Zionist network." Exercising control over more than a thousand newspapers and magazines in "very many countries of the world" with an "unlimited budget," the world Zionist "machine" services the vast monopolies of the West in their attempt "to establish control over the whole world."

If the campaign had its psychological roots in the dark phantasmagoric past, which had been nourished in the climate of Stalin's last years, it also served a pragmatic political purpose. With the Soviet Union's client Arab states suffering a major debacle in the Six-Day War and the Communist regime itself badly thwarted in its diplomatic endeavor at the United Nations to compel an Israeli withdrawal from occupied territory, a convenient scapegoat was needed to rationalize severe setbacks. Tiny Israel and public opinion were surely not the factors behind these failures. The enemy must rather be presented as a hidden, all-powerful, and perfidious international force, linked somehow with Israel. "World Zionism" was the ideological cloth that could be cut to fit the designated adversary. During the months following the Six-Day War, the citizenry of Communist states as well as those of the Arab and Afro-Asian world were literally saturated with this theme. Foreign radio broadcasts beamed from Moscow chattered away endlessly about Zionism as if this mysterious ghost would take on flesh by repeated incantation.

The flight from reality reached its nadir in the USSR in the fall and winter of 1967. In October, *Komsomolskaia pravda,* the mass-circulation newspaper of the Young Communist League, offered its readers a surrealistic description of the enemy: an "invisible but huge and mighty empire of financiers and industrialists," Zionism is the lackey "at the beck and call of the rich master whose nationality is exploitation and whose God is the dollar."[4] With overwhelming economic and political power at its disposal, Zionism is able to exert "effective moral and psychological influence upon the sentiments and minds of people . . . in many countries." About a dozen countries are specifically mentioned, but the author notes that the giant octopus commands "wide possibilities" in almost seventy countries of the globe.

Most notably subject to Zionist influence is the United States. To document his thesis, the author rattled off unusual data: The number of Zionists in America totals twenty to twenty-five million (there are but six million Jews in the U.S.); the percentage of Zionists among American lawyers is seventy; the percentage of Zionists among physicists "including those engaged in secret work on the preparation of weapons for mass destruction" is sixty-nine; and the percentage of Zionists among industrialists is forty-three. Especially strong is Zionist influence in the mass media, where its adherents own 80 per cent of the big publishing houses.

So extraordinarily precise were the Soviet published data that observers speculated about their source. Even a fantasy world draws upon elements of reality. Exhaustive research finally unearthed the basis of the author's figures. It is an obscure pamphlet of eighty-one pages entitled *America—A Zionist Colony,* published in Cairo in 1957. The writer was a certain Saleh Dasuki, who, besides specifying the percentages noted above, explained that "Jews, whether they have preserved their religion or whether they have adopted other religions, are known in the U.S.A. under the collective name of Zionists." Specialists in the field of hate propaganda recalled that in 1957 Cairo had set up a veritable factory for the production of anti-Semitic literature. It operated under the direction of a former employee of Joseph Paul Goebbels' Nazi Propaganda Ministry, Johannes von Leers, who had adopted the Arabic name Omar Amin.

Communist stalwarts were given further insights in December by a key Party organ, *Agitator,* which instructs activists in basic tactical guidelines. The author, Yury Konstantinov, found the "World Zionist Organization" to be a "political, economic and military concern" with broad interests ranging from "religion to intelligence" and having at its disposal "extremely large funds" obtained from "Zionist multimillionaires." The influence of the Zionist operation, according to Konstantinov, is demonstrated by its alleged ownership or control of 1,036 newspapers and magazines published throughout the world. If this failed to stretch the credulity of the reader, the author retreated to the more conspiratorial warning: Zionists work hard to deliberately shield their influence from public view. *Agitator* advised Party activists that anti-Zionist propaganda would be accused of being anti-Semitic. But this, the journal emphasized, was a mere ploy, for the Zionist is the major purveyor of anti-Semitism.

A disturbing if not surprising feature of the propaganda campaign was the rehabilitation of the Soviet Union's leading purveyor of anti-Semitic bigotry, Trofim K. Kichko. His 1963 book, *Judaism Without Embellishment,* was so vulgar and noxious in its language and illustrations that Communist parties everywhere joined a world-wide chorus of criticism demanding the withdrawal of the Soviet publication. In response, the Soviet Party's Ideological Commission condemned the book, and it was removed from bookstalls. But now Kichko reappeared with an article in a Ukrainian Party youth organ (*Komsomolskoye znamya,* October 4, 1967) which described a plot of "international Zionist bankers," including the Rockefellers, to transform the Middle East into "a strategic launching pad aimed against the socialist world, against the international workers' and liberation movements." Curiously, the Rockefellers appear in the writings of Kichko and his colleagues, just as they had in Nazi mythology, as the archetype of the Jewish banker. In January, 1968, Kichko was awarded the highly prized "certificate of honor" by the Supreme Soviet Presidium of the Ukraine.[5]

Having been duly honored, the Ukrainian "authority" on Judaism proceeded to write a new book, *Judaism and Zionism,* published in 1968 in Kiev. The edition was unusually large—sixty thousand copies—and designed "for a wide circle of readers." Kichko's virulent bigotry was again made evident with his description of Judaism as a doctrine which teaches "thievery, betrayal and perfidy" as well as a "poisonous hatred for all other peoples." The ultimate objective of Judaism, it appears, is the fulfillment of God's promise that "the whole world belongs to the Jews." This doctrine, he argued, has been pressed into the service of Zionism in order to help it create a "World Jewish Power" in Palestine and to fulfill "the territorial-colonialist ambitions" of the "imperialist allies and admirers" of Zionism. Zionism, Kichko found, is the reverse side of the coin of "cosmopolitanism," an ideology preaching that "the Fatherland of every person is not the country in which he is born, but the entire world." The author of the *Protocols* could not have found a more apt spiritual descendant than Kichko.

In the early summer of 1968, the theme of the world Zionist plot began to be employed in a new direction. The locus of Soviet concern was no longer only the Middle East, where a scapegoat was needed to explain the failures of Soviet policy. The basic fear of the Communist leadership now centered on Czechoslovakia, where the humanizing and democratic tendencies of the government led by Alexander Dubcek threatened to burst the integument of Soviet totalitarianism. World Zionism would now be depicted as the spearhead of international capitalism engaged in an effort to subvert Communist states and harm relationships between them. (Similarity to the fundamental elements of the old *Protocols* is here especially marked.)

An article in the authoritative foreign policy journal, *Mezhduna-rodnaia zhizn'*, published in June, 1968, signaled the change in emphasis of the Zionist theme. Entitled "Israel, Zionism and International Imperialism," the article was written by a leading Soviet "expert" on the subject of Zionism, K. Ivanov.[6] He recapitulated the international conspiracy thesis, linking world Zionism, Jewish capitalism, Israel, American imperialism, and West German revanchism in a gigantic plot to overthrow Communist rule. Since Western imperialism is unable to destroy by military means the Communist states of Eastern Europe, he argued, it has been forced to rely upon ideological subversion. The key role is played by world Zionists, who "are trying to instill into the minds of Jews in various countries, including the socialist countries, that they have a 'dual citizenship'— one, a secondary one, in the country of actual domicile, and the other, the basic, spiritual and religious one, in Israel."

The potential enemy was clear: a fifth column of Jews who have fallen prey to the "dual citizenship" concept. Ivanov charged that the imperialist intelligence services and psychological warfare agencies were spending hundreds of millions of dollars, utilizing the dual citizenship concept to "subvert and corrupt" the "fraternal militant community of the socialist countries." The target of the subverters and corrupters, it was apparent, was Czechoslovakia.

In August, just a few days before the Soviet invasion of Czechoslovakia, leading Soviet organs, including the important Defense Ministry newspaper, *Krasnaia zvezda* (August 17), as well as *Komsomolskaia pravda* (August 13), dealt at length with mysterious "saboteurs" who threaten to undermine the socialist commonwealth. Judaism was singled out for condemnation as prescribing "racial exclusivism" and as justifying "crimes against 'Gentiles.'" Woven into this warped fabric of thought were such characteristic threads as the sinister role of the "Joint," the danger of the dual citizenship concept, the challenge of the international Zionist conspiracy.

Specific public identification of the names of the "saboteurs" might have proved unseemly at the time. But Moscow, as early as July, had set Czechoslovakia and the world on notice as to whom it regarded as the culprits desecrating the Communist image: Eduard Goldstücker, chairman of the Union of Writers and vice-rector of Charles University; Frantisek Kriegel, Politburo member and chairman of the National Front; Ota Sik, deputy premier and the leading economic reformer; and Bohumil Lomsky, minister of defense. All were considered to be Jews (although Sik has emphasized that he is not).

Kriegel was to receive personal Soviet attention. He was included in the top leadership group that met in Moscow with the Soviet authorities. Premier Kosygin is reported to have refused point-blank to negotiate with Kriegel, snarling, "What is this Jew from Galicia doing here?"[7] Bertrand Russell in a letter to the *Times* of London on September 16 revealed that Kriegel had been subjected to "vicious treatment" in Moscow. It is believed that the Russians wanted to prevent his return to Prague but that Czech President Ludwik Svoboda refused to budge unless Kriegel was allowed to come back with his colleagues. Unlike the other top Czech officials', Kriegel's signature is absent from the Moscow agreement.

No sooner had the Soviet troops crossed the Czech frontier than Soviet organs were set to work to portray Czechoslovakia as the embodiment of a "counter-revolution" in which secret Zionists played a decisive role. On August 23, the government newspaper *Izvestiia* described an omnipresent "counter-revolutionary underground" that included at its core the Club of Non-Party Activists (KAN). The Soviet newspaper charged that three of its leaders— Rybacek, Musil, and Klementiev—were "agents of the international Zionist organization, 'Joint.'"[8] Aside from the fact that the "Joint" has not functioned in Czechoslovakia for twenty years, none of the three "agents" was Jewish.

The next day, a Moscow English-language broadcast to Africa contended that "Zionist elements" had taken control of the Czech information organs and were demanding the establishment of friendly relations with Israel. Listeners were also told that these "'elements' refuse to support the struggle of the Africans against racism and colonialism in Africa."[9]

The official "white book" on the invasion, *About the Events in Czechoslovakia,* a documentary volume published by the Soviet Government on September 10 and distributed widely in several languages (the authors were identified as the "Press Group of Soviet Journalists"), reiterated the theme that KAN was led by agents of international Zionism. It went on to add that an important reason for the intervention of the Warsaw Pact powers was the effort by certain forces "to bring about a change in Czechoslovakia's position with regard to the unanimous condemnation by the Socialist countries of Israel's aggression, and, in particular, to restore diplomatic relations with that country."

The theme of a conspiracy threatening Czechoslovakia was carried into 1969. In March, Tass reproduced in detail a lengthy story which had appeared in a Lebanese Communist newspaper, *Al-Dunia.* The story disclosed the decision of a "secret meeting" that had somehow escaped the attention of the world press: "A secret meeting has recently been held in London. Taking part in it were representatives of the biggest Zionist organizations and supporters of the so-called 'United Organization of Czech and Slovak Politicians Inside and Outside Czechoslovakia.'" The plot involved Jews within Czechoslovakia who held "responsible posts" in political, economic, and cultural spheres, and who maintained "strong contacts with Zionism." The purpose was nothing less than the overthrow of the socialist system in that country and the restoration of capitalism. The Tass dispatch was carried in all the leading Soviet organs and on Radio Moscow.

If the campaign against Zionism served the opportunistic function of justifying the application of brute force, it also reflected a deepseated anti-Semitism in some sectors of the Soviet leadership. Especially revealing of this bigotry was a major *Izvestiia* story of September 4, 1968. It purported to be an exposé of the Czech foreign minister, Jiri Hajek, who had courageously flown to the United Nations on the occasion of the invasion to present his country's desperate situation before the Security Council. To the *Izvestiia* editors and their masters, seeking a Zionist label to pin upon the unreconstructed Hajek, it must have seemed natural that he was of Jewish origin. The article, besides describing a lurid past of Hajek— the details of which were pure concoction—emphasized that he had "changed his name some time ago from Karpeles to Hajek." Karpeles is a characteristic Jewish name among East Central Europeans.

The deliberate malice turned out to be an indelicate journalistic boner for, as *Volksstimme,* organ of the Austrian Communist Party, revealed on September 5, *Izvestiia* had confused Jiri Hajek with another Hajek whose first name was Bedrich and who had previously been named Karpeles. The Czech foreign minister had not changed his name, and he was not Jewish. Hajek was later to comment to the liberal Czech journal *Reporter:* "I should like to emphasize that I would not be ashamed to be a Jew because I think that in this country we discarded racism some time ago."[8] But the "boner" offered a telling insight into what "research" information the Soviet Union relied upon for its campaign against Zionism.

Moscow's charges about a world Zionist conspiracy were echoed by the other major Warsaw Pact powers, Poland and East Germany (although not by Hungary and Bulgaria). Official Polish propaganda took as its point of departure the student uprisings in various Polish cities during March, 1968, and went on to relate these developments, ascribed to Zionist forces, to events in Czechoslovakia. The principal spokesman of Poland on the subject was General Jan Czapla, deputy head of the Political Administration in the Polish Ministry of Defense. In an article in *Trybuna Ludu* on August 25 (and later carried on Radio Warsaw as well as in the Polish army journal), General Czapla stated that revisionist and Zionist forces —the "international bridgehead of imperialism"—had developed to such a point in Czechoslovakia as "to menace directly and effectively the foundations of socialism and strike directly at Communists." In Poland, on the other hand, he declared, these forces had been crushed. And, of course, it was necessary to do the same in Czechoslovakia.

The Soviet analyst K. Ivanov supported Czapla's juxtaposition of the Polish events with developments in Czechoslovakia. In a comprehensive discussion of the steps leading up to and justifying the military intervention, published in *Mezhdunarodnaia zhizn'* in October, Ivanov noted that among the "necessary lessons to be drawn" was that counter-revolution has an attraction for "definite strata of the population." Just as, in Poland in the spring of 1968, "Right-wing bourgeois, Zionist trends" came to the surface, so too, in Czechoslovakia, Zionists, along with Trotskyites, anarcho-syndicalists, and rightists, made themselves manifest.

Walter Ulbricht's propaganda machine in East Germany went even further than either the Soviet or Polish press. If the latter two found that the Zionists were but threatening the foundations of Czech Communism, *Neues Deutschland* argued that "the workers have lost control over the Communist Party of Czechoslovakia, and Zionist forces have taken over the leadership of the Party." The statement appeared on August 25, the same day that General Czapla's article was published in *Trybuna Ludu.* The orchestration of the propaganda effort couldn't have been clearer. Two days earlier *Izvestiia* had launched the official justification for the Warsaw Pact powers.

The more virulent character of the campaign against Zionism in the East German mass media, both during the Czech crisis and going back to the post-Six-Day War period, raised an intriguing question which has been closely studied by Simon Wiesenthal, the celebrated hunter of Nazis. In a press conference on September 6, he told correspondents in Vienna that there was a "great difference in tone between East Germany and the other East bloc states" in the public treatment of the supposed threat of Zionism. He discovered that "the expressions, terms, and ideological categories of thought" employed in the East German press and radio were "much more strongly reminiscent" of the Nazi organs *Völkischer Beobachter, Der Stürmer,* and *Schwarze Korps* than of Communist organs. Wiesenthal did not consider this accidental: thirty-nine persons who occupied influential posts during the Nazi era have today "at least the same influence in the press, radio, and the propaganda organs of East Germany."

There can be little doubt now that the campaign against world Zionism was to have been climaxed with a staged show trial, reminiscent of those of the early fifties. Both *Le Monde* on September 12 and the *Times* of London on September 13 carried an article written by a prominent Czech Communist which disclosed that the Soviets were insisting that an "anti-Zionist trial must be staged, starring Mr. Kriegel and Professor Eduard Goldstücker." The author further stated that Moscow was prepared to "produce evidence" for such a trial within three months. Additional confirmation came from Bertrand Russell in his letter to the *Times* on September

16. On the basis of "excellent authority," he was convinced that the Soviets were "pressing for a trial in the classic Stalinist tradition of the 'Doctors' Plot' " in order to divert attention from the aggression in Czechoslovakia.

A speech delivered by Dubcek on October 11, carried by the Czech press and radio but scarcely noted in the West, strongly suggested that he was vigorously resisting pressure for a staged show trial. The address was devoted to a report on his negotiations with the Soviet Union, held the previous week in Moscow, during which he had been compelled to accede to wide-ranging demands upon Czech freedom. While cataloguing the humiliating concessions, Dubcek digressed to observe that there are "those who believe the moment is propitious for a return to the practices of the nineteen-fifties." The allusion to the notorious Slansky trial was all too clear.

Had the show trial been held, the central figure of the proceedings in absentia would no doubt have been Professor Goldstücker, then teaching at the University of Sussex in England. The Soviet press has hurled more abuse at him than at any other Czech reformer. *Literaturnaia gazeta* on October 2 devoted special attention to him, giving emphasis to his Jewish origin. After noting that Goldstücker had been an "active member" of a Zionist youth organization when he was a teenager, the periodical recalled that he had been appointed by Czechoslovakia as its ambassador to Israel. The article then curiously reminded its readers of an earlier show trial: "But after one year he was recalled; trials in Czechoslovakia had already begun of a number of public figures accused of criminal contacts with world Zionism."

As late as December, 1968, the theme of anti-Semitism continued. *Zpravy,* the Russian occupation newspaper published in the Czech language, carried stories having a "marked anti-Semitic flavour."[9] Yet the Soviet propaganda effort was having little, if any, effect within Czechoslovakia. On the contrary, it evoked the sharpest condemnation from workers and intellectuals, expressed in various forums and in the news media. A comment on "racial prejudice" in the journal *Politika* (October 24) summed up the Czech reaction: "We have had tragic experiences with all sorts of pogroms, whether organized by Hitler or initiated by people who 17 years ago prepared the political trials. That is why we are so sensitive about any anti-Semitic attack." No doubt, sophisticated Russians would react in the same way to ancient myths, were they free to express themselves. But Soviet leaders still drew sustenance from outdated fantasies based on historic prejudices.

During 1969, the official Soviet mass media continued and intensified their drumbeat about omnipotent Zionism. The trade union journal *Sovietskiie profsoiuzy,* in its January issue, accused Zionism of inciting the Polish youth uprisings of the previous year and of exerting a "disintegrating influence" upon Czechoslovak youth. The entire thrust of Zionism, the author argued, was the use of Jewish citizens in all capitalist countries to conduct "subversive work" against the USSR and to "undermine from within" the friendship of the various Soviet peoples. A Soviet newspaper that specializes in anti-Zionist diatribes, *Sovietskaia Rossiia,* carried on January 24 a long exposé which focused upon Zionism's "provocative and treacherous" propaganda campaign to convince Jews that they have a "dual loyalty."

In February, the mass circulation weekly *Ogonek* underscored the massive threat of the Zionists. Having at their disposal vast resources, the Zionists "infiltrated their agents into the press, the radio, the television and the cinema of all States." The impact of that "infiltration" was spelled out in various foreign broadcasts by Radio Moscow during March: encouragement of counter-revolution during "the last ten years" in Hungary,* Poland, and Czechoslovakia; support of "subversive activities in African countries"; propagation of militant anti-Communist and chauvinist propaganda.

The climax of the campaign was the publication of an extraordinary book (in an edition of seventy-five thousands copies) titled *Beware: Zionism!* Written by Yury Ivanov, it wove together into 173 pages the various strands of the anti-Zionist theme spun over the course of the previous three years. Zionism is presented as a giant international "Concern" of World Jewry. With "one of the largest amalgamations of capital" available to it, the "Concern" maintains an extensive "international intelligence centre" and a "well-organized service for misinformation and propaganda." The objective of the "Concern's" various "departments," which are

---

* Strikingly, when Moscow found that it was having difficulties with the Kádár regime in Hungary in early 1972, it once again raised the specter of Zionism. An article in *Pravda* on February 3, 1972, referred darkly to the "intrigues of Zionism" supposedly increasing in Hungary, where they sought out the "places where the bourgeois-philistine way of life still exists."

allegedly operated under a "single management," is "profit and enrichment" aimed at safeguarding "its power." Details of international Zionism's influence on the policy of Israel, which it considers as its own "property," as well as its cunning efforts aimed at subverting both the socialist and new national states, are spelled out. Elaborated, too, is the ramified network of Zionist propaganda organs buttressed by the major mass media, which have been "penetrated" by "sympathizing elements."

The significance of this obsessive and irrational work might ordinarily be minimized as an isolated literary phenomenon were it not that its publication was accompanied by a synchronized campaign of laudatory reviews in almost all the major Soviet newspapers and magazines, and in broadcasts by Tass in numerous foreign languages. The voice of the official Soviet authority was not disguised. It spoke clearly through *Pravda* (March 9): "From the pages of Yu. Ivanov's book emerges the true and evil image of Zionism and this constitutes the undoubted importance of the book."

With the ideology of the Ivanov book so strongly endorsed, Soviet journalists could feel free to give vent to the wildest concoctions. Thus, V. Vysotsky, writing on May 31, 1969, in Byelorussia's leading newspaper, *Sovietskaia Byelorossia,* "discovered" that a secret meeting of Zionists had taken place in London in 1968 at which it was decided to take over the entire Arab world—Lebanon, Syria, Jordan, Iraq, Yemen, Saudi Arabia, and the Arab peninsula. From this base, Vysotsky said, the Zionists planned to attain "mastery over mankind" using all possible devices—"force, bribery, slyness, perfidy, subversion, and espionage."

The themes of the *Protocols* continued into 1970. The newspaper of the Ministry of Defense, *Krasnaia zvezda,* on March 13 observed that the Zionists "are making wide use out of their agents in dozens of countries throughout the world . . . to mobilize the Jews of all countries" in order to serve Israel. Not to be outdone, the Party's principal organ for propagandists, *Agitator,* warned in March that the Zionists are attempting, through radio and "other means of communication," to "brainwash Soviet citizens of Jewish origin." The warning to Soviet Jews couldn't have been more explicit.

Nineteen-seventy was also marked by the publication of a revised edition of Ivanov's *Beware: Zionism!,* lengthy passages of which, especially concerning the House of Rothschild, were widely reprinted in the Soviet press. The Rothschilds, as in Nazi propaganda, were portrayed as the centerpiece of the world Zionist conspiracy. The family became symbolic of a "Jewish world government," with its funds transferred secretly out of France to a Tel Aviv bank. The new edition was especially noteworthy for presenting the Vatican and the Ecumenical Council as instruments of the "Jewish Millionaires' Conspiracy."

Even belles-lettres were infected by the anti-Zionist venom coursing through the body politic. Ordinarily Soviet fiction, unlike the propaganda that fills the pages of Soviet newspapers, periodicals, and political tracts, has been free of anti-Semitism. After all, the tradition of the creative Russian intelligentsia, in the main, has stood in vigorous opposition to overt bigotry, and novelists, however obsequious they might be to the Party line, would rarely be found pandering to that kind of official course that smacked of the obscenities of ethnic hate. A radical break with this humanist tradition occurred in the spring of 1970, with the publication of two viciously anti-Semitic novels by Ivan Shevtsov. They were published in scores of thousands of copies, and under the imprimatur of powerful state agencies.

Shevtsov is a retired naval officer who had acquired a reputation as a hard-line Russian chauvinist and anti-Semite. The publication of the two books was his first venture into the literary world. The first novel, *In the Name of the Father and the Son,* which appeared on March 23, was printed by one of the principal state publishing houses, Moskovskii Rabochii. An edition of sixty-five thousand copies sold out in the course of two days. The second novel, *Love and Hate,* was published several weeks later, in April, in an extraordinary edition of two hundred thousand copies. What made the book even more impressive—and ominous—was the publisher: none other than the Ministry of Defense, an institution that was the very incarnation of official patriotism. Like the first novel, Shevtsov's second handiwork, with the strong patronage it enjoyed, was also sold out in only a few days.

In the Name of the Father and the Son recalls the propaganda of *Der Stürmer* during the Nazi era. Its 399 pages are replete with tales of the "sinister" character of Zionism. Zionism, a character in the novel states, "moves under cover, secretly infiltrating all the life cells of the countries of the entire world, undermining from within all that is strong, healthy and patriotic . . . grasping all the important administrative, economic, and spiritual life of a given country." Echoes of the *Protocols* reverberate through this and similar passages. Zionism, according to Shevtsov, even "sent its agents into the international Communist and workers' movement," penetrating into the leadership of the Russian Communist Party itself. Thus "Judas-Trotsky (Bronshtein), a typical agent of Zionism" entered into the Party leadership and became "international provocateur Number One."

The technique of putting Trotsky's original name in parenthesis to emphasize his Jewish origin recalls the methods used by Stalin's editors during the "anti-cosmopolitan" campaign to identify Jews for the Soviet public. Needless to say, the reference to Trotsky as a Zionist is a gross falsehood, but the author clearly intended, in this way, to associate Zionism with the archetype of villainy (in Soviet mythology) and with Jewry to boot.

The theme of the *Protocols* was made especially explicit in the author's description of the relationship between Zionism and "American imperialism." If Soviet propaganda has, in the main, depicted Zionism as a mere instrument of "American imperialism," Shevtsov reversed the relationship. "You think no doubt that international Zionism is in the service of American imperialism. For my part, I am convinced that it is the other way around. American imperialism constitutes the economic and military base of Zionism. It serves the aims of Zion." Strikingly, Shevtsov put these words in the mouth of a "good" Jew, the character Aron Hertsovich.

The author's bigotry appears to have had few limitations. One of his characters notes that the decorations in a Soviet theater are shaped like six-pointed stars. The character proceeds to enlighten his children with the information that the star of the Soviet flag has but five points, and he cannot but deplore decorations that recall the six-pointed Star of David. The depth of vulgarity is reached through a play upon words, "Unitas" and "Unitaz." The first is the title the author gives to a fictitious Spanish-language Zionist newspaper; the second is the Russian word for toilet bowl. One character, in condemning Zionism, comments that the newspaper's "title fully corresponds to its contents." Whereupon a second character observes, "But someone forgot to flush it."

Characteristically, the author's anti-Semitism is accompanied by a general attack upon liberalism, individualism, and artistic experimentalism. His heroes rail against abstract art, Picasso (who is called a pornographer), modern music, and avant-garde theater and poetry. Two of the most talented and popular Soviet poets, Bella Akhmadulina and Andrei Voznesensky, are subjected, through thinly disguised names, to virulent denunciation. On the other hand, Stalin and super-patriotism are loudly applauded. The attributes of the authoritarian personality find clear expression in Shevtsov.

His second novel was, if anything, more vicious. The arch-villain of the novel is Nachum Holtzer, a pervert, sadist, dope-peddler, and killer. A professional Moscow journalist and off-beat playwright, Holtzer murders his own mother (in order to get her inheritance), disembowels her, and wraps her intestines around her head. He also seduces a delicate and beautiful Russian teen-age girl, whom he had turned into a hashish addict. He later murders her and dismembers her body. The Jewish degenerate was a typical feature of Nazi literature; Shevtsov has given it a Soviet dimension. In addition to Holtzer, the novel contains two other characters with Jewish names: Jacques-Sidney Davey, a foreign journalist who is thrown out of the Soviet Union for the possession of narcotics and "Zionist literature"; and Samuel Peltzig, an American professor of literature who peddles drugs.

Not only must the Jew be associated with drugs, whether through addiction or trafficking; he must be deprived of the symbols through which he has been universally admired. Thus it is essential that Albert Einstein's discovery of the theory of relativity be debunked. Shevtsov writes: "Einstein's role was blown up and he was made a sort of Jesus Christ. (Actually the theory of relativity was suggested long before Einstein.)" And, like his first book, *Love and Hate* pours venom upon liberals, intellectuals, and any cultural influence which may have a Western orientation or inspiration.

The Soviet intelligentsia were stunned by the appearance of the Shevtsov books. They could not recall anything as primitive and crude as his rogues' gallery of Jews.[10] Even a conservative critic, writing in *Komsomolskaia pravda,* found his first novel filled with "banality and ignorance." Shevtsov, the critic observed, had a "sick passion for collecting everyday dirt." Yet the writer for the Young Communist League newspaper was careful to avoid criticizing

Shevtsov's virulent anti-Semitism. And even this limited criticism was taken to task by the important Party newspaper *Sovietskaia Rossiia* for displaying "an unbridled, hooliganistic tone."

Initially, government officials avoided being drawn into the public controversy which was rapidly developing and which threatened to become embarrassing. When the minister of culture, Yekaterina Furtseva, was asked at a press conference on April 16 whether Shevtsov's novels did not contradict the finest traditions of Soviet literature, she responded that the author was an accepted member of the Soviet literary fraternity. She added that "we can't all write classics," and that if some works departed from the usual standards, it was, after all, "a matter of taste."

But, as the criticism mounted and spread abroad in ever-widening circles, high Party officials felt it necessary to take some action which might neutralize the tarnished image acquired by Soviet literature. Finally, on July 12, *Pravda* denounced the Shevtsov novels as "ideologically vicious and artistically weak." But it did not say that the books were being withdrawn from circulation, especially in the military encampments where *Love and Hate* had a particularly strong endorsement. Nor did the *Pravda* criticism make any comment concerning the overt bigotry displayed in both novels' treatment of Zionism and Jews. Indeed, the Party organ could not make such comment without repudiating a four-year-long major Soviet propaganda effort.

The climax of the rapidly rising hysteria in the mass media was reached in 1971, while political trials of groups of Soviet Jews were being held in various cities of the USSR. The endlessly flowing stream of fulminations in the press was gathered up in four "special collections" and published in "mass editions" by the Political Literature Publishing House. Their titles are indicative: *The Aims and Methods of Militant Zionism*; *Zionism Is the Tool of Imperialist Reaction*; *Hotbed of Zionism and Aggression*; and *Anti-Communism and Anti-Sovietism Are the Profession of the Zionists*.[11]

A lengthy and definitive article in *Pravda* on February 18, written by V. Bolshakov, set the tone for the climax. Zionism was now labeled "an enemy of the Soviet people." For the first time in the four-year-long campaign a phrase was used which harked back to the Great Purge of the late thirties. A more threatening reminder to Soviet Jews could not be envisaged. Bolshakov put it bluntly: "A person who turns to the Zionist belief automatically becomes an agent of the international Zionist concern and, hence, an enemy of the Soviet people."

The *Pravda* article recapitulated the old charges: Zionism was the spearhead of imperialism's campaign against the USSR; its "main content" was "bellicose chauvinism, anti-Communism and anti-Sovietism"; at one and the same time, it is "one of the major associations of finance capital, an international espionage center, and a smoothly functioning service for misinformation and slander." Zionism conjoins major monopoly and banking interests—such as Lazard Frères, Rockefeller, Morgan, Kuhn Loeb, and the Rothschilds—not only in a vast effort to weaken the Arab countries but to recover investments these interests had lost in Russia as a result of the October Revolution. Thus Zionism is principally engaged in "subversive operations . . . against the Soviet Union and the other socialist countries."

The entire history of Zionism is portrayed by Bolshakov as given over to destroying Soviet power: it allegedly collaborated with all the counter-revolutionary forces during the Civil War (1918–20); it presumably entered into a "dirty alliance" with the Hitlerites during World War II (even to the extent of collaborating with the Nazis in the holocaust of Babi Yar!); and, finally, after the war, it placed itself wholly at the disposal of "U.S. monopoly capital" in its thrust to destroy socialism. A reading of the *Pravda* article would suggest that Zionism had but an incidental interest in the issue of Palestine, its overwhelming concern being the subversion of Soviet power.

A large section of the Bolshakov essay is devoted to the Zionist "plot" in Czechoslovakia in 1968. Further details were added to the distortions that had been presented in 1968–69: "The Zionists sought to seize the leading posts in all the mass information media of the C.S.R. [Czechoslovak Socialist Republic] in order to conduct frantic propaganda against the socialist system in Czechoslovakia, against the Czechoslovak Communist Party, the Soviet Union, the C.P.S.U. and the Communist Parties of the fraternal socialist countries." Goldstücker, Sik, and Kriegel were again depicted as "Zionist agents" preparing a "counter-revolutionary coup." And when, "at the request of many thousands of Czechoslovak Communists," the Soviet Red Army and other Warsaw Pact powers arrived to rescue the endangered Czech socialist society,

". . . the Zionist underground shifted to illegal methods of struggle. Rabid Zionists, including 'consultants' furnished by Israel, worked at many of the clandestine radio stations that operated on C.S.R. territory in those days and disseminated slander against socialism."

The Bolshakov theme, with a certain extraordinary variation, was to be given international exposure at the United Nations in September, 1971. Addressing the Security Council, the Soviet ambassador to the UN, Yakov A. Malik, declaimed at length on the evils of Zionism, comparing it with the worst elements of Fascism. He then sought to explain the origin of the Zionist ideology in a statement so reeking with overt bigotry that it stunned Western delegates. His "explanation" merits quoting in full:

> Mr. Tekoah [the Israeli ambassador to the UN] was indignant at our parallel between Zionism and Fascism. But why not? It is all very simple: both are racist ideologies. The Fascists advocated the superiority of the Aryan race as the highest among all the races and peoples in the world. The Fascists considered that the ideal was the Aryan with his blue eyes and blond hair. I do not know what the external signs are with the Zionists; but their racist theory is the same. The Fascist advocated hatred toward all peoples and the Zionist does the same. *The chosen people: is that not racism?* What is the difference between Zionism and Fascism, if the essence of the ideology is racism, hatred towards other peoples? *The chosen people. The people elected by God. Where in the second half of the twentieth century does one hear anyone advocating this criminal absurd theory of the superiority of the one race and one people over others?* Try to justify that from the rostrum of the United Nations. Try to prove that you are the chosen people and the others are nobodies. Nobody will support you, and you would be well advised not to try it. [Emphasis added.][12]

The presentation of the Judaic religious concept of "the chosen people" as meaning racial superiority is straight out of the *Protocols of the Elders of Zion*. There it is central to the argument that Jews have concocted a diabolical plot to overthrow the existing order so that they, as "the chosen people" with superior intelligence, can rule mankind. Anti-Semitic writings of the twentieth century have drawn continuously upon this notorious source and repeated endlessly "the chosen people" canard.

Even when spouting vulgarities during the UN debates of the summer of 1967, Soviet delegates eschewed any reference to the "chosen people" concept. Nor can one detect any reference to it in the Soviet mass media before 1968.[13] The first to use it, significantly, was the prominent bigot Trofim Kichko in his book *Judaism and Zionism*, published in 1968. He wrote that "the Jewish bourgeoisie" is motivated primarily by

> . . . the chauvinistic idea of the God-chosenness of the Jewish people, the propaganda of messianism and the idea of ruling over the peoples of the world. Such ideas of Judaism were inculcated into the Jews first by the priests and later by the rabbis for centuries, and are inculcated today by Zionists, educating the Jews in the spirit of contempt and hatred towards other peoples. . . . The ideologists of Judaism, through the "Holy Scriptures," teach the observant Jews to hate people of another faith and even destroy them.

The other subsequent Soviet reference to the "chosen people" that has been located is in an article that appeared in the Kishinev newspaper *Molodezh Moldavii* on July 1, 1971. The article was devoted to an attack upon nine defendants in Kishinev who had been accused and convicted of a variety of "crimes" in connection with the attempted hijacking of a Soviet plane (to be examined in Chapter 12). In the course of its analysis of Zionist doctrine, the newspaper charged that the ideologists of Zionism have invented a "world Jewish nation" that is "chosen" to perform a "special mission." The mission of the "chosen" consists of "nothing less than the claim to rule over the entire world." It is perhaps not accidental that this reference should find expression in a city which experienced the infamous pogrom of 1903. Nor is it accidental that Ambassador Malik should utilize an ancient source of prejudice. During the course of the Security Council meetings, he had no hesitancy about making use of another well-worn stereotype: he told Ambassador Tekoah to keep his "long nose" out of the Soviet garden.

At approximately the same time as Ambassador Malik was excoriating international Zionism at the UN, a publication in Byelorussia (*Belarus,* October, 1971) was delineating another facet of the "world Zionist conspiracy." In an article entitled "The Independent Adviser," the Soviet organ addressed itself to the role of Dr. Henry Kissinger. The article began with a "disclosure" that would surprise scholars of Russian history. It "revealed" that Gregory Rasputin, the notorious adviser to Tsar Nicholas II of Russia, was but "a puppet in the hands of his secretary, Aron Simanovich." Simanovich, in turn, "acted according to a program worked out by Ginsburg, Varshavsky, Brodsky, Shalit, Gurevich, Mendel and Poliakov—a whole gang of Zionists."

The historical "disclosure" was designed to demonstrate a parallel role performed by a present-day Jew, operating under instructions of the "world Zionist conspiracy": "Certain events in history, even though they are far apart one from the other in time and place, are strangely similar. . . . This is particularly so in those cases where the same tactics are used: to influence the government in power with the help of court agents." The author quickly turned to the current scene. The United States was presented as being under the thumb of the Zionists: "America has always supported Israel in everything. American statesmen and diplomats jump out of their skins to please Golda Meir. Whenever Moshe Dayan or Abba Eban go to the United States, they pass their skullcaps around and the skullcaps immediately get filled up with millions of dollars. Whenever the State Department has to appoint an ambassador to a Near Eastern country, it won't appoint one without the consent of the Zionist organizations. That's their *geschaft*." (The Yiddish word *geschaft* is part of the Soviet bigot's lexicon.)

The critical question is then posed: how to explain the conduct of the United States? The answer is simple. The U.S. is covered with the "sticky spider webs" of Zionist organizations which "enjoy unlimited influence in the country and in the Congress." But the Zionists do not act directly. As in Tsar Nicholas' day, "the Zionists, it is evident," have had to entrench "themselves strongly in the American Olympus." This they have done by placing a particular individual at the locus of American power: "He is not a priest, but a professor; he is not a drunkard or a libertine, but an intellectual of the highest caliber. The obligations that Aron and Grishka Rasputin had carried out together, he manages very well to carry out by himself."

The individual, of course, is Dr. Kissinger. His background is elaborated in a characteristically distorted manner. He is described as being in "full charge" of U.S. "intelligence," of the Pentagon, and of the State Department. Not only has he performed this role for President Nixon; he did the same for the administrations of Eisenhower and Kennedy. Dr. Kissinger has been for lo these many years the "filter" of the White House! Dr. Kissinger is presented as the evil genius of American policy—responsible for policy toward Israel, toward Meir Kahane, and toward the Vietnamization program. For good measure, he is portrayed as the originator of "contacts with Mao"—the *bête noire* of the Kremlin. The essence of Soviet ideology is summed up in the penultimate sentence: Everything that Dr. Kissinger does in the White House is "done under the banner" of the "six-cornered Star of David."

It is evident that the fantasy world of the infamous *Protocols of the Elders of Zion* continues to display, in its updated version, a remarkable vitality. Although anti-Jewish discrimination had been an integral part of Soviet state policy since the late thirties and early forties, the policy had lacked an official ideology which would justify focusing suspicion upon Jews and, thereby, rationalizing their exclusion from politically sensitive posts. The "corporate Jew," first as "cosmopolitan" and then as "international Zionist," was transformed into an ideology. The enemy was defined in a fairly clear manner. While the ideology might, on the one hand, be used to justify an invasion of Czechoslovakia, it, on the other hand, could be made to serve internal purposes—the suppression of a burgeoning Jewish national consciousness. Unlike Hitlerism, however, the ideology of the "corporate Jew" is by no means systematically integrated into official Soviet thought. It functions on a purely pragmatic level, performing tasks that satisfy the regime's purposes. To the extent that the ideology functions on that level, it can be and has been set aside when these purposes do not require servicing. For the immediate future, its disappearance into the dustbin of history can scarcely be expected.

Chapter 9
The Silent and
Not-So-Silent Soviet Jews

The twin aspects of Soviet policy on Jews stand in fundamental contradiction to one another. On the one hand, there is the attempt to bring about the forcible assimilation of Jews through the elimination of specific Jewish institutions and the obliteration of references to Jewish tradition and history, especially Jewish martyrdom. On the other hand, there is the enforcement of patterns of discrimination, based precisely upon the nationality identification in passports and questionnaires. And the patterns of discrimination are accompanied by a propaganda campaign which stimulates and strengthens local sources of anti-Semitism, including those sources which give effect to and, indeed, extend the patterns. Discriminatory patterns and overt anti-Semitism cannot but generate a consciousness of one's origins, an awareness of one's identity, and, thereby, create a set of subjective feelings that are the very opposite of what is intended by those promoting the process of forcible assimilation.

This awareness, in turn, produces two opposing results. Some will make a determined and conscious effort to suppress all outward manifestations of being Jewish, even to the extent of denying being Jewish. If this fulfills the aim of those promoting assimilation, it has done so only in consequence of conscious internal repression. The assimilation here is purely artificial. It results not from a lack of awareness of being Jewish but rather from an *acute* awareness that being Jewish carries intolerable burdens which, at all costs, must be avoided.

Others, faced with the same set of contradictory forces, will react with a revulsion against the discriminatory patterns and anti-Semitic propaganda. Instead of desperately trying to escape the discrimination and the propaganda by repressing their identity, they will try to determine what that identity is, its myriad of historical and cultural facets. Instead of holding their nationality in contempt, as might happen with a natural assimilatory process, they take a sudden pride in it. Such a reaction is quite normal for minority groups who are subject to discrimination. Awareness among Negroes of the patterns of anti-black discrimination in the United States, for example, has ultimately given rise to a "black is beautiful" movement, accompanied by a pride in a historical and cultural past that stretches all the way back to African origins. One important difference with the black situation in the United States does appear. In the United States, not only is pride in blackness tolerated, but institutional means are or can be created for its fullest expression. In the USSR, on the contrary, a similar pride among Jews can find no institutional means of expression. Consequently, the pride must seek expression and fulfillment outside the Soviet Union, in a favorable Jewish environment; specifically, in Israel.

How widespread is the process of internal repression of Jewishness, of Jewish identity, in the Soviet Union? Certainly, it embraces what can be called the "Jewish Establishment"—prominent Jews in various, mainly non-political, fields who clearly have a vital stake in the status quo. On March 4, 1970, the Soviet regime assembled over forty prominent Jews at a staged press conference in Moscow designed to counter world criticism that the USSR was hostile to Jews and Jewish interests.[1] They were also called upon to parrot the Soviet line on Israel and Zionism. With rare exceptions, the stellar figures had never been involved with specifically Jewish concerns or interests and did not express any pride in Jewish tradition or identity. Some of them had not even been known to be of Jewish origin.

The thinking of the Jewish Establishment was best expressed in a long article in *Pravda* on March 17, 1970, by I. Braginsky, the editor-in-chief of *Peoples of Asia and Africa*, a leading Soviet journal. Braginsky has often been used by Soviet authorities as a spokesman on the Jewish issue. Two major points were made in his article. First, basing himself upon various statements of Lenin, Braginsky emphasized that assimilation—the tendency toward unity "with the national majority of a given country"—is "progressive," while Jewish "isolation" or "exclusiveness" is regressive. Lenin, indeed, was a vigorous champion of assimilation and considered that Jewish nationality had a caste-like character that would ultimately disappear. On the other hand, he (along with Stalin until the late thirties) permitted, indeed encouraged, the establishment of a variety of Jewish cultural institutions. He would have regarded forcible assimilation as anathema. Braginsky avoided addressing the issue of forcible assimilation—the officially sanctioned program of destroying Jewish institutions and identity.

More important, Lenin made his program of assimilation conditional on the elimination of all forms of discrimination. If assimilation was to be welcomed as "progressive," it would be achieved, he thought, by removing every barrier to participation and advancement in the body politic. It is precisely the erection since the late thirties of discriminatory barriers, and the toleration and encouragement of anti-Semitism, that challenge the assimilatory process. Braginsky blinks the facts when he makes his second major point: "In a socialist society, anti-Semitism is completely uprooted, the conditions for it are liquidated; . . . the Soviet Union has proven historically that the Jewish question can be radically solved and similarly removed from the order of the day. . . ." Roy Medvedev, an orthodox Leninist and strong advocate of assimilation, has called these statements of Braginsky "notorious falsehoods."[2] The Jewish question, he wrote, "has by no means been removed from the order of the day" for the very reason that anti-Semitism persists in Soviet society and is officially practiced in an "especially refined and subtle" manner.

Beyond the Establishment, there are thousands of Jews who, when given the opportunity, would deny their origin. The results of the 1970 census point in this direction. Soviet citizens were not required to offer proof of national origin in answering the enumerator's (census taker's) query on nationality. Enumerators were specifically instructed to accept and list whatever nationality a Soviet citizen might claim. If Soviet Jews so chose, they could lie about their origin, a practice the Soviet regime might, in any case, have desired for reasons of its own.[3]

As compared with the 1959 census data, the number of individuals claiming Jewish nationality in 1970 dropped from 2,268,000 to 2,151,000, a loss of 117,000, or 5.2 per cent. This was the largest decline of the seven Soviet nationalities which showed a drop in population.[4] The total Soviet population increased 15.8 per cent. Intermarriage was undoubtedly a factor explaining the Jewish decline. A study of passport holders carried out in the period 1960–68, in parts of Vilnius, Riga, and Tallinn, the capitals of the three Baltic republics, showed that between 86 per cent and 93.3 per cent of the children of mixed marriages (involving Jews) chose the nationality of their non-Jewish parent when registering for their passports at the age of sixteen.[5] An earlier study of mixed marriages in Kharkov produced the same results, with the authors concluding: "The overwhelming mass of those born from mixed marriages of Jews, Poles, Armenians and others with Russians or Ukrainians indicate themselves to the registration office . . . [as] Russians and Ukrainians."[6]

Moreover, a directive to the enumerator tended to increase the number of non-Jews listed in the census. In a mixed marriage in which the parents did not know which nationality their child or children should be designated as, the enumerator was required to designate the child or children by the nationality of the mother.[7] Since in most mixed marriages involving Jews it is the wife who is non-Jewish, a larger number of non-Jews would automatically emerge.[8]

However, mixed marriages among Jews remain an atypical phenomenon in much of the Soviet Union. The limited data from the Baltic cities suggests that there were far more endogamous marriages than exogamous (mixed) marriages. The same applies to Kharkov. An American analyst of the data concludes that "the high rate of Jewish endogamy" is a product of a strong "sense of group identity."[9] On the other hand, two British analysts estimate, on the basis of 1959 census data, that about one-quarter of Jewish males in the Russian Republic were married to non-Jewish women; but that in the other union republics the extent of mixed marriages was "very considerably less."[10] Whether and to what extent the rate of mixed marriages has increased cannot, as yet, be determined. The British analysts believe that the rate of assimilation produced by intermarriage is "likely to become more or less stable." In any case, it seems apparent that the number of mixed marriages could not have contributed significantly to the statistical decline in the census data on the number of Jews.

A much stronger factor is the probable excess of deaths over births. The Nazis' genocidal program not only wiped out an entire generation of children who in 1970 would have been producing their own offspring, but created a situation "whereby the average age of Jewish men is higher than among the general population."[11] Besides, Jewish birth-rates throughout the world are generally lower than non-Jewish birth-rates. This is no doubt true in the Soviet Union, where the rate of reproduction of urban inhabitants (and Jews are overwhelmingly urban) has shown a marked decline. A demographic specialist speculates that "a sophisticated, highly urbanized, mainly European group like Soviet Jewry could well be in a state of physical decline."[12] Yet, it is questionable whether the natural decrease of the Jewish population would necessarily have shown up in the 1970 census, especially at the rate that it did.

A major Soviet geographical work carrying some demographic information which was published in 1964 appeared to be pointing to a trend opposite to that indicated in the 1970 census. It gave the number of Ashkenazic (European) Jews in the USSR as of January 1, 1962, as 2,300,000.[13] The number of Ashkenazic Jews in the 1959 census was 2,186,100. Thus, the percentage increase of Jews during a three-year period had been 5.2. An official booklet on the Jews in the USSR published by the Novosti press agency in 1965 stated that the Jewish population was increasing at approximately the same rate as the non-Jewish population. As late as 1971, one year after the census, a Novosti publication referred to 3,000,000 Jews in the USSR, approximately 900,000 more than are indicated in the census.[14]

Undoubtedly, the major factor explaining the drastic decline of Jews in the census is the desire of many of them to hide their identity. Indeed, Soviet interpreters of the data speak of "assimilation" as the cause of the percentage drop of Jews.[15] It should be emphasized in this connection that the Jewish identification of those who are "assimilated" remains in the internal passport. Quite possibly, the

Novosti figure of three million is the correct one in calculating the total number of persons identified as Jews in their passports, data which would be available to officials of the Ministry of Interior. Since no proof was required by the enumerators in the census, Jews who chose to repress their identity might have done so, especially in the very big cities or in new Siberian communities where the ethnic origins of people may not have been generally known. There is some oral evidence from recent Soviet emigrants to Israel that, in various instances, enumerators used various forms of persuasion to encourage Jews to avoid listing their real nationality in the census.[16]

The obstacle of the passports, nonetheless, remains. Not that it is an insuperable obstacle. Jews have been known to "lose" their passports, particularly in new areas of Siberia, and to acquire passports carrying a non-Jewish nationality identification. Others, upon registration for the passport at age sixteen, have insisted, upon the advice of their parents, that they are Russians, and, with the connivance or sympathy of local officials, have overcome the technical difficulties involving proof to become identified, formally, as non-Jews.[17] Such practices, it should be noted, are rare. Moreover, even when they are successfully accomplished, as Medvedev indicates, "personnel departments and special departments continue to consider these people as Jews." He observes: "In recent years, in many closed institutions [i.e., closed to Jews], in the hiring for responsible jobs, and even in several universities, a questionnaire is filled out in which there are two columns: 'father's nationality' and 'mother's nationality.'" Although the taint of Jewish origin is almost inescapable, quite a number of Jews, aside from the progeny of intermarriages, have nevertheless taken the path of "assimilation," that is, avoiding a formal identification of themselves as Jewish.

Soviet commentators also point to the data on language in the census as demonstrating "assimilation." According to the census, 17.7 per cent of Soviet Jews named as their mother tongue a Jewish language. (This could mean any one of five languages: Yiddish; Judaeo-Georgian; Judaeo-Tadzhik, spoken by Jews in Central Asia; Tat, spoken by Jews of Dagestan; and Judaeo-Krimchak, spoken by Tatar Jews in the Crimea. Yiddish, of course, is the predominant mother tongue.) This figure constitutes a significant drop from the data of 1959. At that time, 21.5 per cent of the Jews stated that the language which they used was one of the Jewish "mother tongues."

In absolute terms, the figures are 380,000 in 1970 as against 488,000 in 1959.

But the Soviet interpretation of the language data may not be very valid. In the first place, the 1970 Soviet census asked whether the respondents were fluent in another language of the peoples of the USSR; 28.8 per cent of the Jews said that they were fluent in a non-Russian Soviet language, besides their own mother tongue. An unknown number of these must have had a Jewish language in mind when they responded to the enumerator. Secondly, as Yakov Kantor emphasized in his analysis of the 1959 census, the data do not reveal whether Jews were versed, in a general and non-fluent way, with a Jewish language.[18] Finally, there is considerable uncertainty as to whether lack of knowledge of a mother tongue means ethnic assimilation. Thus, the Soviet sociologist I. Kon wrote in 1970:

> First of all, not every linguistic assimilation is voluntary. It happens that minorities are simply deprived of an opportunity to cultivate their languages since they are not taught in schools and are not used in cultural life. . . . But even a complete linguistic assimilation, the loss of one's native language . . . is not tantamount to a disappearance of other ethnic differences. A person may speak the language of the majority and yet consider himself a member of a national minority.[19]

The fact of the matter is—as many of the recent Soviet Jewish emigrants to Israel can testify—a large number of the most militantly conscious European Jews in the USSR are totally unfamiliar with Yiddish.

The internal repression of Jewish identity has been matched, indeed outdistanced, by an extraordinary burgeoning of Jewish consciousness. It was only seven years ago that Elie Wiesel characterized Soviet Jewry as the "Jews of silence" who spoke only with their eyes, and their eyes expressed sadness.[20] If they uttered public sounds at all, it was done anonymously, through a grapevine that carried such anecdotes as the following: A policeman asks a Soviet Jew: "Have you relatives abroad?" The Jew replies, "No." The policeman then asks: "But you have a brother abroad?" To which the Jew replies: "No, my brother is in the homeland. I am the one who is abroad." Or there was the riddle: "Why is the Jew like a sputnik?" "Because he goes round and round and has no place to stop." Both testify to the sense of alienation felt by many Soviet Jews. But fear prevented the taking of any initiative aimed at altering the existing situation.

Wiesel's characterization is no longer valid. The Simhat Torah demonstration in front of the main synagogue in Moscow has become an annual affair, with thousands of youngsters singing and dancing to Yiddish and Hebrew songs. And this phenomenon has tended to spread to the synagogues of other major cities. A specifically Jewish *samizdat*, manuscripts of Jewish substance, poetry and tapes of Yiddish and Hebrew songs, circulates widely in underground fashion. A publication appropriately entitled *Iskhod* (*Exodus*) was surreptitiously launched in 1970, and four issues appeared. They carried detailed information and documents testifying to a resurgent Jewish consciousness. Even *ulpans,* formal centers for the private study of the Hebrew language, were started in various communities.[21]

But the most striking manifestation of the new ferment among Soviet Jews were the literally hundreds of petitions which they wrote and signed, whether as individuals or in groups that numbered as many as eighty or ninety persons.[22] All asked for the right to emigrate to Israel. The individuals boldly listed their names and addresses, and often their ages and occupations as well. Resort to the cablegram was even made, such as the following one sent to Premier Golda Meir on March 22, 1970: "Thank you from all the Jews who want to emigrate to Israel. Mazel Tov for Purim. Shalom Uvracha."

To the extent that the ages of the signers were given, a kind of generation gap became manifest. Most were in their twenties, thirties, and forties. The listed occupations suggested a relatively high degree of education, with considerable skills, mainly in the scientific field, and to a lesser extent in the humanities. On the basis of the limited evidence, one can conclude that a young, highly educated, and intensely motivated group has emerged. But the petitions provided far broader insights.

Some basic data about the petitions is pertinent. Between February, 1968, when the first petition arrived in the West, and October, 1970, a total of 220 appeals had appeared and been studied: 68 were sent to Israel, mainly to high government officials like Premier Golda Meir or President Zalman Shazar; 56 were addressed to the United Nations—to either the secretary-general, the president of the General Assembly, the General Assembly, or the Commission on Human Rights; 51 were addressed to various prominent non-Soviet personalities, ranging from President Richard Nixon to John Gollan, the head of the British Communist Party; and finally, 45 were sent to Soviet officials, principally President Nikolai Podgorny, Premier Aleksei Kosygin, and Party General Secretary Leonid Brezhnev.

The relatively small percentage sent to Soviet officials clearly indicated that Soviet Jews had little faith in obtaining redress from the Communist hierarchs. Indeed, copies of such internal petitions have been deliberately sent abroad so that world public attention might be focused upon them. Many of these internal petitions recapitulate in considerable detail the fruitless efforts made over several years, particularly since Kosygin's public promise of December 3, 1966, that Soviet Jews who wish to be reunited with their families in Israel will be granted exit visas. Having exhausted the means for appealing to internal machinery, these Soviet Jews had embarked upon a strategy of what can be called the *"internationalization of protest."* The fundamental assumption of that strategy was that the Soviet rulers are responsive to world public opinion.

The strategy of the "internationalization of protest" is by no means unique.[23] A hardy and impressive band of Soviet intellectual dissenters had been applying the strategy since the Sinyavsky-Daniel trial of 1966. During 1968, in keeping with International Human Rights Year, they deepened and widened that strategy, with the Universal Declaration of Human Rights, rather than the Soviet Constitution, being made their standard, and the UN Commission on Human Rights becoming the principal target of their appeal. Soviet Jewish petitioners, too, began using international standards. They frequently cited the Universal Declaration of Human Rights, particularly Article 13/2, and the International Convention on the Elimination of Racial Discrimination, particularly Part I, Article 5. Both obligate governments to recognize that "everyone has the right to leave any country, including his own. . . ." The Soviet Union has frequently affirmed its adherence to the Universal Declaration, and the Supreme Soviet formally ratified the International Convention on January 22, 1969. In appealing to such international standards, Jewish petitioners have not neglected to note that Premier Kosygin, at a press conference in Paris on December 3, 1966, said that "the door is open" and that "no problem exists" for all Soviet Jews who wish "to leave the Soviet Union" in order to be reunited with their families in Israel.

The geographical areas from which the petitions came are revealing: 34.3 per cent were from Riga, 26.3 per cent from Moscow, 7.7 per cent from Minsk, 6.4 per cent from Tbilisi, 5.7 per cent from Vilnius, 3.6 per cent from Kutaisi, and 3.1 per cent each from Leningrad and Kiev. The balance of 9.8 per cent came from a variety of other places—some major cities, others smaller towns— in the Russian Republic, the Ukraine, Byelorussia, and Georgia. A few petitions arrived from as far away as Novosibirsk, in Siberia, and Alma-Ata, in Kazakhstan. The pattern of geographical distribution suggests that the militancy of segments of Soviet Jewry is by no means a localized or narrow affair; on the contrary, it is broadly based. On the other hand, certain areas show a particularly intense degree of militancy—Riga, capital of the Latvian Republic; Moscow; the Georgian cities of Tbilisi and Kutaisi; and Vilnius, capital of the Lithuanian Republic.

The intensity of ethnic consciousness in Riga, Vilnius, and Georgia would appear to be explicable in terms of their traditional and historic characteristics, which, incidentally, vary basically between the two Baltic cities and Georgia. In Riga the Jewish population is fairly large—thirty thousand, or 5 per cent of the total city population. Before Riga's incorporation into the Soviet Union in 1940, its Jewish community had a rich complex of educational and cultural institutions, the result of which was to be manifested in the linguistic identification given by Jews in the 1959 census. Almost one-half of the respondents (48 per cent) stated that their mother tongue was Yiddish, fully two and one-half times more than the national average for Jews. When Geulah Gil, the Israeli folk singer, gave concerts there in 1966, tumultuous scenes of applause and welcome occurred, and she was literally mobbed by cheering youngsters.

Vilnius has similar characteristics. Its Jewish population (according to the 1959 census) of seventeen thousand constituted 7 per cent of the total population. An extraordinary percentage of Vilnius Jews considered Yiddish to be their mother tongue—69 per cent, more than anywhere else in the country. The question might be raised as to why Vilnius Jews lagged behind Riga Jews in expressions of outward militancy. The answer, at best, can be only speculative. But it is known that Vilnius Jews had been permitted some channels for expressing Yiddish cultural identity, most notably a Yiddish choir and an amateur Yiddish theater troupe. Such channels have been completely lacking in Riga. Moreover, political discrimination against Jews would seem to be greater in Latvia than in Lithuania. Of the 200 members of the Latvian Republic's Supreme Soviet in 1959, not a single one was Jewish, even though Jews constituted 1.7 per cent of the total Latvian population. On the other hand, 3 of the 209 deputies of the Lithuanian Supreme Soviet were Jews—a percentage (1.44) higher than that of any of the other union republic supreme soviets. (Incidentally, the average percentage of Jews in the various union republic supreme soviets was 0.26 per cent. Latvia and Moldavia were the only ones with fairly sizable Jewish minorities which had no Jewish representation whatsoever.)

Thus, Latvian Jews may have had more sharply defined grievances than Lithuanian Jews. Another factor is suggested by a 1970 Soviet source work which carries some documentation on Latvian Jews. The data showed a relative reluctance on the part of Riga Jews, as compared with other nationalities inhabiting that city, to adopt "Soviet customs" regarding birth and marriage rites and holidays, and to have friends among other nationalities.[24] A third factor could be fear. Popular anti-Semitism in Lithuania has always been especially deep. The petition of twenty-six Lithuanian Jewish intellectuals, some of them Party members, of February 15, 1968— the very first of the petitions to come to Western attention—bitterly related how the anti-Zionist campaign in the Lithuanian press had created "objective conditions . . . for the flourishing of anti-Semitism."[25] The letter disclosed, for the first time, that a "bloody pogrom" against Lithuanian Jews took place in Plunge in 1958. The authors chose not to sign their names to the petition because "we know well how people who had protested against flourishing anti-Semitism . . . at one time or another were dealt with summarily." It was the only petition received from which the surnames were deleted.

The militancy of the Georgian Jews springs not from secular Yiddish sources but rather from religious sources. Jews have been living in Georgia since the early Christian Era. Their religious lore traces an ancestry to the Ten Lost Tribes of the Biblical Kingdom of Israel. A religious conviction which links them to the ancient Holy Land is held with great fervor and is transmitted from one generation to another by means of closely knit family and clan ties. Visitors to the USSR have always marveled at the vigor of religious life among Georgian Jews as compared with its enervated and pathetic character in Moscow, Leningrad, and Kiev. In Tbilisi, the Jews are estimated to total 40,000 out of 861,000; in Kutaisi, 20,000 out of 160,000.[26]

Discrimination is not a driving factor in the Georgian Jewish militancy. Georgian nationalism has vigorously resisted encroachments from the Muscovite center, and anti-Semitic polices in one or another area are blunted upon reaching the Georgian frontier. Significantly, the petitions of the Georgian Jews, with but one exception, specifically deny that either racial or religious discrimination affects them. What principally motivates them is the rebirth of Israel as a mystical phenomenon. As one of the longest petitions of Georgian Jews puts it: "The prophecy has come true: Israel has risen from the ashes; we have not forgotten Jerusalem, and it needs our hands."[27]

If traditional and cultural characteristics can be considered as predetermining the attitudes of Riga, Vilnius, and Georgian Jews, and if similar, especially profoundly secular-Yiddish characteristics in other parts of the USSR (like Kishinev, in Moldavia, or Chernovtsy and Lvov, in the Ukraine) cannot easily be expressed because of a prevailing local anti-Semitism, how is the militancy of Moscow Jewry, especially the young people, to be explained? This is an area embracing (according to the 1959 census) 240,000 Jews who, even before the October Revolution, had been subject to a strong degree of assimilation. Religious consciousness is minimal, as are secular-Yiddish feelings. Ever since the Black Years of 1948–53, Moscow has been without the kind of communal-cultural institutional structure that can sustain a meaningful Jewish consciousness.

How then has the phoenix of Jewish consciousness risen from the ashes of a decimated culture? Petitions from Moscow cast a brilliant light upon the motivations of the petitioners. First, there is the negative factor of anti-Semitism. Personal or group experience with overt forms of bigotry and discrimination which assault the dignity of the Jew is a refrain that runs through many of the petitions. Whether the perception of these experiences is precise is less important than the fact that it exists together with a heavily laden emotional content. Especially resented is the anti-Zionist propaganda campaign unleashed by the state authorities in the summer of 1967. Its anti-Semitic features, both in written form and in illustrative cartoons, are considered as "insults [to] our national feelings and our human dignity"—as a typical petition remarks. A young Kiev Jew in 1968 expressed it pointedly when he was asked why "Jewish boys and girls" have "become proud of their national affiliation." His answer: ". . . anti-Semitism—the new brand which was implanted from above and, as a means of camouflage, is called anti-Zionism. . . ."[28] The sentiment, in a somewhat less explicit manner, is echoed in the letters of the Muscovite Jews.

A second factor mentioned in most petitions, paradoxically, is the very absence of Jewish cultural-communal institutions. One letter, signed by eighty-three Jews of Moscow, vividly summarizes this ever-recurring theme:

> The Soviet Union has long been without any kind of public organizations that could in some measure represent the interests of the Jewish ethnic minority.
>
> We are not permitted this, just as we are not permitted to teach our children the Yiddish language and the history of our ancient and eternally young people.
>
> We are the only people in the Soviet Union who are ordered openly, in plain terms, to assimilate, to dissolve, to disappear among other peoples.

A bursting sense of pride is the third motivation which repeatedly appears in the petitions. "I am a Jew, I was born a Jew, and I want to live out my life as a Jew"—so writes a young petitioner; and his words, in a variety of ways, are repeated by the others. Were the formulation to be set in an American context, it would read: "Jewish is beautiful." Some make references to the achievements of Jews in history, their heroism or their cultural contributions—and some point to the martyrology of Jews. Either explicitly or implicitly, the theme of the unity of the Jewish people is given expression.

But the most distinguishing characteristic of the pride is a love of Israel. An engineer wrote: "Can I, a Jew, not be concerned for my people? I am proud that I belong to such a nation which is fighting for its independence surrounded by so many enemies." Another engineer stated: ". . . we demand that we should be allowed to go to our Jewish country where the children will be able to have their own language, their own culture, and where they will be able to be proud of their nationality. . . ." With an ecstatic emotion, they cry that they will relinquish all their belongings so that they may go to Israel; that they will go even on foot. Israel's victory in the Six-Day War is not specifically mentioned as a powerful stimulus to the emergent pride, but testimony taken from recent Soviet emigrants to Israel gives this point particular emphasis. Israel's ability to survive and prevail inevitably affected what Medvedev has called "the sensitivity threshold" of Jews toward anti-Semitism. If, in the past, Jews in various countries could be threatened with anti-Semitism and still not react, "today even 'moderate' forms of anti-Semitism . . . will elicit sharp protest and will become unbearable."[29] The very existence of Israel produces, Medvedev noted, "a feeling of national self-consciousness and sense of personal worth" among Jews. All the more is this the case when burdensome odds are surmounted and terrible dangers blunted. Courage becomes contagious, even to the point of challenging a major power and demanding the fulfillment of one's rights.

In a very few instances, a fourth factor is mentioned: the religious motivation. Such signers usually declare themselves to be committed to Judaism in a general way; one or two will argue that Soviet society prevents them from observing the Sabbath. But the Moscow petitions, unlike the Georgian petitions, tend to illuminate the high degree of secularization of most centers of Jewish life in the USSR. Finally, many petitions offer as a motivation the desire to be reunited with one or another relative living in Israel. But this motivation, humanitarian as it may be, is also the principal formal means by which exit visas can be secured. Deeper motivating forces are clearly at work to power the humanitarian aspiration.

The Moscow petitions were unique only in their number. The same characteristics are to be found in the petitions of Jews from Minsk, Kiev, Leningrad, and other urban areas (except, of course, Georgia). If there were many more from Moscow, it is probably due less to the size of its Jewish community than to the fact that Moscow is the most public place in the USSR, made so by the large number of Western correspondents and foreign embassy officials stationed there, and the masses of tourists visiting the city. Restraints upon overt official pressure, lest it mar the image of the regime, may very well contribute to a greater sense of security among Muscovite Jews and, thereby, weaken inhibitions that might be manifested in other places. Other tourist centers, such as Minsk, the capital of Byelorussia, Kiev, the capital of the Ukraine, and Leningrad, the Soviet Union's second largest city, also provide a certain minimum of security, although, obviously, far less than Moscow's. From the smaller communities of Soviet Russia, petitions were either minimal in number or non-existent.

The many hundreds of signers, it must be emphasized, constitute but a tiny minority of the Soviet Jewish population. Yet, it is clear that they were the tip of the iceberg. How large the iceberg was nobody really knew. The anonymous Lithuanian petition states categorically that 80 per cent of the Jewish community of that Soviet republic would leave if given the opportunity. Medvedev has calculated that between two hundred thousand and three hundred thousand Jews would seek to emigrate.[30] Others speculate that one-half million would seek to leave.[31]

During February and March, 1971, the "not-so-silent" Soviet Jews embarked upon even bolder steps. They were keenly aware that the Soviet Communist Party was to hold its Twenty-fourth Congress from March 29 to April 7. Foreign Party delegations would be arriving in Moscow throughout March. In addition, world press attention would be focusing upon developments surrounding the Party Congress. The militant Jews were determined to dramatize their plight. First, they assembled the largest single petition yet drafted. No longer limited to one city, the massive petition effort accumulated signatures from various parts of the USSR. By mid-March, when the petition was ready for mailing to the United Nations Commission on Human Rights and to the governments of the United States, United Kingdom, France, Italy, and Japan, a total of 1,185 families comprising 4,056 persons had signed it. The regional breakdown was as follows: Georgia, 116; Latvia, 67; Lithuania, 19; the Ukraine, 309; Byelorussia, 183; Moldavia, 141; Bokhara, 61; Tashkent, 88; Leningrad, 79; Moscow, 113; the Urals and Siberia, 109. The large number of signatures from the Ukraine, Byelorussia, and Moldavia testified to the growing wave of activism there.

The giant petition complained that Soviet authorities were "crudely and forcibly" imposing assimilation by the destruction of Jewish cultural and religious institutions. It complained further that the harassment and arrests of those seeking emigration had reached a level which can be considered a "police-gendarme terror that repeats the darkest times of the Stalin-Beria period. . . ." Insisting that "our life in the Soviet Union has become absolutely intolerable," the petitioners appealed to the UN and to Western governments to aid them in their desperate desire to leave. At approximately the same time—on March 18—one hundred Riga Jews addressed a letter to leaders of twenty-three Western Communist Parties. Their appeal was similar.

Far more spectacular was the decision to use a completely new technique, a sit-in in the Presidium of the Supreme Soviet. No one had ever dared challenge Soviet power in this way. And the challenge was to be conducted in the very heart of Soviet authority—the Kremlin. It reflected both the desperation and the courage that had escalated among Soviet Jews in the winter of 1970–71. A fairly small sit-in involving twenty-two Jews from Moscow and eight from Lithuania which took place on February 28 provided a testing ground for the technique. The demonstrators refused to budge unless assured of a definite reply to their demands for emigration. After the authorities committed themselves to making such a reply, the demonstrators dispersed.

When the technique proved successful, others decided to develop it on a much larger scale and to add to it a hunger strike. On March 10, 156 Soviet Jews—from eight cities—assembled in the reception room of the Supreme Soviet to begin a two-day demonstration that would attract world attention. A detailed memorandum by an organizer and participant in the sensational effort illuminates the motivations of those involved, as well as the events which occurred during the two days.[32]

The unique challenge was prompted by the failure of the USSR to respond to earlier protests: "In the winter of 1970–71, it seemed that nothing touched the Soviet giant, neither the unceasing flow of letters and petitions to Israel, to the UN and to the international councils with appeals for help. . . ." A dramatic and original publicity-oriented gesture had to be planned, but one that would be within "the limits of official laws." The emphasis upon lawfulness was a crucial one; it had characterized the preceding petition campaign. The question of timing was vital for maximum public exposure: the action should come after the commemoration of the first 1917 revolution (March 8) and before the Twenty-fourth Party Congress. March 10 was chosen. The initiators were to be, not surprisingly, the Jews from Riga, where "Jewish national anger and protest" was throbbing. On February 26, a group of fifty to one hundred Jews had gone to the reception rooms of the Latvian Council of Ministers and to the Latvian Ministry of Interior to demand exit visas; they had received a sharp refusal. The Riga contingent left the city on the evening of March 9 in order to be in Moscow the following morning.

At 11 A.M. on March 10, the Riga group, numbering fifty-six persons, assembled in the reception room of the Presidium of the USSR Supreme Soviet. At noon, they delivered to the Secretariat a document addressed to the Presidium requesting exit visas for Israel and asking for the release of those who had been arrested. Shortly afterwards, they were joined by one hundred Jews from Vilnius, Kaunas, Lvov, Berdichev, Tallinn, Kislovodsk, and Daugavpils. At 2 P.M., after it was apparent that no official would meet with the group, they turned in to the Secretariat a statement signed by each which read that "in sign of protest against our forcible detention on the territory of the USSR we declare a HUNGER STRIKE."

The unprecedented hunger strike was to last twenty-six hours. The group was seated on the benches along the walls and at tables in the middle of the reception room. Western correspondents entered and interviewed several of the strikers. The correspondents were shortly afterwards removed, and the entrance was closed by 4:00 P.M. Busloads of police converged on the street outside. Employees left at 5:00 P.M., and the room was then dark. Suddenly, the lights went on and the director of the reception room and his deputy entered. A sharp confrontation occurred, with the director advising the group that their statement had been sent to the Ministry of Interior for response, and the group insisting that they wanted to learn what "principles" guided the authorities on the question of emigration. Many spoke up, telling of personal experiences in trying to obtain exit visas. When the director told them to "go home," they responded: "Our home is Israel! Let us go home!" To which he angrily retorted: "You were born in the Soviet Union, this is your Fatherland, and you are obliged to obey Soviet laws."

The demonstrators were adamant and demanded to receive "a representative with greater competence" so that they might receive a "proper explanation." The director and his deputy left, and the lights were turned off. Someone read from the Book of Exodus, in the Old Testament. At 7:00 P.M., the lights again went on, followed by the entrance of the commandant of the reception room. He demanded that the Jews leave; otherwise they would face grave consequences. Nobody moved. Suddenly, at 7:25, some 200 to 250 policemen burst into the hall, stationing themselves in a circle along the walls and in cross-wise positions, thereby separating the demonstrators into isolated groups. The deputy chief of the Moscow police, a lieutenant general, entered and gave the Jews exactly two minutes to leave; "otherwise we shall be obliged to apply to you all the severity of the Soviet laws."

Resistance seemed senseless. The demonstrators moved out to the street and then proceeded to the telegraph office, where they composed an urgent telegram to President Podgorny recapitulating their demands and announcing that they would continue their hunger strike. The following day, at 11 A.M., the group reassembled at the reception room. Warned again, they drafted a new statement asking for "reasons" that motivate refusal of exit visas and declaring their intention of continuing their hunger strike until an answer was received. After delivering the statement to the Secretariat, they decided to go to the Ministry of Interior by marching through the streets of Moscow. Spectators were stunned.

At the Ministry of Interior the Jews were told that they would be received on an individual basis. They refused, saying that at stake was a matter of principle affecting all. They would meet jointly with a "responsible representative" who could "explain the matter to us." Confusion seemed to reign as police officers went to and from various bureaus. Finally, the head of the visa section of the ministry, together with two deputies, appeared. He promised to review their cases, but only on an individual basis. The Jews found this procedure unacceptable.

The officials left, while the recalcitrant Jews remained alone in an empty reception room. After some time had elapsed, the director of the Administrative Department, a major general, was announced. Accompanied by high-ranking officials, he entered into another confrontation with the group. Sharp exchanges took place over the validity of the Soviet attitude on the right to emigrate, the irrational character of decisions on passport applications, and the harsh consequences that had befallen those making applications. The major general would not commit himself to anything beyond the promise to reexamine, on an individual basis, requests for exit visas.

Unsuccessful, he too left, along with his aides. The obdurate strikers, expecting the worst, held their ground. Tension mounted as high-ranking officials passed in and out of the reception room. The major general again appeared, this time with a formal announcement: "You will now be addressed by the member of the Central Committee of the CPSU, deputy to the Supreme Soviet of the USSR, Ministry of Interior of the USSR, Colonel General Shchelokov." A parade of colonels and majors of the ministry stood at attention as Shchelokov entered. He jousted with the Jews, at first delicately: he had one and one-half hours before giving a scheduled lecture at the university. "Perhaps there is someone among you who is the head?" There was no "head," no organization. They wanted answers to the question of principle on the right to leave: "What categories of Jews will be given permits and what categories will be refused?"

The minister, mixing humor and anger, spoke at length. Several considerations guiding policy-makers on emigration were elaborated.* He answered inquiries; assured those present that "Socialist laws" would be strictly observed; and, finally, promised to send, within a month, "special representatives" with wide powers to various localities so that applications would be reexamined in the light of the "principles" he outlined. It was 4:00 P.M. when the interview ended. The demonstrators had achieved their objective. The hunger strike was halted.

The minister was as good as his word. By June, 1971, almost all the participants in the hunger demonstration had arrived in Israel, together with several thousand more. It was clear that great concern was felt in the highest Party circles that the Twenty-fourth Party Congress, with its numerous Communist dignitaries from abroad,

---

* These will be discussed in the next chapter.

might be tarnished were demonstrations to occur during the sessions of the congress. The pressure of dissent had to be relieved, especially in Latvia. There, ten days after the demonstration, many Jews who had applied for exit visas were granted them; all who had applied were summoned to local offices of the Ministry of Interior and asked to sign statements saying either that their families had been granted permission to leave or that their cases were being reexamined. A firm answer on the latter cases would be given after the end of the Party Congress, on April 15. Signers were advised not to take any trips to Moscow, and, indeed, strong detachments of police remained at the Riga train station and at the airport, checking passengers' documents. Those of Jewish nationality who were traveling to Moscow on any but official business were turned back.

The lesson of the hunger strike had not been lost upon militant Jews. On the Jewish holiday of Tishah Ba'av early in August, 1971, fasting and demonstrations took place in at least three cities. Ten Jews of Kiev marched to Babi Yar to fast; three hundred Jews of Vilnius walked four and one-half miles to Ponary, another Nazi execution site; and an undetermined number in Tbilisi, Georgia, staged a sit-in in the offices of the Central Committee of the Georgian Party. But, without the public focus that Moscow provides, let alone the absence of a major event carrying international implications, the demonstrators exerted little impact. Many were arrested; others dispersed. But the challenge of the "not-so-silent" Jews continued.

Chapter 10
Emigration or "Collective Claustrophobia"

A central problem on the agenda of the world struggle for human rights during 1970–71 was the right of Soviet Jews to emigrate to Israel. This cry emanated from the several hundred petitions that had been sent by Soviet Jews during the previous three years to leading world bodies and figures. The petitions, with their many hundreds of signatures, constituted but a token of the pressing character of the problem. Tens of thousands of Soviet Jews had applied for exit visas on the grounds that they sought reunion with their families in Israel. Two questions immediately arose: (1) How do international opinion and international law address themselves to the issue of the right to leave a country? (2) What legal and moral obligation has the Soviet Union assumed in respect of this right?

International opinion was perhaps best expressed in a study conducted by an important United Nations organ, the Sub-Commission on Prevention of Discrimination and Protection of Minorities. Entitled "The Study of Discrimination in Respect of the Right of Everyone to Leave Any Country, Including His Own, and to Return to His Country," the 115-page document was completed and published in 1963, after three years of exhaustive research.[1] The Special Rapporteur of the sub-commission in preparing the study was the distinguished jurist and statesman of the Philippines, Judge José D. Inglés.

The Inglés study is probably the most important work ever prepared by the Sub-Commission on Prevention of Discrimination and Protection of Minorities, and, indeed, it constitutes a landmark in the evolution of human freedom. Its principal theme runs as follows: Next to the right of life, the right to leave one's country is probably the most important of human rights. For, however fettered in one country a person's liberty might be and however restricted his longing for self-identity, for spiritual and cultural fulfillment, and for economic and social enhancement, opportunity to leave a country and seek a haven elsewhere can provide the basis for life and human integrity.

Judge Inglés begins by noting that the right to leave "is founded on natural law." He calls attention to the fact that Socrates regarded the right as an "attribute of personal liberty," and that the Magna Carta in A.D. 1215 incorporated the right to leave for the first time into "natural law." The French Constitution of 1791 provided the same guarantee, and an act of the United States Congress declared in 1868 that "the right of expatriation is a natural and inherent right of all people, indispensable to the enjoyment of the rights of life, liberty and the pursuit of happiness."

It is the contention of Judge Inglés that the right to leave is "a constituent element of personal liberty" and, therefore, should be subject to "no other limitations" besides the minimal ones provided in Article 29 of the Universal Declaration of Human Rights.[2] That article stipulates that all rights are subject only to such limitations as are needed "for the purpose of securing due recognition and respect for the rights and freedoms of others and of meeting the just requirements of morality, public order and the general welfare in a democratic society." It will be noted that Article 29 precludes limitations based upon the foreign policy of a country. So concerned was Judge Inglés that the phrase "public order" may be arbitrarily interpreted in a restrictive manner that he advocated as "the best safeguard against arbitrary denial of the right" the showing of a "clear and present danger to the national security of public order."

The UN study makes the right to leave a precedent for other rights.[3] Judge Inglés notes, for example, that if a person is restrained from leaving a country, he may thereby be "prevented" from observing or practicing the tenets of his religion; he may be frustrated in efforts to marry and found a family; he may be "unable to associate with his kith and kin"; and he could be prevented from obtaining the kind of an education which he desires. Thus, the jurist concludes that disregard of the right to leave "frequently gives rise to discrimination in respect of other human rights and fundamental freedoms, resulting at times in the complete denial of these rights and freedoms." To this, Judge Inglés adds that for a man who is being persecuted, denial of the right to leave "may be tantamount to the total deprivation of liberty, if not life itself."

The sub-commission document goes even beyond this point, to the area of psychiatric disturbances. It contends that denial of the right to leave has a "spiralling psychological effect" leading to "a sort of collective claustrophobia."[4] This happens particularly to those individuals seeking to leave who "belong to a racial, religious or other group which is being singled out for unfair treatment." They develop a "morbid fear of being hemmed in," with consequent serious mental distress. Readers of the petitions of Soviet Jews will recognize the pertinence of Judge Inglés' findings.

In completing his study, Judge Inglés prepared a set of "Draft Principles on Freedom and Non-Discrimination in Respect of the Right of Everyone to Leave Any Country, Including His Own, and to Return to His Country."[5] The preamble to the Draft Principles carries a major statement that places the right to leave at the heart of all other rights. The preamble notes that the right to leave and to return is "an indispensable condition for the full enjoyment by all of other civil, political, economic, social, and cultural rights."

Among the Draft Principles, two stand out. One stipulates that "the right of every national to leave his country shall not be subject to any restrictions except those provided by law, which shall be only such as are reasonable and necessary to protect national security, public order, health or morals, or the rights and freedoms of others." The second has a distinctive humanitarian bent that goes to the very heart of modern civilized society. The Draft Principles would require governments to give "due regard . . . to facilitate the reunion of families." Draft principles concerning the right to leave any country and to return to that country are now on the agenda of the UN Commission on Human Rights. It will probably take a considerable period of time before such principles are adopted by the commission and the higher UN organs—the Economic and Social Council and the General Assembly. Nonetheless, there already exists a body of international law on the subject, one which conforms to international opinion as expressed in the Inglés study.

Article 13/2 of the Universal Declaration of Human Rights reads: "Everyone has the right to leave any country, including his own, and to return to his country." The text was adopted by the Third Committee of the General Assembly, meeting in Paris in the fall of 1948, by a vote of thirty-seven in favor, none against, and three abstentions. The Universal Declaration was adopted by the General Assembly on December 10, 1948, by a vote of forty-eight in favor, none against, and eight abstentions. U Thant has called the Universal Declaration the "Magna Carta of Mankind." It is far more than a mere moral manifesto. According to leading international lawyers who assembled in Montreal in March, 1968, the Universal Declaration "constitutes an authoritative interpretation of the [UN] Charter of the highest order, and has over the years become a part of customary international law."[6]

As early as December, 1960, the General Assembly adopted by a unanimous vote of 89 to 0 a Declaration on Colonialism which specifies that "all States shall observe faithfully and strictly the provisions of the . . . Universal Declaration of Human Rights."[7] In 1961, the Assembly voted 97 to 0 that all the provisions of the Declaration on Colonialism, including the specific reference to the Universal Declaration, be faithfully applied and implemented without delay. In 1962, it reaffirmed this resolution by a vote of 101 to 0. That same year the UN Office of Legal Affairs ruled that a UN declaration "may by custom become recognized as laying down rules binding upon States."[8]

A second body of international law bearing upon the subject is the International Convention on the Elimination of All Forms of Racial Discrimination. This treaty, the culmination of three years of drafting work, was adopted unanimously by the General Assembly on December 21, 1965. Article 5, paragraph d, subsection 2, provides that contracting parties to the treaty "guarantee the right of everyone" to enjoy, among various rights, "the right to leave any country, including his own, and to return to his country." The third major international legal document is the International Covenant on Civil and Political Rights. The result of eighteen years of preliminary drafting work in various UN organs, the Covenant was adopted by a unanimous vote of the General Assembly on December 16, 1966. Article 12, paragraph 2, of the Covenant reads: "Everyone shall be free to leave any country, including his own."

Clearly, then, both authoritative world opinion and international law consider the right to leave a country as a fundamental human right binding on all governments. What is the expressed position of the Soviet Union relative to this right? When Judge Inglés was gathering material for the trail-blazing sub-commission study, he asked every government to submit information concerning its law and practice governing the right to leave. The USSR submitted a body of information which is incorporated in *Conference Room Paper No. 85/Rev. 1* (February 7, 1963). It specified that the Soviet Government may refuse a travel document under three circumstances: (1) if a person has been charged with an offense and judgment is yet pending; (2) if a person has been convicted and is serving a court-imposed sentence; and (3) if a person has yet to discharge his obligation of service in the Soviet army or navy.

These are universal reasons for refusal to grant an exit visa. It is significant that the USSR offered publicly *only* these reasons for rejecting an application for an exit visa. The Soviet document went on to state that "citizens may not be prevented, by membership in a particular racial, linguistic, political, religious or other group, from entering or leaving the USSR."[9] In a further comment, the Soviet Government noted that it exercises "no discrimination of any kind . . . as regards the procedure and formalities connected with entry into or departure from the USSR. . . ." Finally, the USSR told the UN that with reference to appeals "through administrative channels" for exit visas, no discriminatory restrictions are permitted, "and any person who curtails that right [of appeal] is liable to a penalty."

If the Soviet Union publicly attempted to place itself in full accord with prevailing world opinion concerning the right to leave, it also assumed binding and even contractual obligations under international law to fulfill that right. In the first place, the USSR proclaimed itself to be a strong adherent of the Universal Declaration of Human Rights. It is true that the USSR abstained on the vote on December 10, 1948, which adopted the Universal Declaration, but it vigorously championed the 1960 Declaration on Colonialism, which required all states to observe "faithfully and strictly" the Universal Declaration of Human Rights, and it supported General

Assembly resolutions in 1961 and 1962 which reaffirmed this purpose. The Soviet Union also actively endorsed a 1963 UN Declaration on Racial Discrimination which called upon "every state" to observe "fully and faithfully" the provisions of the Universal Declaration of Human Rights.

When Article 13/2 was discussed by the Third Committee of the General Assembly in the fall of 1948, the USSR expressed no opposition to a person's right "to leave any country, including his own," but it proposed an amendment which would add the words "in accordance with the procedure laid down in the laws of that country."[10] In introducing the amendment, the USSR delegate argued that it "in no way modified the basic text of the article [13/2]." He went on to make this interesting comment: "In the Soviet Union . . . no law prevented persons from leaving the country, but anyone desiring to do so had, of course, to go through the legally prescribed formalities."[11]

Only Poland and Saudi Arabia spoke up in favor of the Soviet amendment. Most delegates felt that it would be unnecessarily restrictive, and it was rejected by a vote of seven in favor, twenty-four against, and thirteen abstentions. The article, as amended by Lebanon with the additional phrase "and to return to his country," was then unanimously adopted, with the USSR in favor. The USSR delegate later said that he had misunderstood the issue and that he "would certainly have voted against" the article.[12] Yet, since then, the USSR has not raised its earlier objection and proposed modification.

Indeed, the USSR voted for two binding international treaties which carry specific reference to the right to leave—the International Convention on the Elimination of Racial Discrimination and the Covenant on Civil and Political Rights. The USSR went further: it assumed a contractual obligation to give effect to the right to leave by ratifying the International Convention on the Elimination of Racial Discrimination. This was done by the Presidium of the Supreme Soviet on January 22, 1969. Further evidence of the Soviet Union's obligation to fulfill the right to leave was provided a year earlier when, on March 18, 1969, it appended its signature to the Covenant on Civil and Political Rights. (Byelorussia signed on March 19, and the Ukraine on March 20.) The act of signing a convention or covenant is indicative of a government's general agreement with and support of the provisions of the treaty as well as its intent to consider submitting the treaty to its appropriate domestic organ for ratification.

The USSR has also obligated itself to observe the humanitarian principle enunciated in the Inglés study: special consideration should be given to the reunion of families. This obligation emerges in statements of Soviet leaders, in exchanges of official correspondence between the Soviet foreign minister and the vice president of the United States, and in unpublished diplomatic agreements with Australia as well as, apparently, other countries too. At a press conference in Vienna on July 8, 1960, as reported in *Pravda* the following day, Nikita Khrushchev stated that "we do not object to the reunion of any persons if they want this."[13] In the fall of 1959, Foreign Minister Andrei Gromyko told Vice President Richard Nixon in a telegraphed letter that "requests" aimed at permitting Soviet citizens to obtain passports in order to be united with their families in the United States "will be considered with proper attention as is always the case in consideration of such affairs."[14] Gromyko's letter in part constituted a response to a letter of Nixon addressed to Khrushchev on August 1, 1959. The letter stated:

> In the interest of continuing improvement in relations between the United States and the Soviet Union, I believe that matters such as this involving *principles of nonseparation of families which we both support* should not persist as irritants to larger solutions.
>
> In this regard, I can state that the United States Government does not stand in the way of persons including its own citizens who desire to depart from the United States to take up residence in the USSR. [Emphasis added.]

In June, 1959, following the resumption of diplomatic relations between Australia and the USSR, the Australian Government reported that twenty-one Soviet citizens would be permitted to join their relatives in Australia.[15] The Australian minister of immigration, Alexander R. Downer, stated that the Soviet Government considered this group of emigrants as but a beginning. The prospect that Operation Reunion—as the new policy was termed in Australia —might bring one thousand Soviet citizens to Australian shores was considered likely. In March, 1960, Western diplomats in Moscow were quoted by the Associated Press as saying that the USSR had quietly allowed about one thousand citizens to emigrate during the previous six months in order to rejoin families abroad. In addition to the United States and Australia, the other countries to which the Soviet emigrants had gone were England, Canada, Sweden, and Argentina.

In some instances, the Soviet Government goes beyond the principle of the reunion of families and endorses the principle of the reunion of entire ethnic groups. The attitude to Spaniards living in the Soviet Union is one example. In the fall of 1956, Spaniards, most of whom, as youngsters, had been sent to the Soviet Union in the late nineteen-thirties by the Spanish Republic, began being repatriated to Spain by the Soviet Government. A *New York Times* dispatch from Spain on January 23, 1957, reported that, since the previous September, 2,106 Spaniards had been repatriated. A *Times* dispatch on May 30, 1957, reported that four successive groups of repatriates had arrived in Spain since September, 1956. On May 4, 1960, the Spanish Government issued a note announcing that 1,899 adults had been repatriated from the Soviet Union between 1956 and 1959. If one adds to this the children—offspring of the Spanish refugees—who had been repatriated, the total number of Spanish repatriates may have come to three or four times this figure. An article in the important Soviet journal *Literaturnaia gazeta* showed that the Soviet regime was sympathetically disposed to the aspirations of the Spanish ethnic group to join with its brethren abroad. It explained that many of the Spanish repatriates want "to live with their own people, to share its destiny, its struggle as hard as it may be. Let us wish them luck."[16]

The Russo-Polish repatriation agreement of March 25, 1957, is another example. The agreement provided for the return to Poland of Poles who had been living in the Soviet Union since 1939, together with their children. The agreement was extended until September 30, 1958, and then again until March 31, 1959. It is estimated that since 1957 some two hundred thousand Poles have been repatriated to Poland. A third example are Greeks. While the subject is shrouded in some mystery, it is known that many Greeks who had been living on Russian soil from Tsarist days, and possibly even from pre-Tsarist days, have been permitted to leave for Greece in order to be reunited with their kin. Germans, Mongolians, and Koreans have similarly been beneficiaries of the favorable Soviet attitude toward reunion of families.

The Soviet Union itself has encouraged former Soviet citizens, as well as persons who emigrated prior to World War I from lands now part of the Soviet Union, to "return to the homeland." This campaign was led by the Committee for Return to the Homeland, founded in March, 1955. The committee published a newspaper, *For Return to the Homeland,* in Russian, Ukrainian, Byelorussian, and Georgian, urging readers to return to Soviet Russia. Several thousands of older pre–World War I émigrés—together with their offspring—left for the Soviet Union from Argentina. Particular attention was given in the years 1946–47 to urging Armenians living abroad to return to Soviet Armenia.[17] *Izvestiia* on November 20, 1946, carried a dispatch from Yerevan, the capital of Soviet Armenia, reporting that the government had allocated "huge sums" for the purpose of resettling Armenian repatriates. An article in *Pravda* observed that fifty thousand Armenians had returned to the USSR from Europe and the Near East.

During 1947, the campaign to attract Armenians abroad continued. On June 11, the Associated Press reported from Salonika that a Soviet Armenian delegation had arrived there to supervise the removal to the USSR of about seventeen thousand Armenians who had been in Greece since their expulsion from Asia Minor in 1922. An Associated Press report from Haifa on October 20, 1947, indicated that eleven hundred Armenians in Palestine were awaiting the arrival of the Soviet ship *Pobeda,* which was to take them to the USSR. In the previous month, the Tass news agency charged that Iran was refusing to permit the repatriation of ninety-seven thousand Armenians. And, in December, the Soviet Government asked France not to bar Armenian repatriates waiting at Marseilles to sail to the USSR. On October 21, the *New York Times* reported that Armenian-born citizens of the United States had been encouraged to renounce their citizenship rights and return to Soviet Armenia. On October 31, the *Times* reported that one thousand of these citizens were ready to leave for the USSR.

Although the Soviet Government has been sympathetically disposed to the principle of reunion of families and some ethnic groups, it made, until December, 1966, an exception in the case of Soviet Jews. In three interviews in 1956–57, Khrushchev revealed the official Soviet position with reference to the right of Jews to leave the USSR. One interview, with a delegation of the French Socialist

Party in May, 1956, was printed in the Paris journal *Réalités*.[18] One of the members of the French delegation, M. Deixonne, asked: "Is a Jew permitted to go to Israel, either on a visit or to emigrate there?" Khrushchev responded: "I shall tell you the truth. We do not favor these trips." After Foreign Minister Dmitry Shepilov interjected to disclaim the existence of the problem, Khrushchev went on to say: "At any rate, we don't favor them [trips to Israel]. We are against it. . . ."

In the second interview, in 1957, American pacifist leader Jerome Davis asked whether it was true "that Jews are not permitted to go freely to Israel."[19] Khrushchev answered: "It is true to some extent and to some extent not true." He explained to what extent it was "not true" by noting that as part of the Russo-Polish repatriation agreement, the Soviet Government had permitted Polish Jews to return to Poland even though "we knew that many of them would go to Israel from there." This assertion avoided the issue of the right of Soviet Jews—in contrast to Polish Jews—to leave. (In May, 1959, Khrushchev refused to respond directly to a question put to him by a delegation of American veterans as to whether the Soviet Union permitted Jews to go to Israel.) The third interview was with Eleanor Roosevelt in the summer of 1957. She asked him in the Crimea whether it wasn't "very difficult for any Jew to leave the Soviet Union to settle or even visit Israel."[20] Khrushchev acknowledged the fact and went on to say: ". . . the time will come when everyone who wants to go will be able to go."

The inconsistency between the stated policy on the reunion of families and the stated (as well as actual) policy toward the reunion of Jewish families created an obvious embarrassment. A resolution of the inconsistency had taken the form of denying that Soviet Jews are desirous of leaving the Soviet Union to rejoin relatives elsewhere. On July 13, 1959, the Cairo newspaper *Al-Ahram* printed an exchange of messages between Khrushchev and the Imam of Yemen in which the Premier assured the Imam that no Soviet Jews had ever applied for leave to Israel. The Cairo story was carried in the *Manchester Guardian* on July 14. On July 8, 1960, at a press conference in Vienna, the following question was put to Khrushchev: "Is the Government of the Soviet Union prepared to agree, within the framework of solving the question of reuniting families, to granting permission to persons of Jewish origin in the Soviet

Union to resettle in Israel?" Khrushchev first implied that while Israeli relatives of Soviet Jews may want the latter to go to Israel, the Soviet Jews were reluctant to do so. He said: ". . . the term 'reuniting families' is a rather conditional concept. Probably even today one can read many advertisements in the Vienna papers to the effect that a rich widow is looking for a husband or an old man for a young wife." He then went on to say that the Soviet Ministry of Foreign Affairs has "no requests of persons of the Jewish nationality or of other nationalities wishing to go to Israel."[21] At the time, it was known that 9,236 Soviet Jews had asked for documents which would enable them to obtain exit visas.[22]

A major change in the Soviet formulation of its policy concerning emigration of Soviet Jews was enunciated by Premier Aleksei Kosygin on December 3, 1966, in the course of a press conference in Paris. As recorded verbatim in *Izvestiia* on December 5, 1966, the journalist's query and Kosygin's response appear below:

Q: "The destruction of the war separated many Jewish families and a part of these families are found in the USSR. A part are abroad. Could you give these families the hope of coming together as had been done for many Greek and Armenian families?"

KOSYGIN: "As regards the reunion of families, if any families wish to come together or wish to leave the Soviet Union, for them the road is open and no problem exists here."

This statement of policy by no means offers any insight into the enormous number of obstacles that have to be hurdled. The process of applying and obtaining a visa for Israel is an extraordinarily cumbersome one and needs elaboration. The first step involves obtaining a *vyzov*—an affidavit—from a relative in Israel which states the relationship of the relative to the Soviet citizen, invites the Soviet citizen to join him, and promises to support the emigrant after his arrival. The *vyzov* has to be notarized by the relative in Israel and taken to the Finnish Embassy, which represents Soviet interests in that country. There the affidavit is certified, and the relative mails it to the Soviet Jew. The year 1971 was marked by an unknown number of affidavits that had somehow been "lost" in the mails en route to the USSR.

The Soviet Jew, upon receiving the notarized and certified affidavit, takes it to the local Office for Visas and Registration (OVIR) of the Ministry of Interior, where he is given a form to fill out. He then must proceed to get appropriate documentation. The most important document he needs is a *kharakteristika,* a kind of evaluation précis, made at his place of work and signed by the director of the plant or office, the local Communist Party official, and the trade union representative. Should the applicant have children in school or university, he must obtain a *kharakteristika* for them as well.[23] Requests for such documents become the basis for considerable social pressures upon the applicant. He may quickly find himself without a job or subjected to taunts and ostracism by his co-workers. Finally, a document is required from the local committee that supervises the house in which the applicant has an apartment. The issue may thereby become a neighborhood matter, with the inevitable social consequences.

Once all the documentation has been assembled and given to the local OVIR, the applicant is required to pay a filing fee of forty rubles (about forty-five dollars). He then has to wait for up to six months before an official from OVIR informs him that he is either eligible or not eligible for an exit visa. If not eligible, he can appeal and obtain a decision within three months. Should the decision be firm in rejecting the application, the Soviet Jew must wait a full year before applying again. Many Soviet emigrants are known to have applied numerous times before finally receiving approval.

If the applicant's request for an exit visa is finally granted, he faces additional burdens. Within a period of ten to twenty-five days, he is required to bring further documentation showing that he has resigned his job, that his children have withdrawn from school or university, and that he has left his apartment in proper order. Beginning in January, 1971, he was required to assume an especially heavy financial burden. The regime required him to pay the sum of nine hundred rubles (about one thousand dollars) for each adult member of his family who would be emigrating. The sum covers a five-hundred-ruble charge for "renunciation" of Soviet nationality and a four-hundred-ruble charge for an external passport. Jews have had to borrow from one another to accumulate the necessary sum. In August, 1972, the burdensome payment was enormously increased.

Even for those willing to run the gauntlet, the difficulties in the past have been great, if not insuperable. Prior to 1965, only a relatively small number, mostly aged, were permitted to reunite with their families in Israel.[24] From the middle of 1965 until June, 1967, a small spurt of emigration totaling four thousand, approximately two thousand per year, was permitted. Kosygin's statement of December, 1966, was a formal expression of the new policy. The change was no doubt a concession to world public opinion, rather than to internal pressures exerted by Soviet Jews, who were at that time still "silent." Criticism of Soviet policy on emigration was widespread in the international arena, embracing broad sectors of opinion, including the left. The number permitted to leave, however, did not completely correspond with the number who had made application for exit visas.

Between June, 1967, and October, 1968, no exit visas were allowed. For undetermined reasons, the door was then again opened, to a modest degree. Perhaps the regime was trying to assess the extent of Soviet Jewry's loyalty. Rumblings of alienation, in reaction to general patterns of discrimination as well as the deepening anti-Semitic press campaign, were becoming apparent. The response of Soviet Jewry must have stunned the authorities. Between October, 1968, and the middle of 1969, nearly thirty thousand Jews applied for exit permits. The Soviet leadership reacted by permitting only a trickle to emigrate—two thousand in 1969, one thousand in 1970.

Placing a cover on the pressure cooker could only lead to an explosion of emotions. Made hopeful by the seeming leniency of the regime on emigration, great numbers of Jews were cruelly disappointed to find that their applications for exit visas were either rejected or not acted upon at all. Moreover, those who had applied found that they entered into a thicket of burdensome problems: many were dismissed from their jobs; others saw their children ousted from universities; all faced social ostracism and a myriad of petty harassments. The inevitable consequence was what Judge Inglés had predicted: "collective claustrophobia." And the reaction was similarly predictable. The momentum of struggle escalated, with petitions to international organs and personages multiplying and culminating in sit-ins and hunger strikes. The point of no return had been reached.

What compounded the "morbid fear of being hemmed in"—as the Inglés study put it—was the apparent irrationality of the method of granting exit visas. No pattern could be detected, whether in terms of age brackets or occupations or regions or any of a variety of conceivable categories. It was the psychological need for rationality that helped prompt the spectacular Jewish sit-in in the Kremlin in March, 1971. Soviet Jews finally extracted the presumed guiding "principles" from the Minister of Interior, General N. Shchelokov. He told the demonstrators that the following categories of persons could not obtain exit visas: (1) those who work at an occupation having a direct connection with state secrets (an applicant for an exit visa would have to quit his job for a period of three to five years before becoming eligible); (2) "valuable" specialists; and (3) those who had just graduated from universities (an applicant would have to work for some undefined time to "pay his debts to the state"). He also explained that, in the case of doctors, if too many from any particular locality were desirous of leaving, not all would be permitted to go.

General Shchelokov clearly had added considerably more limitations on exit visas than those which the USSR had formally set in its report to the UN. Those categories—persons serving in the armed forces and persons under investigation for alleged criminal offenses —were, indeed, mentioned by him. What was significantly new were the new categories. Shchelokov placed particular emphasis upon the category of "valuable" specialists, noting—according to an eyewitness—"We cannot supply specialists with higher education to Israel. We need them ourselves." This statement clearly underscored the point made by John Armstrong that the demand for "captive" scientific and technological labor is a critical factor bearing upon decisions involving emigration of Jews.

Another factor had also been alluded to in various Soviet official and unofficial statements. At the staged press conference of "Establishment" Jews in March, 1970, Professor Mikhail Strogovich, a leading authority on jurisprudence, explained that the USSR would not permit sizable Jewish emigration to Israel while the Middle East conflict was unresolved because emigration would augment Israel's armed forces.[25] In February, 1971, the spokesman of the Soviet delegation to the United Nations, Nikolai Loginov, declared that his government, in dealing with requests for exit visas, takes into account "not only the interests of the applicant, but those of the Soviet state and our friendly Arab allies."[26] Both General Shchelokov and his top aide told the Moscow demonstrators that the USSR was concerned that emigration would contribute to the strengthening of Israel at the expense of the Arabs.

Indeed, when fabricated rumors spread in mid-March, 1971, that the USSR was prepared to allow three hundred thousand Jews to leave, the Lebanese premier, Saeb Salam, openly addressed Soviet Ambassador Sarvar Azimov: "This is a very serious matter indeed because every Jew who enters Israel constitutes a more serious threat to the Arabs than a tank or a plane."[27] Jordan's leading daily, *Al-Destour,* complained that such emigration "meets the manpower requirements Israel needs to carry out expansionist and aggressive schemes." The Kremlin rulers were sufficiently concerned to have one of their diplomats in the Arab world, Boris Khalyzov, officially state in the weekly *Akhbar al-Usbu* that the Soviet Union, "which supports the Arabs without limits or restrictions, knows the extent of the effect of Jewish emigration to Israel on the Arab case, and accordingly banned emigration completely." He went on to tell his readers that the number of Jews who emigrated from the USSR since 1967 "does not exceed a few hundred . . . all of them old."[28]

The dissembling was a rather artless indicator of the fact that Soviet foreign policy considerations involving the Arab states are scarcely a decisive factor in dealing with the question of Jewish emigration to Israel. The Soviet rulers certainly placed no obstacles in the path of Communist Poland when it permitted, during the fifties, thousands of its Jewish citizens—most of whom had been repatriated by the USSR—to leave for Israel. And when Poland virtually compelled most of the remainder of its Jewish community to emigrate in 1968–69—after the Six-Day War—the Kremlin did not appear to raise any objections.

There was yet an additional consideration to which Roy Medvedev referred. If a significantly large number of Jews are permitted to emigrate, then the illusion that the Soviet Union is a utopia for its nationalities—so repeatedly articulated for internal and external consumption—will have been punctured.

On the other hand, international moral and legal standards carry a certain weight with the policy-makers of the Soviet Union. The extent to which the Soviet regime conforms to these standards is a measure of the image which it is attempting to project on a world scale. The USSR has accepted authoritative world opinion that the "right to leave" is a fundamental human right; it has obligated itself in a variety of ways to international law, which requires it to give effect to the "right to leave"; and it has accorded recognition, in both principle and practice, to the idea of reunion of families and even of entire ethnic groups. With various international forums debating the issue in 1970–71, the spotlight could not but focus upon how the USSR handled the requests for emigration on the part of its Jewish community.

Khrushchev Remembers addressed the moral issue in a very pointed manner. The book records the following line of thought, which is attributed to the former premier in the late nineteen-sixties: If the Soviet Union is attempting to build a "paradise," why should it keep its borders "bolted with seven locks"?[29] Opening the borders for emigration is both "theoretically" and "practically" feasible. If it is not feasible, "then what kind of freedom would we have?" Were the USSR to continue to bar those seeking to emigrate, then "we will discredit the Marxist-Leninist ideals on which our Soviet way of life is based."

Beyond the moral concern, although intimately related to it, was the growing internal pressure of a strongly disaffected segment of the population. Its agitation continued to make itself felt in key sectors of opinion abroad which the USSR had to take into account. These ranged from left-wing movements, including Communists, to governments with which the Kremlin was striving to establish or deepen friendly relations or to reach a *modus vivendi*. Some of that internal pressure has been defused by a decision taken on the eve of the Twenty-fourth Party Congress—and no doubt related to the *public* aspects of the Congress—to allow approximately one thousand Jews each month to emigrate. From March through December, 1971, almost 13,000 Jews received exit visas for Israel—a thirteen-fold increase over 1970.[30] But the 1971 emigration figures constituted only a token of those seeking the right to leave in order to be reunited with their families in Israel. The problem of dealing with the unceasing internal pressure as well as with international moral forces, including "the Marxist-Leninist ideals" to which *Khrushchev Remembers* alluded, had yet to be tackled meaningfully by the Soviet leadership.

Indeed, the modest, though significant, steps that the Kremlin finally took in the latter part of 1971 regarding emigration of Jews came only after it had made an intense effort to stifle completely the Jewish national movement and its striving for exodus. That effort was to make itself felt first on June 15, 1970, with a series of dragnet arrests, and then by four subsequent trials. Repression and intimidation of Jewish activism were the hallmarks of the campaign, and the Soviet authorities would feel obliged to seek an alternative policy only in the event of its total failure.

Chapter 11
The First Leningrad Trial

"On June 15, a group of criminals trying to seize a scheduled airplane were arrested at Smolny Airport. Investigations are in process." This short item appeared in *Leningradskaia pravda* on the morning of June 16, 1970. A similar reference had appeared the night before in the evening newspaper *Vecherny Leningrad*. The reported event signaled a large-scale crackdown on Soviet Jewish activists. From it were to flow four major trials of Jewish militants —two in Leningrad, one in Riga, and one in Kishinev. Several lesser trials were to unfold in various other cities simultaneously. By the summer of 1971, a total of forty-two Jews were languishing in prison.

The developments of June 15 require elaboration, for they reveal the real purpose of the authorities as distinct from that which would be presented later for public consumption both within and without the Soviet Union. At 8:30 A.M., twelve persons, mostly from Riga, who were crossing the tarmac at Smolny Airport were arrested. They were about to board as passengers a twelve-seat AN-2 plane scheduled to leave Leningrad at 8:35 A.M. for Priozersk (formerly called Keksholm), a city on the outskirts of the province of Leningrad, forty miles from the Finnish border. There, according to the authorities, the twelve had planned to seize control of the plane, tie up the two pilots "without causing a single scratch,"* and place them into sleeping bags under a tent. The twelve were allegedly to have

---

* The quoted statement was made by a defendant who insisted that this was a principle to which all the participants were obliged to adhere.

been joined by four others, all from Riga, already waiting at Priozersk. With one of the twelve being an experienced pilot, they would then fly to Sweden. (It was never made clear how sixteen persons were supposed to fit into a plane containing fourteen seats —twelve for the passengers and two for the pilots.) Four and one-half hours before the arrests at Smolny, at 4:00 A.M., the four persons at Priozersk were arrested. They had arrived by train from Leningrad and were sleeping in the woods not far from the airport when the police arrived.

More significant than the arrests at Smolny was what happened immediately afterwards. Within a two-hour period, and in some cases within a forty-five-minute period, eight Leningrad Jewish activists were arrested. None of them were near the airport. One was on vacation in Odessa, 850 miles away; a second was on vacation in a Leningrad suburb; a third was on an official business trip sixty miles outside of Leningrad; the others were at home or at work. Within approximately the same time period, about forty houses were searched in a number of cities, including Moscow, Riga, and Kharkov. Everything related to Israel and Jewish culture was confiscated. Included in the material taken were poems by the Hebrew writer Chaim Bialik, translations of writings by the American novelists Leon Uris and Howard Fast, picture postcards of Israel, and copies of petitions addressed to the United Nations. During the next few weeks, the dragnet spread to others in Leningrad and Riga, and to several other cities, including Kishinev and Odessa. More arrests and searches took place. A *samizdat* document reveals the types of items that the secret police seized upon for evidence in Kishinev: books on Jewish history, textbooks on the Hebrew language, recordings of Jewish songs, and copies of *Folksstimme*, the Yiddish newspaper of Communist Poland.

That the swift, nationally coordinated effort had taken on the form of a pre-planned, concentrated drive to intimidate and smash Jewish activism was not lost upon Jews, especially Jewish militants in various cities. How else could one explain the widespread arrests of Jews who were not directly connected with the contemplated seizure of a plane? Three letters focusing upon the arrest of the Leningrad Eight and appearing in the second edition of the underground journal *Iskhod* (*Exodus*) testify to this awareness. One was written on July 8 by a close friend of the Leningrad Eight, Viktor

Boguslavsky, a brilliant young bridge engineer, who addressed his letter to R. A. Rudenko, procurator-general of the USSR. Noting that none of his arrested friends were even present at the airport on June 15, he asked: "What relation could they have with the incident at Smolny Airport?" He pointed to the "evidence" seized at their homes: ". . . Hebrew-language textbooks and self-teaching manuals, sent by post from Israel and, in part, photo-copied. All these together with letters and articles on Jewish history, novels, Jewish songs on tapes. . . ." Then he asked, "What is their crime?"

Boguslavsky answered his own theoretical queries: "Their own 'guilt' was that they were born Jews and longed to remain Jews. They learned their own language and greedily swallowed a few facts about the history of the Jewish people. They were worried about the fate of their relatives in the State of Israel. . . ." After observing that most of them had applied for exit visas for Israel and had been refused, he went on: "So it is clear that the guilt of my arrested friends lies in the fact that they wanted to live in their historical homeland, their own national state, amongst their own people." Finally, he called attention to the children of his friends, and concluded:

> My friends dreamed of hearing their own Jewish language from the mouths of their children. Is that a crime? No.
> A keen interest in the fate of one's own people, love of one's people, cannot be considered a criminal offense.

For his pains, Boguslavsky would himself be arrested shortly after writing the letter and would be placed in the dock with his friends the following May.

The second letter, written on June 28, was addressed to both Rudenko and the Presidium of the Supreme Soviet. Its authors were two Leningraders—Grigory Vertlib, a lawyer, and Hillel Shur, an engineer. They emphasized that "a trial is being prepared of those [in Leningrad] who wanted only one thing—to leave for Israel." After relating how most of the arrested Leningraders had repeatedly applied for visas and been rejected, Vertlib and Shur asked: "What is this, is it the revenge of the political authorities for being unable to break the spirit of those people?" Insisting that the Leningraders never intended to commit any actions contravening the law or harming the Soviet people, they posed the critical question: "We ask of you, can it be that the Soviet Government wants to frighten those Jews who wish to leave for Israel?"

Vertlib and Shur cautioned that Jewish activists "will not be frightened by any repression." They reminded the authorities of previous trials against Jews—Dreyfus and Mendel Beiliss—as well as the Doctors' Plot, and warned that the trial being prepared against the Leningrad group "may enter history side by side with these infamous cases and it may cause untold and irretrievable harm to the Soviet state." Besides, they asked, where will it end? "Shall we have to face another trial? And then more trials—concerning other people who wish to leave for Israel?" Their predictions proved to be correct, even to the extent of including one of them—Hillel Shur —in the Kishinev trial. (Vertlib was eventually allowed to go to Israel.)

The final letter was written by the Moscow activists and was addressed to the deputies of the USSR Supreme Soviet. Commenting on the arrest of the eight Leningrad Jews, the letter called attention to the fact that none of them were "at the airport and nowhere near the airport" at the time of the planned hijacking. The ten signers observed: ". . . the real motives for these arrests became obvious very soon: during the house searches . . . the authorities . . . discovered and confiscated such *real* evidence as textbooks of the Jewish language, applications concerning departure for Israel and so on. The reasons for the arrests are now evident to us, the more so because we are guilty of the same crimes." If the Moscow signers hadn't been arrested, it was only because the "competent powers" had yet to "choose a given moment" in order "to frighten" some "given people" and "edify others."

But the intimidation will not succeed, except through an endless series of reprisals, said the signers: "History now demands that you choose, and you have only two possibilities: either let us depart in peace, or enter onto the well-trodden path of mass reprisals. Because as long as we exist, we will continue to demand the freedom to depart—and we will raise our voice louder every day and our voice will become intolerable to you." The challenge, at least until the spring of 1971, fell on deaf ears. There would then be a partial response, in the form of a significant increase in the number of exit visas granted. But even then, the concession would go hand in hand with the intimidating force of political trials.

Still, for those in the Kremlin who sought to crush the Jewish national movement once and for all, the attempted hijacking offered an effective weapon. "Flight abroad" was a Soviet crime that conceivably might be covered by Article 64a of the Russian Republic Criminal Code, which deals with "betrayal of the fatherland." Moreover, world public opinion, particularly after the experiences of the summer of 1970, when several major international hijackings occurred, could hardly be expected to be sympathetic. If, somehow, the Jewish national movement as a whole could be tarred with the hijacking brush, then the authorities would have, on the one hand, a legal mechanism with which to convict and isolate the militant leaders and, on the other hand, a moral mechanism with which to intimidate Jewish activism.

The timing of the incident was especially convenient for the authorities. Only one day earlier, on June 14, thirty-seven Leningrad Jews had completed an appeal addressed to U Thant, the United Nations secretary-general, who was at the time in Moscow on an official visit. The appeal, which emphasized that the "motives" of the signatories "are not social or political" but rather "deeply national," asked Thant to intercede with the Soviet Government to allow the emigration of those Jews seeking to do so. Had the appeal reached Thant in Moscow or had it reached Western correspondents in Moscow, who in turn might have queried Thant about his reaction, it might have exercised an important public impact. The arrests in Leningrad halted, for the time being, the delivery of the appeal.

Who, then, was involved in the hijacking incident and what were their motivations? A *samizdat* document, *Iskhod*, no. 4, which covers, in considerable detail, the trial held in Leningrad from December 15 to 24, 1970, provides much of the data on which an analysis can be based.[1] Further information can be drawn from Tass and Novosti dispatches, reports of Western correspondents in Moscow, articles in the Soviet press, and accounts in other *samizdat* literature, especially those in *Khronika*. There are, of course, gaps in the documentation. No Western observer or correspondent was permitted to enter the courtroom. While *Leningradskaia pravda* on December 15 declared that the case would be considered in "open" court, admission to the two-hundred-seat courtroom was carefully restricted to security and other government officials and to direct relatives: parents, children, brothers, sisters, wives. And the Soviet authorities have meticulously avoided presenting a full summary of the proceedings.

Not all of the sixteen people apprehended at the airport or at Priozersk on June 15 were placed on trial. The following eleven persons were in the dock:

> Mark Y. Dymshits, a forty-three-year-old former pilot in Bokhara who worked as an engineer in Leningrad.
>
> Eduard S. Kuznetsov, a twenty-nine-year-old former philosophy student at the University of Moscow who had spent seven years in a forced labor camp for "anti-Soviet" democratic activities and who worked at the time as a "methodologist" in a Riga psychiatric hospital.
>
> Silva I. Zalmanson, Kuznetsov's twenty-six-year-old wife, who, as a graduate mechanical engineer, worked as a designer in a Riga factory.
>
> Israil I. Zalmanson, Silva's twenty-one-year-old brother, a student at the Riga Polytechnical Institute.
>
> Iosif M. Mendelevich, a twenty-three-year-old who had spent four years at the Riga Polytechnical Institute but had left before completing his course of studies.
>
> Anatoly Altman, a twenty-eight-year-old Riga resident who had been born in Chernovtsy and had lived for a while in Odessa. He had worked as a lathe operator, a driver, and a wood engraver.
>
> Arie G. Khnokh, a twenty-six-year-old electrician who had completed seven years at a Railway Technical Institute.
>
> Boris Penson, a twenty-five-year-old artist.
>
> Mendel Bodnia, a thirty-two-year-old invalid with an eye injury.
>
> Aleksei Murzhenko, a twenty-eight-year-old factory worker. A friend of Kuznetsov, he too had been convicted of and had served time for anti-Stalinist utterances.
>
> Yury Fedorov, probably in his late twenties. He had been convicted of "anti-Soviet" offenses.

Those not placed on trial included an older brother of Silva Zalmanson, Vulf, a thirty-year-old mechanical engineer then serving as a lieutenant in the Red Army. He would later be tried and convicted by a military court. Dymshits' divorced wife and two daughters were released shortly after their arrest at the airport.

Apparently, Mrs. Dymshits, of Russian national origin, was initially unwilling to join the hijacking attempt but felt pressured to do so in order to be reunited with her ex-husband. Mrs. Arie Khnokh, a sister of Mendelevich, had been apprehended at Priozersk but was released because of her advanced state of pregnancy.

Of the eleven in the dock, nine were Jews who had planned to flee to Israel. One of the nine, Kuznetsov, was a product of a mixed marriage (his mother was Jewish), but although *Russian* was listed as his nationality in his passport, he considered himself Jewish and evidently made an unsuccessful effort to change his official nationality identification. The two non-Jews, Murzhenko and Fedorov, apparently joined the plan with the hope of seeking asylum in Sweden.

What had motivated the Jews to take an extreme and illegal recourse? With the exception of Dymshits and Israil Zalmanson, all of them had made application for exit visas, and all had been refused. The result, inevitably, was a profound frustration, the character of which is indicated in an open letter sent by Silva Zalmanson to U Thant at the beginning of 1970 (it appeared in *Iskhod*, no. 3):

> . . . I want to leave the country where much is inimical and alien to me despite the fact that I was born and have lived in it to this day. Alien, because I regard only Israel as my spiritual homeland and the people among whom I live consider me an alien element. . . . I believe that there will come a day and the happiness which now seems to me unbelievable will come true. But while I am outside Israel the awareness that my homeland is being created without my participation gives me *unbearable pain and helplessness* . . . [and] *drives me to despair.* [Emphasis added.]

Helplessness and despair would appear to have been particularly characteristic of those with an intensely Jewish background. It was true of the Zalmansons (the young Israil had not applied for an exit visa because he feared expulsion from the Riga Polytechnical Institute). Mendelevich, who was fluent in Hebrew and deeply read in Jewish culture, was similarly affected. He had deliberately withdrawn from the university lest his being a student be considered an obstacle to obtaining an exit visa, and since 1967 he had repeatedly appealed for permission to leave.

The background and experience of Khnokh were pretty much the same. According to a footnote in *Iskhod*, no. 4, he was brought up in a Yiddish-speaking family where national traditions and festive days were strictly observed. He became increasingly convinced that the future of the Jews as a people could be realized only in Israel, and he often said that the absence of Jewish culture in the USSR "was making his life impossible." Having made repeated applications for exit visas, he gradually came to the conclusion that the officials didn't even bother to read his requests. He helped draft various appeals by Riga Jews to Kosygin, to U Thant, and to foreign Communist Party secretaries. While less is known of Altman, he appears to have had an outlook similar to that of Khnokh. Altman was active in helping reproduce in Riga material of Jewish content.

The reasons Penson and Bodnia applied for exit visas were far less nationalistically intense. Penson's parents, both old, were the ones primarily interested in exit visas. Penson thought that the visas might be granted if he fled. Bodnia simply wanted to join his parents, both living in Israel. During the trial, he collaborated with the prosecution and spoke of his co-defendants in hostile tones.

The sense of being helplessly hemmed in had already been described in the Inglés study for the United Nations Sub-Commission on Prevention of Discrimination and Protection of Minorities. Judge Inglés referred to an extreme psychological distress flowing from "collective claustrophobia." Silva Zalmanson's letter to U Thant is symptomatic of this extreme distress, reflected in the terms "unbearable pain" and "despair." It will be recalled, in this connection, that the hopes which had been allowed to be cultivated among Jews seeking exit visas during the latter part of 1968 were sharply punctured when the Soviet regime ended its liberalized policy and, once again, in late 1969, severely limited the number of exit visas. The sudden collapse of expectations could not but feed the frustration.

That the acute frustration of the activists might make them prone to accept a wild scheme for leaving the USSR is by no means implausible. The role of Mark Dymshits is critical here. For it is he who played the key organizing role in the hijack attempt. Several characteristics distinguish Dymshits from the Jewish activists— Zalmanson, Mendelevich, Altman, and Khnokh. In the first place, he is much older than they and, therefore, beyond the age group generally involved in the national movement. More important, he does not appear to have sprung from a strong Jewish background. Not until the autumn of 1969, when he was introduced to a circle in Leningrad studying Hebrew, is there any important indication that he had any interest at all in Jewish culture and tradition.

Dymshits' motivation was different from the others'. He was not impelled by either ethnic-cultural consideration or the desire to be reunited with relatives. Rather, personal experience with anti-Semitic discrimination was the vital factor. While he elaborated, in his opening statement to the court, three motives for his action—"(1) anti-Semitism in the USSR; (2) the foreign policy of the USSR in the Near East; and (3) the internal policy of the USSR on the nationalities question in relation to the Jews"—he went on to point to the triggering act for his decision to leave the USSR. Because of his "Jewish origin," he stated, he had been unable to find work in his profession of airline pilot in Leningrad and was obliged to go to Bokhara to obtain a job. Although he later worked in an agricultural institute and as an engineer, he dreamt always of flying. His final statement to the court reads quite differently from those made by the militants: "What a pity, though, that the people from the personnel department [in charge of airline positions] whom I so often asked for work—unsuccessfully, for some reason—were not sitting beside him [the public prosecutor]; after all they are the ones who could have stopped me before the autumn of 1969."

Dymshits appears to have been totally obsessed with flying, a passion which his wife underscored in her testimony. The realization that with his advancing age he had but few years left to pilot a plane probably made him desperate. Unlike the others, who had made application for exit visas, he refused to go through the required procedures, which would have meant perhaps endless delays. As early as 1967–68, he began to concoct exotic schemes for escaping: first he thought of building a balloon and then he conceived the idea of building an aircraft. Finally, he conjured up a plan to hijack a plane. But, convinced that he could not accomplish a hijacking by himself, he began to look for others who might be prevailed upon to join him.

At this stage—a close reading of the trial proceedings, as recorded in *Iskhod*, no. 4, indicates—a mysterious, unidentified figure entered the case. A person called "Venya," evidently a neighbor of the leader of the Leningrad Zionist group, Hillel Butman, introduced Dymshits to Butman. "Venya's" surname was never mentioned in the case, nor is it clear that "Venya" was a real name and not a pseudonym. According to a footnote in the *Iskhod* account, "nobody knows him [Venya]," and, when a defense counsel in the hijacking case asked that "Venya" be summoned as a witness, the chairman of the court, Yermakov, turned the request down. Was "Venya" a police agent? More precisely, was he an *agent provocateur* who engineered a vast entrapment process? Aware of the obsession of Dymshits, did he hope to introduce him to persons who might fall easy prey to his scheme, thereby setting in motion a widespread police action?

Certainly, without the intercession of "Venya," Dymshits' obsessive idea might never have fallen on fertile soil, to be nourished, and then to blossom forth in a "conspiracy." The *agent provocateur* has often played a prominent role in major police and juridical cases during the course of Russian and Soviet history, and may very well have done so in the hijacking plot.[2] "Venya" was, after all, the indispensable link between a purely latent "criminal" idea and the core of the Jewish national movement, which, the authorities believed, lay in Leningrad. The authorities would have found especially convenient the seduction and corruption of that core. If the national movement was to be finally discredited and smeared, a legitimate pretext was essential to the regime. The deliberate pairing of Dymshits with Butman could ultimately provide that pretext. That pairing could not have occurred without the mysterious "Venya." The fact that the Soviet regime has meticulously shielded and hidden his identity from public view cannot but reinforce this hypothesis of how the plot was originally triggered.

In any case, shortly after the meeting, which occurred sometime in the late fall of 1969—probably in December—Dymshits informed Butman of his plan for an organized escape. The initial scheme that Dymshits projected was the hijacking in mid-air of a TU-124 plane (48 to 52 passengers) that flies the Leningrad-Murmansk route. Butman apparently agreed to the plan. Two of his Leningrad colleagues, Lev and Mikhail Korenblit, also initially appeared interested. There are some indications that the plan involved the notion of Jewish activists purchasing all of the seats on the plane (similar to the AN-2 plan). To allay suspicion, the affair was to be disguised as a trip to the wedding of Mikhail Korenblit. The plan was dubbed "Wedding," and Korenblit was referred to as the "groom."

Butman brought Dymshits to Riga sometime after the beginning of 1970 and introduced him to Silva Zalmanson. She and Butman were known to each other as a result of their mutual interest in the publication of Jewish and Zionist materials. She in turn had them meet Kuznetsov, whom she had married in January, 1970, as well as others in Riga who she thought would be interested in the escape plan. Kuznetsov seems to have been apprised of the plan by one of the Korenblit brothers, even before he met Butman in Riga.

The attempted hijacking was scheduled for May 1–2. But two obstacles had intervened. Dymshits, in striving to acquaint himself with the controls of a TU-124, prevailed upon a former fellow pilot from Bokhara, now on the Moscow scheduled line, to let him sit in the cockpit. Dymshits concluded that the controls were too complex for him. Far more important was the fact that leaders of the Leningrad group, who had either supported the idea or had expressed an interest in it, developed second thoughts about its feasibility. Its "criminal" character no doubt disturbed them. After considerable internal discussion, they came to the sober decision to abandon the plan. By April 10, the idea was formally dismissed by the Leningrad group.

Significantly, they took a further crucial step. Fearful that Dymshits might seek to carry out this or a similar plan, which they were now convinced would be hurtful to the cause of the activists, they made a determined and vigorous effort to convince Dymshits to halt the pursuit of his chimerical scheme. In the hope of convincing a doubtful Dymshits, the Leningraders made inquiry of "official" sources in Israel—who these may have been is not indicated in *samizdat* literature—and received a firm negative response. The Israeli reaction did not budge Dymshits. He told Mikhail Korenblit that he had already resigned from his job and had, therefore, no alternative but to pursue his aim. Dymshits was quoted by Mikhail Korenblit as asking: "What should I do now?" To which the latter replied: "Get a job, and that immediately." Lev Korenblit had a heated but unresolved argument with Dymshits on either May 24 or 25 urging the latter to drop his escape project. On the following day, however, Dymshits assured Butman that he would no longer seek to give effect to his idea. Butman immediately informed Lev Korenblit about this.

Some of the Leningraders had their doubts about Dymshits' promise, and well they might. The ex-pilot was convinced that his personal Rubicon had been crossed and there could be no turning back from the course he had chosen. At the end of May, he devised a variation of his original plan. He (it is not clear whether he was to be joined by others) would attempt, in the dark of night, to steal a twelve-seat AN-2 plane from the Leningrad airport and fly away without passengers. The leap into a fantasy world could not have been more evident. At Dymshits' urging, Kuznetsov and his wife Silva came to Leningrad at the end of May. A cursory canvassing of the security precautions at Smolny Airport convinced even the fixated that the idea was crazy.

Kuznetsov returned to Riga assuming that the project was at an end. But the fertile, if feverish, brain of Dymshits could not be stopped. On June 5, he called Kuznetsov and asked him to come again to Leningrad as a new variation of a hijacking had been conceived. The new plan was the one that they would try to implement on June 15. On June 8, Dymshits and Kuznetsov, joined by Fedorov, on a kind of "dry run," flew the Leningrad-Priozersk route on the AN-2 plane. The die was cast.

To avoid the possibility of the Leningrad group's interfering with the contemplated hijacking scheme, Dymshits and Kuznetsov deliberately chose not to tell its leaders anything about their plan. They had already concluded that the Leningraders had no stomach for high adventure. A *samizdat* document which carried the proceedings of the later Leningrad trial reveals that Dymshits deliberately assumed a posture of "deviousness" toward the Leningrad group. He was already angry with them for making inquiries in Israel concerning his proposed hijacking. In his view, the negative Israeli response was a certainty. In the same *samizdat* document, Kuznetsov was quoted as saying that he and his friends from Riga were so convinced that the Leningrad group would strive to sabotage their efforts that "in our trips to Leningrad we tried to avoid being seen." The document attributes to Silva Zalmanson the following view: "After finding out that the Leningraders were categorically against this idea of crossing the border illegally, we concealed our preparations from them carefully. We told them that we too had given up the project, because we were afraid that they might cause our plans to fail."

In turn, some of the Leningrad leaders, aware of Dymshits' pro-clivities, sensed that something stronger than his assurances was necessary to prevent him from taking a precipitate action. If he were to be prevailed upon to sign a public document, they reasoned, he would then know that his name was available to the KGB, and he would be reluctant to take on an illegal and conspiratorial role. Butman asked him to sign a telegram expressing condolences to the mothers of the Israeli children who had been killed by an Arab terrorist ambush near the Lebanese border. Dymshits refused. In-stead, he asked that affidavits be obtained for him from fictitious relatives in Israel, and, he promised, these would be used by him to make an official and legal request to emigrate.

While Butman strove to "find" relatives for Dymshits, others in the Leningrad group decided to put him to the test of a firm com-mitment. An auspicious occasion presented itself on June 13. The Leningrad group was accumulating thirty-seven signatures for the petition to U Thant. Mikhail Korenblit, at Mogilever's request, went to Dymshits' home to ask for his signature. What followed next, as described in the *Iskhod* record of the court proceedings, is especially puzzling. Korenblit told the court that although he was a familiar face at Dymshits' home, he had been astonished to find that at first he was not allowed in, and that only after the doors to all the rooms had been closed had he been led into the kitchen. Korenblit then started to say, "and I saw. . . ." At that point he was interrupted by the chairman of the court and by the prosecutor, while policemen rushed to him and led him out of the courtroom. On the way, Korenblit shouted: "I ran off at once to phone Kaminsky [a Lenin-grad Jewish leader] and the boys and told them: 'You've got to ring Edik [Kuznetsov] in Riga urgently—everybody knows every-thing. . . .' " Korenblit was rushed out of the courtroom without the defense counsel or defendants being asked whether they had any questions for the witness.

Whom or what Korenblit "saw" (or "understood"—a possible interpretation suggested in a footnote in *Iskhod*) is unknown. Korenblit's testimony, in general, had opened up avenues in the courtroom which the authorities were determined not to have explored. At one point, when Korenblit was going to say something about Dymshits ("I considered Dymshits a decent man who had suffered for the Jewish people, but . . ."), he was halted by the prosecutor. In any case, Korenblit's mission to Dymshits was too late. The attempt at a hijacking was scheduled for two days later—June 15. As in a Greek tragedy, the denouement was inexorably unfolding.

A critical point which emerges clearly from the evidence requires emphasis. The Leningrad group leaders, however seductive they initially found the schemes of Dymshits, in the end not only rejected them but moved with a vigorous, almost fanatical, determination to thwart them. Mature, rational judgment overcame a deep-seated, desperate desire to emigrate. In keeping with the Jewish national movement as a whole, they pursued their objectives within the clearly defined framework of legality. Illegality must be firmly and deliberately eschewed lest the movement itself be placed in jeopardy. Yet, the Soviet authorities, disregarding the overwhelming weight of the evidence at their disposal, utilized the initial interest of the Leningrad group in the Dymshits proposal to smear and, thereby, attempt to destroy it and the national movement to which it was inextricably linked.

The Riga group blindly followed Dymshits into the trap that would quickly be sprung. A few of them, central figures in the Jewish national movement, must have had moments of doubt. Silva Zalmanson, in her final statement to the court, gave expression to such moments:

> Some of us did not believe in the success of the escape or believed in it very slightly. Already at the Finland [Railroad] Station [in Leningrad, before traveling to Priozersk], we noticed that we were being followed, *but we could no longer go back . . . go back to the past, to the senseless waiting,* to life with our luggage packed. Our dream of living in Israel was incomparably stronger than the fear of suffering we might be made to endure. [Emphasis added.]

It was as if, having been stirred to envision a dream about to be fulfilled, they felt emotionally compelled to advance to that dream however illusory their reason showed the dream to be. This may have been especially true of the younger Zionists. The final statement of the twenty-three-year-old Mendelevich bares the inner comprehension that was ultimately reached: ". . . I am also guilty of having allowed myself to be indiscriminate in choosing the means of achieving my dream. These past six months have taught me that emotions must be subordinated to reason."

That the defendants had intended to seize a plane and flee abroad is clear. What is, however, open to serious question and considerable doubt are the charges that were brought against them. This, indeed, was a central issue in the court proceedings and in the punishment that would be rendered. (It should be emphasized that Soviet law did not specifically cover hijacking.) As regards the attempted plane seizure, the defendants could have been tried under two alternative sections of the Criminal Code of the Russian Republic. One of the two is Article 83, which deals with "illegal departure abroad" and carries a modest penalty of deprivation of freedom for a period of one to three years. The other is Article 64a, which deals with the far more dangerous crime of treason: "Betrayal of the Fatherland, an act deliberately committed by a citizen of the USSR to the detriment of the national independence, territorial integrity or military might of the USSR. . . ." "Flight abroad" is listed as one such act. The commission of a crime under the treason article is subject to the heaviest penalties, including death.

(Of course, the planned plane seizure and flight abroad did not occur. They were interrupted and thwarted well before the planners had even set foot on the plane. However, Article 15 of the Criminal Code, under which the defendants were also tried, deals specifically with "the preparation of a crime and . . . an attempted crime.")

The treason charge was the one chosen by the authorities. But was there an *intent* by the defendants to hurt or weaken the security and integrity of the Soviet state? This is the decisive question, for the crucial words "deliberately committed" clearly refer to "intent." Repeatedly, throughout the trial, the defendants vigorously denied such an intent. All of the Jews stated that their only purpose was to settle in Israel. Typical was Mendelevich's reply to a question about his intentions: "I had only one aim: to reach Israel." The defendants objected to any suggestion that they had anti-Soviet political motives. An exchange between Kuznetsov and his defense counsel was characteristic:

> Defense counsel: Did you commit this crime out of political motives?
> Kuznetsov: No, I was guided by considerations of a spiritual and moral nature.

> Defense counsel: Did you intend to bring harm to the USSR?
> Kuznetsov: Not at all.

A number of defense attorneys gave strong emphasis to the problem of intent. Mendelevich's attorney was especially insistent that "the question of the motive is essential." After reminding the court of his client's deeply Jewish cultural and religious family background, and his repeatedly expressed desire to live in Israel, he contended that it was impossible to consider that Mendelevich had wished to damage the independence, territorial integrity, and military power of the Soviet state. *Iskhod* summarized a particularly critical point made by the defense counsel: "Even if Mendelevich had escaped to Israel to pray to his God and maybe even revile the USSR—even that could not have damaged our external security. The defense submits that our country's 'prestige' is *not* external security. . . ." Denying that his client had a "direct intent" to commit injury to the USSR, he concluded that Mendelevich's purpose did not come under Article 64a. Altman's attorney stressed the same argument: his client had no intention of undermining the power of the USSR; neither he nor his accomplices had the "direct intention" of damaging the prestige of the USSR; and, therefore, his client had not committed any action punishable under Article 64a.

The final statements of the Jewish defendants address the question of intent with a meticulous care that at the same time provides an insight—at times eloquent—into their motives. According to a summary in *Iskhod,* Silva Zalmanson said:

> I don't think that Soviet law can consider anyone's "intention" to live in another country "treason." . . .
> Let the court at least take into consideration that *if we were allowed to leave* there would be no "criminal collusion" which has caused so much suffering. . . .
> Israel is the country with which we Jews are bound spiritually. . . .
> By going away, we would not have harmed anybody.
> I wanted to live over there with my family, work there. I would not have bothered about politics—all my interest in politics has been confined to the simple wish to leave. Even now I do not doubt for a minute that some time I shall go after all and that I *will* live in Israel. . . . This dream, illuminated by two thousand years of hope, will never leave me. NEXT YEAR IN JERUSALEM!
> And now I repeat:

". . . if I forget you, Oh, Jerusalem, let my right hand wither away. . . ."

She repeated the words in Hebrew.

A section of Altman's statement reads:

> I have no possibility of avoiding punishment, but one thing puzzles me: I applied for permission to go to Israel as far back as 1969. At that time my wish to leave brought me contempt and no more; while now—a trial. . . .
>
> Today, on the day when my fate is being decided, I feel wonderful and very sad: it is my hope that peace will come to Israel. I send my greetings today, my Land! Shalom Aleichem! Peace be unto you, Land of Israel!

The statement of Khnokh is precise and explicit:

> I can only repeat once more that my actions were not directed against the national security of the USSR. My only wish is to live in the state of Israel, which I have long considered my own country, the country where my people originated as a nation, where a Jewish state, Jewish culture used to be and where it is developing today and where my mother tongue is spoken. Where my relatives . . . live.
>
> I have no anti-Soviet intentions whatever.

Only two specific examples allegedly showing hostile political intent of the defendants were offered by the state. The prosecutor contended that upon arriving in Sweden, the "criminals" planned to hold a press conference designed to place the Soviet Union in an embarrassing light. Evidently, Butman had suggested such an idea to Kuznetsov while the former was still a part of the original hijacking scheme. Butman appears to have been motivated by a desire to respond to the large-scale press conference staged by the Soviet authorities in March, 1970, to "prove" that Soviet Jews were totally committed to Soviet society and contemptuous of Israel and Zionism. With the thought of dispelling any illusions that the outside world might entertain in consequence of the official press conference, Butman probably conceived of another press conference by the would-be hijackers to show that the Jews at the official conference did not, by any stretch of the imagination, represent Soviet Jewry.

Within the Leningrad group, Butman's proposal met stiff resistance. Lev Korenblit, his closest collaborator, vigorously opposed the idea on the ground that such a press conference would not help the Jews desirous of leaving the USSR. Rather, he argued, it would draw world attention away from the emigration problem to the unlawful act of a plane seizure. He was no doubt correct. But the vital question was not how Korenblit felt about the proposal, but how Kuznetsov regarded it. The testimony of Kuznetsov suggests that the idea was not even taken seriously. When asked whether he intended "to arrange a press conference in Sweden," he answered: "For some reason, Butman mentioned this, but I thought this was not a serious thing and *there was no specific* talk about it." (Emphasis added.) His defense counsel, who was himself sharply critical of Kuznetsov's views, told the court that his client considered politics a "vanity," and that he was interested solely in "going to Israel." *Iskhod* quotes Kuznetsov as saying in his final statement:

> I had no intention of causing harm to the Soviet Union. I have always wanted to live in Israel. . . . I have never expressed the wish to speak at a press conference anywhere and never discussed the question with anyone. Without going into the reasons why I have no such intentions, I will only say that my ironical turn of mind would have prevented me from making any political speeches.

The second example to which the prosecution pointed as showing an alleged anti-Soviet political motive was a "testament" that had been prepared by Mendelevich and signed by the others. It was to have been left behind for publication if the hijacking failed. While the prosecutor described the "testament" as "a slanderous anti-Soviet document," there is no copy available from which to make an independent judgment. The defense attorney for Mendelevich insisted that, in essence, it contained nothing more than the statement that Mendelevich and all who signed it simply want to leave the USSR. Besides, according to the testimony of Kuznetsov, the "testament" was to be circulated only in the event of the death of the hijackers. Thus, only in the remotest of circumstances would it have seen the light of day. And, indeed, no one outside of the USSR has seen a copy. According to an informed source who had been told the essential contents of the "testament," it simply stated that the signers had acted out of desperation, with the hope of demonstrating to the world that the right of Jews to leave was being abridged.[3]

The prosecution, no doubt fully cognizant of its weakness in documenting concrete examples of anti-Soviet political intent from the very beginning of the case, made another issue, unrelated to the case, its central focus. Indeed, that issue became central to all the trials of Jews that were to follow. The issue was "international Zionism." If it could be demonstrated that "international Zionism" was by definition "anti-Soviet," and that the Riga defendants had become decisively influenced by and subordinated to "international Zionism," it could then be argued that the intent of the accused, or at least most of the accused, was clear: as Zionists, they planned to hijack the plane for self-evident political and anti-Soviet reasons. The flawed character of this circular reasoning did not make it any the less deadly.

The motivation factor was incorporated into the formal charges leveled against seven of the defendants—Dymshits, Kuznetsov, Mendelevich, Silva Zalmanson, Israil Zalmanson, Altman, and Khnokh. They were accused, under Article 70 of the Criminal Code, of "anti-Soviet agitation and propaganda . . . conducted with the aim of undermining or weakening Soviet authority. . . ." They were further accused, under Article 72 of the Criminal Code, of "participation in an anti-Soviet organization." "Anti-Soviet" activity here was to be interpreted as Zionist propaganda and organizational activity.

The principal speech of the prosecutor, in its opening section, was devoted largely to the "intrigues of international Zionism," and throughout the case he tenaciously pursued the subject of the defendants' Zionist views. Thus, for example, when Silva Zalmanson acknowledged from the very start she was a Zionist, the prosecutor asked her whether she "knew" that Zionism was "hostile" to Marxist-Leninist ideology. She replied that Zionism was not hostile to Soviet ideology as its main idea was the reunification of the Jews in a single state. The prosecutor inquired as to whether she understood that Zionism was hostile "to us." She answered in the negative.

The prosecutor's malice emerged distinctly during the questioning of Mendelevich. The latter was asked whether he was "a Zionist or a person of Jewish nationality." After Mendelevich answered simply, "I am a Jew," and went on to say that he sought only to find himself in his "homeland," Israel, the prosecutor declared: "The Russian people has allotted to you Birobidzhan and you can go there." The young Zionist would not permit himself to be badgered. He replied: ". . . permit me to decide for myself which state and not which 'province' is my homeland."

A vulgarity born of ignorance and prejudice entered into the prosecutor's exchange with Kuznetsov:

> Prosecutor: Explain the meaning of the word *Zionism*.
>
> Kuznetsov: I do not agree with Marxist-Leninist philosophy on its general definition of Zionism as "an agent of imperialism."
>
> Prosecutor: Do you not consider that Zionism generates anti-Semitism?
>
> Kuznetsov: Zionism has existed since the nineteenth century and anti-Semitism has always existed. Didn't you know that?

Kuznetsov then reached for a note in order to quote from *The Nuremberg Trial,* published in Moscow in 1970 under the editorship of the procurator-general, Roman Rudenko. The prosecutor, however, prevented him from reading it. It may very well have contained a statement which would have shown that the anti-Semitism of the Nazis could hardly be ascribed to Zionism.

In the hope of documenting the alleged link between Zionism and anti-Soviet propaganda and organization, the prosecutor turned to materials which were either read, reproduced, typed, or distributed by the defendants. Some of his efforts would have evoked hilarity or disbelief in courts elsewhere in the world. Illustrative was the questioning of a Riga militant, Arkady Shpilberg (he was to be placed on trial in May, 1971), who was called in to testify about the alleged anti-Soviet activity of Silva Zalmanson. Shpilberg made repeated attempts to explain to the prosecutor what was meant by the term *Zionism,* but in vain. The prosecution would not permit him to address himself to this question. When the prosecutor asked him to describe the contents of a suitcase full of literature which he and Silva Zalmanson brought to Leningrad, Shpilberg insisted that the materials were neither slanderous nor anti-Soviet. He then proceeded to describe them: (1) a collection of verse by Jewish poets, including Bialik and S. Frug; (2) some books of Bialik's poetry; (3) the novel *Exodus*, by Leon Uris; (4) a Hebrew textbook. The prosecutor significantly halted the further enumeration of these innocent titles. Perhaps he thought it would be difficult to use such books to document anti-Soviet subversion.

Reference was also made to two leaflets, "Nekhama Has Returned" and "Your Mother Tongue," which some of the Rigaites were involved in preparing and reproducing. The first, no doubt a discussion of Nekhama Lifshitz, the great Soviet Jewish folk-singer, who was finally allowed to emigrate to Israel in 1970, is unavailable for independent content analysis. The second appeared as a principal factor in the later Riga trial of May, 1971, and will be discussed in Chapter 13, which deals with that trial. Finally, much was made of two issues of *Iton*, a journal with whose production a few of the Rigaites were involved. Since this journal was the central element in the Riga trial, it too will be analyzed later. At this point, perhaps a broad generalization can be made about the character of *Iton*. It is drawn from comments made by Altman's defense attorney, as recorded in *Iskhod*. After saying that his client's involvement with *Iton* did not show anti-Soviet motives, he went on: ". . . although the paper did pursue Zionist aims we must remember that at all times and in all currents there were people who did not necessarily accept all the commitment and all the postulates of that current but only a part. Altman took only one postulate from Zionism—*return.*"

The most perceptive comment on these published materials was made by Khnokh's attorney. *Iskhod* quotes him as saying: "It is absurd to think that the Soviet state system can be weakened by the dissemination of documents like 'Nekhama Has Returned' or 'Our Native Tongue,' let alone by their possession."

But the prosecution, desperately in need of a motivation for the defendants, continued to allege violations of Articles 70 and 72. A witness who was a member of the Leningrad Zionist group with which Dymshits was linked was asked: "Are you a member of an anti-Soviet organization?" To which he replied: "I am a member of an educational organization whose aim is the study of the Jewish people's language, history, and culture." A hostile witness in the case of Khnokh was asked about the latter. When the witness, a relative of Khnokh, accused him of harboring anti-Soviet views, Khnokh said to him: ". . . Tell me if we discussed the Soviet Union or if we only talked about Israel." The witness's response was fascinating: "Although only Israel was discussed, I understood straightaway that you were an anti-Soviet person."

The court's verdict was predictable. Seven of the defendants—Dymshits, Kuznetsov, Mendelevich, Silva Zalmanson, Israil Zalmanson, Altman, and Khnokh—were found guilty under Articles 64, 70, and 72; the others, except Bodnia, were found guilty under Article 64. (Due to Bodnia's "repentance" and his cooperation with the prosecution, he was found guilty of lesser offenses. Instead of Article 64, he was judged under Article 83, dealing with "illegal departure abroad," and Article 43, which requires a lighter punishment than that which ordinarily might be imposed.)

In addition, all were found guilty under Article 93(1): "Misappropriation of state or public property on an especially large scale." This charge was also subjected to important challenges by the defendants. In the first place, no actual stealing had occurred. As Silva Zalmanson's lawyer noted, "We have been speaking about the theft of a plane, but it is standing at the airport. We have been speaking about what might have been." Secondly, there was the important question of intent. Khnokh, in his testimony, emphasized that the defendants had no intention of keeping the plane: "What use would it have been to us?" Dymshits' attorney underscored the point: "In essence, my disagreement with the indictment refers to Article 93(1). The objective aspect of this article is theft. Yet the defendants *did not even have the intention of stealing.* From the moment of their arrest on June 15 up to this day the accused have always given the same answer to this question: the aircraft was of no use to them and they knew that it would be returned." (Emphasis added.) The defense attorney called attention to the Tokyo Convention on air piracy, which has been in force since December 4, 1969, and which obligates contracting parties to return hijacked aircraft.

The court proceedings revealed that the charge under Article 93(1) was, curiously, not introduced until October 14, 1970, four months after the arrests were made. This suggests that the state was determined to "throw the book" at the defendants, using every conceivable means at its disposal. The judgment of the court on December 24, 1970, reflects this supposition. Dymshits and Kuznetsov were condemned to death. Mendelevich received a fifteen-year "strict regime" sentence, Fedorov a fifteen-year "especially strict regime" sentence, Murzhenko a fourteen-year "especially strict regime" sentence, Altman a twelve-year "strict regime" sentence, Silva Zalmanson and Penson ten-year "strict regime" sentences,

Israil Zalmanson an eight-year "strict regime" sentence, and Bodnia a four-year "intensified regime" sentence.[4]

A horror-struck world, already stunned by information from the courtroom that was made available to Western correspondents during the trial, reacted with outrage to the ferocious sentences. No hijacking, after all, had actually taken place. Why, then, the death sentences? Why the harsh prison sentences? From virtually every sector of Western society, not excluding fellow-travelers and Communists, protests poured into the Kremlin. The response of the Italian Communist Party newspaper, *L'Unità*, on December 27 was typical of left-wing reaction. Under a headline which read "An Incomprehensible Judgment," the editors wrote: "There are many things which are difficult to understand in the proceedings and conclusions of the Leningrad trial against a group of Soviet citizens who had the intention—not accomplished—of diverting a plane. . . ." In addition to criticizing the Soviet authorities for holding the trial virtually *in camera,* thereby putting into question "principles of personal guarantee for every prisoner," *L'Unità* denounced the imposition of the death penalty.

To deal with both the escalating foreign criticism during the trial and the furor raised by the verdict, the Soviet mass media practiced a monumental deception. While directed mainly at the non-Soviet public, the deception was also geared to the Soviet populace. The official line comprised three crucial elements: (1) the trial was not directed against Jews; (2) the issue in the trial was exclusively a question of hijacking; and (3) the plans for the hijacking, to a decisive extent, involved the use of violence.

From the very opening of the trial, the Soviet regime was concerned that the transparent anti-Jewish character of the trial would be, and indeed, was being, exposed. Every conceivable precaution was taken to prevent access to information or to the court by Western correspondents or observers. On the very day when the courtroom proceedings were launched, the deputy public prosecutor of Leningrad refused to acknowledge to a correspondent of the *Jewish Chronicle* (London) that he knew about a trial involving Jews taking place.[5] All information was to be managed through the government news agency Tass, and through the official press.

Leningradskaia pravda on December 16 carried the first press item on the case. As if to disguise the character of the trial, it placed three non-Jewish names—Kuznetsov, Fedorov, and Murzhenko—first among the defendants it listed. A Moscow radio broadcast in Hebrew on the same day said that only "some Jews" were on trial. Kuznetsov, of course, considered himself Jewish, but the prosecutor was determined to have him identified as a Russian (in accordance with the listing in his passport). In the same way, he was anxious—in response to a concerned world opinion—to deny the anti-Jewish motivation on the trial. On December 21, he angrily told the court (according to *Khronika*): "Some say that this trial is against Jews, but that is untrue. The trial is not about Jews. This is a criminal trial in which the majority of the criminals are Jews. But Kuznetsov I do not consider a Jew. I consider that Kuznetsov is a Russian."[6]

On December 23, Tass carried the first lengthy commentary on the trial. In it, Tass responded to world concern by declaring that "Zionist circles abroad are whipping up anti-Soviet propaganda" on the "pretext" that the defendants include "a number of persons of Jewish origin." To counter this "propaganda," Tass observed that the Leningrad city prosecutor had chosen not to press charges against "several citizens of this Jewish nationality" who were involved in the hijacking plot. As examples, it listed Dymshits' wife and two daughters, none of whom, however, were or considered themselves to be Jewish. The only Jew against whom charges were not pressed was Khnokh's wife, and the reason—as Tass admitted —was that fact that "she is an expectant mother."

A Tass broadcast by Radio Moscow on December 26 returned to the same theme. It declared that only "several Jews" were involved in the court proceedings. Their presence in the courtroom, Tass announced, had become a "pretext" for "Zionist circles in the United States . . . to whip up an anti-Soviet hysteria." Two days later, a lengthy Tass dispatch written by Yury Kornilov insisted that just "some of the criminals were persons of Jewish nationality." Kornilov added: "The slanderers are trying to give credulous readers the impression that the Soviet court judged the criminals not for the crime they committed, but for their nationality." Again, Zionist propaganda was found to be the inspiration for the "slander" in the foreign press.

In a round-up of the case, *Novaia vremia* on January 8, 1971, reiterated the familiar argument. The accusation that "the Soviet court had indicted the defendants not for their crimes but for their nationality" was simply a concoction of the Zionist press. The author of the article was Yevgeny Yevseev, one of the USSR's leading "specialists" on Jews and Zionism. He said that he himself had attended the proceedings, hardly an indication that the trial had nothing to do with the Jewish nationality question in the USSR.

The treatment of the trial itself by Tass and the Soviet press was deliberately simplified to focus attention upon the attempted hijacking. In the December 16, 1970, issue of *Leningradskaia pravda*, it was noted that the accused had long plotted to hijack the plane in order to escape abroad. The Kornilov article for Tass on December 28 restated the "facts" of the case thus: ". . . several traitors to the country formed a criminal group and made preparations to seize an aircraft and fly it abroad. . . ." On December 31, *Izvestiia* summarized the basic point: "Certain circles in the West are trying to depict this crime as an innocent attempt by eleven persons to leave this country, but this has nothing in common with the facts. It is a far cry from wanting to move to another country to forming an armed gang and carefully planning an attack on people with arms."

Not even the ultimate destination of the Jews among the accused —Israel—was mentioned. No indication was given of the motivation of the defendants, as seen from their own viewpoint. Perhaps it was too dangerous or too embarrassing to reveal to the Soviet public and the world at large that there existed Soviet citizens who desired to leave the Socialist Utopia. Even more significant was the failure to specify in the press something that, in fact, had been essential to the indictment and that the prosecution had gone to great lengths to develop—the intent of the defendants as comprehended by the prosecution. Entirely deleted was the "evidence" of the "testament," books, leaflets, and newspapers, which were supposed to show the anti-Soviet and political intent of the accused. Indeed, there was almost no indication in the Soviet press that the principal figures in the trial had been indicted and convicted under Articles 70 and 72. Did the Soviet authorities fear that public elaboration of the "evidence" of intent would evoke either wry amusement or rollicking guffaws everywhere, including places where their foreign support was strongest?

Having launched a public relations campaign that made the attempted hijacking the focal point, the Soviet authorities felt compelled to embellish the press treatment by stressing alleged plans of violence which the defendants were accused of harboring. The Tass dispatch of December 23 listed the "weapons" carried by the "criminals"—a revolver, ammunition, axes, knives, brass knuckles, rubber truncheons, a laundry cord, nooses, and gags. The defendants were said to have had "specially drawn-up instructions" showing the angle from which to shoot at the pilot's back. But then, in the Tass outline of the expected procedure of the hijacking, nothing was mentioned of shooting; instead, the Soviet pilots were to have been knocked out with brass knuckles, bound and gagged, and left at Priozersk.

Izvestiia, on December 31, did little to clarify this discrepancy. While alleging that the plan had been for Kuznetsov to deal with the first pilot using "his brass knuckles," and Bodnia with the second pilot, *Izvestiia* nonetheless contended that a spot had been chosen from which the defendants were to shoot the pilot in the back. Emphasis was given to the presence of a revolver among the items confiscated by the authorities from Fedorov. But, as the proceedings and notes of the trial in *Iskhod* made clear, the pistol was not in working order, and the defendants had been perfectly aware of the fact. Fedorov had told Dymshits (to whom the gun belonged) that he conceived of using the pistol only as a means of scaring the pilots in the event that they had to fly with them to Sweden. Kuznetsov was quoted as telling Bodnia that "they must try and avoid violence, the pilots must come out of this without a scratch." Khnokh emphasized in the courtroom: "We are not bandits. None of us has ever had any intention to kill or assault and injure anybody." Kuznetsov's attorney, in keeping with the demonstrated fact that no shooting had been or could have been contemplated, called upon the court to "exclude from the accusations any plan to threaten the life of the pilots."

The position of the authorities in asking for the maximum penalties, including death, however, required that violence and contemplated murder be stressed in the mass media, even if it meant a gross distortion of the facts. In keeping with the distortion, the defendants, from the very beginning of the trial, were presented (in *Leningradskaia pravda* on December 16, for example) as incorrigible "criminals" and "idlers." The previous incarceration of Kuznetsov, Murzhenko, and Federov for "anti-Soviet" political activities was emphasized, as was an earlier prison sentence imposed upon Penson, for rape. Mendelevich, Khnokh, and Bodnia were described as people who "refrained from doing an honest job," while Dymshits was characterized as "a man of exaggerated pride" who "lately" was unemployed.

In the end, the deception did not succeed. The shock felt in all foreign quarters manifested itself in mounting mass demonstrations in numerous cities, in the intervention of prominent international figures and Western Communist parties, and in appeals by various governments. When, by a coincidental set of circumstances, the Fascist ruler of Spain, General Francisco Franco, commuted on December 30 the death sentences that had been imposed upon Basque nationalists, the Soviet regime found itself in a profoundly embarrassing and even indefensible position. Its press had violently denounced the trial of the Basque nationalists, and its leading cultural figures had issued public statements calling for the ostracism of the Franco regime from civilized society. To have let stand the death penalty in the Leningrad trial would have run the risk of making the USSR, not Spain, the moral outcast from the world community.

On December 29, 1970, one day before Franco's act of commutation, Soviet authorities, no doubt in response to the world outcry, hastily arranged for an appeal of the Leningrad verdict. The Collegium for Criminal Cases of the Supreme Court of the Russian Republic was assembled in Moscow to hear the appeal. So short an interval from the verdict to the appeal—only five days—was unprecedented in Soviet legal practice. Indeed, according to legal sources cited in *Khronika*, the earliest an appeal could technically be heard under Soviet law would be January 5, 1971.[7] The Moscow prosecutor himself on December 30 asked for mitigation of the sentences of Dymshits and Kuznetsov on the grounds—as *Izvestiia* later reported—that "their criminal activity was cut short in the stage when they were attempting to commit the crime, and capital punishment under the Soviet Criminal Code was an exceptionable measure." On December 31, at 11:00 A.M. the Supreme Court of the Russian Republic bowed to world opinion. The death sentences were commuted to fifteen years—Kuznetsov was to serve in a "special regime" camp under especially severe work and discipline conditions, while Dymshits was to serve in a "strict regime" camp.

The sentence of Mendelevich was reduced from fifteen years to twelve, of Altman from twelve to ten, and of Khnokh from thirteen to ten.

But the government's commitment to the intimidation of the Jewish national movement was not to be halted or modified. *Izvestiia*'s article on January 1, 1971, announcing the appeal court's reprieve, made that clear when it once again emphasized that "international Zionism" is "the source of anti-Sovietism."

Chapter 12
The "Ominous Chain of Rigged Trials": Leningrad II and Kishinev

The belief that the Jewish national movement would be intimidated by the trial in December proved to be as monumental a form of self-deception as the deception the Kremlin rulers attempted to perpetrate upon world public opinion. Open telegrams and letters written immediately after the verdict was announced testify to the refusal of the leaders of the movement to acquiesce in the intimidation process.[1]

On December 26, two days after the trial ended, seventeen Moscow Jews prominent in the national movement wired President Podgorny: "Shaken by anti-humanism of Leningrad Tribunal. Demand immediate quashing and granting right free departure to all Jews wishing to go to Israel." The same day, a leader of the Jewish national movement in Moscow, Meir Gelfond, a forty-year-old doctor, sent an open letter to Amnesty International which declared that "the real reason" for the trial was "the wish to terrorize tens of thousands of Jews who are longing to leave for Israel." Dr. Gelfond noted that the convicted had been for years exercising their "elementary right" to seek permission to leave the USSR. Only when they had "lost hope" of their rights being fulfilled did they take the "desperate step" of planning a hijacking. The trial, he stated, was but a "pretext" for crushing the national spirit. He recalled previous trials of the Black Years that had the same objective. Then, too, "cosmopolitans without a homeland," "agents of world Zionism," and "doctor saboteurs" had been arrested.

The implication was obvious: the movement would not be broken. It was made explicit the next day, on December 27, when fifty-nine Moscow Jews wrote to the UN Commission on Human Rights. After charging that "the judges' bloodlust is revolting" in that they imposed the death penalty upon Jews who *"did not kill anybody* and who *did not cause harm to anybody,"* they threw down the gauntlet to the authorities:

> We, the undersigned, have the same ardent desire to go to our home-land, Israel. We declare that *we will not be stopped or intimidated* even if our brothers' blood is shed.
> *We are ready to lay down our lives* for our rights to live in our own country. [Emphasis added.]

The resistance was not restricted to Moscow. On December 28, ten Jewish activist leaders from Minsk, the capital of Byelorussia, dispatched a letter to the procurator-general of the USSR charac-terizing the "cause and essence" of the trial as *"anti-Semitism."* The Minsk signers, like the Muscovites, declared that "the purpose of the Leningrad trial is to deter Jews wishing to go to Israel to be reunited with their near ones, with their people." They saw the trial as but the "first link in an ominous chain of rigged trials" which could be compared to earlier "judicial reprisals against Jews" —the Dreyfus case, the Beiliss case, the Mikhoels case, and the Doctors' Plot.

Earlier, in the fall, three Jewish leaders from Riga, anticipating the outcome of the trial, reached the same decision to resist. In a letter addressed to both the Central Committee of the Party and its General Secretary, Leonid Brezhnev, they recalled the arrests, searches, and interrogations of the summer of 1970 and then con-tended that "this cannot be understood otherwise than as a desire to exert pressure on the Jewish masses who want repatriation to Israel, to make them give up their intentions."[2] But, the letter went on: ". . . no repressions, no intimidation and no blackmail can force the Jews to give up the path chosen by them."

For a moment, the Kremlin seemed to have entertained second

thoughts about proceeding with further trials. Would they serve the purpose for which they were intended? some in the Soviet leadership may have asked. Moreover, account had to be taken of the massive criticism throughout the Western world that had greeted the first trial. Significantly, the head of the Leningrad Party organization, Vasily Tolstikov, was removed from his post in September, 1970, and sent to China as ambassador. It was a clear demotion by the Party leadership. A second trial of nine Leningraders, most of whom had been rounded up on June 15, was scheduled for January 6, 1971. But, on that day, after only an hour of court hearings, the trial was suddenly adjourned. (The grounds for the adjournment were not made public; instead, the authorities leaked "information" that one of the defendants, Lev Yagman, was suffering from a "cold.") The Moscow correspondent of the Italian Communist Party newspaper, *L'Unità*, reported that further "Jewish trials" would not be held, and the French Communist Party organ, *L'Humanité,* quoted "well-informed sources" as saying that additional scheduled trials against Jews had been canceled.[3]

In the end, those in the Soviet leadership who insisted upon the trials had their way. The halting of the trials would have provoked a crisis of credibility and a serious loss of face. Besides, there was the unfinished task of destroying the Jewish national movement. On May 11, five months after its initial scheduling, the second Leningrad trial was started. The advocates of additional trials must have accepted the compromise that they would take place only after the Twenty-fourth Soviet Party Congress had ended early in April. Thus, acute embarrassment could be avoided, especially in view of the fact that observers from numerous Western parties would be present at the Congress. The hard-liners must have also accepted a second compromise: a limited number of the activist Jewish elements would be allowed to leave in the interval. And, finally, it was recognized that the application of the death penalty would have to be avoided lest it spur the same kind of world outcry that distinguished the first trial.

For those pursuing the objective of liquidating Jewish militancy once and for all, the second Leningrad trial was as critical, and perhaps even more so, than the first. Indeed, it had been central to the planning of the massive arrests and searches of June 15. The reason is not too difficult to fathom. The Leningrad group constituted the only *organized* sector in what essentially was an amorphous and spontaneous national Jewish movement. Launched as early as the winter of 1966, the Leningrad Zionist organization actually functioned under a charter of its own.[4] It elaborated a full-fledged program which included the operation of several *ulpans* where Hebrew and Jewish history were taught, and the distribution of Jewish literature. The group's public activity, to be sure, was carefully conducted within the confines of Soviet legal norms. It was undoubtedly for this reason that no arrests occurred during the four-year period 1966–70. That the organization was, however, under extensive police surveillance is certain.

The attempted hijacking offered a unique opportunity to strike at the one organized group which may well have seemed to the authorities to be the central nervous system of the Jewish national movement as a whole. Remove the nervous system, they probably reasoned, and the movement will wither and die. The Leningrad group, after all, had close contacts with Jewish activists everywhere. Moreover, it was deeply versed in Jewish matters, with some of its members speaking fluent Hebrew. Almost all of them had made repeated applications for exit visas to Israel.

Of significance, too, was their proficiency in using legal measures to dramatize the Jewish problem in the USSR. Thus, one of them, Vladimir Mogilever, in order to show that facilities for the study of the Jewish language and culture are unavailable in the USSR, made formal inquiry of the authorities in Birobidzhan and of the Soviet minister of culture, Yekaterina Furtseva. Birobidzhan replied that no Jewish school existed. The letter to Furtseva was responded to by the head of the Culture Department of the Leningrad City Soviet, who said that "to open a Jewish school in Leningrad was inappropriate."[5] The replies enabled Mogilever's colleague, Lassal Kaminsky, to write to *Pravda*: "Where, may I ask, can a Jew in the USSR teach his children their mother tongue? Where can his children learn the long-suffering history of their people?"[6]

A particular irritant to the regime were the numerous petitions demanding exit visas drafted by the Leningrad group and sent to Soviet authorities and to the United Nations. It was precisely the petition signed by thirty-seven Leningraders on June 13–14, 1970, and scheduled for delivery to U Thant, then visiting the USSR, that may have helped prompt the Soviet authorities to crack down the following day on the entire Jewish national movement.[7]

One further consideration is likely to have made the Leningrad group especially important in the eyes of the Kremlin. Unlike the defendants in the first trial, the Leningrad group was composed of highly educated and highly skilled men in the sciences. If a "brain drain" of Jewish scientists was the dominant factor in the reluctance of the Soviet authorities to grant exit visas, then what more effective means to intimidate and frighten that segment of the Jewish intellectual elite, potentially susceptible to nationalist sympathies, than by making an example—a harsh example—of the Leningrad group?

Sketches of the professional backgrounds of the nine placed on trial illuminate the above point. Thirty-nine-year-old Hillel Butman was a graduate of both the Leningrad Law Institute and the Leningrad Northwestern Polytechnic Institute. When arrested, he was working as an engineer at an electrical-welding equipment plant. Lev Korenblit, forty-nine, graduated with distinction from the University of Chernovtsy and then went on to win a doctorate in mathematical physics. He was a senior scientific worker at the Institute of Semi-Conductors in Leningrad. Thirty-four-year-old Mikhail Korenblit, a younger brother of Lev, was an oral surgeon. Vladimir Mogilever, thirty years old, had won a silver medal upon graduation from school and went on to take courses at an electrical-technical institute and the University of Leningrad. A mathematician and engineer, he was senior worker at the Geological Research Institute. Thirty-eight-year-old Solomon Dreizner was a graduate of an engineering-construction institute who had become a chief engineer at the Leningrad Housing Design Center. Lassal Kaminsky, forty years old, was an engineer at a design institute. Lev Yagman, thirty, was a silver medal winner who was a graduate of the Leningrad Shipbuilding Institute. He was employed as an engineer-designer at the "Russian Diesel" Works. Thirty-year-old Viktor Boguslavsky graduated from the Leningrad Engineering-Building Institute. A building engineer with training in architecture, he worked as head of a group in the Leningrad Transport Design. Viktor Shtilbans, thirty, was a physician.

If because of internal political considerations it was considered vital to place the Leningraders on trial, it was also essential that the real aims of the trial be hidden from the world press lest the already marred image of the USSR be damaged beyond repair. Thus, what Tass and Novosti reported about the proceedings from May 11 to May 20 was significantly different *in emphasis* from what actually took place in the courtroom (as recorded in a *samizdat* document). The distortion was facilitated by the exclusion, once again, of all Western correspondents and observers.

Official Soviet reportage stressed the attempted hijacking theme. It was the only theme that could conceivably evoke a sympathetic response from public opinion abroad. On the opening day of the trial, Tass avoided specifying the charges against the nine defendants. Instead, it stated that Butman and Mikhail Korenblit, "together with other persons on trial, were actively involved in preparing the seizure of a passenger plane, in order to flee abroad." Novosti, the same day, said that Butman and Korenblit were charged under Article 64 (the treason clause) of the Criminal Code for "having taken direct part in the scheming and financing of the hijacking attempt of an AN-2 aircraft at Leningrad airport on June 15, 1970."

The Soviet public was treated, though briefly, to the same theme. On May 12, *Izvestiia* reprinted on the last page a dispatch that had appeared earlier the same day in *Leningradskaia pravda* saying that the Leningrad defendants were connected with the hijacking plot.

Over and over again, throughout the nine-day trial, the already worn and shabby record would be replayed in official governmental dispatches. The deception was, if anything, greater than that attempted in the first Leningrad trial. The fact was—as the *Iskhod* record of the earlier trial had indicated—the Leningrad group, after April 10, had striven to halt Dymshits from carrying out his plan. Indeed, the long testimony at the second Leningrad trial of Dymshits, and the shorter testimony of Kuznetsov and Silva Zalmanson—all given on May 14—underscored the evidence that the former pilot and his Riga associates did everything possible to shield their planning from the Leningrad group and to fool the latter into thinking that no hijacking would be attempted. A *samizdat* document covering the proceedings of the second Leningrad trial provides the essentials of their testimony.[8] Tass and Novosti instead extracted material from testimony about discussions that took place prior to April 10 and consciously juxtaposed this material with the June 15 incident. The result was a fabrication as gross as one might find in the annals of judicial processes.

The actual charges brought against the Leningrad nine further highlight the crudity of the deception. Only Butman and Mikhail Korenblit were charged under Article 64. If others were involved in "preparing the seizure of a passenger plane in order to flee abroad"—as Tass claimed—why were they not charged under the same treason clause? In its concluding report of the trial on May 20, Tass overlooked the question. All but Boguslavsky, it said, were implicated in the hijacking plan in "one way or other."

The particular charges against Butman and Mikhail Korenblit spring in part from a fact mentioned in Dymshits' testimony. According to Tass, the judge asked him whether Butman and Korenblit knew that, after the initial hijacking plans had been discarded, a new hijacking plan had been projected. Tass reported that Dymshits had answered: "Yes, they did." The *samizdat* summary of Dymshits' testimony indicates that he related the following: "M. Korenblit saw me at the beginning of June and asked that if we do anything to inform him beforehand by a pre-arranged sentence over the phone so that they should have time to make ready for possible searches. At about 6 A.M. on June 15, I phoned Korenblit, could not get him on the phone and phoned to Butman's wife and asked her to transmit the pre-arranged sentence to Korenblit." While the statement showed that Korenblit continued to be intensely suspicious of Dymshits' plans, it hardly suggests that he and Butman were certain more than two hours prior to the attempted hijacking that it would occur. Most of Dymshits' testimony, in fact, was devoted to cataloguing the efforts of Butman to "dissuade" him from the hijacking. According to the *samizdat* account, Dymshits was asked in the court "as to what other pressures Butman could have exerted," and he answered, "None."

Butman apparently lived in a fool's paradise. He must have been certain, after bitter quarrels with Dymshits, that he had convinced the latter (by May 26) to desist from his plan. Immediately thereafter, he went on vacation with his daughter outside of Leningrad and remained there until his arrest on June 15. Would he have gone on vacation if he had had an inkling of what would happen? A further question arises: if Mikhail Korenblit suspected that a police action would occur on June 15, why wasn't he at home to receive the pre-arranged call from Dymshits? The most that could legitimately be claimed by the prosecution was that within an hour or two of the attempted hijacking, Butman and Korenblit learned of the plans.

The Novosti round-up story of May 17 gave the question of Butman's and Korenblit's involvement an entirely different twist. And, for good measure, it distorted the role of the others in the Leningrad group: "Having inspired Dymshits and Kuznetsov to to hijack a plane, Butman and [the] others did not desist from similar steps later on. . . . They knew of all steps made by Dymshits. Before boarding the plane they planned to hijack, Dymshits notified M. Korenblit by phone about the beginning of the operation by a coded message. Sending Dymshits to commit a crime, Butman and his accomplices were already planning to exploit his experience."

The distortion was compounded by a crude and misleading effort to introduce the State of Israel as a factor in the hijacking scheme. It was the first time that Israel's alleged role had been mentioned. The press coverage of the first trial avoided reference to that country. Now, with the egregious need to underline the allegedly treasonous character of the Leningrad groups, Tass on May 11 baldly charged that the Leningraders "used their contacts with foreign tourists for communication with Israeli authorities so as to *coordinate with them the criminal actions.*" (Emphasis added.) The following day, Tass went further. It declared that Mogilever had informed Israel about "the criminal plot" and made "requests for instructions."

The principal Novosti story of May 17 detailed the following: "It was revealed at the court that Zionist quarters in Israel were well informed about this [Leningrad] group and not only subsidized it but also directed its activities. The group informed the Israeli special service of its subversive activities and received from the latter instructions and recommendations." The Novosti account reported a phone call received by Butman from his contact in Tel Aviv, one Osher Blank, which provided Butman with "recommendations given by the Israeli intelligence." While describing the telephone discussion in some detail, Novosti significantly failed to indicate precisely what Israel recommended. Novosti simply concluded that "the trial in Leningrad is revealing new irrefutable facts on the participation of . . . Israeli special services in inspiring and subsidizing the criminal activities of the defendants and in giving guidance to the latter."

The reason that the Novosti story was less than complete in its report of Israel's "recommendations" is apparent from the *samizdat* record of the trial proceedings. Dymshits related that inquiry had been made as to the Israeli Government's attitude on the proposed hijacking, and that the Israelis gave a "negative answer." *Leningradskaia pravda* on May 18, in its summary of the trial, felt compelled to acknowledge the fact that, although the defendants might have consulted Israel about the hijacking idea, Israel did not support it. But neither Tass nor Novosti retreated from the fanciful accusations it was propagating to the world press.

The linkage of the Leningrad group with Israel intelligence through "tourists" raised further questions. Novosti on May 17 carried an extensive description of the activities of one of these "tourists"—Donald Melament. He was described as a "Zionist" and a United States citizen "who received the necessary training in Israel." It was claimed that Melament was a Yale University postgraduate student who had taken a special course in "subversive sciences" and was advised that he would receive one thousand dollars for every Soviet scientist whom he succeeds "in persuading to go to the United States." He came to Leningrad State University, where he pursued advanced work in the chemistry faculty.

Besides supposedly making efforts—unsuccessfully—to recruit Soviet scientists, according to Novosti, Melament was alleged to have established contact with Mogilever. The latter saw the American as a potential "liaison man" between Israeli intelligence and the Leningrad group. Melament was alleged to have agreed to the assignment and "was prepared to do everything to facilitate the carrying out of the criminal plans of Mogilever and others." Upon leaving the USSR, Melament—according to Novosti—received from Mogilever a "large envelope" addressed to "Sasha"—the alleged alias of Osher Blank. It was supposed to contain "slanderous" letters, appeals, and other "documents" on the position of the Jews in the USSR. Also included was "a report on the activities of the conspirators and the actions they were planning."

The portrait of Melament as sketched by Novosti (presumably based upon Mogilever's testimony at the trial) no doubt struck an amused response among those who might fancy spy thrillers. Here was a "greedy" agent working for the United States, and, at the same time, acting as a contact man between "subversive" Soviet

Jews and Israeli intelligence. A more disciplined imagination would have been required to make the "contact man" theory plausible. Melament, until recently living in Cambridge, Massachusetts, in a letter to the *New York Times* provided a few details that devastated the portrait and, together with it, the Novosti report.[9] He had not been in Israel since 1964. How could he then have transmitted the envelope to "Sasha"? Moreover, the only request that Mogilever had made of him was to send "intermediate-level Hebrew texts" by "open mail" so that Mogilever's "meager library of Hebrew books" might be augmented. Melament's letter ended with the observation that "the false charges made by the prosecution concerning me and the closed door nature of the trial indicate that the case against the Leningrad Nine may be very flimsy."

In addition to the hijacking accusation, Tass and Novosti gave emphasis to another crime with which seven of the defendants were charged. All but Boguslavsky and Shtilbans were accused of having engaged in the theft and hiding of state property and, therefore, were subject to penalties under Article 189 of the Criminal Code covering such crimes. (Later, during the trial, the prosecution dropped that charge from the indictments against Mikhail Korenblit, Kaminsky, and Yagman on the ground that they knew nothing about the stolen property.) The specific item said to have been stolen was a duplicating machine which was the property of a government office in Kishinev, Moldavia. The reason for the theft, according to Tass, was that the Leningrad group wanted "to print and distribute slanderous materials against the Soviet Union."

However, according to the *samizdat* account, Dreizner testified that the stolen machine was never actually used.[10] Furthermore, he said, the group had contemplated its use only for the purpose of reproducing Hebrew textbooks. Other defendants were said to have given similar testimony (according to a *New York Times* dispatch from Moscow that cited "Jewish sources"). The Tass report is especially puzzling since the Leningrad Nine were also charged with publishing and distributing "slanderous materials." If they could do it without a duplicating machine, why run the risk of stealing the machine? The episode, which was considerably enlarged upon in the later Kishinev case, is unclear. If it indicates a blunder, having criminal implications, on the part of some in the Leningrad group, the intention could not have been what Tass reported it to be. In any case, the seriousness of the charge is open to question in view of the fact that the stolen property was never used. But, given the intention of Soviet officialdom to generate in the outside world a hostile attitude toward the defendants, it is hardly surprising that emphasis would be placed on such criminal charges as hijacking and stealing.

Far less stress was placed by Soviet press agencies upon the two key charges against all the defendants: anti-Soviet propaganda (Article 70) and anti-Soviet organization (Article 72). Novosti referred vaguely to the "printing and distributing [of] anti-Soviet documents and publishing an illegal anti-Soviet newspaper." It also emphasized that the "underground" group had "issued false 'letters' and 'appeals' on behalf of Soviet Jews and distributed them among various organizations abroad." But the Soviet organ failed to identify or define the contents of the "slanderous" documents and the newspaper. Nor did it indicate in what way the "letters" and "appeals"—which the Leningrad group are known to have signed—were false. Did Soviet officialdom fear that an identification and summarization of these materials would reveal to the world that they were in no way "slanderous," "false," and "anti-Soviet"? Certainly, the Kremlin appeared unprepared to run the risk of weakening the image it was attempting to create—hardened "criminals" planning a hijacking and engaging in theft—by a forthright elaboration of the critical charges on anti-Soviet propaganda and organization.

A principal thrust in the courtroom, in sharp contrast (according to the *samizdat* account) dealt precisely with alleged violations of Articles 70 and 72. Not that the attempted hijacking issue was excluded. Considerable attention was given it. But the question of propaganda and organization assumed at least equal, if not greater, importance. Thus, the "charge sheet,"* as quoted in the *samizdat* document, read:

---

* Early in 1973 the author came into possession of the first part of the "charge sheet" copied from the original indictment. Comparison with the *samizdat* account of the "charge sheet" indicates that the latter is accurate. There does appear, however, a striking additional point in the original indictment: "Existing facts irrefutably prove the direct involvement of the Zionist centers with the events in Hungary in 1956 and with the activation of the counter-revolutionary forces in Poland and Czechoslovakia in 1968." This absurd allegation corresponds with the accusations made by Soviet propaganda agencies as examined in Chapter 8 of this study.

> International Zionism is conducting subversive activity against the socialist countries . . . they distribute slanderous articles. . . . This has helped the creation of a Zionist anti-Soviet organization in Leningrad.
>
> It has been established by the investigation that persons who entered the organization, maintained ties with the Zionist circles of Israel, actively engaged in hostile activity, slandered Soviet domestic and foreign policy and developed emigratory feelings, persuading persons of Jewish nationality to emigrate to Israel, using for this anti-Soviet Zionist literature, including that published in the capitalist countries.

Five specific items of "Zionist anti-Soviet literature" which the Leningrad group distributed were then listed in the *samizdat* account: (1) the Leon Uris novel *Exodus;* (2) a *feuilleton* by the Israeli left-wing journalist Amos Kenan; (3) the two issues of *Iton*; (4) a brochure "For the Return of Jews to Their Homeland"; and (5) a collection of "slanderous letters" in *Iskhod.* How Uris' popular novel about the formation of Israel can be considered "anti-Soviet" defies rational analysis. Nor can the next two items be reasonably considered anti-Soviet. (A content analysis of these items appears in Chapter 13, since they figured prominently in the Riga trial. The brochure, unknown in the West, is also dealt with in the context of the Riga trial.)

As for the letters which have appeared in *Iskhod,* most of them—notably—avoid general political criticism of Soviet policy. Instead, they draw attention to the fact that Jewish cultural opportunities and institutions are non-existent in the USSR, and, therefore, the signers seek visas to go to Israel, where they might live a full Jewish life. The letters are basically apolitical in the sense that Soviet institutional, economic, and political structures are not discussed. Only one objective is expressed, and that repeatedly—that the signers be permitted to be reunited with their families in Israel. Besides, it is by no means clear whether the letters contributed to undermining and weakening the Soviet state. Proof that they would do so is essential to demonstrating the validity of the charge under Article 70.

Assuming, moreover, that the USSR somehow regarded the letters as "slanderous," why was the Leningrad group held responsible for those that did appear? Did the act of distribution itself transform innocence into guilt? The signers, in the last analysis, are responsible for what they signed. Yet, only a handful of the signers were arrested, and many, during the course of 1970–71, have been permitted to leave the country. These questions go to the very heart of the Kremlin's motivations. It may be assumed that the authorities believed that, without an organizational base, the Jewish national movement as expressed in letters and petitions for exit visas might disintegrate. A greater misconception could not have been entertained.

Throughout the questioning of the defendants the theme of the alleged anti-Soviet materials was hammered upon. On the second day of the trial, for example, Mogilever acknowledged that he had engaged in cultural and educational work for the Leningrad group and that he had taken part both in the preparation of collective letters to Soviet organs and in transmitting copies abroad. In preparing literature, he tried to prevent the intrusion of anything that smacked of an anti-Soviet tone. If, in individual cases, "anti-Soviet expressions" crept in, it was accidental.

Yagman, on the third day, admitted that he and his colleagues wrote collective letters, including the letter to U Thant, seeking permission to emigrate. But he did not consider the literature anti-Soviet. The Leningrad organization, he said, was not anti-Soviet; it had not pursued anti-Soviet aims, for it did not seek to undermine and weaken the Soviet state. Kaminsky said much the same thing. He did not consider the organization anti-Soviet. It was a Zionist organization whose aim had nothing to do with the USSR; it sought only the return of Jews to Israel. The literature which they prepared and distributed was not meant to undermine and weaken the Soviet system. Anti-Soviet references may have appeared in the material—for which he expressed regret—but they were incidental and did not reflect their basic content; the distributed material dealt fundamentally with the history and life of Israel.

There was a certain irony in charging the Leningrad group with the "slander" and "anti-Sovietism" that allegedly appeared in *Iton*. As will be made clear later, it was precisely the Leningrad group, and particularly Lev Korenblit and Boguslavsky, who were critical of certain articles that had appeared in *Iton* as being too harsh with reference to the USSR. *Iton* was published in Riga (although much of its material was assembled by the two Leningraders) and one of those responsible for its publication, Boris Maftser, appearing as a witness in the second Leningrad trial, declared that the Leningraders had demanded that *Iton* should be carefully edited and contain nothing that reviled Soviet power. Boguslavsky told the court that he and Korenblit were sufficiently dissatisfied to consider halting its publication altogether. The irony did not seem to penetrate the prosecution.

One comment of Kaminsky was especially perceptive. He observed that the undermining and weakening of the Soviet system were well beyond the strength not only of the small Leningrad organization but of many "imperialist" states. The comment echoed a theme which had been developed by a defense attorney in the first Leningrad trial. But it fell on deaf ears. The authorities had their own definition of "anti-Sovietism," and what their definition encompassed was staggering.

The testimony of Lev Korenblit, as recorded in the *samizdat* account, was particularly revealing:

> I want to say something about anti-Soviet literature. As it transpired during the investigation, I had an absolutely false idea of the term "anti-Soviet." I thought that anti-Soviet literature could be considered literature that calls for the overthrow of the Soviet power and for the change of the Soviet regime. As has been dinned into me in the time that has passed since my arrest, "anti-Soviet" is any suggestion that differs from the official Soviet line, anything that does not coincide with or is contrary to the letter of the Soviet newspaper article. In this sense, those articles that expressed sympathy for Israel and support for its struggle for existence are really "anti-Soviet," even though the Soviet Union might not even be mentioned in them. Therefore I admit that I am guilty in the distribution, preparation, and keeping of "anti-Soviet" literature, and I am prepared to bear punishment for this.

The "admission" of guilt was extraordinarily striking. It constituted a rare but incisive commentary upon the substance of the charges in the trials against the Jewish militants.

Korenblit's message was clearly designed for the Jewish national movement. The intimidation effort was obvious: any deviation from the Party line, even a mere expression of sympathy for Israel, was, on its face, anti-Soviet. But why did Korenblit decide to accept the definition that the authorities offered? Almost all involved in the first Leningrad trial had refused to accept the official definition of "anti-Sovietism." Most in the subsequent Riga trial would also refuse.

Korenblit's testimony unwittingly disclosed, at least in part, a powerful factor: the definition had been "dinned into him" from the time of his arrest. The arrest had taken place eleven months before the trial. (Incidentally, Soviet law requires that a maximum of nine months' incarceration is permitted before trial. Incarceration of eleven months would appear to be a violation of Soviet legality.) Under circumstances of almost total isolation, and faced with the constant bombardment—as implied in the words "dinned in"—by interrogators of official definitions and official "truths," Korenblit succumbed. It may be that one of the reasons for the delay from January to May in opening the trial was to permit the persuasive powers of the prosecution to leave a strong impact. None of the defendants displayed the vigorous resistance shown by the accused in the first Leningrad trial.

Korenblit's disclosure also helps throw light upon the strange behavior that marked the "final statements" of the accused. Like the defendants in Soviet trials of an earlier era, and like the defendants in the Slansky trial, which had been engineered by the Soviet secret police in November, 1952, each defendant now rose to abjectly admit his guilt under Articles 70 and 72, and to throw himself upon the mercy of the court. Even Yagman and Kaminsky, who had initially refused to acknowledge any guilt in the courtroom, now joined in the common *mea culpa*. Yagman said: "I am guilty, but it is only now that I have met with a different evaluation of my activity." Kaminsky said: "I understand that I am tried not as a Jew, and not because I had applied for emigration to Israel, not for my convictions, but for concrete crimes."

Butman, the leader of the group, joined in agreeing that "our organization reached anti-Sovietism," but he then went on to say that "we had not wanted that. I always told my comrades that we should not allow any anti-Soviet statements." As during the Stalinist epoch, guilt was determined not by "subjective" intent but by the "objective" standards set by the Party as to what act constitutes a violation of revolutionary legality. Butman was even willing to acknowledge "that at one time I intended to commit a terrible crime [of hijacking]. . . ." An unimplemented intention, indeed a discarded intention, was also an "objective" form of guilt. Butman merely asked that the punishment be mitigated because he had "renounced the plans for the hijacking. . . ."

Boguslavsky's admission of guilt must have been particularly painful. His courageous letter of July 8, 1970, was among the first significant documents that exposed to the world the real purpose behind the massive raids and arrests of June 15. In his earlier testimony in the court, he avoided making a statement of guilt. Now, he declared: "I admit my guilt. For a long time, even during the investigation, I could not understand what the crime was, but after my talks with investigators and in the court I understand and I consider that in my letter in defense of my comrades I had been wrong." If he "understood" what his "crime" was, it is not apparent in his statement, as reported in the *samizdat* account. What is, however, apparent is that the "investigators" had given him considerable attention for a long period. The pressure may have been intensified during the trial.

Judging from the statements by Lev Korenblit, Yagman, and Boguslavsky, one can speculate that a myriad of forms of psychological pressure were exerted upon the Leningrad defendants. The imposition of other types of pressure, too, cannot be excluded. It is not unreasonable to assume that the pressures were greater than in the first Leningrad trial or in the later trials. For, in the last analysis, the second Leningrad trial was regarded as crucial by those who strove to crush the Jewish national movement. World reaction to the first trial had been sharply negative, while the Jewish national movement, instead of diminishing, was accelerating and taking on new and more militant forms. Confessions of guilt may have appeared essential to the prosecution, especially in view of the flimsiness of the attempted hijacking charges.[11]

Moreover, the initial round-up (and, perhaps, the frame-up) of the Dymshits-Kuznetsov group had been but the pretext for a vast, coordinated police effort to arrest key Leningrad militant elements. This group, which the authorities conceived to be the fulcrum of the entire national movement, was to be isolated, while their associates, supporters, and sympathizers everywhere were to be intimidated. The courtroom case against the Leningrad group (as distinct from the press case) focused upon two elements, both essential to the aims of the regime. First were the collective letters and petitions concerning exit visas which were sent abroad. If the defendants in the second Leningrad trial would admit that such activity was recognized by them as anti-Soviet, it might halt the spread of the petitions. The second element was the translation, duplication, and distribution of material with a distinctly Jewish or Zionist content. If these activities, too, were admitted to be anti-Soviet, then other Jews might be reluctant to engage in them.

The Leningraders may have also been "persuaded" to make abject confessions by promises of less severe sentences. If so, they were misled. The penalties, except for Shtilbans', were heavy. But-man received ten years for "being one of the initiators in forming the criminal group and an active participant of a particularly grave crime against the state." Mikhail Korenblit was given seven years for "participation in preparations to hijack a passenger plane." Kaminsky and Yagman received five years; Mogilever four years; Dreizner, Lev Korenblit, and Boguslavsky three years; and Shtilbans one year. (Shtilbans had been a member of the Leningrad group for but a short time. In addition, he appears to have collaborated with the prosecution.)[12] The sentences of Lev Korenblit, Mogilever, and Dreizner might have been higher had they not confessed and aided the prosecution. Tass noted that they received lesser penalties because of their "sincere repentance and the fact that they helped uncover the crime at the stage of preliminary investigation."

As early as August, 1970, there appeared a hint that the Lenin-grad group was undergoing the kind of pressures that would elicit the confessions that ultimately emerged. At that time (August 19), the wives and mothers of most of the defendants wrote to Procurator-General Rudenko. Noting that they had been informed that their spouses and sons had "confessed their guilt," the authors declared that their loved ones ". . . have not and could not have done any-thing unlawful; and we cannot imagine what circumstances could have forced them to engage in self-incrimination. . . ." Their letter asserted that "the whole of the 'anti-Soviet activity' [of their hus-bands and sons] consists of the fact that . . . [they] sought to realize their cherished dream by entirely lawful means." The cherished dream was "to live in our historical homeland and to educate our-selves and our children in the spirit of our people." They pursued that objective by the "lawful means" of submitting applications for exit visas and, when refused, by writing complaints to the Soviet Government and to the United Nations. As for the charge of attempted hijacking, this was "a monstrous error."

The wives and mothers, joined by numerous friends, wrote a second letter to President Podgorny just prior to the trial. In pleading for the release of the defendants, they said:

We are convinced that the people under arrest are not guilty and that the charges submitted by the investigation cannot be true. They are trying to accuse our friends and relatives of anti-Soviet propaganda. But can the desire to live in our historical Fatherland, with our people, the desire to learn about our rich cultural heritage and the unconcealed interest in the life of Israel, and the fact that we are clearly worried about the situation in the Near East be considered as anti-Soviet activity? Is it possible that this can be classified as subversive and the weakening of the Soviet regime?

The Soviet Government answered yes to these questions. Tass, in its final report on the trial, said that the sentences had received "general approval" when announced in the courtroom. The comment was gratuitous, for the final judgment had been rendered as early as June 15, 1970.

Intimately linked to the second Leningrad trial was the trial of nine Jews which opened in Kishinev, Moldavia, on June 21 and ended on June 30. While the Kishinev trial was the fourth and last trial connected with the attempted hijacking, and while it was preceded by the Riga trial (May 24–27), the issues in the Kishinev courtroom were precisely the same as those in the second Leningrad trial. Unfortunately, no *samizdat* document is as yet available on the proceedings in Kishinev, and, therefore, any analysis must be limited. However, a brief account in *Khronika* (no. 20) and a few second-hand reports by Jewish sources in Kishinev provide some pertinent information on what took place in the courtroom.[13] They supplement the official dispatches from Tass.

As in Leningrad, the charges included attempted hijacking, the theft of a government-owned duplicating machine, and the preparation and dissemination of "anti-Soviet" literature. The Kishinev group of nine was said to have had the closest of ties with the Leningrad group particularly through David Chernoglaz, a thirty-one-year-old Leningrad agronomist who was alleged to have acted as the contact between the two groups. To sharply demonstrate the linkage, the authorities included among the defendants three Leningrad residents. In addition to Chernoglaz, they were Anatoly Goldfeld, a twenty-five-year-old engineer, and Hillel Shur, a thirty-four-year-old engineer. The six Kishinevites were twenty-five-year-old Aleksander Halperin, twenty-four-year-old Semyon Levit, twenty-five-year-old Khary Kizhner, twenty-five-year-old Arkady Voloshin, twenty-four-year-old Lazar Trakhtenberg, and twenty-four-year-old David Rabinovich.

The emphasis of Tass in its reportage on the trial was exactly the same as in its reportage of the second Leningrad trial. The attempted hijacking was the dominant theme. According to the government news agency, "three [sic] years ago," Goldfeld, Halperin, Voloshin, and Kizhner "got in touch with a group of criminals [recently] convicted at Leningrad and agreed to take part in hijacking an Aeroflot aircraft so as to defect abroad." The details of "Operation Wedding" were once again recapitulated, with Dymshits, Butman, and Mikhail Korenblit brought in to supply the evidence. Evidently, the four mentioned Kishinevites had agreed to participate in purchasing an agreed-upon allotment of tickets for the TU-124 airliner flying the Leningrad-Murmansk route.

The fact that the entire plan was discarded was not mentioned in the Tass dispatches. Mere consideration of the project was sufficient to demonstrate guilt under Article 61 of the Moldavian Criminal Code (similar to Article 64 of the Russian Criminal Code). A Tass quotation from the testimony of Goldfeld is revealing. Although, he "had doubts" about the plan, Goldfeld said: "I am guilty of taking part in the discussion of hijacking a plane. The very discussion was against the law. By this, I violated the law, which I regret."

The second principal theme in the official reportage concerned the theft of the duplicator. Because Kishinev had been the locus of the theft and eight of the defendants were charged with involvement in it—only Levit was not charged—more stress was placed upon the theft than in the Leningrad case. How the duplicator was stolen, dismantled, transported, and brought to the apartment of Shur's mother for temporary lodging was discussed in the most elaborate detail. That the machine was never used went unreported in the Tass dispatches. Instead, the dispatches attempted to leave the impression that the machine had actually been used for the "clandestine production of slanderous literature." The official reports of the trial testimony repeatedly linked the theft with the preparation and distribution of anti-Soviet propaganda by the Kishinev group.

As in the Leningrad trials, Tass gave very little attention to the other two charges under which the Kishinev groups were tried—anti-Soviet propaganda (Article 67 of the Moldavian Criminal Code, similar to Article 70 of the Russian code) and anti-Soviet organization (Article 69 of the Moldavian Criminal Code, similar to Article 72 of the Russian code). References were made to "slanderous" and "anti-Soviet" materials, but nowhere was there mention of a single specific item of this nature, even though all of the defendants except Rabinovich were accused of these "crimes."

The brief *Khronika* account indicates that the preparation and dissemination of "anti-Soviet literature" played, indeed, a prominent part in the courtroom testimony.[14] It listed the following items as having been featured: Leon Uris' novel *Exodus,* two issues of *Iton,* Howard Fast's novel *My Glorious Brothers,* and "The Six-Day War." (The last item was not further identified.) In addition, the prosecutor focused upon the *ulpan* in Kishinev. While presumably created to study Hebrew and the history and culture of Israel, the *ulpan* in fact was a cover for an anti-Soviet organization, he charged. The Moldavian press was to give emphasis to this point, arguing that "the *ulpans* are a school for future anti-Sovietists."[15]

Jewish sources reported that the defendants told the court that they never had any intention of weakening or undermining the Soviet regime, and that their involvement with the Leningrad group and their reproduction and distribution of books and articles had solely an educational and cultural purpose. *Khronika* indicated that Chernoglaz, while denying guilt under Articles 61 and 119, said that if he had violated Articles 67 and 69, he had done so unwittingly and without anti-Soviet intent. Trakhtenberg also denied culpability under Articles 67 and 69, while Goldfeld acknowledged only "partial guilt." Voloshin, Halperin, Kizhner, Levit, and Rabinovich pleaded guilty, but there is no precise indication of whether they pleaded guilty to "anti-Soviet" propaganda and organization or to the theft of the duplicator. Jewish sources reported that Levit, Trakhtenberg, and Kizhner rejected the charge of "anti-Soviet" propaganda. Goldfeld is said to have declared that the alleged anti-Soviet material which had been in his possession had been approved by the censorship agency of the Soviet Government.

Hillel Shur openly defied the court. Refusing to take part in the trial, he said (according to *Khronika*): "The Kishinev Court is not legally entitled to judge me; I was never in Kishinev, nor is there a single witness concerning the accusation against me from Kishinev." His statement was remarkably blunt. It charged that the chief investigator of Moldavia, in the presence of the prosecutor, had offered him a "judicial bribe." If he admitted guilt, he was told, he would be released on probation; otherwise a severe punishment would be imposed upon him. He concluded: "I refuse to have my fate decided by people who at the very beginning violate Soviet laws themselves. I refuse to take part in this trial." Shur followed the statement with a hunger strike that lasted until the end of the trial.

The authorities in Kishinev received little, if any, collaboration from the local Jewish community. Even before the trial, eight Jewish residents who were close friends of the defendants wrote to Brezhnev: "We declare with utmost responsibility that our friends never sought or intended to undermine the Soviet laws. They never agitated against the USSR. They never slandered the USSR." The letter contended that the defendants' only desire was to participate in a "reborn [Jewish] culture" and to "return to their homeland, Israel." What laws, the signers asked, "would sanction trials for harboring such desires?"

During the trial, four Kishinev witnesses refused to testify altogether. A fifth witness demanded that the court permit him to testify in his "native tongue"; otherwise he would not testify. Jewish witnesses from Kishinev who did appear said that the defendants had never engaged in anti-Soviet activity, never forced anti-Soviet literature on people, and never incited anyone in an anti-Soviet spirit. The precise statements of these witnesses is not known. They may have taken a form not dissimilar from the statement of Levi Latzman, a Kishinev resident who sought to be a witness at the trial but was refused. Instead, since he had earlier made application for an exit visa, the authorities acted upon that application and required him to leave immediately for Israel. From Israel, he wrote that one of the defendants was his "personal friend" whose only "crime" was "the study of his ancestral language [Hebrew] and culture." Latzman said: "I myself suffered many hours of interrogation as a material witness in this case. The authorities tried to get me to testify that the defendants' intentions were directed against the Soviet state, and I refused, testifying only that the defendant wished to help himself, along with several others, to emigrate to their historic homeland, Israel."

The verdict of the court was in keeping with a predetermined decision. The Kishinev proceedings were but another link in "the ominous chain of rigged trials"—as a letter from Minsk protesters in December, 1970, had predicted. The heaviest sentences were imposed upon those active in the Leningrad group—five years for Chernoglaz and four years for Goldfeld. Rabinovich, who was accused only of theft, received one year. The others received two years. In the courtroom, largely packed by members of government agencies, there were overheard threatening shouts: "They got too little"; "They ought to be shot." But neither the threats nor the attempt at intimidation through the trial would prove effective against the militants in the Jewish community.

Chapter 13
How "Spiritual Emigrants" Threaten Soviet Might: The Riga Trial

It was in the Riga trial, May 24–27, 1971, that the intimidation campaign of the Soviet authorities became clearly pronounced. The attempted hijacking, which had been the rationale for the large-scale round-up and incarceration of Jews during 1970, could not be made the basis of the Riga case since not a single one of the four Riga Jews who were placed on trial—as a careful reading of all the Tass and Novosti dispatches and of a lengthy commentary in *Sovietskaia Latvia* on May 29 makes clear—had anything to do with the attempt. Nor had the Riga group ever even considered a hijacking. Indeed, they do not seem to have had the slightest inkling that a hijacking was contemplated elsewhere. The mask which shielded the authorities' real purpose—crushing the burgeoning Jewish spirit—was, in the Riga case, ripped from the face of the Soviet judicial apparatus.

The travail of the Riga group began, as it did for all the others, on June 15, 1970. That day, the secret police swooped down on the homes of the fifteen Riga Jewish families. An eyewitness described the search: "They found neither arms nor bombs, but they confiscated Hebrew books and dictionaries, private correspondence, copies of our letters to the Supreme Soviet concerning our [requests for] repatriation to Israel, Israeli postal cards. Even the Bible caused grave suspicions, and they left it with me only after long discussions."[1]

The searches were followed by daily interrogations. One of those who would later be arrested, Ruta Aleksandrovich, a twenty-three-year-old nurse at the Twelfth Riga Polyclinic, was called to KGB headquarters and asked questions about her "friends," with the warning that she would be arrested unless she told "the truth." In August, two of her friends were arrested—Boris Maftser, a twenty-four-year-old engineer at an art accessories factory, and Arkady Shpilberg, a thirty-three-year-old engineer employed in the construction bureau of a railway-car building plant.

Ruta Aleksandrovich was arrested by five KGB agents on October 7. Of delicate health, with a medical history of asthma and nephritis, she must have sensed that her period of incarceration might be long even as the KGB agents promised her parents that she would be released in a few hours. At the doorway, she paused: "Mother, if something happens, don't wait for me. Go to Israel." Later, her parents would be told by a KGB major that she was accused of anti-Soviet agitation and propaganda, and that because "she refused to give us evidence during the interrogations . . . she is now arrested."

A strong-willed, romantic girl with a circle of friends which extended into numerous Soviet cities, Aleksandrovich was keenly aware of the fate that threatened her. Shortly before her arrest, she composed a statement remarkable for its clairvoyance:

> One after another my friends are arrested, and evidently, it will soon be my turn. Of what am I guilty? I don't know how the charge will be formulated and what statute will come to the mind of my accusers. I only know that my conscience is clear.
>
> I shall be put on trial only because I am a Jewess and, as a Jewess, cannot imagine life for myself without Israel.[2]

In essence, this is what she would be convicted of, as would Maftser, Shpilberg, and a third friend, Mikhail Shepshelovich. The last was a twenty-eight-year-old who had studied for four years in the physics and mathematics department of the Latvian State University. Misha —as he was affectionately called—was arrested one week after Aleksandrovich went to prison.

The Riga Four, as the evidence submitted to the court indicated, constituted themselves in 1969–70 as a core of Jewish activists in touch with other Jewish activists in various cities throughout the USSR. Even earlier, Shpilberg had displayed a keen interest in Jewish causes. Having graduated from a Leningrad institute of engineering, Shpilberg, in November, 1966, helped organize the Leningrad Jewish group in which Butman was the principal figure. He arrived in Riga in 1967 and found others who shared his strongly Jewish viewpoint.

Maftser revealed to the court the purpose that was to motivate the group: "My wish was, after having made acquaintance with the history and culture of the Jewish people and of Israel, to make other people acquainted with them." Clearly, a pride in their own Jewishness inclined them to stimulate a similar pride in others. Maftser had been friendly with the deeply committed Iosif Mendelevich (who was convicted in the first Leningrad trial) and, through him, had met Shpilberg. Maftser was also acquainted with Ruta Aleksandrovich.

From one of Aleksandrovich's friends in Moscow, a certain Khavkin who later emigrated to Israel, Maftser apparently received the idea of setting up a small publication operation which would reproduce Jewish books and materials. Since Shepshelovich, another friend of Maftser, was technically skilled in photography, he joined the circle to photocopy the typewritten material. Their first book was—according to the Riga newspaper—a "Zionist brochure received from Israel." The name of the brochure was not revealed in Soviet published reports. Other books that were reproduced, according to press accounts, dealt with the Jewish language and the history of Israel.

The intense Jewish commitment of the Riga group went further. Acting upon their inner convictions, three of them repeatedly applied—unsuccessfully—for exit visas to Israel. Only Maftser does not appear to have applied for a visa. It is probable that one member of the Riga group even refused to complete his formal schooling and to take highly skilled positions lest his opportunity for leaving the USSR be foreclosed. Thus Shepshelovich received four years of university training in highly technical fields, but left without graduating. Instead, he took a minor job as a metal-fitter in the Riga Manufacturing combine. (Aleksandrovich may have been similarly motivated. After completing her nursing training, she went to the Moscow Pedagogic Institute but dropped out for "personal reasons." She later transferred to the Latvian State University and then quit because she "was not interested in the study of foreign languages.")

The authorities took their time in preparing the case, assembling twenty-one volumes of "evidence." Two of the prisoners were held incommunicado for ten months, one month longer than the maximum permitted under Soviet legal procedures. If this could hardly be termed lawful, it was consistent with a determination to break the spirit of the arraigned. In fact, one of them, Maftser, did become a virtual witness for the prosecution. In keeping with a long tradition of Soviet judicial cases of this type, he stated: "I deeply regret the damage caused by my actions to the Soviet state," and "no matter what the punishment is, I can only say that I shall never again commit the errors I committed before and shall never again step on the path of crime." The commentator for *Sovietskaia Latvia*, V. Strokolev, was unintentionally revealing in the following disclosure of Maftser's reasons for confessing: "Maftser . . . had been made to do a lot of thinking by his preliminary detention and his meetings with the state investigator. He realized his guilt and felt remorse for what he had done."

None of the others would confess. The authorities, acutely aware of the difficulties this posed, took extraordinary steps to isolate the case from the public. The trial was held at "Fisherman's House," far from the center of Riga. Admission to the courtroom was as restrictive as in the previous trials. Especially poignant was the exclusion of Aleksandrovich's fiancé, Isai Averbukh. When he insisted on his right to be present, he found himself under arrest and sentenced (on May 17) to fifteen days' imprisonment on charges of "hooliganism." Thirty-three of his friends, unavailingly, complained in a telegram to the Soviet procurator-general that Isai's arrest was illegal.

Concern over public reaction was a palpable consideration. Sixty-seven Riga Jews had sent an open letter to the KGB and the municipal authorities, announcing their intention to hold a peaceful demonstration on the day the trial opened. With an extraordinary display of the boldness characteristic of Latvian Jews, they re-

quested the authorities—in keeping with the Soviet Constitution—
to provide them with a place to hold their demonstration as well as
with appropriate protection by the militia.[3] Suggesting that the
Soviet press be invited, the letter added that "we ourselves will
arrange for the presence of foreign press representatives." The
response of Soviet officialdom was hardly unexpected: no demonstration would be tolerated lest it pressure the court!

With the isolation of the courtroom virtually complete, the
official press organs of the Soviet state felt free to foster, by unsubtle
hints, the illusion, both at home and abroad (through the reportage
of Novosti and Tass), that the four defendants were linked with
the attempted hijacking. Thus, Novosti, on May 24, reported that
"From the testimony of Maftser direct ties of the accused with the
members of the criminal group of Butman and his accomplices in
Leningrad became clear. Butman's group prepared the hijacking
of a civil aviation plane to escape abroad." Tass reported the same
day that Maftser "testified that he had joined this unlawful activity
[of the Riga group] under the influence of Iosif Mendelevich, who
was convicted in Leningrad last December together with Mark
Dymshits for the attempted hijacking of an AN-2 plane."

On May 26, Novosti reported that Mogilever, from the Leningrad group, who was called to appear, "testified that as long ago
as 1966 Shpilberg, who lived in Leningrad, organized an underground anti-Soviet group which later prepared an action to hijack
a Soviet airplane for making a flight abroad." The round-up story
in the leading Latvian newspaper on May 29 stressed the following:
"Perhaps everything began from the fact that . . . Boris Maftser
made acquaintance with I. Mendelevich, who has now been convicted by a Soviet court for an attempt, together with a group of anti-
Soviet-minded persons, to hijack a passenger AN-2 plane in Leningrad to escape abroad."

The technique was familiar: the guilt-by-association technique
was used to establish that the Riga Four had something to do with
the hijacking. But nowhere was there advanced even a suggestion
that the Riga Four had known, let alone participated in, plans for
a hijacking. The cleverly worded hints were but a device to influence public opinion at home and abroad, and to generate the notion
that those on trial were connected with the contemplated hijacking.

The allegation that links existed between the Leningrad and Riga group required something more substantive lest belief in the conspiracy theory crumble. An attempt to buttress the charge was, indeed, made. Novosti reported on May 25 that "it was precisely their [the Riga group's] joint criminal activities that created that atmosphere in which plans were hatched for committing this especially dangerous state crime [attempted hijacking]." What were the "criminal activities" which "created that atmosphere" conducive to the attempted hijacking? Novosti reported that the prosecution had called attention to "an illegal printing base . . . set up in Riga which was used for duplicating a considerable part of the slanderous writings, fabricated by the criminal group in Leningrad." Tass, on May 28, put it somewhat differently: "Chibisov [the prosecutor] believes that the evidence shows convincingly the guilt of everyone of the group which fabricated and circulated the seditious literature that prepared the ground for Mark Dymshits, Gilya Butman, and their accomplices to attempt a particularly dangerous crime—treason."

Whether the Riga group fabricated "seditious" literature or merely circulated it was not the critical point here. What is critical is the question: Precisely how did such literature create an "atmosphere" or "prepare the ground" for an attempted hijacking? There is nothing in the courtroom proceedings, as reported by Tass, Novosti, or *Sovietskaia Latvia,* that touches on the question. Clearly, the dark hints of conspiracy and the shadowy allusions to creating an "atmosphere" were careful verbal maneuvers designed to bias the public against the Riga group. Indeed, the charges against the Riga Four were Articles 65 and 67 of the Latvian Criminal Code, which are the same as Articles 70 and 72 of the Russian Criminal Code (dealing with anti-Soviet propaganda and organization). No reference was made in the formal charges to treason or flight abroad, for the obvious reason that the twenty-one volumes of testimony could not sustain such charges.

The vital issue was then the so-called slanderous or seditious literature that the Riga group had produced and distributed. When the prosecutor, Dmitry Chibisov, was quoted in the press organs as saying that the defendants were guilty because they had committed "concrete punishable crimes" and not because they sought to go to Israel, he was referring to this literature and the organizational structure erected for its production and distribution. Not surprisingly, the official reports of the trial are extraordinarily vague in describing the contents and character of the literature. *Sovietskaia Latvia* made reference to "textbooks for the study of the Jewish language" and "books on the history of Israel." Were these "seditious" or "slanderous"? The press stories do not answer this question.

More pointedly, the mass media referred to "Zionist literature" that carried "slander against the Soviet people and against the internal and foreign policy of the Soviet Government. . . ." Only two items of this type of literature were mentioned. One was the newspaper published by the Riga group, *Iton*. Its contents were not described. At one point, Novosti noted that it contained "an assertion . . . about the forced assimilation of Jews which allegedly exists in the USSR." Needless to say, this type of assertion has been made by many Western scholars, by numerous foreign Communists who have commented upon the Soviet Jewish scene, by such Jewish specialists as Yakov Kantor, and by the Soviet historian Medvedev, in *samizdat* literature. Was this assertion slanderous?

The fundamental enigma concerned the failure of the official reports to list "slanderous" "Zionist" materials which were submitted in evidence, to summarize their contents, and to indicate how many were produced and distributed. Such materials were, after all, the only "evidence" advanced by the prosecution. In the case of the previous Leningrad trials, the official reports at least did not hesitate to spell out, in considerable detail, the hijacking schemes for which the defendants were tried and convicted. Why the absence of concrete details in the Riga case? Would a listing or characterization of the literature introduced as evidence have evoked public disbelief or even amusement?

If the official reports of the trial were vague and raised even more questions than they answered, a lengthy *samizdat* document which has but recently surfaced in the West throws a brilliant light upon the courtroom proceedings.[4] The document is an eyewitness account of the trial. When it is examined together with other *samizdat* materials which had been used as evidence in the court, an insight can be obtained into these questions: (1) Precisely what kind of materials prepared by the Riga Four did the prosecution regard as "slanderous"? (2) What was the intent of the Riga Four in preparing the materials? (3) How widespread was the distribution of the materials? (4) What kind of organizational set-up was created for the distribution of the materials?

From the point of view of the prosecution, the most important of the "slanderous" materials prepared by the Riga Four was *Iton* (the Hebrew word means "newspaper"), which was, in fact, a collection of articles, most of which were translations from the foreign press. Much of the prosecution's effort (and, earlier, that of the investigatory agencies) was devoted to determining who selected the materials for inclusion, how the material was prepared for publication, and how and to whom *Iton* was distributed. *Iton* was a central element in both the Leningrad and Kishinev cases.

The idea of preparing *Iton* was decided upon at a meeting of several Jewish activists from three or four Soviet cities, held in Riga during the second week of November, 1969. The choice of materials for *Iton* was to rest with the Leningrad group, mainly Lev Korenblit and Boguslavsky, although Mendelevich also had a hand in the selection process. The Riga group was to be responsible for its typing, photocopying, and printing. According to Maftser's testimony, *Iton*'s "editorial board" met in Leningrad on January 10, 1970, and Mendelevich then returned to Riga with the selected articles, which he dictated to Silva Zalmanson, who typed them. Shepshelovich and Maftser, with the assistance of several others, photographed the typed pages and arranged for the printing of the plates. By the middle of February, the first issue of *Iton,* known as *Iton Aleph* (*Aleph* is the first letter of the Hebrew alphabet), was ready.

Not until the fall of 1971, almost eighteen months after it was printed, did a copy of *Iton* become available in the West. A careful reading of its contents proves especially instructive. Seven of the articles comprising *Iton Aleph* have nothing to do with the Soviet Union at all. Four concern Israel, one deals with Zionism, one commemorates the Warsaw Ghetto uprising, and one describes the historical significance of the Jewish holidays of Purim and Passover.

Of the articles concerned with Israel, the first is a translation of a *Time* magazine piece of March 14, 1969, on Golda Meir, the Israeli premier; the second, entitled "The Israeli People's Army," is a sympathetically written short excerpt translated from a book by the American military historian Brigadier General S. L. A.

Marshall. The third is a translation of an article that appeared in *Midstream* magazine (October, 1968), written by the left-wing Israeli author Amos Kenan and entitled "A Letter to All Good People: To Fidel Castro, Sartre, Russell, and All the Rest." The last of the articles about Israel is a very amusing *feuilleton* written by Israel's most prominent humorist, Ephraim Kishon, over a decade ago and entitled "How Israel Lost the Chance to Acquire the Sympathy of the Entire World."

The article on Israel which received the most attention in the courtroom was the one by Kenan. It is a poignant essay written from a strongly leftist point of view which, with sardonic wryness, criticizes other "progressives" because of their negative views on Israel's victory in the Six-Day War. While vigorously appealing for negotiations between the Arab states and Israel and proposing a variety of concessions to the Arabs, Kenan opposes any attempt to compel a one-sided withdrawal by Israel without a peace treaty. If critical references are made to the open-ended Soviet support of the Arabs—and it is these references which evoked the hostility of the prosecution—they are balanced by harsh remarks about the West, especially about the United States (which "kills the Vietnamese," "tramples on the poor," and "oppresses the Negroes"). Kenan's caustic comments extend to "chauvinist" elements in Israel's leadership, who are referred to as "hysterical, mad militarists."

The Zionist piece has few contemporary political overtones. It is a short, laudatory sketch of an early Zionist leader, Joseph Trumpeldor, written by the prominent revisionist-Zionist V. Jabotinsky several decades ago. The reason for its inclusion in *Iton* was the fact that March, 1970, marked the fiftieth anniversary of Trumpeldor's death in Palestine at the hands of the Arabs. The article on the Jewish holidays, which was said to be written by Mendelevich, is composed in the spirit of Jewish tradition. The first holiday, Purim, the author writes, commemorates the lifting of the threat of a Persian holocaust, and the second, Passover, celebrates the liberation of Jews from Egyptian slavery. In keeping with the Zionist orientation of the militants, the closing sentence of the article read: "And there, behind the desert, is your home!" The reference, of course, is to Israel. The Warsaw Ghetto essay, entitled "May the Jewish People Live!" (also attributed to Mendelevich), is an elegaic commentary on the heroism of the ghetto fighters of April, 1943. After a description of the planning and character of the uprising, which drew upon the research of the Polish Marxist historian B. Mark, the essay concludes: "These young men and girls were called to battle by the pride for the Jewish people and by the anger for degraded honor. They fought and they won. To them, the dead, we shall be eternally grateful."

The single article in *Iton Aleph* which deals specifically with the Soviet Union is called "About Assimilation." Only recently has it been learned that almost all of it was drafted by Professor Mikhail Zand, the brilliant Orientalist and Jewish scholar from Moscow whose difficulties in receiving an exit visa from the Soviet regime in order to move to Israel attracted world-wide attention. Oddly enough, the court attributed the article to Mendelevich, But, then again, the prosecution's accuracy in regard to other allegations had been repeatedly shown to be open to question.

The article examines in general the process of physical, linguistic, and cultural assimilation of Jews in the Diaspora, contrasting that process with the one occurring specifically in the Soviet Union. Much of the material in the article is generally known and could have been written, with some variation in style, by a Soviet ideologist on the nationalities question. In only two instances is there any criticism of Soviet practice. The article observes that questions on the nationality of parents inserted in questionnaires for hiring personnel in government institutions and departments have been used to discriminate against the progeny of mixed marriages who are registered in their passports as non-Jews. In addition, the author characterizes the linguistic assimilatory process in the USSR as "forced," a product of the destruction by the regime of Jewish educational and cultural institutions.

The essay concludes with a fascinating digression on the subject of Judaism in the USSR. After noting that after the October Revolution most Jews lost interest in the synagogue, the author points out that post-war developments have led to a certain renewed interest in that institution. The particular developments to which the author alludes are anti-Jewish discrimination and the liquidation of all forms of national existence. Both led to a revitalization of Jewish "national feeling" which "turned towards the sole [Jewish] institution remaining—the synagogue. Against its [the synagogue's] will and even contrary to it, the synagogue became the center of the spiritual life of Jewry. . . ." Yet the author is convinced that Judaism, as a religion, will not attract Jewish intellectuals and that therefore, even were the Soviet regime to take the very unlikely step of granting complete religious freedom, this "cannot solve the Jewish question." What the article clearly implies is of the utmost importance: no national Jewish objective can be served by striving for internal political reforms in the area of religion. In essence, the essay eschews a strategy oriented to changing the policy of the Soviet Government.

An analysis of the contents of *Iton Aleph* shows that it does not, by any reasonable definition, constitute "slander" of the Soviet Union, let alone suggest an anti-Soviet orientation. Only the article on assimilation carries a mild, if oblique, criticism of Soviet practices regarding Jews, and, as the testimony of Lev Korenblit showed, the Leningrad group would have preferred a revision of that particular article to modify its tone. But Korenblit also emphasized that those responsible for *Iton* did not have "anti-Soviet aims," and that, "on the whole," they were convinced its contents were "not anti-Soviet."

Shepshelovich, who was largely responsible for the photographic reproduction of *Iton*, was particularly clear on the question of motivation and intent. According to the *samizdat* account, he said that he had "no anti-Soviet convictions and had never had them." Indeed, on the "public and social" plane he considered himself a "socialist," although on the "national" plane he was a "Zionist." His "sole aim" in reproducing materials in *Iton* was "the desire to study the history and the cultural heritage of the Jewish people" and to have a "better knowledge of the problems of Israel and of the situation in the Near East." As for the charge of slander, Shepshelovich commented that "slander is deliberate lies used for the attainment of definite aims." What he reproduced was, therefore, not slander, only "facts" which had occurred or "interpretations" that are "objective." He reiterated: "The sole aim of our publications was to inform Jews who wished to know the truth about Israel, and this aim is not criminal. I do not consider myself guilty."

Especially pertinent in demonstrating the apolitical character of *Iton* was the quantity prepared for distribution. If the Riga and

Leningrad groups had intended to mount a challenge to the regime, they would have prepared and distributed a great number of copies of *Iton*. Instead, the number produced was incredibly tiny—a little over one hundred copies, fifty of which were taken by the Leningrad group, and another fifty given to a Moscow colleague, a certain Malkin, who also served on the "editorial board." A few more were reproduced in May, 1970, and given to Shpilberg. To whom were individual copies to be given? Boguslavsky's testimony emphasized that they were to be allocated exclusively to "those interested in them." The objective, clearly, was to provide those who already had a keen interest in Jewish matters with additional information. As noted by Shepshelovich, *Iton* was "addressed exclusively to Jews, and mainly to those Jews who want to go to Israel."

The testimony of Aleksandrovich, as recorded in the *samizdat* account, underscores both the extremely limited quantity produced and the purpose of distribution. "I first saw *Iton-1* in March, 1970. Maftser showed it to me in my house. He said that this was the first issue of a periodical publication. I received from him three to four copies. Later, I asked for a few more. . . . In all I received five to six copies. I gave a few copies to Rosen and one to P. Khnokh. My mother gave two copies to her acquaintances. I don't remember whether I gave any to anyone else. Probably not." She went on to state that her sole purpose in receiving and distributing *Iton* was her desire "to acquire knowledge of Jewish culture and of Israel," and to spread this knowledge; she did not have any intention of "undermining and weakening the Soviet regime."

Soviet authorities attempted to assign to the producers and distributors of *Iton* a more insidious purpose. Not only did it contain "vile, slanderous fabrications," according to the prosecutor, but the judge surmised that the use of the Hebrew word *Aleph* (and *Bet* for the second issue) to designate the issue numbers had an ulterior aim. The *samizdat* account records the following exchange:

Lotko [the judge]: Why were the *Itons* called *Aleph* and *Bet*?

Maftser: This corresponds to the figures one and two. In the Jewish alphabet figures are denoted by letters.

Lotko: Was this intended to conceal the periodical nature of the publication?

Maftser: *Aleph* and *Bet* are the same as one and two.

The official Latvian newspaper report of the proceedings gave emphasis to the alleged surreptitiousness: "The numbers of the *Iton*, in order to conceal the fact that this was a periodical publication, were identified not by number, but by letters of the Jewish alphabet. . . ."

Iton Bet was prepared in May, 1970, from materials received from Leningrad the previous month.[5] Its character was similar to that of the first *Iton*, but with a somewhat bolder and sharper nationalist edge. Of eight articles, four concerned Israel. The first was a Russian translation of Israel's Declaration of Independence of May 14, 1948 (the obvious intent was to commemorate Israel's twenty-second anniversary). The second article, entitled "The First of the Six Days," was a translation from an Israeli newspaper of June 20, 1968. The third article, entitled "Israeli Raid on the West Bank of the Suez Gulf," was a translation of three separate items from *Le Monde*, September 11, 1969. The fourth was the translated text of an interview with Premier Golda Meir that had been printed in *U.S. News and World Report* on September 22, 1969. None of the articles commented upon the internal policy of Soviet Russia, although the Meir interview did make observations about Soviet foreign policy with regard to the Mideast—observations that were universally known.

A fifth article might have stirred some Soviet irritation. It was a translation from a story that appeared in the *Jerusalem Post* of September, 1969, which reported upon a speech of Golda Meir at a Tel Aviv mass meeting. The newspaper headline read: "The Soviet Authorities Will Not Be Able To Break The Jewish Spirit." The quotation was the Israeli premier's; it summed up her speech. The aim of the reported speech and assemblage was to rally public support on behalf of Soviet Jewry. Militant Soviet Jews must have already been aware of the event, since Israel's foreign broadcast beamed to the USSR undoubtedly carried it in full. Thus its reprinting in *Iton* could scarcely be considered new or threatening.

Three items in *Iton Bet* dealt with the Soviet Jewish situation. An anonymously written and eloquently phrased article entitled "September 29, 1969—Babi Yar" reported upon efforts made by some two hundred to three hundred Jews to commemorate the massacre by assembling at the murder site. The obstacles placed in their path by the militia, which had deliberately been stationed at Babi Yar that day, are related in a moving and sympathetic manner. Certainly, the article reflected Jewish national sentiment; it was written in the tradition of Yevtushenko's poem, the opening lines of which were quoted at the beginning of it. (Interestingly, the article refers to the presence at the site of the writer who had in 1959 raised the issue of Babi Yar, Viktor Nekrasov, although his name is not specifically mentioned: "But there was an extraordinary person there. . . . Once he had already written about Babi Yar when an amusement park was intended to be opened there. . . . He did not consider this somebody else's affair, even though he does not have a drop of Jewish blood.") But to consider these comments anti-Soviet would strain the imagination. It is significant that the prosecution did not choose to make specific reference to them.

A seventh item, entitled "Letters," comprised several Soviet Jewish petitions which had already been published abroad. Most of them constituted a sharp response to the officially organized press conference of March 4 and concluded with a ringing declaration on behalf of the right to leave for Israel. The introduction to the collection of petitions—the final item in *Iton Bet*—was the only article which openly criticized the Soviet regime. Entitled "The Jews Break Their Silence," the article had as its epigraph the Hebrew phrase *Shlakh Et Ami* ("Let My People Go"). The essay began with a quotation from Elie Wiesel's book *The Jews of Silence*, and then proceeded to spell out the evidence showing the remarkable transformation among young Soviet Jews. Citing the numerous petitions signed by young Soviet Jews, the writer boldly commented: "And so in this manner, making sacrifices step by step, the Soviet Jews have revealed the anti-Jewish and anti-humane policy of the Soviet Union [while] trying to attain the right to live in the land of their ancestors, in their Homeland."

As with the article "About Assimilation" in *Iton Aleph,* the prosecution mistakenly attributed the authorship of the introductory essay to Mendelevich. In fact, the author of the unsigned essay was Mikhail Zand. Why the authorities continued to pin responsibility of writing so many articles upon the youthful Mendelevich is unclear, but it suggests that meticulousness and accuracy were not their strong points.

It is reasonable to assume that the introductory essay was particularly disturbing to the prosecution. At one point in the *samizdat* account of the trial, Lev Korenblit referred to the essay's "sharp tone," bracketing it with "About Assimilation" as unnecessarily troublesome. Yet, the prosecutor refrained from specifically referring to it or to any other piece in *Iton Bet*. Besides, the seriousness of the challenge to the regime posed by the entire issue of *Iton Bet* was open to question by any reasonable standard. The proceedings revealed that the number of copies of *Iton Bet* which had been produced totaled a mere 130 to 140. The output was almost as minuscule as that of *Iton Aleph*. How big an impression could have been made upon the Jewish community by this type of material, with its incidental critical reference to internal Soviet affairs, was certainly open to question. Excessive concern with it hardly reflected a sober assessment of its impact.

The third issue of *Iton* never saw the light of day. It had been prepared exclusively by the Leningrad group. This probably means that no specific article on Soviet Jewry would have appeared. The material that was to be included in the third issue was decided upon at a meeting in Leningrad on June 13–14, 1970. But on June 15, the dragnet arrests of Jewish activists were initiated.

Besides *Iton,* only two other items introduced by the prosecution have become available. One, mentioned earlier, is the leaflet "Your Native Tongue," which, according to the prosecution (as quoted in the *samizdat* account), had been prepared in October, 1969, by Shpilberg, Maftser, and "others of the same opinion." The leaflet was geared to the forthcoming January, 1970, census in the USSR, and urged Jews to tell the census-taker that their mother tongue was Yiddish, even if they no longer used Yiddish. The appeal called attention to the fact that previous censuses had shown a decline in the number of Jews speaking Yiddish and that these statistics had been utilized by the authorities to prove the linguistic assimilation of Jews. It charged that the Soviet regime was forcing the assimilation process.

The idea advanced in the leaflet was naïve. Did the Riga group seriously believe that enough Jews would be influenced by the leaflet to alter the census data in any meaningful way? Certainly, the number of copies of the leaflet produced by the group was scarcely conducive to producing such a result. According to the prosecution, "several tens" of copies were typed by Silva Zalmanson, of which twenty-one were taken by Shpilberg and thirty by

Khnokh. Shepshelovich ran off twenty photocopies and gave them to Maftser, who, in turn, passed them on to Aleksandrovich for distribution.

Evidently, there was a second variant of the leaflet which has not as yet appeared. According to Judge Luka Lotko (as quoted in the *samizdat* account), it contained the assertion that "all the workers of the Jewish culture" had been "annihilated absolutely." He asked Shepshelovich whether this was not "slander," and the latter replied that these "repressions" did, in fact, occur during the nineteen-thirties and -forties. No other reference to slander was made. If the entire project lacked sophistication, it also lacked a hostile attitude to the current Soviet regime.

The second item which figured in the trial and which has subsequently appeared abroad was a questionnaire on anti-Semitism. It is the kind of questionnaire which a human rights agency, voluntary or governmental, might have prepared in many Western countries. The questions are about various types of anti-Jewish discrimination, overt forms of anti-Semitism, problems in observing the Jewish faith, violence against Jews or Jewish institutions, and difficulties in obtaining exit visas.

It was drafted by Mendelevich in May, 1969, and was apparently designed to develop a picture of the extent and character of anti-Semitism in the USSR. In the context of Soviet society, the idea was even more naïve than the appeal about the mother tongue. Who would fill out the forms? What evidence would they use? How would it be evaluated? There is no indication in the *samizdat* account of the methods to be used. Indeed, when Maftser was pressed on the matter by the judge, he stated (according to the *samizdat* account) that "the very idea of this plan [was] unrealistic. We did not even see any aim or sense in its realization. The questionnaire was compiled by Mendelevich. None of the other defendants had seen it. We received no material for this plan."

However, the prosecution gave considerable attention to it. Apparently, Maftser had in late May, 1969, gone to Moscow and discussed the plan—he called it by the code name "Pushkin"—with several Jewish activists, including Khavkin and Svechinsky. Maftser was quoted in the running account as saying that "all of them expressed doubts concerning the desirability of collecting the material." Khavkin, he said, "did not approve" and was "first and foremost" interested in the question of emigration. Maftser had initially reached Khavkin through Aleksandrovich, to whom he had described the plan.

According to her testimony, as described in the *samizdat* account, she had described the plan to Mogilever "but I received no material from him. Since then and up to May, 1970, I did not go back to this plan and had no information about the 'Pushkin' plan." The only time she was reminded of the plan, she said, was when Mogilever in May, 1970, told her that he had asked in various places in the USSR whether his son could obtain a Jewish education. When she started to testify that Mogilever had received a negative response from Birobidzhan, she was cut off by the judge.

Because Aleksandrovich had expressed an interest in the plan when Maftser told her about it, the judge appeared to give the issue some priority in her case. He asked why she "approved the idea of collecting slanderous information" about anti-Jewish discrimination. Her response was unhesitating: "Because such facts exist. In the Soviet Union there are no Jewish schools. In the times of the personality cult, among the workers of Jewish culture there were relatively more victims than among the workers of culture and art of other nations. In the Soviet newspapers, they write with bias about Israel, [and] as for the situation of Jews in the USSR. . . ."

At this point, the Judge halted her testimony. He was obviously determined to avoid having the courtrooom become the arena for spelling out egregious forms of anti-Jewish discrimination. If anti-Semitism was officially unrecognized, contrary testimony was impermissible. Even a study of anti-Semitism by a Soviet scholarly institution is totally unacceptable. But for the court, it was sufficient to demonstrate "slander" by dredging up a naïve plan that, in fact, was moot almost from the beginning. To have made the discarded questionnaire a factor in the prosecution is an indication of the determination of the authorities to convict the defendants, however groundless the case proved to be.

Three other "slanderous" items were introduced, none of which is available for an independent content analysis. One was called "The Biography of the Poems of a Soviet Jew." Evidently, selections were made from this book by Maftser, who testified that he did not consider the poems to be "criminal." A mere ten copies were typed by Silva Zalmanson; one she kept, and nine were given to Maftser.

The second was a brochure entitled "For the Return of the Jewish People to Its Homeland." According to Shepshelovich's testimony, it "shed light on certain aspects of the situation of Jews" in the USSR and contained an appeal to the Soviet Government to permit Jews who so wished to go to Israel. Shpilberg's testimony indicates that the text made an analogy between the desire of Jews to "return to their homeland," Israel, and the repatriation to the USSR of Armenians. The "analogy is obvious," he added. Apparently only twenty copies of the brochure were made—ten photocopies by Shepshelovich and ten typewritten copies by Silva Zalmanson. Maftser told the court that the brochure "was printed exclusively for the information of a narrow circle of persons." Evidently, the group had come to the conclusion that the brochure was too critical of the USSR to be widely distributed. Of the ten photocopies, seven were burned—according to Maftser—and of the ten typewritten copies, seven or eight were destroyed by Shpilberg after he had read the brochure. Thus, only four or five remained in the USSR.

The third item was a brochure called "Home." It is clear that this particular piece was regarded as excessively harsh—a "marked atom," in the words of Maftser. Aleksandrovich told the court that it contained the "exaggeration" that all Soviet Jews wanted to go to Israel. After Silva Zalmanson had typed ten copies, it was agreed by the Riga group that all the copies ought to be destroyed. Silva Zalmanson's testimony suggests that there remained only two copies, which she gave to her brother, Vulf.

The evidence strongly indicates that the Riga group was especially careful to avoid printing and distributing anything that might have anti-Soviet overtones. The authorities were somewhat less meticulous in their characterization of the intent of the Riga Four. They were regarded simply as anti-Soviet. Nor were the authorities especially selective in deciding which materials confiscated from the defendants were to be used as evidence of their motives. Maftser related that an abridged version of Leon Uris' novel *Exodus* and some thirty pages of Howard Fast's novel about the Maccabees, *My Glorious Brothers,* were taken from him. References to these novels recurred in the courtroom proceedings. Both novels, which had been popular in the West, were clearly regarded with the deepest suspicion by the Soviet police. But suspicion extended far beyond these books. According to Shpilberg's testimony, the works of Chaim Bialik and Sholem Aleichem, together with dictionaries and textbooks in the Hebrew language, as well as postcards with Israeli landscapes, were taken from him by the police.

The prosecution attempted to portray the Riga group as part of a closely linked national conspiracy committed to anti-Soviet activity. In its opening statement, the prosecution spoke of the creation in August, 1969, of an "All-Union Coordinating Committee." Maftser told the court that "approximately" ten persons were present at the meeting, including two from Leningrad, two from Moscow, and one from Kharkov. He himself represented Riga. While the prosecution, throughout the proceedings, sought to show that the "committee" was a tightly knit group which directed broad underground activity, Maftser—hardly a witness hostile to the prosecution—offered a very different impression. Only the Leningrad representatives, he said, wanted to establish a central "Zionist" organization; the others rejected the idea because, aside from the Leningrad group, no local organizations existed. According to Maftser, the "committee" was established simply to maintain some form of contact and coordination between activists in various cities. The first meeting, he testified, was devoted principally to the exchange of information about emigration and the signing of collective petitions.

Maftser further testified that the first formal meeting of the "committee" took place in Riga on November 8–9, 1969. He went on to say that "in Moscow, Kiev, Riga, there was no disciplined connection," and that "the question of funds was not discussed, because we did not have one single organization." Apparently, the only thing agreed upon was the publication of *Iton*. Suggestions were advanced for funding it from voluntary donations and the sale of literature.

The second and last meeting of the "committee" was scheduled for February, 1970, in Kiev, but it was called off because those involved suspected that the police were shadowing them. The meeting was finally held five months later, on June 13, in Leningrad. Three or four people from that city were present, and one came from each of the following cities: Moscow, Kharkov, Kiev, Riga, Minsk. Maftser told of a report on the Leningrad organization and of a decision to write a letter in defense of two Jews who had been arrested in Tbilisi. No other activities or decisions were reported by him as having taken place.

The sketch of the "committee's" activities hardly suggested a tough core of anti-Soviet revolutionaries. Indeed, Maftser's further testimony indicated an even more anemic quality than was first intimated by him. He now acknowledged that the "committee" had not been responsible for the assembling of collective petitions, that they were accumulated "in spite of the 'committee.'" The court sought to learn whether the "committee" did not try to obtain funds from parcels sent from abroad. Maftser answered in the negative. Repeated efforts by the prosecution or the court to ascertain whether funds for the "committee" or for travel by the various activists came from outside sources foundered on the flat statements of the defendants and witnesses that they themselves were the contributors.

Whether the "committee" was anything more than the loosest kind of gathering for the exchange of information is questionable. Aleksandrovich related that she knew nothing about it. Shpilberg testified that he had never heard of it. The latter insisted, in response to a query of the judge as to whether there was not discussed an "amalgamation of the groups from various towns," that "we had no groups." When Silva Zalmanson, in testifying, openly acknowledged her participation in various printing activities, she too stated that she knew "nothing about the existence of any organization."

Besides Maftser, only Mogilever, who had been called by the prosecution to testify, referred to the "committee," but in a way that hardly fitted the image that the prosecution was attempting to create. In his testimony, Mogilever described the August, 1969, founding meeting as entirely accidental. He and another Leningrader had gone to Moscow to see off a third friend who had been permitted to go to Israel. There he met a Moscow activist, Khavkin, who invited the two Leningrad activists to meet with some "people of the same mind." The conversation that took place was about "Jewish life" in various towns, about literature, and about emigration. Finally, according to Mogilever, after some discussion of the need to "exchange information," it was decided to "hold periodic meetings of

Jews from various towns of the Union and name these conferences the VKK. [The All-Union Coordinating Committee]."

As the trial proceeded to its denouement, the state's charge of anti-Soviet activity on the part of the Riga Four was emptied of meaning. The prosecution concentrated particularly on Shpilberg (who would be given the maximum sentence) apparently because he had been linked with and had helped establish in 1966 the Leningrad group. But Mogilever thoroughly punctured the state's case. The running account records his testimony:

> I know Shpilberg from 1965. At that time my comrades in Leningrad and I had incorrect views in that we concentrated our attention mainly on the internal problems of the Soviet Union. We considered that in the USSR democracy is not sufficiently developed and we discussed these questions. *Shpilberg immediately began to persuade me insistently not to be attracted by the so-called "democratic" activity and argued against anti-Sovietism.* He said that we, Soviet Jews, who do not know either the language or the historical past of our people, should concentrate on the study of our national culture, language, and history. He strove to create a Zionist organization solely with the aim of studying and propagandizing Jewish culture, and of helping the emigration of Jews to Israel.
>
> Shpilberg's entire activity was exclusively of a cultural and educational character. [Emphasis added.]

Mogilever went on to say that after Shpilberg moved to Riga, he knew nothing of any anti-Soviet activity on Shpilberg's part. Shpilberg's lawyer emphasized, unavailingly, that his client had vigorously discouraged others from anti-Soviet activity, had belonged to no "committee" and had been exclusively devoted to the "narrow" cause of Jewish national awareness.

The testimony of other witnesses called before the court unintentionally contradicted the picture of Shpilberg as a political conspirator. An engineer named Karantaer, who had known Shpilberg since 1956, could not offer the court any evidence that Shpilberg had criticized the nationalities policy of the USSR or that he had propagandized among others concerning emigration. Under questioning by the prosecutor and the judge, Karantaer recalled only that Shpilberg was "nationalistically inclined" and desired to emigrate to Israel.

A second witness, Matseichik, also an engineer who had known

Shpilberg at his place of work since 1967, remembered no instance of Shpilberg's referring to the Soviet nationalities policy or to assimilation. Matseichik did characterize Shpilberg as a "fanatic," but on the grounds that "he was possessed by a wish to go to Israel."

A third witness, Korshunov, who had worked at the same Leningrad plant as had Shpilberg prior to the latter's move to Riga, remembered that Shpilberg had told him that Israel had fought a "just war" in 1967. He could recall no example of Shpilberg's discussing Soviet anti-Semitism or engaging in any "public" activity. A fourth witness from the Leningrad plant, Rutenberg, also testified that Shpilberg had said that Israel had conducted "a just defensive war." When the prosecutor asked him whether Shpilberg had referred to anti-Semitism in the USSR, the witness related that Shpilberg had said that admission to "certain institutions of learning" was closed to Jews. When the judge asked the witness whether Shpilberg had said that Zionists welcomed anti-Semitism because it prevented assimilation, Rutenberg replied: "I don't remember exactly."

An especially hostile witness, Abramov (a Tat Jew who considered himself completely assimilated to Russian society) told the court that Shpilberg had said that "as a Jew he wanted to live in Israel and would try to get permission to emigrate." He further quoted Shpilberg as saying: "Anti-Semitism was, is and will be. In the USSR there are also anti-Semites who sometimes infringe the rights of the Jews." A final hostile witness, Mikhailov, who had been a co-worker of Shpilberg in Leningrad, described him as being a "pro-Zionist" who had found "no Jewish national culture" in the USSR.

Significantly, almost all of the witnesses characterized Shpilberg as an excellent worker. None could fault him for his technical contribution at the plant; none referred to him as an organizer of any kind of political activity, including propagandistic activity; and none spoke of him as a conspirator. His pro-Israel statements, privately made, hardly appear particularly subversive, especially since the recent disclosures of the *Politicheskii dnevnik* show that pro-Israel sentiment was fairly strong among the Soviet intelligentsia during and after the Six-Day War.

The attorney for Shpilberg, named Rozhansky, put the defense case in a nutshell. According to the *samizdat* account, he told the court:

> In the actions of the defendants there had been no deliberate intent aimed against the Soviet regime or against its economic foundation—the socialization of the means and the tools of production; or against its political form—the Soviets of Workers' Deputies.
>
> There had been only a narrow purpose—the development of national self-awareness and departure to Israel.

Even if, Rozhansky continued, the literature which the Riga Four produced and distributed did contain "slanderous fabrications," that literature, nonetheless, did not "touch upon the regime" itself; it merely touched upon "individual facts"—i.e., individual instances of discrimination. The argument was a significant one, but it was lost upon the Soviet court.

The state's case was summed up in the prosecutor's concluding comments, which repeated the charge that the defendants "conducted and directed activities aimed at the undermining and the weakening of the Soviet regime." Aleksandrovich, in her final statement, spoke eloquently in rebuttal. Acknowledging that she participated in distributing some of the Zionist literature produced in Riga, she said: ". . . but I had never pursued the aims of undermining and weakening the Soviet regime. My aim is the self-determination of the Jewish nation, and in this sense I am a Zionist. The spirit of socialist ideas is dear to me and I do not see any contradiction here with my desire to go to Israel."

But it was Shepshelovich's final statement that most sharply punctured the state's flimsy indictment. Like the child in the fairy tale who commented upon the emperor's nakedness, the young militant asked: ". . . can it really be said in seriousness that several home-made printed publications of an informative and educational nature can undermine the might of such a state as the USSR?"

The query was fundamentally rhetorical. The investigation and the prosecution of the Riga group could not be understood in the context of a genuine threat to the Soviet state. Rather, it can be grasped only in terms of the determination of the Soviet regime to obliterate Jewish national consciousness. Activists seeking either to perpetuate Jewish identity or to encourage emigration to Israel must be silenced. Their influence, potential or actual, on Soviet Jews generally must be neutralized. For these reasons, they must be presented as villains of the worst type. Novosti reported that the prosecutor told the court that by "preparing and distributing slanderous literature," the defendants had "turned into a tool of international Zionism. . . ." *Pravda* had already warned in February, 1971, that any Soviet citizen associated with "international Zionism" was thereby transformed into the vilest of Soviet citizens—"an enemy of the people."

It was echoed in *Sovietskaia Latvia,* which said of the defendants: "Pitiful renegades, spiritual emigrants, they have slandered the Soviet country which has raised them. . . . They have received their just deserts." The "just deserts" were imprisonment in forced labor camps under the harsh "strict regime": three years for Shpilberg, two years for Shepshelovich, and one year each for Aleksandrovich and Maftser. Other "spiritual emigrants" could expect the same, or worse.

In the Riga case, as in the previous trials of Jews, the central issue revolved about the interpretation of the article of the various union republic criminal codes dealing with propaganda. On the basis of what criteria can the material produced and distributed by the activists be considered "slanderous" and "anti-Soviet"? Roy Medvedev, in a recent work,[6] cites a responsible Soviet "legal commentary" on the application of Article 70 (and, by implication, on the same type of article in other criminal codes) which casts serious doubt on the judgment rendered in the trials of Jews. According to the legal commentary, the prosecution of people who espouse "criticism, dissatisfaction, or disagreement with some measure or another of the Party and government authorities is impermissible and contradicts the substance of the laws." An individual can be charged with "anti-Soviet agitation and propaganda only *in those cases* when he *deliberately* disseminates views about the Soviet state or society that he knows to be false, and that defame or discredit. . . ." Moreover, for a person to be found guilty, "it must be established that the slanderous fabrication, discrediting the Soviet social and political order, has been disseminated by him with the intention of undermining the Soviet system."

Did the activists disseminate information about the Soviet state which they knew to be false? Did they, with malice aforethought, try to discredit Soviet society? Did they have the intention of under-mining the Soviet system? The *samizdat* accounts of what transpired in the various trials demonstrate unequivocably that these accusa-tions were without substance. The Soviet courts, in applying Article 70, sought objectives not covered by legal niceties. It was hardly accidental, then, that in the official reportage of the trials, the cen-tral issue would be completely skirted or blatantly distorted.

Chapter 14
"A Free Country
Cannot Resemble a Cage"

On the day that the second Leningrad trial ended and just before the Riga trial started, an especially significant letter was forwarded to the Presidium of the Supreme Soviet. It was written by one of the Soviet Union's distinguished physicists, Valery N. Chalidze, who was also a co-founder of the recently formed Soviet Committee on Human Rights.[1] Accompanying the letter was a signed statement by two other members of the committee—Andrei D. Sakharov, the co-discoverer of the hydrogen bomb, and Andrei N. Tverdokhlebov, another prominent physicist. In their statement, the latter two associated themselves with the comments made by Chalidze.

Those comments must have stunned the Party leadership. Not only did they challenge the carefully elaborated arguments presented by the Soviet state in the trials; they questioned the very principle upon which the Kremlin had operated in dealing with the Jewish question since 1967 and which served as the rationalization for the trials. The Chalidze letter showed that a critical segment of the Soviet intelligentsia rejected the propaganda line which the Soviet state was foisting upon both world and Soviet public opinion. More important, the letter suggested that this segment of the intelligentsia was prepared to do battle on behalf of those seeking emigration and, thereby, to actively oppose a basic state policy.

Chalidze called the charges of "anti-Soviet activities" in the

Leningrad and Riga trials "ridiculous." A harsher criticism for a Soviet citizen to make would be difficult to conceive of. The "only aim" of the defendants, the physicist asserted, "was to protest against the unlawful refusals to issue them visas for repatriation." It was state officials who engaged in "unlawful" acts by refusing visa requests, not the accused. Chalidze rejected the charge that the defendants were hostile to the Soviet system and desired to weaken or undermine Soviet power. "Their main principle," he wrote, "is non-interference in [Soviet] affairs here." He continued with an interesting observation: "They have one aim—to go to Israel—and they observe the non-interference principle so painstakingly that they are sometimes reproached for egoism by those who are concerned with the defense of human rights in our country." The oblique criticism referred to the regret felt in some sectors of the democratic movement in the USSR that Soviet Jewish activists were so apolitical that they deliberately avoided involvement even in the struggle for general political reform in the USSR.

The prominent physicist and his associates went beyond the immediate issue of the trials to question the official position on Zionism. Aside from the actions of Soviet Jewish militants, the Chalidze letter constituted the sharpest challenge to fundamental Kremlin ideology. After noting that "official propaganda" disseminates "unfriendly and unsubstantiated reports" about Zionism, and that the Soviet press portrays Zionism as a "reactionary" and "practically Fascist" political movement, Chalidze wrote: ". . . Zionism is no more than the idea of Jewish statehood, and one can only admire the persistence of an ancient and persecuted people, who in very difficult circumstances have resurrected a long-vanished state. It is precisely such rebirth and elimination of the tragic consequences of dispersion for the Jewish people that constitute the goal of Zionism." Zionism was not only defended as a legitimate national movement, it was actually lauded. This in the face of the most vituperative onslaught upon an ideology ever mounted by the Soviet state since the end of World War II. The official charges that Zionism is "anti-Communist" and "anti-Soviet" were vigorously contested. The "concerns of Zionism" have nothing in common with anti-Communism, Chalidze wrote. Those "concerns," on the contrary, "are entirely national."

The co-founder of the Soviet Committee on Human Rights proceeded to raise the critical issue of emigration. The right to leave a country was held to be fundamental, and the actions taken by the authorities to hinder and frustrate the exercise of this right were termed "illegitimate," "arbitrary," and without a "basis in law." Indeed, the entire procedure for making application for exit visas was denounced as "excessively cumbersome." Chalidze held that "violations" of the "obvious right of men to leave any country" constituted "persecution of Jews" and resulted in "forcible detention of people." He called for an end to this "persecution" and urged the Presidium to "pardon" those already convicted and those yet to be placed on trial. In his request for pardon, he recommended that the Presidium "take into account the legitimacy of the repatriates' desire to emigrate" and thereupon "dismiss the . . . criminal cases."

The statement of Sakharov and Tverdokhlebov accompanying the letter read: "We agree with the arguments in V. Chalidze's letter and join in the appeals to end the persecution of repatriates and to stop violating the right to leave the country. We join in the appeal for dismissal of the mentioned criminal cases by act of pardon."

Ten days later, on May 31, Chalidze again turned to the theme of emigration rights for Jews. He addressed to both Premier Kosygin and Premier Golda Meir of Israel a letter which urged the Soviet leader to simplify the procedures for consideration of exit visa requests and to issue a declaration "that the desire of Jews to go to Israel is their own private affair and should not be examined in connection with the difficulties of ideological rivalry or political events." Premier Meir was asked to take steps to halt "extremist manifestations" by Jews outside the USSR against the Soviet Government. He suggested the establishment of "direct consular relations" between the two governments to facilitate the fulfillment of the principle of family reunion. A copy of the letter was forwarded to the UN Secretary-General U Thant with the recommendation that he assist in establishing "non-political" relations between the USSR and Israel in order to expedite the desire of those seeking "the realization of their dreams" to be reunited with their families.

The Committee on Human Rights, of which the three scientists (none of whom were Jewish) formed the central core, was launched on November 4, 1970.[2] From its very origins, it became heavily involved with the trials.[3] Three days after the court in the first Leningrad case handed down its harsh sentences, Chalidze and

Tverdokhlebov were joined by mathematician Aleksander Yesenin-Volpin and two other physicists in sending a telegram to President Podgorny asking him not to "permit the murder of Kuznetsov and Dymshits!" The telegram stated that "their attempt to break the law was motivated by extreme necessity. . . ." The motivation, it went on, was a result of a government policy that "holds the people in the country by force." The plea was then made that the "Jews' right to *repatriation*" be recognized and that all who want to go be permitted to do so.

Sakharov did not sign the telegram. Instead, he sent an "open appeal" to Podgorny on the next day, December 28, asking him to prevent the execution of Dymshits and Kuznetsov. "I categorically reject the charge of treason to the homeland as irrelevant to the actions of the condemned persons," he wrote. Sakharov further pointed to "alleviating circumstances" with regard to the attempted hijacking. He noted that the group "did not endanger anybody's life," thereby challenging the state's contention that Dymshits and his associates planned to murder the plane's pilot. Even more important was the following "alleviating circumstance": "It should be noted in particular that the defendants made the attempt because the authorities had restricted the lawful right of tens of thousands of Jews to leave the country."

So that his plea would not be regarded as unpatriotic, Sakharov at the very same time sent an "open appeal" to President Richard M. Nixon asking that United States courts consider the Angela Davis case "with full objectivity" and "humaneness." His "impartiality" was evidently taken seriously. When the appeal of the first Leningrad case was heard before the Supreme Court of the Russian Republic in Moscow, on December 29–30, Sakharov was given the privilege of being allowed in the courtroom. He was able to inform Western correspondents and other observers waiting outside the Supreme Court building of the revocation of the death penalty and the reduction of several sentences.

The indomitable Sakharov ceaselessly pursued the attempt to win justice for the imprisoned Jews and to obtain for all Jews seeking emigration the right to leave. Following the Chalidze letter of May 20, Sakharov, in the first week of October, 1971, sent an eloquent "open appeal" to the Supreme Soviet in which he outlined three crucial aspects of the emigration problem in the USSR. The point of departure for his appeal was "the trials of recent months." The first aspect relates to the psychological effects upon Soviet citizens who desire to emigrate but face virtually insurmountable difficulties. Echoing the Inglés UN study, Sakharov's appeal noted that the lives of these would-be emigrants are "transformed into constant torture by years of expectation only to receive unjustified refusals." The second aspect of the problem flows inexorably from the psychological "tortures." Having "lost hope of satisfying their aspirations within the framework of the law," the would-be emigrants attempt "to break the law in one way or another." Their acts, "prompted by extreme necessity," are considered by the courts as "betrayal of the motherland," with the result that severe punishments have been imposed.

A third aspect of the problem relates to the socio-economic effects upon Jews who make formal application to emigrate. Obliquely referring to the chauvinist and anti-Semitic elements in Soviet society, Sakharov wrote: "Persons attempting to leave, usually without success, find themselves in doing so in the position of second-class citizens with regard to retaining a number of their rights—because of prejudices, traditions and conformism in our society." He specifically referred to ouster from universities or the loss of one's job. Even "judicial prosecution," Sakharov noted, has been used. Two cases were cited—those of Raiza Palatnik in Odessa and Valery Kukuy in Sverdlovsk.

After contending that the "freedom to emigrate" is an "essential condition of spiritual freedom" and that "a free country cannot resemble a cage, even if it is gilded," Sakharov appealed to the Supreme Soviet to take three actions: (1) adopt legislation "so that anyone who desires to leave the country will be given the opportunity to do so"; (2) amend the treason clause of the Criminal Code to the end that it be interpreted more narrowly; and (3) grant "amnesty to all citizens sentenced in connection with attempts to leave the country."[4]

Svetlana Alliluyeva, in her book *Only One Year*, recalled that during the pre-revolutionary era "one's attitude toward Jews had always been the great divide between the liberal intelligentsia and the reactionary bourgeoisie."[5] It continues to be "the great divide." The liberal Soviet intelligentsia have reacted vigorously to anti-Semitism and to official patterns of anti-Jewish discrimination.

Nowhere was their concern made more manifest than in the remarkable critique of the trials by the prominent scientists comprising the Soviet Committee on Human Rights.

Russia's most outstanding man of letters in the nineteenth century, Leo N. Tolstoy, set the tone for a kind of Judophilia that still characterizes segments of the Soviet intelligentsia and that is mirrored in the poetry of Yevtushenko.[6] In a private letter which achieved wide circulation several years before his death in 1910, Tolstoy wrote: "The Jew is that sacred being who has brought down from heaven the everlasting fire and has illumined with it the entire world. He is the religious source, spring and fountain out of which all the rest of the peoples have drawn their beliefs and their religions. The Jew is the pioneer of liberty. . . . The Jew is the pioneer of civilization. . . . The Jew is the emblem of civil and religious toleration. . . . The Jew is the emblem of eternity. . . ."[7]

Shortly after the pogroms of 1881–82, which had stirred the conscience of many liberal intellectuals, Tolstoy joined one hundred other distinguished members of the intelligentsia in a petition to Tsar Alexander III protesting the massacres of Jews. The petition effort had been organized by one of Russia's leading thinkers, Vladimir S. Soloviev.[8] Following the Kishinev pogrom in 1903, Tolstoy again made his anger felt. "The outrages of Kishinev," he declared, "are but the direct result of the propaganda of falsehood and violence which our Government conducts with such energy."[9]

Maxim Gorky, the forerunner of "socialist realism," pursued the Tolstoy tradition. As a youngster, he had been outraged by the 1882 pogrom in Nizhny-Novgorod, and he would later depict it in forceful terms. The Kishinev pogrom spurred Gorky to react strongly. He denounced the upper classes as being "no less guilty of the disgraceful and horrible deeds committed at Kishinev than the actual murderers and ravishers."[10] Their guilt lay "in the fact that not merely did they not protect the victims, but that they rejoiced over the murders." Gorky wrote extensively on anti-Semitism, and it is a commentary on the thinking of Soviet officialdom that some two hundred to three hundred pages of Gorky's comments on Jews and the Jewish question were deleted from both a thirty-volume edition of his works published by the Soviet Academy of Sciences from 1948 to 1956 and from an eighteen-volume edition published from 1959 to 1963.[11]

What prompted Gorky's most vigorous intervention and the intervention of scores of other Russian intellectuals was the Beiliss blood libel case of 1911–13. In December, 1911, they issued a manifesto the current relevance of which is obvious:

> The eternal struggle of humanity for liberty, legal equality and fraternity and against slavery, hate and social discord has been with us from ancient times. And, in our times, as always, the same persons who uphold the rightless condition of their own people are the most persistent in exciting among them the spirit of religious and racial enmity. . . . The false story of the use of Christian blood by Jews has been broadcast once more among the people. This is a familiar device of ancient fanaticism. . . .[12]

It was signed by 150 leaders in the arts and sciences, including Count Ilya Tolstoy, the president of the Academy of Science, and Gorky.

A key figure in the drafting of the manifesto was the prominent novelist Vladimir G. Korolenko. He had joined with Soloviev in 1882 in protesting against the pogrom of that time. Later, his novel *Yom Kippur* would sympathetically portray various Jewish characters. He gave special attention to the Beiliss trial, commenting pointedly, if somewhat optimistically, that "evidently Russian citizens finally understand that the Jewish question is not only a Jewish but also a general Russian question; that the untruth and corruption uncovered at the Beiliss trial is an all-Russian untruth and corruption. . . ."[13] Liberal lawyers from St. Petersburg gave expression to Korolenko's opinion by condemning "the slander of the Jewish people" and the attempt to propagate "racial and national animosity."

Sakharov's "open appeal" to the Supreme Soviet singled out two particular trials, aside from the attempted hijacking case, for special comment. He noted that the trials of Valery Kukuy in Sverdlovsk and Raiza Palatnik in Odessa illustrated the "unjust approaches" of Soviet authorities. Neither trial received coverage in the Soviet press, but *samizdat* literature provides considerable information on them. Their egregious character attracted considerable interest among members of the Soviet dissenting intelligentsia and prompted their active intervention.

The thirty-two-year-old Kukuy was a senior planning engineer at the Sverdlovsk design institute for agricultural machinery.[14] His difficulties began at the end of December, 1970, when he joined nine other young Jews from Sverdlovsk in writing a letter of protest to President Podgorny concerning the verdicts imposed in the first Leningrad trial. His name appeared first on the letter. After being summoned by the KGB on January 10, 1971, and interrogated about "Zionist activities," Kukuy became the target of a vituperative attack in the local Party newspaper. He was accused of trying to obtain Zionist literature, listening to Israeli radio broadcasts, gathering with others to study Hebrew, and discussing the "development of national awareness." The local newspaper charged him with "treason" because he wanted to emigrate to Israel.

There followed a KGB search of his home in which all materials in which the words *Israel* or *Jew* appeared were confiscated. Also confiscated was a typewritten copy of the well-known Soviet novel *A Dog's Heart* by Mikhail Bulgakov, published in the USSR in 1925. On June 15–16, Kukuy was placed on trial and charged with slander. The major evidence was the Bulgakov novel, which the defendant had lent to a friend, as was acknowledged in the testimony of the friend. The book was judged by the prosecution to be "anti-Soviet" even though it had earlier been published in the Soviet Union. Kukuy was found guilty and sentenced to three years' imprisonment. The harsh punishment prompted his friends and relatives to ask: "Can it be that the time has again come when people are tried for their views?" They considered the conviction on the flimsiest of charges as "another link in the long chain of reprisals and persecution to which persons who have expressed a desire to emigrate to their spiritual and historical homeland, Israel, have been subjected. . . ."

Sakharov and Chalidze wrote to the Supreme Court of the Russian Republic on July 16, 1971, urging it to reverse the lower court's decision.[15] Terming the Sverdlovsk proceedings "a strange trial," the two scientists pointed out that: (1) the witnesses were asked totally irrelevant questions; (2) the witnesses directly or indirectly repudiated earlier statements which the KGB investigators had extracted from them in pre-trial interrogations; (3) the conviction was based on "the evidence of a single witness," Kukuy's brother, Anatoly, while the evidence of all the other witnesses was disregarded, which seemed to indicate "discrimination on the basis of Party membership" (Anatoly was a Party activist); and (4) the prosecution's superficial evaluation of the Bulgakov novel as "anti-Soviet" was open to serious question. After concluding that "there was no *corpus delicti* in V. Kukuy's actions," Sakharov and Chalidze found it especially strange that his attorney should have asked "the court for clemency." Without proof of guilt, they implied, not clemency but rather the dismissal of case should have been demanded.

The other scandalous case, the Palatnik trial[16] and conviction, prompted another prominent Soviet intellectual—Lydia Chukovskaya[17]—to enter the list of protesters. Chukovskaya is a noted Soviet writer whose novel *The Deserted House,* dealing with Stalinist terror, received world-wide plaudits.

Raiza Palatnik, a thirty-four-year-old Odessa librarian, was arrested on December 1, 1970. What had sparked the interest of the authorities were her repeated requests for an exit visa to Israel. In October, 1970, the KGB had searched her home and confiscated "over fifty copies of anti-Soviet literature." Tried on June 22–24, 1971, Raiza Palatnik was found guilty of slander and sentenced to two years. In an extraordinarily moving final statement, she firmly denied the accusation. She acknowledged that her personal library contained various types of literature but observed that "I collected this literature exclusively as a result of my personal interests and tastes and pursued no other aims by it." The librarian posed the central issue of the trial: "Surely nobody would think of arraigning a person for his likes and tastes. Why then, in my case, should this be used against me to support charges of anti-Soviet views?"

Lydia Chukovskaya was stunned by the kind of literary materials which the court had found to be "slanderous" and "anti-Soviet" in convicting Raiza Palatnik. The prominent Soviet author pointed to two examples: (1) "Requiem," a poem by Anna Akhmatova which expressed revulsion against Stalinism; and (2) a poem by Osip Mandelshtam which had sketched Stalin in sharply critical terms. She commented: "Observing court practice in recent years, one involuntarily comes to the conclusion that 'anti-Soviet' is gradually approximating the concept of 'anti-Stalinist.'"

She was particularly shocked that two of her own letters condemning Stalinism, written in 1966 and 1968 and circulated in *samizdat* fashion, were taken from Raiza Palatnik's home and used by the prosecution to bring about the conviction of the librarian. Lydia Chukovskaya, acutely aware that she herself had not been prosecuted for writing these letters, insisted that "I cannot allow some other person to answer for my actions and not myself"; it is not the reader but the writer who is "wholly responsible."

In the fall of 1971 she appealed to a higher regional court in Odessa to overturn the Palatnik conviction. Emphasizing that "anti-Stalinist" writing is not equivalent to "anti-Soviet" writing, she insisted that the basis of the Palatnik case was unwarranted. For, as she explained, the relevant documents in the trial contain "not a single word of slander."

As in the Beiliss case, criticism of the recent trials of Jews has not been limited to the most prominent intellectual dissenters. In addition to those comprising the Soviet Committee on Human Rights, who have been dubbed "legalists" (*zakonniki*), a much broader, if less well-known, group identified by Zand as pragmatists have been concerned with trials of Jews since 1969. Some have participated openly in protest activities. On May 22 of that year, fifty-two dissenters made available to Western correspondents a petition that they planned to forward to the United Nations criticizing, among other violations of human rights by Soviet authorities, "trials of Soviet Jews demanding the right to depart for Israel."[18] The reference was to the Kochubiyevsky case. The signers noted that Kochubiyevsky was one among those "defending national equality and the preservation of national culture" who had been subjected to judicial harassment.

But most of the activist democratic dissenters prefer to operate anonymously. The *Khronika tekushchikh sobytii* (*Chronicle of Current Events*) is the principal organ of the "pragmatists." Published six times a year since early 1968, the *Khronika* has focused to a considerable extent, particularly during and after mid-1969, upon the plight of Soviet Jewry. Thus, the eighth issue of *Khronika* (June, 1969) carried a lengthy firsthand account of the Kochubiyevsky trial, elaborating especially upon the virulent anti-Semitism manifested in the courtroom. The twelfth and thirteenth issues of *Khronika* in early 1970 contained several pages exclusively devoted to letters by Soviet Jews protesting against the anti-Semitic and anti-Israel campaign waged by Soviet authorities.

With the fourteenth issue of *Khronika*, in June, 1970, reportage of the large-scale arrests and trials of Jews was begun in earnest. In that issue the details of the Smolny Airport incident were bared. Because *Khronika* has played a critically important role in both sensitizing the democratic-minded in the USSR to the plight of Jewry and arousing public opinion in the West, it would be useful to summarize the contents of a typical issue.

Khronika, no. 18, devoted some two thousand words to the subject of the Jewish national movement. The section began with a brief report on the trial of Vulf Zalmanson by a Leningrad military tribunal on January 5–6, 1971. Then it sketched specific accounts of "extrajudicial persecutions" connected with the first Leningrad trial: relatives of a number of the defendants in that trial were dismissed from their jobs. There followed a short note on the Raiza Palatnik case which revealed that the "investigation" had been concluded. A similar, though longer, note on the Riga case came next. A fairly detailed account of the difficulties plaguing Arkady Raikhman followed. This biophysicist, who was director of a hospital laboratory in Odessa, had repeatedly applied for an exit visa. Interrogated by KGB officials who "made fun of his religious and national feelings," he was threatened with an army draft notice. *Khronika* ended its report with the note: "At the present time, Raikhman is working in Odessa as a longshoreman."

Next came the disclosure that 433 Georgian Jews from Tbilisi, Kutaisi, Poti, and Kulashi appealed to the Twenty-fourth Congress of the CPSU asking that their repeated requests since 1969 for exit visas be acted upon. This was followed by a lengthy exposé of the travail of the prominent movie producer Mikhail Kalik. After he applied for an exit visa, his property was confiscated and criminal proceedings were launched against him. *Khronika* disclosed that seven prominent dissenters protested to the procurator-general about the persecution of Kalik, observing that "already once, during the years of the cult [he] was subjected to unfounded repressions."

The case of Semyon D. Mak was then elaborated upon. He had been an author for Central Television and had won two awards for his nearly one thousand film subjects. In 1970, he found himself the subject of "gross and unfounded repressions by the management of Central Television which clearly is anti-Semitic in character." Dismissed from his job, he had appealed to President Podgorny for an

exit visa. Next came the case of a teacher in aesthetics, Aleksander
A. Gittelson, who had completed his doctoral work in the faculty
of languages at Leningrad State University. The obstacles placed
in the path of Gittelson and his family when they applied for exit
visas were described.

Khronika then reported at length on the demonstration of twenty-
four Soviet Jews at the offices of the Presidium of the Supreme
Soviet on February 24, 1971. Details on the scandalous Kolchinsky
case followed. Leonid N. Kolchinsky had been dismissed from
school for defending the dissident writers Sinyavsky and Daniel, and
for opposing the invasion of Czechoslovakia. After making efforts
to apply for an exit visa for Israel, he was drafted into the Red
Army. *Khronika* reported that fifty Jews from Moscow and Kharkov
petitioned the Presidium of the Supreme Soviet to let Kolchinsky
emigrate, charging that the use of the military draft against him
was illegal.

The section on the Jewish national movement concluded with
three items: (1) an appeal of March 5, 1971, by twenty-three
Kharkov Jews to the Congress of the Ukrainian Communist Party
that they be allowed to leave for Israel; (2) a disclosure that in
February, 1971, an order appeared to "remove from the public
libraries all publications which might be of assistance in studying
the Hebrew language"; and (3) a list of prominent Jewish activists
who had been permitted to emigrate.

Besides the "legalists" and the "pragmatists," there is yet a
third group among the intelligentsia which is vitally concerned with
the Jewish question.[19] Referred to as "neo-Communists," they seek
to restore Soviet Russia to its Marxist-Leninist origins. Like their
counterparts in Dubcek's Czechoslovakia, they have sought to give
socialism a "human face." The central figure in the group, Roy A.
Medvedev, has provided what is both the most detailed exploration
of the multifaceted Soviet Jewish problem by a contemporary non-
Jewish Soviet analyst and an elaborate prescription of how to solve
the question.[20]

Medvedev, like Lenin, regards the assimilation of Jews as "historically progressive." But he is vigorously opposed to the policy of
forcible assimilation pursued by the Soviet authorities since the
latter years of Stalin. In his view, the Kremlin should return to the

policy of the nineteen-twenties and -thirties, when Jewish cultural institutions, including schools, were permitted and were provided with the necessary state support. Medvedev also recommends, though with regret, that Jews seeking to go to Israel—his estimate puts the total at two hundred thousand to three hundred thousand —be allowed to leave.

However, the principal aim of Medvedev is the elimination of the myriad forms of civil discrimination against Jews. It is the state policy of anti-Semitism, he believes, which has generated a profound ethnic consciousness among Jews; it has, thereby, on the one hand, militated against the "historically-progressive" assimilation process and, on the other, stimulated emigrational tendencies among Jews.

After observing that "there has grown up a whole generation of young Jews who have never breathed the pure air of national equality, who have never felt themselves Soviet citizens enjoying full rights," Medvedev offers his solution:

> We simply need to carry out consistently the most important instruc-
> tions of V. I. Lenin, and . . . the program of the CPSU on the nation-
> ality question. All manifestations of open and secret discrimination of
> Jews . . . must be unconditionally abolished. Quotas on admission of
> youth of Jewish descent to institutes of higher education must be
> abolished. Citizens of Jewish descent must be guaranteed equality of
> rights to participate in political, cultural and economic affairs. It is
> necessary to abolish the fifth point in questionnaires and the third
> point in passports. The question about nationality of one or another
> citizen of the USSR should only be posed during a census. All these
> "reforms" ought to be proclaimed in some kind of special address of
> a responsible Soviet leader, for example, at the congress of the CPSU,
> during which our leadership should openly confess the mistakes and
> misrepresentations of the past years, and disassociate itself from them.

The abolition of anti-Jewish discriminatory measures, Medvedev concludes, "will lead to a significant acceleration of the process of assimilation which corresponds completely with the Leninist national policy on this question."

The Medvedev thesis rests upon an undeclared fundamental assumption: that anti-Semitism is a perversion of Soviet society and history and not an integral product or an inevitable consequence of them. This assumption is open to question, given the deep roots of popular anti-Semitism and the totalitarian and xenophobic features of current Soviet society which feed upon those roots. At the very same time that Medvedev's essay was written, another formulation of the Soviet Jewish problem which took sharp issue with his approach was drafted.

The document, which also appeared in *samizdat* form, was entitled *The Jewish Question in the USSR (Theses)*. Although unsigned, the document is now known to have been written by Professor Mikhail Zand, a key figure in the Jewish national movement in the USSR.[21] The *Theses* deny the possibility of an autonomous Jewish existence in the USSR, an alternative which Medvedev considers at least feasible for a limited, though undetermined, time period. For Zand and the Jewish activists, so pulverized are the former Jewish institutional and communal structures in Soviet Russia that their restoration is inconceivable.

The *Theses* posed two inexorable choices for Soviet Jews: either total assimilation with the majority population or emigration (the term *repatriation* is preferred by the activists). In either case, the Soviet Jewish population will have ceased to exist as a distinctive group within the USSR. The *Theses* grant that there is a large group of Soviet Jews who "have not yet realized the inevitability of a choice between assimilation and repatriation." With time, that group will be obliged to choose, Zand insists.

If there is a certain similarity between Medvedev's and Zand's respective solutions to the Jewish problem, the similarity disappears when their respective assumptions are highlighted. Zand agrees that were Jewry to have "a real opportunity of dissolving itself within the majority population," the Jewish problem could be resolved for those seeking assimilation. But his *Theses* question, in an oblique form, whether "dissolution" or "total assimilation" will be tolerated by the Soviet authorities: whether, in fact, they can or will end anti-Jewish discrimination and bigotry. Thus, the *Theses* state: "All sections of Soviet society are infected with anti-Semitism in everyday life." Indeed, the *Theses* argue that official anti-Jewish discrimination is but "the tool used by the authorities in their assimilationist policy."

It is precisely because the assumption of Medvedev that assimilation offers a solution to the Jewish problem in the USSR is open to considerable doubt that Jewish nationalism continues to grow. In a lecture at Columbia University on October 6, 1971, Zand observed:

"There are Jews, for example, who wished some two or three years ago, to become fully assimilated, and now they want to emigrate to Israel because they feel now that there is no possibility to become assimilated. So it is a process of growing national feeling among the Jews, of the first pole, of the Jews wanting repatriation; and the pole of the Jews wanting assimilation is now losing."

Roy Medvedev is of course aware of this polarizing phenomenon. His twin brother, Zhores, a distinguished geneticist, wrote a poignant description of his travail in a mental institution (published in 1971) in which he said: "A medical record . . . may cause a man as much trouble as . . . Jewish origin."[22] Zhores' "medical record" was, of course, a product of his dissent, a voluntary act; "Jewish origin," on the other hand, is an involuntary, objective phenomenon, from which there is no escape and no alternative. In Soviet society, it spells trouble. Recently, Aleksander Solzhenitsyn, in an interview with the *New York Times* (April 3, 1972), disclosed how Party propagandists tried to create trouble for him among the population by suggesting that he was really Jewish (and with a name said to be "Solzhenitser or Solzhenitsker").

Of whatever of the above-indicated categories into which they might fit, the Soviet intelligentsia, "with its democratic and liberal traditions," as Zand declared in his Columbia University address, is the "best friend" of the Jewish national movement. "For Russian intellectuals," he said, "to be an anti-Semite is a shameful thing, and to be a friend of Jews is a matter of honor." The Soviet intelligentsia has exposed to the world, whether in letters by the Soviet Committee on Human Rights or in disclosures in *Khronika*, the massive deception propagated by the Kremlin in its attempt to justify the trials. The "legalists" and "neo-Communists" have documented widespread official anti-Semitism and have seen to it that this documentation has become available to international opinion. Some who retain a certain influence with Soviet authorities have played the role of public defender of the Jews within the context of the struggle to protect human rights.

The democratic intelligentsia, in a sense, has been the teacher of the Jewish national movement. It was the dissenting intelligentsia who, in 1966, first formulated the tactics of protest through petitions and letters addressed to Soviet leaders. In 1968, they "internationalized" the protest by addressing their petitions to United Nations organs. The Jewish national movement borrowed these tactics and implemented them on a large scale beginning in late 1969. If, in 1971, the Jewish movement went beyond these tactics to demonstrations, sit-ins, and hunger strikes, its debt to the intelligentsia remains immense. It is for this reason that certain actions in the West which alienate the Soviet intelligentsia can only prove hurtful to the Soviet Jewish movement. Among these actions are violence and appeals to violence.

But it was less what the Soviet intelligentsia did, however valuable its role may have been, than it was what Soviet Jews themselves did and how world opinion reacted to such efforts that would affect the outcome of the Soviet Jewish struggle. One fact would clearly emerge: Soviet Jews not only refused to bow to official intimidation, as reflected in the now-notorious trials of 1970–71 but, instead, they intensified their attempts to attain exodus. The number of signers of petitions continued to grow. On the eve of the General Assembly session in September, 1971, a petition carrying over a thousand names from some twenty communities was transmitted to UN officials. Other petitions in 1971 reflected a passionate determination not to retreat. Some of them conclude with the words: "Israel or Death."

The petitions were accompanied at times by direct confrontations with Soviet officials. Details of one of the most important of these confrontations is recorded in a *samizdat* document.[23] On September 20, 1971, at 3:00 P.M., ninety-three Moscow Jews, after sending a telegram to Brezhnev requesting a meeting, went to the offices of the Central Committee of the Communist Party. The chief of the reception office told them that an answer to their petition would be given at 5:30 P.M. Promptly at that hour, the head of the administrative section of the Central Committee, A. I. Ivanov, arrived and met with five spokesmen for the group. Ivanov was accompanied by two high officials of the Ministry of Internal Affairs (MVD).

The discussion lasted two and one-half hours. The Jewish representatives set forth four complaints:

1. The documents from Israeli relatives which are required in order to set in motion applications for exit visas are frequently delayed in the mail or do not reach the persons to whom they are addressed.

2. The requirement of a *kharakteristika* from an applicant's place of work is an unnecessary burden and should be eliminated.

3. Jews who have applied for exit visas are faced with "massive extralegal persecution" such as demotion, dismissal from work, and exclusion from academic institutions.

4. The length of time taken to examine requests or exit visas is "mechanically stretched out," and many applicants receive groundless refusals.

Ivanov responded by saying that "the decision of the question of whether to allow Jews to go or not is not the right of the Jews but of the government." He emphasized that "the interests of the state" are given and will continue to be given "primary consideration." With regard to postal delays or non-delivery, he suggested that complaints be directed to the Minister of Communication. The *kharakteristika* will be retained, he told them, "whether you like it or not." He denied that "extralegal persecution" exists, but should there be instances of such persecution, he recommended that they be brought to the attention of local courts and the public prosecutor.

The Central Committee official did acknowledge that requests for *kharakteristiki* in factories and enterprises are met "without enthusiasm." The Jewish representatives then cited instances of beatings and anti-Semitic threats and warned about the development of "pogrom feelings" through the heating up of public opinion. Ivanov's MVD colleague, in response, stated that "outrageous cases" should not occur and that appropriate measures will be taken to halt them.

Significantly, in emphasizing that the interests of the state will determine which applicants receive exit visas, Ivanov called attention only to a "brain drain." He said nothing about Middle East considerations. (A month later, Premier Kosygin, on a visit to Ottawa, told members of the Canadian House of Commons that the USSR's major concern was that "we don't want to supply soldiers to Israel's army." Only when peace comes to the Middle East, he stated, will the situation regarding exit visas "radically change." The emphasis is clearly different when Soviet officials address foreign audiences. When meeting with Soviet Jews, the primary state interest is revealed to be a basically domestic consideration, not a foreign one.)

At the end of the meeting, Ivanov warned that further gatherings of Jews at the Central Committee will be regarded as "conscious pressure" on the Soviet leadership and that this will "negatively influence" the fate of persons applying for exit visas. The Jewish representatives rebuffed the threat. They stressed that the right of Soviet citizens to appeal to Party and governmental organs is provided for by Soviet law. And should they receive no assurances on the various problems connected with the right to depart for Israel, they intended to reserve their right to appeal again to all organs upon whom their fate depends. Subsequently, most of the ninety-three participants, despite the various forms of harassment to which they were subjected, did receive exit visas. No doubt this sequel had not gone unnoticed in the Soviet Jewish community.

However courageously unbending the Jewish activists may have been, world opinion remained a decisive consideration in their aspirations. If the death sentences in the first trial were commuted, if the punishment imposed in subsequent trials was less severe, and if the barriers to exodus were significantly, although still incompletely, lifted, it was in large part because key sectors of world opinion reacted with revulsion to the trials. It was all too apparent to the Kremlin that its official reportage of the judicial proceedings had fallen on deaf ears. So tarnished had its image become, so exposed its Achilles' heel—the plight of its Jewish community—that the very conduct of its diplomacy was deleteriously affected. And this at a time when it sought, for a variety of reasons of state, to reach a *détente* with the West.

Soviet embarrassment reached a climax in October, 1971, when its two top leaders, Kosygin and Brezhnev, traveled to the West, the former to Canada and Denmark, the latter to France. In Canada, the Soviet premier was greeted with giant, though orderly, demonstrations. He found himself especially on the defensive when questioned in closed session for two hours by the House of Commons External Affairs and Defense Committees, and at press conferences. Kosygin felt compelled to justify at length Soviet policy toward the Jews and to provide assurances on exit visas: "We are opening doors and will go on opening them."[24] (In Denmark, the challenge and response would be the same.)

Stung by the Canadian demonstrations and no doubt fearful of seeing them duplicated in France a week later, when Brezhnev was scheduled to arrive in Paris, the Soviet Foreign Ministry instructed its French ambassador, Piotr Abrassimov, to attempt to placate French-Jewish opinion. The ambassador took the surprising and totally unprecedented step of inviting one hundred Jewish leaders to a meeting, where he appealed for a cessation of demonstrations.

The conduct of the Soviet ambassador was fascinating.[25] Trying to demonstrate good will, he related stories of his childhood in the Jewish district of Vitebsk, where he had learned, he said, to speak Yiddish fluently. To prove it, he spoke a few words in that language and even sang a Yiddish tune. The ambassador referred to his military service during World War II, when "I went to the front with my three best friends, Levin, Berman, and Rosenblum." The disclaimer of anti-Jewish prejudice was remarkably unsophisticated. Several of his responses to questions were even more revealing. Queried as to whether there was anti-Semitism in the USSR, the ambassador responded that some isolated groups had anti-Semitic feelings, "but perhaps these were engendered by the fact that certain people of Jewish nationality conduct themselves in such fashion as to bring about a negative reaction, though unjustifiably, among certain groups in the population."

The answer to a second question was still more provocative. Asked about the anti-Semitism in Poland that resulted in the expulsion of Jews from Poland in 1968, Ambassador Abrassimov observed: ". . . I was ambassador of the USSR in Warsaw and, insofar as I could observe life in Poland, I drew the conclusion that Poles and Jews lived in good friendship. During the period of certain complications in Poland, a small part of the Jews did not show themselves in the best of lights. And when these Jews wanted to leave the country they were given authorization to do so."

Rarely was what Einstein had called "the shadow of the Russians" more sharply delineated. At one point, even the velvet glove was discarded. "One must stress, gentlemen, that an unhealthy state of mind, the drumbeat of propaganda around the alleged question of 'Jews in the USSR,' the indecent demonstrations and terrorist acts *put millions of Soviet Jews in a more and more false situation*." (The emphasis is in the official Soviet text.) Abrassimov went on to say that the propaganda and demonstrations have as their purpose to "create distrust towards the Jews among all people of the Soviet Union, to arouse hostility towards them. . . ." The warning was made explicit: "Representatives of the Jewish communities in the

West who understand this problem even partially should reflect on this in more profound fashion."

Still, the meeting was significant in revealing the responsiveness of Soviet officialdom to world opinion. If, as one leftist participant commented, "many questions remain unanswered" and "the problem has not been solved," the number of exit visas granted shot up to eighteen hundred during November, 1971, and to three thousand during December. The Kremlin was moving with a certain vigor to blunt the sharp edge of world concern.

Chapter 15
Epilogue

The year 1972 constituted a watershed in the struggle of Soviet Jewry to emigrate. The stream that had carried about 13,000 Jews to Israel during 1971 was transformed into a fairly fast-moving current, with the average monthly number of recipients of exit visas increasing from more than 1,000 to approximately 2,500. A total of almost 32,000 Jews were allowed to leave in 1972. It was, of course, true that the Soviet regime was determined to dam the flow, or at least to alter its character by preventing educated segments of the Jewish population from leaving. Still, the size of the exodus testified to its historic importance.

Soviet foreign-policy needs no doubt contributed heavily to the partial opening of the "gilded cage." The Kremlin vigorously sought *détente* with the United States as well as with the NATO powers in order to serve three principal objectives: (1) defuse international tensions; (2) stabilize the status quo in Central and Eastern Europe; and (3) open up an extensive amount of trade and commercial relations with the industrial capitalist powers. Especially was trade sought with the United States. Both advanced technology, including computer items, and large-scale quantities of grain were desired. An agreement to limit the escalating arms race would enable the Soviet leadership to shift, to some extent, its priorities to consumer goods, light industry, and public services. Besides, there was the looming power of China, with which the Kremlin was profoundly concerned. *Détente* with the United States would facilitate the objective of protecting the Soviet Union's western flank in the event of a possible conflict with China.

Thus, international events in 1972 fortuitously conspired to assist the movement of exodus. For, as long as the issue of the right to leave occupied a central place on the agenda of the Western conscience, discussions leading to *détente* would inevitably be strained. It was in this context that world public opinion played a critical role. The USSR was anxious, if not to shelve the burning human rights issue of 1970–71 concerning Jewish emigration, at least to reduce its intensity and remove it to a far less pronounced sector of priority items in *détente* negotiations.

Those who doubted the value of world public opinion pointed to the invasion of Czechoslovakia by the Red Army in August, 1968, to destroy the Dubcek regime, then striving for "communism with a human face." Did not the Kremlin totally disregard world public opinion at that time? Indeed it did, but the question is fundamentally irrelevant. In matters involving the *vital* interests of the Soviet state (or, indeed, of any state), international opinion will be disregarded. Not only was the Czechoslovak experiment seen as potentially challenging, at its very heart, the security system of the Soviet Union in Eastern Europe (the Warsaw Pact structure); it constituted an ultimate threat to the internal power of the Communist oligarchs in Moscow. For, if permitted to develop, the Czechoslovak "spring" would have stirred latent and, indeed, emerging reformist forces throughout East Europe, including the USSR itself. The Jewish nationalist movement within Russia was of an entirely different order insofar as the vital interests of the USSR were concerned. That movement did not seek internal changes within the USSR. Indeed, it carefully eschewed such an objective. It was not reform within Soviet society which was sought; rather escape from that society (to Israel) was the goal. In this sense, the Jewish movement was completely different from the other national stirrings within the USSR (such as those among the Ukrainians or among the Baltic peoples). For the ultimate success of these stirrings might alter or at least affect the distribution of power within Soviet society. In the same way, the Jewish movement had a fundamentally different character from that of the democratic dissenters, whose aspirations were regarded by the narrow and parochial occupants of the Kremlin as genuinely threatening to their power.

Moreover, allowing several tens of thousands to emigrate would, it was hoped, ease explosive internal tensions. These would-be émigrés had shown themselves to be indigestible to the assimilation process, and their alienation and disaffection could not be stilled except by massive total suppression. Not only would such a hypothetical alternative fly in the face of foreign policy objectives; it would pose unacceptable internal risks. Any significant return to Stalinism, which massive suppression would have required, could have unleashed totally unpredictable consequences that might challenge segments of the ruling bureaucracy itself. Since 1953, and especially since 1964, the Soviet hierarchs have been inclined to play it safe, to maintain a certain semblance of order and legality, to "manage" events in a more or less rational manner so that uncontrollable developments and utter chaos are precluded.

Once the policy decision was taken to increase Jewish emigration significantly in 1972, the Kremlin was necessarily confronted by three tasks: (1) how to explain and justify the policy both to the Soviet public and to Russia's Arab allies; (2) how to administer the emigration policy in such a way as to minimize the losses to the Soviet economy and social structure; and (3) how to bring about a halt ultimately to the exodus process without resorting to the unacceptable forms of massive suppression.

Justifying the policy to a Soviet public composed of numerous nationalities, many of whom were restive under the Kremlin's general Russification policy, was a delicate problem. If Jews, by their clamor, could require appeasement by being granted the right to leave, might not other nationalities be stimulated to strive militantly for greater internal cultural and even political rights? (The question of the right to leave for most of them was less pressing, there being no "homeland" to which they might legitimately go. An exception were the Germans in the Soviet Union. Following *détente* discussions between officials of the Federal Republic of Germany and of the USSR in the summer and fall of 1972, Soviet authorities, just prior to the West German elections in November, permitted approximately one thousand Soviet Germans to emigrate.) Clearly, a meaningful explanation to the Soviet public was crucial and perhaps even essential. The Arabs, too, had to be mollified, if only as a matter of face-saving (since, as has been shown, Soviet policy toward its Jewish community is almost completely unrelated to its

Middle East policy). An Arab spokesman, the Premier of Lebanon, on December 16, 1971, complained to a visiting Soviet delegation to his country that "every new Jew who arrives in Israel is more dangerous than a tank, cannon, or fighter plane."

The formal justification of the policy to fit the concerns of both Soviet nationalities and Arab leaders came in the spring of 1972. At the end of March, Tass carried on its foreign service a lengthy interview that a key Soviet official, Boris T. Shumilin, the Deputy Minister of Interior, gave to a correspondent of Novosti. The same interview was then published in the national weekly *Nedelia,* April 10–16, 1972. Shumilin denied as "provocative rumors" that "emigration has acquired a mass character and even strengthens Israeli military potential. . . ." He went on to say that "really a small number of persons of Jewish nationality apply" for exit visas. The main rationale thus took the form of sharply minimizing the extent, and therefore the significance, of the exodus.

A masterful juggling of statistical data was required. The deputy minister asserted that in 1971 "approximately 10,000" (the "approximation" was 3,000 less than the actual number) emigrated from the USSR to Israel, "out of whom approximately two-thirds were elderly people and women." He then offered data on the total number of Soviet Jews who had been permitted to go to Israel since World War II—21,000—and contrasted this figure with the 800,000 Jews who emigrated to Israel "from the Arab countries alone." The comparative data was clearly designed to deprive the Arabs of their major complaint.

As for the 1972 data, the Soviet official was notably obtuse:

> I can say that in such large centers of the Soviet Union as Moscow, Leningrad, Kiev, Odessa, and such regions as the Moldavian SSR and others, the organs of the Ministry of Interior of the USSR have up to the present received a very insignificant number of applications for emigration: in Moscow—285 persons, Leningrad—50 persons, Kiev —119 persons, Moldavia—124 persons, and so on.

He deliberately chose not to mention the great number of applications from Georgia, Lithuania, and Latvia, as well as the considerable number from Byelorussia. Nor did he give data for a great number of other cities in the Russian Republic and the Ukraine. And the data which he did provide are open to the key question: "As of precisely when?"

The deputy minister offered a second important rationale, principally designed for his Soviet audience:

> The main reasons for such applications for emigration to Israel are religious views, the desire to reunite with relatives, survivals of the past and mercenary, private property interests. A definite part is also played by the Zionist propaganda, which influenced individual unstable elements.

The implication was obvious. It was not genuine Soviet citizens who aspired to leave the Socialist society. Rather, the applicants were those who were essentially and fundamentally alien to that society and its ideals. Shumilin all but exclaimed, "Good riddance to bad rubbish!"

Managing the exodus process in such a way as to minimize its impact upon the economy and the social structure was, of course, more important than how it was justified. Inferences from Shumilin's statement offer an insight into the overall handling of the problem. Especially instructive was his lack of reference to Georgia and the Baltic republics. Indeed, until January, 1972, almost 50 per cent of the number of those permitted to go to Israel came from Georgia and perhaps as many as 40 per cent came from the Baltic republics. These were areas in which, as noted earlier, the process of assimilation, for a variety of reasons, had had a minimal impact. In Georgia a special religious factor exerted a potent influence. And in Lithuania and Latvia it may be that a burgeoning native nationalism (along with local anti-Semitism) was a factor that motivated provincial officials to facilitate the exodus of Jews.[1]

It was apparent that the Soviet authorities were desirous of keeping down the number of Jewish applicants from the central parts of European Russia, especially from its major cities, which were inhabited by many of the Jewish intelligentsia. That was the import of a statement made early in 1972 by a high Soviet diplomatic official in Washington, when he told the correspondent of an Israeli newspaper that "most of the Soviet Jews leaving Russia this year would be from rural and outlying areas, not Moscow, Leningrad, or Kiev." Shumilin too gave expression to this view. If a certain liberalization in granting exit visas took place in 1972, it was largely extended to Moldavia, the Ukraine, Uzbekistan, and Tadzhikistan. According to a Reuters dispatch on July 11, 1972, Georgian Jewish emigrants now constituted only 20 per cent of all emigrants to Israel. The majority were coming from the Baltic states, Moldavia, and the Ukraine. Even the number of Jews permitted to leave from Moscow increased. A *New York Times* story on July 8, 1972, based upon State Department information, reported that "the largest group of Jews leaving the Soviet Union are managers, service personnel, merchants, salesmen and clerks." But the *Times* also noted that those with skills in the basic sciences, physics, and space were being prevented from emigrating.

Ironically, a particular group of Soviet Jewish intelligentsia, tiny in number, that was singularly uninterested in Zionism benefited from the liberalized policy. Its members had been active for some years in the democratic movement of dissent. What happened to four of five signers of a letter to the *Times* of London published on March 9, 1972, is illustrative. The signers were prominent dissenters, well known in the West: Yury Stein, a film producer; Yury Glazov, a linguist; Yury Titov, an artist; Aleksander Yesenin-Volpin, a mathematician and poet; and Vladimir Gershovich, a mathematician. Their letter expressed solidarity with "the victims of recent repressions [of democratic elements in Soviet Russia] and our most profound concern at the turn which the internal political wheel may take." Soon afterward, four of the "troublemakers" were given exit visas for Israel (although none have gone there). Only Gershovich was refused on grounds that his wife was once engaged in "secret work."[2] Another who benefited was the brilliant poet Yosef Brodsky, who was at one time convicted of "parasitism." Although he was not an activist in the democratic movement, his type of often abstract poetry was held to be taboo. Since he refused to reform his ways, it was more convenient to let him go—some bureaucrats may have thought—than to arouse world-wide protests by exerting overt forms of pressure upon him.

Several who had been active in both the Zionist movement and the democratic movement similarly found a positive response from Soviet officials. Typical was the case of Boris Tsukerman, a prominent physicist who had acted as a legal adviser to the Sakharov-Chalidze group. As early as February, 1971, he was granted an exit visa. It is not unreasonable to assume that the Kremlin hoped to weaken seriously the movement of democratic dissent within the USSR by allowing Jewish activists in it to emigrate. In the late sixties, as many as one-third of the signers of petitions calling for internal democratic reforms within the USSR were Jews.

For a considerable number of the Jewish intelligentsia who had been active or interested in the democratic movement, the Soviet invasion of Czechoslovakia in August, 1968, marked a decisive turning point. From that moment on, they saw little hope for reform within Russia and turned to Zionism. Characteristic were the observations of Roman Rutman, a leading Jewish scientist and activist in the Soviet Union, who has been repeatedly refused an exit visa. He told a correspondent of the New York weekly the *Village Voice* (December 30, 1971) that the Czechoslovak experience radically changed his initial orientation to democratic reform:

> I realized that we had been lying to ourselves about the future all along, that Russia would never have more freedom than she has now. Her tradition has always been one of absolute power to the state. Her people have no tradition of being independent. They have always let themselves be led by one tyrant or another.

The partial opening of the "gilded cage" inevitably generated forces which had an inner dynamic of their own. If heretofore any thought about leaving was rejected as chimerical and an exercise in futility, it now seemed a real possibility. Earlier fears eased. Courage became contagious. The movement for exodus struck sparks in numerous directions, not least among highly assimilated sectors of urban Jewry, including those who were members of the valued scientific and technological elite. Each month brought thousands of new applications for exit visas; the average, it is estimated, was 6,500 monthly. A backlog still remained from previous years. During the four-year period from 1968 to 1971 there had been 75,000 applications, and more than 17,000 received exit visas. Now the backlog was greatly increased even as the exodus multiplied. For Soviet officialdom, the escalation of requests for exit visas must have been perceived as indication of a hemorrhage that needed stanching. Managing and restricting the flow in order to limit the impact upon the economy and the social structure became linked with a determined effort to halt the exodus altogether. But such an effort had to be consistent with an overt display of Soviet willingness to permit emigration in order to satisfy world opinion. Intimidation and harassment had to be intensified.

A critical feature of the process of intimidation of Soviet Jewry was the stepped-up vehemence of anti-Zionist propaganda in books and publications. The notorious "specialist" on Jewish questions Ye. Yevseev was unleashed in two books offered to the wide reading public in late 1971: *Zionism: Ideology and Politics,* and *Fascism under the Blue Star. Pravda,* on February 3, 1972, hailed the works as disclosing "the true face of Zionism," its "chauvinist, racist dogma of the 'chosen people' " and its advocacy of "dual loyalty" in order to promote "subversive activities." *Fascism under the Blue Star,* 75,000 copies of which were published by the Central Committee of the Young Communist League, was especially vitriolic. It charged that Judaism "zealously dinned into the heads of the young generation . . . hatred of man . . . genocide . . . love of power . . . criminal methods of attaining power" (p. 46). A characteristic element of Yevseev's vulgarity was displayed in the manner in which he praised those assimilated Jews who had acquired public fame. If a prominent Jew had become internationally "beloved," it was "not at all because he had gone to the synagogue and had liked 'fish' or 'tsimes' " (p. 58).

The organs of the Young Communist League were particularly given to publishing formulations that carried a pronounced anti-Semitic innuendo. Thus a not atypical article in *Komsomolskaia pravda* on November 27, 1971, observed that Zionism strives to inculcate among Jewish youth everywhere "racial hatred of 'goyim' " and the "spirit of the superiority over all mankind."

It remained for the publishing house of the Young Communist League of the Ukraine, Molod, to have the final word by printing in mid-1972 a new work of that arch-bigot Trofim Kichko, entitled *Zionism—the Enemy of Youth.* Two quotations from the book are perhaps sufficient to illumine its nature:

Human sacrifices were evidently so customary among ancient Jews that strong young men who were doomed to be killed for the sake of the God Yahve remained absolutely calm. . . . The idea of sacrificing the young is now being used by the Israeli rabbinate with the aim of inculcating indifference to the suffering not only of people of other faiths, but also of Orthodox Jews. Some militant servers of Judaism bless not only the steady violence against the Arabs but also atomic weapons, [thereby] nurturing plans of destroying the entire world. These and similar plans emanate from the foundations of Judaic teachings. . . [p. 40].

The Zionists intend to carry out the social order of imperialism—to conquer first the Arab world and then the entire globe. . . [p. 148].

The bigoted vulgarities of the anti-Zionist campaign even spilled over into the literary world, which, except for the Shevtsov novels, had been almost immune from them. In September, 1972, the prominent conservative literary periodical *Oktiabr'* began serialization of a new novel, *The Promised Land,* by Yury Kolesnikov. His plot recalls earlier writing of Kichko. A central figure in the novel is a rabbi in Cyprus, Ben-Zion. Besides operating in the late thirties a cheap tavern which is the locus of extensive smuggling activities, the rabbi acts as agent for Zionist plotters from a so-called Action Committee. The Committee pursues the task of purchasing, with money supplied by American Zionists, Czech-made weapons from Romanian prostitutes for Palestinian Jews. The object of the exercise is the destruction of the Arabs. At the same time, the Nazis, through a secret deal with the Zionists, also supply the Palestine Jews with weapons from the same Czech factories. Hitler and Mussolini are portrayed as allies of the Zionists, who, in turn, deliberately provoke pogroms in order to compel Jews to go to Palestine.

Some Soviet foreign propaganda, distributed through its information agencies abroad, also echoed Kichko's themes. Especially notorious was an article "The School of Obscurantism," published on September 22, 1972, in the official bulletin of the Soviet Information Office in Paris. According to the article, Judaic religious works teach that "the world should belong" to the Jews; that "other peoples" will be delivered by God to the Jews "so that they may be finally slaughtered"; that pagans and Christians "are not to be considered as men"; that Jews are forbidden to save the life of a pagan although they are allowed "to test the effect of a drug on him"; and that Jews are "required to rejoice" when witnessing the last moments of a pagan's life. The article concludes: "Of such religious commandments . . . the 'moral' code of the Zionist society is composed." The target, however, extends beyond Zionism to all of Jewry:

These repugnant and odious regulations—the hatred of other peoples —have been inculcated from the cradle into entire generations of Israelis to whom it is prescribed to "massacre the goyim under divine sanction."

The Novosti agency fully endorsed the article in a statement distributed on October 11, 1972. The Soviet organ contended that the article accurately "exposed" the "ideas which inspired Zionists" to commit their "crimes" against Arabs. According to Novosti, the " 'sacred' books of Judaism" studied by "each child in Israeli schools" are the source of the "racism" and "atrocities" perpetrated by Israel and "international Zionism." The Soviet press agency did not restrict itself to handouts. Toward the end of the year it released a lengthy report called "Anti-Communism, the Main Line of Zionism," written by V. Bolshakov, the author of the notorious article on international Zionism in *Pravda* in February, 1971. The essential feature of the new report was summed up in the opening section: "Hand in Hand with Pogrom-Makers." The nearly endless fulmination against Zionism in the document ran for 88 pages.

While such officially endorsed writings could only intensify anti-Jewish prejudice and legitimize the growing number of vicious libels hurled in public places against Jews, the objective of silencing Jewish militants proved to be singularly unsuccessful. Indeed, the militants openly demanded that the state authorities take action to punish those who incite by their writings racial or national hatred. Typical of the reaction of Jewish activists was a petition sent by thirty-five of them in early 1972 to the procurator-general and to the Party Central Committee's Department of Agitation, commenting upon the Yevseev book. After a detailed analysis of its contents, they wrote: "We demand that Ye. Yevseev be brought to justice and that measures be taken to prevent the appearance of books containing anti-Semitic propaganda, which is forbidden by the laws of the Soviet Union." According to *Khronika*, no. 24 (dated March 5, 1972), a group of Baltic Jews demanded that similar action be taken against Ivan Shevtsov, the author of the anti-Semitic *Love and Hate*.

A more analytical response came in the form of a lengthy book review published in the *New York Review of Books* on November 16, 1972. The author was Mikhail Agursky, a cybernetics engineer living in Moscow. While the book he chose to review was Ivanov's *Beware: Zionism!*, his lengthy analysis could have just as easily applied to almost any work in the anti-Zionist campaign. Agursky noted that the Ivanov work is "couched in an intricate Aesopian language" where the word "Zionist" means "Jew." As in the *Proto-*

cols of the Elders of Zion and in similar "Black Hundred" literature of the Tsarist era, the Jews are endowed by Ivanov—and by the other Soviet anti-Zionist pamphleteers—with "a sort of cosmic power of evil." Holding such virtually "divine" attributes as "omnipresence, omniscience . . . and extraordinary guile and perfidy," the Zionists have pitted their power against Soviet Russia in an effort to destroy her. The links which Agursky has traced briefly between Soviet anti-Semitism and Tsarist anti-Semitism are more fully explored and elaborated upon in an as yet unpublished work, *The Trojan Horse of Fascism,* by Vitold Kapshitser. Reference has earlier been made to his mother's moving plea that he be allowed to leave for Israel, which was read to the UN General Assembly in September, 1969. Vitold was finally allowed to leave in 1972. His mother, Elizaveta, died in September, 1972.

The distinctive anti-Semitic element in the propaganda campaign against Zionism did not go unnoticed in some foreign Communist Party circles. A top Italian Communist, Senator Umberto Terracini, told an interviewer of *La Stampa* (published on November 18) that Soviet authorities are responsible for the publication of anti-Semitic literature in an ever-growing volume. Specifically referring to a recent Novosti publication attacking Zionism and Judaism, he denounced it as "a heap of idiocies built on rotting quotations." The party official went on to say that the propaganda is a product of the anti-Semitism "stirred up" by the Six-Day War. Differences between anti-Zionism and anti-Semitism become blurred and "responsible men" in the Soviet Union make no effort to "end the confusion." Terracini observed that the propaganda is "the reason why so many Jews want to leave the Soviet Union. . . ."

Intellectuals in the USSR no doubt were similarly revolted. Soviet anti-Zionist propaganda, together with the Kremlin's increasing repression of dissent, may have prompted the following statement of Sakharov issued in June, 1972:

> Our society is infected with apathy, hypocrisy, narrow-minded egoism, hidden cruelty. The majority of the representatives of its highest stratum—the party and government administrative apparatus—are deeply indifferent to violations of human rights. . . .

Accompanying the anti-Zionist campaign was a massive effort to depict Israel in the blackest of terms. Life in the Jewish state was portrayed as a veritable hell with no redeeming qualities. This strategy was initiated in mid-January, 1972, with articles in *Literaturnaia gazeta* (January 15), *Sovietskaia Rossiia* (January 16), and *Izvestiia* (January 19), and continued throughout the balance of the year. The principal feature of the new effort was the use of letters from Soviet Jews who had left for Israel but wrote of their disillusionment with what the Soviet press called "the Promised Land." According to *Literaturnaia gazeta,* more than 1,500 former Soviet Jews in Israel had sent individual and collective letters to Moscow seeking permission to return. But no list of names was published by the Soviet journal, and this claim does not appear to have been published elsewhere or again in *Literaturnaia gazeta.* The basic source for the newspaper articles, a booklet, *Deceived by Zionism*, written by B. Prakhye and published by Novosti in 1971, cited from about a dozen letters of disillusionment. The booklet, incidentally, received maximum publicity both within and without the USSR. Published in a number of different languages and in vast quantities, it was widely promoted by Tass.

Where Soviet propaganda organs could seize upon and exploit stories appearing in the Western press which dealt with difficult problems of adjustment for Soviet emigrants in Israel, they did not hesitate to do so. But obvious distortions entered into the retelling of the stories. A characteristic, if amusing, example was the publication in the widely read weekly *Za rubezhom* (July 15, 1972) of portions—heavily edited—of an article by Sol Stern that originally appeared in the *New York Times Magazine* on April 16, 1972. While the Stern article had examined in some detail the various dissatisfactions of groups of Soviet Jewish emigrants with Israeli life, he noted that only "a small trickle" sought to return to the USSR. The censors deleted the quoted phrase. In keeping with the official effort to play down the number of Soviet Jews who were actually emigrating, the *Za rubezhom* version substituted the phrase "immigrants from European countries" for the word "Russians" that Stern had reported were coming in planeloads from Vienna.

A corollary of the anti-Zionist and anti-Israel propaganda was the attempt by Soviet authorities to portray the Jews as perfectly satisfied in the USSR. This theme was especially emphasized when they addressed Western opinion. A notable example was the May, 1972, issue of *Soviet Life,* which is designed for an American audience. Two of its thirteen articles were devoted to presenting Jewish life in the USSR in a favorable manner. One celebrated the thirty-eighth anniversary of the Jewish Autonomous Region of Birobidzhan; the other dealt with "Places Shalom Aleichem Loved." American correspondents flying to Moscow to cover the visit of President Nixon were each given a copy of the issue. And at various press conferences held in Moscow Soviet spokesmen gave expression to the oft-repeated assertion that a "Jewish problem" did not exist in the USSR. Minister of Culture Furtseva, for example, told the correspondents that "most Soviet Jews are busy building the Soviet society" and "we do not have the Jewish problem which is attributed to us."

But the "Jewish problem" continued to remain a stubborn fact of life. In order to prevent its expression in the form of demonstrations during President Nixon's visit, the authorities had taken a number of steps. One involved the sudden calling up to army duty of some two dozen Jewish activists, including David Markish, the son of the great Yiddish poet Perets Markish, who had been among the Jewish cultural leaders executed by Stalin on August 12, 1952. (David, also a poet, went into hiding and was later arrested and detained for a short period. He and his mother, Esther, had for several years unsuccessfully applied for exit visas.)[3] A second device was to keep Jews of other cities from entering Moscow. An appeal, entitled "Against the New Wave of Repression" and signed by thirty-three Soviet Jews, including Valery Panov, a former leading dancer of the Kirov ballet, described the technique:

> . . . every Jew was under suspicion in those days in May. In Riga, Vilnius, and a number of other cities, the KGB officers took Jews off plane ladders, off inter-city buses, and off trains, preventing them from going to Moscow, Leningrad, and Kiev even on official business. *There was only one basis for the detention: a Jewish appearance and the registration in the passport of the word "Jew."*

Several Jewish militants in Moscow were arrested.

Another form of intimidation was to hold trials of a few of the activists. Their convictions were to serve as an object lesson for other militants. Yuly Brind, a machine builder and operator in Kharkov who, during and after the Six-Day War, had openly supported the Israeli cause, applied in January, 1972, for an exit visa. At first placed in a mental institution, he was tried in June for "slandering" the Soviet system and was given a sentence of two and one-half years. Vladimir Markman, a senior engineer from Sverdlovsk, who was a close colleague of the convicted Valery Kukuy, was similarly charged with "slander" in April and given a three-year sentence in August. Ilya Glezer, a prominent biologist in Moscow whose work on the structure of the brain had received international recognition, was arrested in February, 1972, and sentenced the following August to three years, also on grounds of "slander." *Moskovskaia Pravda*, on August 23, 1972, called Glezer a "moral degenerate" who was behind a "filthy, disgusting" letter-writing campaign directed toward the Soviet Government, foreign embassies, and editorial boards. The newspaper comment constituted a clear warning to the militants.

But the most widely used method for discouraging Jews from seeking exit visas was to compel them to run an obstacle course of prolonged torment. Only the most tenaciously determined could withstand the seemingly endless series of enormous difficulties and harassments placed in the path of applicants. An extraordinary fifty-thousand-word document prepared by Jewish activists in Russia in April, 1972, then reduced to microfilm and smuggled out to the West, spelled out the burdensome obstacles that had to be hurdled. The document, entitled *White Book of Exodus* and released by the National Conference on Soviet Jewry, incorporates scores of letters and appeals, as well as valuable primary source materials.

The *White Book* was divided into four chapters, each revealing the "administrative obstacles . . . arbitrariness and lawlessness" associated with applications for exit visas. The first chapter describes the complicated difficulties in collecting the essential documents required for taking the initial step of applying for an exit visa. Thus the preliminary invitations (*vyzov*) needed from Israeli relatives were repeatedly, if conveniently, lost in the mails. So many invitations had gone astray that, in July, 1971, 155 Jews from Moscow, Riga, Minsk, Odessa, Derbent, and Georgia formally complained to the Universal Postal Union that the USSR was violating the Universal Postal Convention, which it had ratified.

Obtaining a character reference—the *kharakteristika*—from

one's place of employment was doubly difficult; the individual was obliged to suffer vicious anti-Semitic slurs at public hearings in the trade union or collective, ostracism as a "traitor," serious demotion, or loss of job. A classic example was the treatment meted out to a star performer of the Kirov Ballet Company in Leningrad, the previously mentioned Valery Panov, and to his wife, Galina Rogozina, who was also a soloist with the company. On March 30, 1972, a meeting of the company was called to discuss their requests for *kharakteristiki*. The authorities had evidently planned it in a manner calculated to carry the maximum impact: one performer spoke of "crime and treason in the theater"; another said there was "betrayal in the temple of love and creative art"; a third commented that "we made him, we must destroy him." On April 7 the trade union committee of the Kirov theater voted to discharge Panov because of "his amoral behavior [and] treason, which are incompatible with his presence in the theater company." (Later, on May 26, he was thrown into prison on trumped-up charges of "hooliganism" and compelled to share for seven days a cell "with amputees, cripples, invalids with crutches." A more inhuman disposition of the case, for a ballet dancer, is hard to contemplate.)

(*Khronika*, no. 23, dated January 5, 1972, provided numerous examples that underscored the theme of the *White Book*. Typical of persons dismissed from their positions after applying for exit visas were an artist in the All-Union radio symphony orchestra, the head of the surgical department of the Moscow Railway Hospital, the senior scientific worker in the Literary Museum, a senior scientific worker in the Institute of Biological and Medical Chemistry of the Academy of Medical Sciences, a prominent mathematician from the Scientific Research Institute of Mechanics, a leading engineer at the All-Union Scientific Research Institute of Oil Refining. Demoted were the head of the All-Union Scientific Research Institute of Machine-Tool Construction, a senior worker at a shoe factory, and chief engineers in Simferopol. Dozens who fall into similar categories were also listed.)

An additional burden resulted from the application of so-called Rule 7 imposed by OVIR, which required that applicants must "submit a witnessed statement from parents remaining in the USSR, giving their attitude to the applicant's emigration." Fears and anxieties of elders, together with factors frequently flowing from the generation gap, all too often acted as hindrances. A variety of poignant illustrations of such hindrances were documented in the *White Book*.

The second part of the *White Book* is entitled "At Work, in the Street, and in Reception Offices." It examined in detail the heavy pressures borne by applicants once they had successfully received the necessary preliminary documents. (Many, of course, were not so fortunate.) The section began with the following warning:

> You have been to the mountains and you know that one must not trust the deceptive proximity of the mountaintops which you have to cross. When you get to that top, you find that it is not a top at all but only a place from which you can see a new ascent.

The critical problem was trying to earn a living, since the loss of one's previous position was certain. Some worked as dishwashers or unskilled laborers. Others, less lucky, were threatened with prosecution for being "parasites." A few tried to eke out an existence as private tutors but frequently found themselves harassed by the police.

Various documents elaborate upon insidious and open forms of threats: anonymous telephone calls; arrests and questioning; stones thrown through windows; beatings by unknown persons, at times involving deadly weapons; and obscene and abusive verbal attacks on members of the applicants' families. "Especially difficult conditions" were described as prevailing for Jewish applicants living in small towns or villages. The most disturbing form of intimidation was the sudden incarceration of a number of Jews in mental institutions.

The second part of the *White Book* concluded with a host of examples of official rejections given by authorities to various applications. What appeared to be particularly exasperating, from a psychological viewpoint, was the apparent total arbitrariness of the decisions rendered. A petition signed by eighteen people and sent to the UN Commission on Human Rights (included in the *White Book*) is illuminating:

> . . . of two families in approximately the same situation, one may receive permission to emigrate and the other may be turned down. One person with an academic degree is allowed to go, another is not because of that same degree. . . . In some scientific and academic institu-

tions a person is arbitrarily declared "capable of increasing the scientific or military potential of the enemy State of Israel." In other institutions, under the same circumstances, such statements are not made.

Part 3 of the *White Book* was called "Permission Has Been Received But . . ." The fortunate ones continued to face an "obtuse arbitrariness." A violinist was not allowed to take his professional instrument with him. Others could not carry specific items of their personal property. Harassment at the airport included the removal of photographs, letters, and mementos. The sudden imposition of additional financial charges increased the difficulties, while a constant flow of abuse augmented personal tensions. The last section of the volume dealt with those who not only failed in reaching the "mountaintop" but were the unfortunate ones who reached "instead of the homeland—Mordovia." The section's title refers to the Soviet area that contains the prison camp in which those Jews convicted in 1970 and 1971 were incarcerated.

When UN Secretary-General Kurt Waldheim visited the Kremlin in mid-July, 1972, 254 Soviet Jews forwarded to him a petition which expressly complained about the "humiliating procedure, comparable to a moral inquisition," that is involved in seeking an exit visa. A new item was also noted: "Persons receiving military pensions are deprived of their rank and pensions, and they and their families are thereby doomed to hardship." A typical example was the case of retired and highly decorated Colonel Lev Ovsishcher. After applying for an exit visa, he was called on May 10, 1972, to the district military office in Minsk, where his decorations and rank were removed while his name was struck from the list of veterans receiving state pensions.

The UN petition also complained of the financial charges imposed on persons receiving exit visas. The 900 rubles ($1,000) for each adult family member was described as "enormous," since it was "equal to the average eight months' earnings of a citizen of the USSR." The complaint was premature, for the 900-ruble levy turned out to be but a fraction of the costs that would be imposed in August, 1972.

The petition to Waldheim included a significant disclosure that bore upon the critical subject of the arbitrariness of decision-making in granting exit visas. According to the signers, "commissions" whose memberships are "kept secret" (but apparently are chosen by the Ministry of Internal Affairs) examine applications "in secrecy" and make decisions on the basis of "secret instructions." The mysterious labyrinthine process evoked the nightmare world of Kafka's novels.

The nightmare was especially traumatic for those Jews in the scientific and technological elite who sought exit visas. (To some degree, this also applied to highly specialized talents in the ballet field and to not easily replaceable professionals in the humanities, such as curators of rare objects in museums.) Earlier analysis had indicated that it was precisely this segment of the Jewish community, with its specialized skills, that profoundly concerned the Kremlin. The possible loss of this pool of talent was a vital, if not decisive, consideration in the formulation of the emigration policy. In most instances involving the elite, Soviet authorities imposed a ban that was almost total.

A list of some of the more prominent names that were subject to the ban is illustrative: Vladimir Slepak, an electronics engineer who worked on automatic control for TV research; Viktor Polsky, a physical engineer with a doctorate in photo-electronics; Aleksander Lerner, a world authority on cybernetics; Roman Rutman, a specialist in automation control with a doctorate in technical sciences; Herman Branover, an expert on hydrodynamics; Ilya Glezer, an authority on brain morphology; Yevgeny Ratner, a top researcher in plant physiology; Viktor Yakhot, a specialist in solid-state physics; and Pavel Abramovich, a radio engineer whose expertise extended to the field of computer research.[4]

The most outstanding example was Dr. Veniamin Levich, an internationally renowned authority on physical chemistry and, more important, a corresponding member of the prestigious Academy of Sciences. Although his outlook was completely non-political, the mere act of applying for an exit visa for Israel had, in the words of his wife, "transformed [him] into a pariah, a non-person." His scientific papers were no longer published, he was not invited to attend scientific meetings, and he was stripped of his important teaching and research positions. Abuse and social ostracism accompanied him everywhere, while his two sons were compelled, too, to suffer their father's "sin." Yevgeny, a top astrophysicist, was threatened with induction into the armed forces even though he had serious chronic illnesses. Aleksander, a corrosion engineer, was immediately discharged from the institute in which he worked. The requests of the sons for exit visas were also rejected.

On April 27, 1972, Veniamin Levich and another distinguished scientist, Professor Aleksander Voronel, wrote a joint letter addressed to the Academy of Sciences of the USSR, to similar bodies in Great Britain and the United States, and to international associations of physicists and chemists, in which they warned against scientists being turned "into an exploited and discriminated-against minority, into bondsmen of the twentieth century." Their letter continued:

> The sole rightful owners of their [the scientists'] hands or their brains are the people themselves. No references to government interests can forbid the scientists to feel that they are free people, and, in particular, prevent them from going, together with their brains, to their historical homeland if such is their desire.

The letter ridiculed the all too frequent reason offered by the OVIR authorities for rejecting the visa applications of scientists: that they presumably were in possession of state secrets. Such reasons, the joint letter emphasized, "are without any real foundation." Indeed, many of the scientist applicants either worked on purely theoretical questions unrelated to defense work or had left several years earlier any position that either was regarded as involving "secret" work or might be so considered. Even more absurd was another justification offered by the state authorities: that the work of the scientists was too valuable to the Soviet regime. If this were the case, they would not be dismissed or demoted from their positions—the characteristic way in which the Kremlin treated scientist applicants for exit visas. The Levich-Voronel letter noted that as soon as a scientist "announces his desire to go to Israel [he] is automatically deprived of the possibility to continue his scientific activity . . . [and] nobody is interested in using him."

A similar point was made in a letter written on February 21, 1972, by the automation-control expert Roman Rutman, and sent to various international bodies. After pointing out that his application for an exit visa was rejected on grounds that "he is a highly qualified specialist" (Rutman cited from the official test itself), the expert caustically observed: "This high evaluation of my abilities did not prevent the administration from removing me from being in charge of the laboratory [and] forbidding me to teach in the Institute of Radio Engineers. . . ."

The real motivation for the harsh punitive actions taken by the Soviet authorities was spelled out by Levich and Voronel. They wrote:

> . . . the authorities have in mind not us *but those of our colleagues whom they intend to frighten* with the sight of our being made out-casts. . . . The scientists must see in our example what awaits them in case of disobedience—the loss of work, the end of a scientific career, personal insecurity, and a quite doubtful possibility of emigration. [Emphasis added.]

With the rationale for barring emigration of scientists revealed to be so transparently specious, the Kremlin sought a new device to thwart the clamor for exit visas. International opinion among academics and scholars had to be assuaged, but, at the same time, the "brain drain" must be plugged. It was not uncharacteristic for the Soviet bureaucratic leadership to select a method which it may have thought to be clever but which enlightened opinion would inevitably regard as a relic of feudal society.

On August 3, 1972, the Presidium of the Supreme Soviet enacted a decree (No. 572) which required that "citizens of the USSR leaving for permanent residence abroad in other than socialist countries . . . compensate the State for their education received from institutions of higher learning. . . ." Eleven days later, on August 14, the Council of Ministers of the USSR affirmed the decree and directed "the Ministries of Finance and Higher Educa-tion to institute education fees as compensation for the expenditures for education in institutions of higher education. . . ." The Council order further authorized the organs of the Ministries of Finance and Internal Affairs "to grant in exceptional cases partial or full exemp-tion from payment of these fees." Neither the August 3 degree nor the August 14 order was published in the Soviet press or in any official organ. Information about the new edicts and their implemen-tation could be obtained only from Soviet Jews who were seeking exit visas.

Public disclosure of the contents of the edicts might have proved most embarrassing. First, they had an *ex post facto* character. Not only were new applicants for exit visas subject to the new fees; earlier applicants who had already been approved for visas were suddenly faced with the added taxes. Second, the "diploma tax"—as it came to be called—was extraordinarily exorbitant. The scale, according to Viktor Perelman, who had earlier worked on *Literaturnaia gazeta,* ranged from 4,000 to 25,000 rubles. (Other Soviet sources have advised that the tax imposed in some communities upon those holding a doctorate of science went as high as 35,000 rubles. Apparently, the scale varied from city to city.) Some thirteen separate rate schedules were established for graduates of differing technical schools, institutes, and universities as well as for separate types of diplomas and degrees.

Since the average annual income for a technically trained person in the USSR ranged from 2,400 to 3,600 rubles,* it was apparent—as Perelman observed—that "had the repatriates even wished to pay them [the taxes], they would anyway be unable to do so without help from the outside." He calculated that the cost of an emigration visa for an engineer was equal to his salary earned during five to seven years; for a physician six years; and for a scientist six to eight years. Moreover, for a family in which the wife and son (or daughter) were university graduates—a by no means infrequent circumstance—the required payments become virtually prohibitive. Approximately one-half million Soviet Jews who are either specialists with a higher education or graduates from a technical institute could be affected. Potentially affected, too, were 150,000 Jewish students attending higher-education or specialized schools.

The reason for the "diploma tax" as given by the authorities to applicants for exit visas was that the latter should "pay back the working class" for their state-financed education. *Izvestiia,* on September 29, put it this way: "The training of skilled personnel costs the state and the people many millions of rubles." It was "logical," the newspaper argued, to require the exit visa tax. The logic was tortured. Not only had the Soviet Constitution, in Article 121, assured citizens the right to a free education without qualification but a leading Soviet demographer, B. T. Urlanis, had earlier made clear that five or six years of labor for the state, on the aver-

---

* The estimate was made by three Soviet mathematical physicists in a letter dated September 3, 1972, and sent to participants in an international conference on high-energy physics held in Batavia, Illinois. They asserted that a Soviet Candidate of Sciences (equivalent to a Ph.D.) earns 200 to 300 rubles a month. Available data approximate this estimate.

age, provided adequate compensation to it for the cost of education. Writing in *Literaturnaia gazeta* July 29, 1970, Professor Urlanis asserted: "A person pays his debt to society in full in about five or six years of work, after which he is producing over and above what he took from the state. . . ." Applicants for exit visas, in the main, had given more than six years of service to the state.

Besides, the "diploma tax" far exceeds the actual costs of education. An authority on Soviet education costs, V. A. Zhamin, writing in 1969, stated that the annual cost of university training was 1,000 rubles, while that of graduate school was 1,700 rubles. And at the graduate school level candidates for advanced degrees both work and study simultaneously. Thus the cost of an advanced degree is only partly borne by the state. Indeed, if the state does incur any losses, it is more than compensated by the forfeiture by emigrants of their pensions, interest on bonds, savings (above $100), and apartments.

To the outside world, through Novosti, the Kremlin attempted to justify the August 3 decree by contending that it was in consonance with a UNESCO resolution (No. 1243) of November 14, 1970, and with practices of the French and Swedish governments. The contention had no foundation in fact. The UNESCO resolution dealt exclusively with the "brain drain" from *developing* countries, not industrially developed countries such as the USSR. In France higher education is free. The only exceptions are certain institutes of higher training for government service, where students are admitted on the clear understanding, agreed to beforehand, that upon completion of their studies they will serve the state for a period of time equal to the amount of their schooling. Only 5 per cent of the total French university student body is involved in this program. No limitations of any sort are imposed on the balance of French students when they graduate. Swedish officials publicly and vigorously denied that any regulation existed in their country requiring taxes for exit visas.

The contrived explanations, whether directed toward Soviet Jews or toward world public opinion, in fact shielded the real purpose of the new decree: to discourage and halt the exodus of Soviet Jews, especially those who were technical and scientific specialists. It was but one more deterrent augmenting a host of others designed to stop the Jewish "brain drain." Professor Levich, joined by nine other Soviet Jewish intellectuals, forcefully posed the issue in a press conference on August 15. He emphasized that Soviet policy was transforming Soviet Jews into "a new category of human beings—the slaves of the twentieth century." The Soviet biologist Viktor Zaslavsky termed the tax decree "monstrous," for it reminded him "of World War II deals of exchanging trucks for Jews. . . ."

Other aims may have been served by the August 14 order. Some people in the Kremlin may have considered that Jews abroad would fill Soviet coffers with desired dollars. That a form of blackmail and extortion was decided upon is not inconceivable. This was the argument advanced by Perelman, who had been fired from his position on *Literaturnaia gazeta* after he had applied for an exit visa. In a document circulated in Moscow on August 27, Perelman contended that the Kremlin was trying to convert Jews who wanted to emigrate into a "commodity on the international financial market" in order to obtain hard currency. He stated that a Ministry of Finance official had told a group of Jews on August 15: "We are not so naïve as to suppose that you have as much as this [to pay for exit visas]. But you know where to get it. . . ." Calculating that the total cost for an estimated 80,000 applicants would be one-quarter billion dollars, he urged Soviet Jews to refuse to pay. In Perelman's view, if the tax was maintained it would doom thousands of Jews to years of waiting as "unsold slaves" until ransom money could be raised abroad.

It was also possible that some people in the Soviet administrative apparatus hoped to use the steep fees as a means of discouraging Jews from applying for university admission. Quotas have been the principal method of limiting the number of Jews attending Soviet universities. A *samizdat* article written in November, 1971, by the prominent Jewish literary critic Grigory Svirsky called attention to a newly authorized Soviet book published in Gorky in 1970, which advocated a sharp reduction in the number of specialists with higher education and endorsed the *numerus clausus*. The author was the philosopher V. Mishin; the book's title was *Social Progress*. Jews who might entertain thoughts of someday applying for exit visas were apt to buttress the discrimination process by voluntarily withdrawing from the competition for university admission.

The escalation of the costs in acquiring exit visas could not and would not stymie aspirations of educated Jews seeking to emigrate. Hundreds signed petitions. Typical was one signed by two hundred Moscow Jews on September 3, which called the "diploma tax" "contrary to a number of legal, social, and economic norms and principles . . . of modern society." The petitions were accompanied by demonstrations and organized efforts to meet with Soviet officials.

In the world's scientific and academic community, the reaction to the Soviet decree was one of shock and revulsion. Twenty-one Nobel Laureates, in a public statement on October 1, expressed "dismay" with the "massive violation of human rights" implicit in the policy of "exorbitant head taxes." They warned that the "diploma tax" would have "a depressing effect on the possibility of expansion and enhancement of academic, cultural, and scientific exchanges and contact between the peoples of the United States and the Soviet Union." On October 31, six thousand professors from some two hundred American and Canadian universities took out a two-page advertisement in the *New York Times,* urging that "the Soviet Government rescind this benighted decree and remove all arbitrary bars to the free movement of people." When M. V. Keldysh, president of the Soviet Academy of Sciences, paid an official visit in mid-October to the American scientific community, he found only disdain and contempt for the Soviet tax decree.

The public anger in the United States was reflected in an amendment to the East-West Trade Relations Act submitted to the Senate by three-quarters of its members (seventy-six Senators) which served notice that Congress would not approve a proposed Soviet-American trade package unless the "diploma tax" was dropped. The amendment specified that "no nonmarket economy shall be eligible to receive most-favored-nation treatment or to participate in any program of the Government of the United States which extends credits or credit guarantees or investment guarantees" if that country "imposes more than a nominal tax on emigration, for any purposes or cause whatsoever. . . ." Senator Henry M. Jackson, the author of the amendment, emphasized that it was "a clear signal to the Soviet Union" that it will have to deal "not only with the Administration but also with Congress." Earlier he observed that "the greatest crime is the indifference and the failure to act." "People must not be denied individual rights and freedoms for economic concessions," Jackson stressed.

With negotiations for a vastly stepped-up trade agreement between the Soviet Union and the United States well advanced, the "clear signal" of the Jackson amendment did not go altogether unheeded in Moscow. In late October and early November, Soviet authorities granted exemptions from the "diploma tax" to approximately 190 educated Jews and their families who had applied for exit visas. The August 14 implementing order of the Council of Ministers had provided for such exceptions. Among those exempted was the automation-control expert Roman Rutman, an activist in the Jewish national movement.

But even as the exemptions were granted, the chief of the visa department of the Soviet police, Colonel Andrei Verein, told Soviet Jewish activists—as reported in a letter signed by forty-seven of them on October 31—that the waiver of the tax in certain cases was "not . . . a change of the authorities' approach to the emigration problem, but . . . a gesture toward a certain foreign power with which the Soviet Union is seeking to develop commercial and economic relations." The allusion was to the United States. The letter went on to quote the Deputy Minister of Interior, Boris Shumilin, who had also met with the Jewish activists, as saying that Soviet policy "has not changed and will not change." It was apparent that, for the time being, the Soviet edict would not be withdrawn even in the face of an aroused world opinion.

International morality on the question of the right to leave a country was forcefully expressed in a colloquium sponsored by the International Institute of the Rights of Man held at the University of Uppsala in Sweden from June 19 to June 22, 1972, and attended by seventy distinguished international legal authorities from twenty countries. The colloquium adopted a "Declaration" which a moving spirit at the meeting, Nobel Laureate René Cassin, said added "flesh and bones" to Article 13/2 of the Universal Declaration of Human Rights.

Among the twenty Articles of the Uppsala "Declaration," three were particularly pertinent. Article 2 stated: "Every State shall recognize, implement and enforce the right of any person to leave its territory, temporarily or permanently." Article 4 specified: "No State shall subject a person to reprisals, sanctions, penalties, or harassment, for seeking to exercise or for exercising the right to leave a country." A crucially relevant point was made in Article 5:

"No special fees, taxes or other exactions shall be imposed for exercising . . . [a person's] right to leave a country "

The same month that the Uppsala "Declaration" was issued, Academician Sakharov publicly released a memorandum he had originally sent Leonid Brezhnev in March, 1971, and which also addressed itself to the issue: "It is essential to pass laws ensuring the free and unimpeded exercise by citizens of their right to leave the country and return to it freely. It is essential to abolish the illegal regulations containing limitations of that right." Sakharov's view, which paralleled almost exactly that of the Uppsala "Declaration," represented enlightened public opinion within the USSR. Whether its crude abridgment by the Kremlin rulers can stand the test of time and widespread indignation is open to question.[5] The outstanding fact of 1972, after all, was the acquiescence of the Soviet leadership to world opinion by allowing a considerable number of Jews to leave.

In view of the limited breakthrough achieved with respect to emigration, all the more ironic and poignant is the plight of the approximately thirty-five militants who had been incarcerated during 1970 and 1971 only for the reason that they desperately sought to emigrate, and who were still held in forced labor camps. Their spirit had by no means been broken. On December 24, 1971, twenty-four of them smuggled out a joint letter which testified to the unquenchable striving of man for freedom:

> Today, on December 24, 1971, the first anniversary of the passing of the sentence on Jews who wished to go to Israel, handed down at the first Leningrad trial, we the victims of this and of the subsequent trials, proclaim a three-day hunger strike as a sign of protest.
>
> We state that neither malice nor hatred ever guided our actions in connection with the Soviet State, and that we never had any intention of undermining it.
>
> We considered and consider Israel as our Homeland, and it is only our fervent desire to live there that has brought us into conflict with the Soviet authorities.

Soviet activists continued to remind their fellow Jews that they owe a debt of gratitude to those still languishing in labor camps. Their *White Book* concluded with the observation that the efforts of the imprisoned "gave a tremendous push to the common cause." "Your road," the book reminded its readers, "is strewn with years of their [the prisoners'] lives, their health, and their convict labor."

Justice demands that these political prisoners, together with those sentenced for the same "crimes" in 1972, be pardoned.[6] This was the plea of Soviet Jewish activists, seventeen of whom wired President Podgorny on December 22, 1971, urging him to "liberate these Jews, whose only aim is to go to their national Homeland." It was also the plea of the world Jewish community and of men of good will everywhere. It was eloquently echoed by the Soviet Committee on Human Rights in May, 1971. The Committee's co-founder, Chalidze, posed the issue in a broader and sharper form in a provocative essay written on May 7, 1972, and submitted to the Uppsala colloquium. He argued that "generally speaking, a State should not have the right to punish . . . a person who has committed a crime if this individual does not want to live in the [particular] society. . . ." The argument has particular merit, he observed, where the State has "distinctive criminal laws." What the USSR may consider "anti-Soviet agitation" aimed at "defaming the social and state system" would be regarded in the West as a "normal public exchange of opinion." Thus, he concluded, "justice would be served" in convictions of this kind "by guaranteeing the right of convicted persons to leave the country."

On September 13, fifty-one leading Soviet scientists and artists submitted an appeal to the Supreme Soviet, asking it to grant amnesty to all political prisoners on the occasion of the fiftieth anniversary celebration of the formation of the USSR (on December 30). Signatures for the petition were collected between May 4 and September 5. Sakharov was its prime mover. (Chalidze had resigned from the Committee on Human Rights in the fall. He wished to receive official permission to lecture at New York University and Georgetown University and must have felt that continued involvement with the Committee would compromise his efforts to obtain an exit visa.[7]) Other signers included the prominent physicist Mikhail Leontovich and the leading mathematician Igor Shafarevich, both members of the Academy of Sciences. The noted cellist Mstislav Rostropovich and the writers Lydia Chukovskaya and Viktor Nekrasov also joined in the appeal. Veniamin Levich and Aleksander Lerner added their names to the joint effort.

Beyond the question of the right to leave, there remain other facets of the unresolved Soviet Jewish problem. For even if Med-vedev is correct in estimating that those who seek to emigrate num-ber between 200,000 and 300,000, the bulk of the Soviet Jewry—85 to 90 per cent—apparently, and for the foreseeable future, in-tends to remain. Its rights, whether in the cultural and religious area or in the civil area, have yet to be restored. In the cultural sphere, no positive response has been made by the Soviet Govern-ment in the past few years, despite concessions concerning emigra-tion. The absence of Jewish communal institutions and Jewish schools is especially painful, as many of the petitions testify. A con-siderable number of Jews would be prepared to utilize such insti-tutions and schools if they existed. The 1970 census revealed that a minimum of 315,000 Jews considered Yiddish their native tongue. No doubt, many more have some familiarity with the language or might very well be interested in subjects that bear upon Jewish his-tory and cultural heritage even if these were taught in the Russian language.

Soviet Jewish activists have especially focused upon a new de-mand—the right to study Hebrew. On February 1, 1972, forty-nine Moscow Jews wrote to the Municipal Department for People's Edu-cation, noting that interest in the Hebrew language "has steeply risen among a part of the Jewish population in Moscow," and requesting that courses be established for the teaching of that lan-guage. One month later, on March 1, forty-seven Jews of Minsk wrote to the Central Committee of the Byelorussian Communist Party and to the Ministries of Education and Culture in Byelorussia, asking that "evening courses for the Hebrew language" be allowed. They bitterly complained that two private study groups for the learning of Hebrew, established in Minsk at the end of January, 1972, were halted by the local authorities.

The condition of Judaism remains desperate, despite two positive, though minor developments in 1972. On May 15, the Central Synagogue in Moscow finally obtained a new rabbi to succeed Rabbi Yehuda Leib Levin, who had died the previous November. The vacant post had meant that the Soviet capital, with several hundred thousand Jews, had been without a single rabbi for six months, a fact which caused some embarrassment to Soviet authorities. The new rabbi was fifty-nine-year-old Yakov L. Fishman, who had not officiated as a rabbi since 1964 and who lacked the scholarship and learning of his predecessor. In March, the Yeshiva was finally re-opened. It had but six students, none of whom was studying for the rabbinate (they were training to be either cantors or ritual slaughterers).

The current tragic situation of Judaism was revealed in a lengthy, frank "appeal" written on March 31, 1971, by a long-time member of the Moscow congregation, G. M. Manevich, and addressed to the late Rabbi Levin. It called attention to "the total lack of a central Jewish religious administration" in "contrast to other religions practiced in the Soviet Union." The "appeal" further noted: "All Jewish communities are in acute need of rabbis"; the single Yeshiva "is in a deplorable state"; kosher meat is obtainable in only "a very few towns"; valuable religious scrolls "are rotting and becoming unfit for use"; Jewish cemeteries are maintained in "fewer and fewer towns"; and "every year it becomes increasingly difficult to acquire prayer shawls, phylacteries . . . and other vital religious articles."

Discrimination against Jews in a variety of areas of employment has become especially pronounced. The Svirsky *samizdat* article throws a glaring light on the subject. The "fifth point" in the internal passport (identifying nationality), he observed, is universally used and is often accompanied by vulgar expressions of anti-Semitism. Already in 1965, Svirsky had vigorously condemned the growth of anti-Semitism in a presentation to the Moscow Union of Writers, a speech which Roy Medvedev had called attention to and warmly endorsed in his own *samizdat* essay on the Jewish question. From the time of Svirsky's speech, he ceased to be published and became virtually a "non-person."

The Moscow Union of Writers itself fell prey to open bigotry. On December 29, 1971, it expelled Aleksander Galich, a distinguished playwright, song-writer, and film scenarist who also served as a "corresponding member" of the Soviet Committee on Human Rights. He was accused of trying to persuade Russian Jews to emigrate to Israel. More pertinent than this unlikely charge was the manner in which the discussion concerning his expulsion took place. In a throwback to the format of the anti-"cosmopolitan" campaign of the late forties, Galich was repeatedly referred to as "Comrade Ginzburg," his original name. The play upon a person's name for purposes of evoking prejudicial associations was by no means unusual. Solzhenitsyn related how the authorities, in their smear effort against him in 1971 and 1972, suggested at various meetings that his real name was the Jewish-sounding "Solzhenitser." Listeners to such rumor-mongering were clearly expected to respond negatively to someone presumably "alien" in origin.

Medvedev had documented the deepening of discriminatory practices in the political-security areas as well as in the broader fields of economic life. But a letter circulating in *samizdat* form which came to light in May, 1972, indicates that even appointment to that prestigious and sacrosanct body the Academy of Sciences is no longer immune to ethnic bias. The letter was written in Moscow on October 10, 1970, and was signed by I. S. Narsky, a doctor of Philosophical Sciences, Professor at Moscow State University, and a part-time senior scientific worker at the Academy of Sciences. Addressed to the Academy President M. V. Keldysh, the letter, in its first paragraph, was instructive:

> Recently I have frequently come across allegations about me which are being spread among members of the Department of Philosophy and Law of the USSR Academy of Sciences saying that I am concealing my true nationality, as supposedly I am really a "Polish Jew." I could have ignored these rumors if it were not for the circumstances that they are transparently connected with the fact of my promotion to candidate status for election as a corresponding member of the USSR Academy of Sciences.

The writer took elaborate pains, drawing upon fairly extensive genealogy, to demonstrate that his parentage was exclusively Russian in origin.

This and similar developments may have prompted Sakharov, in his June, 1972, "postscript" to the "Memorandum" he had initially written to Brezhnev in March, 1971, to express "alarm" about an "intentional exacerbation of national problems" as well as about other recent anti-democratic phenomena in the USSR. In his "Memorandum" he reiterated his earlier view that the internal passport system must be gradually abolished, "since it is a great hindrance to the development of the country's productive forces and a violation of the rights of citizens."

It is quite likely that the movement for exodus has intensified suspicion about Jews in general, which finds expression in the erection of even stronger barriers against employment and promotion of

Jews. A recent disturbing development affecting the All-Union Radio and Television Orchestra may be indicative of the trend. After its conductor, Yury Aronovich, was allowed to leave, a re-examination of the "musical capabilities" was ordered of all members of the orchestra. Thirty musicians, of whom twenty-five were Jewish, were dismissed. Only four Jews remain, and there is no certainty that their jobs are secure. The renowned film director Mikhail Kalik, who after much personal travail was finally allowed to emigrate to Israel in November, 1971, revealed later that he had been reproached by various Soviet Jews, after he had applied for an exit visa, on grounds that supposedly "things had been quiet until the agitation to emigrate to Israel began . . . [which] reactivated the 'Jewish question.' "

If, for the activists and the broad stratum of the Jewish population which supports, through personal commitment, their aims, the burning issue is the right to leave, for the majority of Soviet Jews, who appear to seek assimilation, the question of anti-Semitism remains pressing. Obstacles to full assimilation in the form of discrimination must be lifted if the natural human right to integration is to be achieved. Inevitably, this requires that the forces which nourish the roots of discrimination, particularly propaganda campaigns that carry distinctive anti-Semitic overtones, must be eradicated. Furthermore, numerous Jews, whether or not they seek integration, also desire fulfillment of their natural right to give expression to the great Jewish cultural and religious heritage of their forefathers. Opportunities, including the essential institutional means, for realization of this normal human aspiration must be provided. Only when the options of emigration, assimilation, and maintenance of Jewish identity are permitted and kept open can it be said that "the shadow of the Russians" will have passed.

Jean Paul Sartre, in his January 7, 1971, speech in Paris, succinctly summed up the character of today's Soviet Jewish problem:

> We must also work, so far as we can, to bring [it] about that the Soviet Union develops a policy which gives Soviet Jews their full rights as citizens and as humans. Actually, there is only one such policy; it is composed of three options among which the [Soviet] bureaucracy continues to vacillate: (1) for those who wish it, to facilitate assimilation; and toward this end to launch a campaign against anti-Semitism, and to tackle the problems of anti-Semitism head on. (2) For the

Jews who require a Jewish national culture inside the Soviet Union, to permit such a culture to develop. . . . (3) Finally, when these measures have borne fruit, to open the doors and permit all those, not only Jews, but all Soviet citizens who wish to leave Soviet soil to depart.

The sentiments were the same as those expressed by Roy Medvedev. Even if some of them were seriously questioned as a possibility by Jewish activists, they continue to be the goal of enlightened opinion both within and outside the Soviet Union.

There can be little doubt that ending Soviet anti-Semitism and restoring Jewish cultural and religious rights are far more difficult objectives to attain than the right of Jews to leave for Israel. For these purposes presume a fundamentally different set of ideological assumptions and beliefs of a socialist character from those now subscribed to by the occupants of the Kremlin. Discrimination and forced assimilation continue to be integral elements of Soviet policy on the Jewish question. That is the reason why the thoughtful Mikhail Zand has so vigorously demurred at the hopes projected by Roy Medvedev.

Yet modest progress is conceivable. More overt forms of discrimination and vulgar anti-Semitism can be reduced, and some specifically Jewish institutions can be provided. The history of the Soviet Union since the middle nineteen-fifties is not without examples, however minor, of one or another concession to Jewish integrity, especially when the outcry from abroad has had a loud and sustained character.

To maintain and maximize that outcry is the responsibility of civilized society. Solzhenitsyn, in a somewhat different but related context, expressed it movingly in his undelivered Nobel lecture, published in August, 1972, in the Nobel Foundation *Yearbook*:

And mankind's sole salvation lies in making everything everyone's business: in the people of the East being vitally concerned with what is thought in the West, the people of the West vitally concerned with what goes on in the East.

Even if no positive response is immediately forthcoming, the concern must be made real and palpable. Especially is this the case at a time when the United States and the USSR are striving for agreements in a variety of fields—commercial, cultural, and scientific.

For, as Sakharov recently observed, Soviet authorities "seem more impudent because they feel that with *détente* they can now ignore Western public opinion." That "everyone's business" necessarily and particularly includes the condition of Soviet Jewry need not be underlined. For the Jews of the Soviet Union have a special claim on mankind's conscience: they constitute the surviving remnant of that spiritually rich and culturally prolific East European Jewish community that was decimated during the Holocaust. They warrant what their kin had not been fortunate enough to receive: the care and vigil of civilization.

Notes

CHAPTER 1

1. The statement was made by Kosygin at his press conference in New York and reported in the *New York Times,* June 27, 1967. He delivered the same comment at a press conference in Ottawa, Canada, in October, 1971 (see *Chicago Tribune,* October 21, 1971). The same comment was made in Copenhagen by Kosygin (see *Jewish Chronicle,* London, December 10, 1971).
2. Ilya Ilf and Yevgeny Petrov, *The Complete Adventures of Ostap Bender* (New York, 1962), p. 294.
3. Lewis S. Feuer, "Meeting the Philosophers," *Survey: A Journal of Soviet and East European Studies,* April, 1964, pp. 10–23.
4. Raymond A. Bauer, Alex Inkeles, and Clyde Kluckhohn, *How the Soviet System Works* (Cambridge, Mass., 1956).
5. Professor Alex Inkeles extended me the privilege of examining the interview material concerning nationalities in the winter of 1960. The analysis of the data is my own.
6. The study, entitled "The Nationality Questionnaire," appeared in mimeographed form as part of the Harvard Project. It was written by Sylvia Gilliam.
7. Jesse D. Clarkson, *A History of Russia* (New York, 1961), pp. 333–35.
8. Cited in Lucy S. Dawidowicz, ed., *The Golden Tradition* (New York, 1967), p. 406. The early Social-Democrat Pavel B. Akselrod wrote: ". . . the majority of this Russian society . . . as a matter of fact . . . considered all Jews . . . as kikes, [and] harmful to Russia . . ." (*ibid.,* p. 410).
9. Salo W. Baron, *The Russian Jew under Tsars and Soviets* (New York, 1964), pp. 220–22.
10. Paul Avrich, *Kronstadt 1921* (Princeton, 1970), pp. 178–80. Evidence about the widespread character of popular anti-Jewish stereotyping in Soviet Russia during 1920–21 is to be found throughout this study.
11. Mikhail Gorev, *Protiv antisemitov* (Moscow, 1928), p. 9.

12. *Pervyi vsesoiuznoi s'ezd OZET v Moskve, 15–20 Noiabria 1926 goda* (Moscow, 1927), p. 65.
13. Yury Larin, *Yevrei i antisemitizm v SSSR* (Moscow, 1929), p. 241–44.
14. *Ibid.,* p. 238.
15. *Pravda,* February 19, 1929.
16. Solomon M. Schwarz, *The Jews in the Soviet Union* (Syracuse, 1951), pp. 254–56.
17. Merle Fainsod, *Smolensk under Soviet Rule* (Cambridge, Mass., 1958), p. 445.
18. The uncensored and expanded version of Kuznetsov's documentary novel is especially useful with regard to the Ukraine. It was published under his newly adopted name, A. Anatoli, in 1970 by Farrar, Straus & Giroux. Anti-Semitism in the partisan units is treated in Schwarz, *op. cit.,* pp. 322–30.
19. Schwarz, *op. cit.,* pp. 342–48.
20. Ilya Ehrenburg, *Post-War Years: 1945–54* (Cleveland, 1967) pp. 131, 298.
21. Harrison E. Salisbury, *To Moscow and Beyond* (New York, 1960), p. 77.
22. Isaac Deutscher, *Stalin,* 2nd ed. (New York, 1967), p. 627.
23. *Réalités,* no. 136 (May, 1957), p. 104.
24. Sally Belfrage, *A Room in Moscow* (London, 1958).
25. The episode, which is based upon an eyewitness report of M. Tatu, *Le Monde*'s correspondent in Moscow, is discussed in William Korey, "A Soviet Poet as Rebel," *New Republic,* January 8, 1962. See *Le Monde,* October 10, 1961.
26. The Yevtushenko-Khrushchev exchange appears in "Russian Art and Anti-Semitism: Two Documents," *Commentary,* December, 1963, p. 434.
27. Earlier, Premier Aleksei Kosygin had denounced overt manifestations of anti-Semitism in a speech in Riga. See *Pravda,* July 19, 1965.
28. *Novyi mir,* no. 9 (September, 1966), pp. 187–205. For a summary, see *Patterns of Prejudice,* vol. 1, no. 2 (March–April, 1967), pp. 15–17.
29. Moshe Decter, ed., *Redemption! Jewish Freedom Letters from Russia* (New York, 1970), pp. 10–14.
30. *Yevreiskii vopros v SSSR (Tezisy).* This document, written in the spring of 1970, was recently revealed to have been drafted by Professor Mikhail Zand.
31. Andrei D. Sakharov, *Progress, Coexistence, and Intellectual Freedom* (New York, 1970), pp. 54, 65–66.
32. Andrei Amalrik, *Will the Soviet Union Survive Until 1984?* (New York, 1970), p. 38.
33. Einstein's comments were made to Shlomo Mikhoels. See A. Sutzkever, "Mit Shlomo Mikhoels," *Di Goldene Keit,* no. 43 (1962), pp. 165–66.
    The "shadow" hovers over the reminiscences attributed to Nikita Khrushchev. He is quoted as saying: "Unfortunately, the germs of anti-

Semitism remained in our system, and apparently there still isn't the necessary discouragement of it and resistance to it. My guards aren't bad fellows, but anti-Semitism crops up even in my conversations with them." *Khrushchev Remembers,* introduction, commentary, and notes by Edward Crankshaw, translated and edited by Strobe Talbott (Boston, 1970), p. 269.

Deutscher noted: "Despite all that the Bolshevik Governments have done, in their better years, to combat these [anti-Semitic] prejudices, enmity towards Jews was almost unabated." He traced its sources to Greek Orthodoxy and the "native tradition of pogroms." See Deutscher, *Stalin, op. cit.,* p. 604.

CHAPTER 2

1. A recent careful and provocative analysis casts doubt upon the thesis that the Tsarist state organized most pogroms. The extent to which they were spontaneous or encouraged, especially by local Tsarist officials, remains a mystery. The regime, of course, tolerated and sponsored anti-Semitic propaganda. And some of its officials assisted pogrom-oriented activists. See Hans Rogger, "The Jewish Policy of Late Tsarism: A Reappraisal," *The Wiener Library Bulletin,* vol. 25, nos. 1 and 2 (1971), pp. 42–51.

2. Hans Rogger, "The Beiliss Case: Anti-Semitism and Politics in the Reign of Nicholas II," *Slavic Review,* vol. 25 (December, 1966), p. 629.

3. *Ibid.,* p. 626.

4. See George Lichtheim, "Socialism and the Jews," *Dissent,* July–August, 1968, pp. 314–42. Marx, in his *Zur Judenfrage* (1944) did, however, use certain stereotypes about Jews (and their relationship to capitalism) that were to become part of the lexicon of such Soviet bigots as Trofim K. Kichko.

5. V. I. Lenin, *Collected Works,* 4th ed., English translation (Moscow, 1965), vol. 29, p. 253.

6. V. I. Lenin, *Sochineniia,* 3rd ed. (Moscow, 1937), vol. XVII, p. 292: The decree banning anti-Semitism was published in *Izvestiia,* July 27, 1918. Lenin's role is noted in Anatoly V. Lunacharsky, *Ob antisemitizme* (Moscow, 1929), p. 38.

7. For references, see Joel Cang, *The Silent Millions* (New York, 1969), pp. 170–73. At the Twenty-fourth Party Congress in March–April 1971, Leonid Brezhnev placed greater stress on "monolithic unity," although he made the usual bow to the blossoming of national cultures. See his speech in *Pravda,* March 31, 1971.

8. See, particularly, J. Stalin, *Marksizm i natsional'no-kolonialnyi vopros* (Moscow, 1937), pp. 6, 8.

9. Lenin, *Sochineniia,* 3rd ed. (Moscow, 1937), vol. 24, p. 96.

10. Stalin, *op. cit.,* p. 209.

11. Andrei Vyshinsky, *Sovetskoe gosudarstvennoe pravo* (Moscow, 1938), p. 247.
12. *Izvestiia,* June 19, 1919.
13. From Semyon Dimanshtein's speech to a Party caucus at a Conference of Jewish Sections and Jewish Commissariats in October, 1918. Cited in Schwarz, *op. cit.,* p. 97.
14. *Pravda,* December 28, 1932.
15. This point is discussed in Chapter 3.
16. Tsentral'noe statisticheskoe upravlenie, *Itogi vsesoiuznoi perepisi naseleniia 1959 goda: SSSR* (Moscow, 1962), p. 204. Data on the region's representatives in the Soviet of Nationalities are derived from *Deputaty Verkhovnogo Soveta SSSR* (Moscow, 1962).
17. The data are calculated from the census results reported in *Izvestiia,* April 17, 1971. The 1959 census results are in *Pravda,* February 4, 1960.
18. The five recognized Jewish languages in the USSR are Yiddish, Judaeo-Georgian, Judaeo-Tadzhik, Tat, and Judaeo-Krimchak. The number of Jews considering Yiddish their native tongue, according to the 1970 census, is probably close to 315,000.
19. Yakov Kantor, "Aynike Bamerkungen un Oisfiren tsu di Fareffentlichte Sachhakalen fun der Folks-tselung in Ratenverband dem 15 Yanuar, 1959," *Bleter far Geshichte* (Warsaw, 1962–63), Vol. 15, pp. 146–47. This work appeared in early 1964.
20. In 1959, 69 per cent of the Jews in Lithuania considered Yiddish their native tongue, 48 per cent in Latvia, and 50 per cent in Moldavia. In 1970, the percentage in Lithuania dropped to 62 and in Moldavia to 45. No figures were given for Latvia.
21. M. Friedberg, "Slozhno-podchinennoe predlozhenie v idish-taich, XVI–XVII vv," in *Voprosy sintaksisa romano-germanskikh iazikov* (Leningrad, 1961). Only the pertinent section of this article was examined.
22. *Pravda,* July 1, 1944.
23. Commission on Human Rights, *Study of Discrimination in the Matter of Religious Rights and Practices, Conference Room Paper,* no. 35 (hereafter referred to as *Conference Room Paper,* no. 35).
24. *Jewish Telegraphic Agency,* January 13, 1960.
25. Lenin, *Sochineniia,* vol. 17, p. 141.
26. Maurice Hindus, *House Without a Roof* (Garden City, 1961), p. 73. The role of Point 5 in alienating Soviet Jews is examined in the chapter entitled "Jew—Russia's Stepson," pp. 297–325.
27. Lenin, *Sochineniia,* vol. 14, p. 18.
28. *Sobranie uzakonenii i rasporiazhenii rabochego i krest'ianskogo pravitel'stva Ukrainskoi SSR* (Kiev, 1922), no. 41, item 598. See also the *Sobranie* of 1927 (Kiev, 1927), no. 34, item 157. For Byelorussia, see *Prakticheskoe reshenie natsional'nogo voprosa Belorusskoi SSR,* part 1 (Minsk, 1927), pp. 120, 133–39.
29. Cited in Solomon M. Schwarz, *The Jews in the Soviet Union* (Syracuse, 1951), p. 137.

30. *Novaia sistema narodnogo obrazovaniia v SSSR* (Moscow, 1960), p. 79.

31. Joseph B. Schechtman, *Star in Eclipse: Russian Jewry Revisited* (New York, 1961), p. 151.

32. *Pravda,* November 2, 1961.

33. *Report of the American-European Seminar on the U.S.S.R.* (West Haven, Conn., n.d. [1957]).

34. *Vedemosti Verkhovnogo Soveta SSSR,* no. 52 (1293), p. 931. Signed on August 29, 1964, the decree was published on December 28, 1964.

35. *Uchitel'skaia gazeta,* March 12, 1964.

36. *Neues Leben,* January 20, 1965.

37. *Neues Leben,* January 27, 1965. Three years later, the same journal reported that after numerous complaints by German parents in Kazakh-stan, a greater number of hours for the teaching of German as the mother tongue were instituted in that republic. See *Neues Leben,* October 16, 1968.

38. *Réalités,* no. 136 (May, 1957).

39. Kantor, *op. cit.,* p. 148.

40. *Ibid.* The blow also fell on the specific Jewish culture in Bokhara and Georgia. Their respective literatures were forbidden, and in the case of Georgian Jewry, their cultural leaders were executed. See the address of Mikhail Zand at Columbia University on October 6, 1971 in *Soviet Jewry Today,* vol. 1, no. 1 (November, 1971).

41. B. Z. Goldberg, *The Jewish Problem in the Soviet Union* (New York, 1961), pp. 59–73; see also C. Szmeruk, "Soviet Jewish Literature: The Last Phase," *Survey,* April–June, 1961, pp. 71–77.

42. For details see Yehoshua Gilboa, *The Black Years of Soviet Jewry* (Boston, 1971).

43. `American Jewish Year Book 1971` (Philadelphia, 1971), vol. 72, p. 408.

44. An analysis of the Yiddish journal can be found in Joseph and Abraham Brumberg, *Sovietish Heymland—An Analysis* (New York, 1966). A recent survey of its character is in Elias Schulman, "A Jewish Journal in the Soviet Union," *Reconstructionist,* June 11, 1971, pp. 13–17.

45. *Jerusalem Post,* February 3, 1961.

46. *Jerusalem Post,* December 1, 1961.

47. Stalin, *op. cit.,* p. 209.

48. *Ibid.,* p. 194.

49. *Pravda,* November 2, 1961; *Materialy XXII s'ezda KPSS* (Moscow, 1961), pp. 190–92.

50. Dzhunusov's article, as translated from the Russian (*Istoriia SSSR,* no. 3, 1962) is in *Soviet Sociology,* vol. 1, no. 2, pp. 10–28; the report to the UN is in United Nations General Assembly, *Manifestations of Racial Prejudice and National and Religious Intolerance,* Doc. A/5473/Add. 1, September 25, 1963, p. 48 (hereafter referred to as *Manifestations*).

51. Richard Pipes, "The Forces of Nationalism," *Problems of Communism,* January–February, 1964, p. 6.

52. *Pravda,* September 21, 1948.
53. Cited in Gilboa, *op. cit.,* pp. 209–10.
54. See Daniel P. Moynihan, "Breakthrough at Ljubljana," *National Jewish Monthly,* September, 1965, pp. 15–17; and *Seminar on the Multinational Society,* Doc. ST/TAO/HR/23.
55. *Izvestiia,* July 16, 1963.
56. *Conference Room Paper,* no. 35.
57. J. Meisel and E. Kozera, eds., *Materials for the Study of the Soviet System* (Ann Arbor, 1953), p. 241.
58. John Curtiss, "Religion as a Soviet Social Problem," *Social Problems,* vol. VII, no. 4 (Spring, 1960), pp. 328–39.
59. Walter Kolarz, *Religion in the Soviet Union* (New York, 1961), p. 388.
60. Goldberg, *op. cit.,* p. 295. However, on March 23, 1971, the Soviet Government organized a conference of representatives of Jewish religious communities at the Moscow Choral Synagogue. Some thirty-five rabbis and congregation leaders from a number of communities assembled in order to condemn Israel and Zionism. A longtime member of the Moscow religious community, G. M. Manevich, complained in a letter to the chief rabbi of Moscow on March 31 that the conference failed to take up the pressing need of creating a "Union of Jewish Religious Communities of the USSR, with a permanent central administrative board and rabbinate." A copy of Manevich's lengthy and profoundly moving letter finally reached the West early in 1972.
61. *Manifestations,* Doc. A/5473/Add. 1, pp. 52–53.
62. *Ibid.*
63. *Conference Room Paper,* no. 35, p. 12; G. Anashkin, "O svobode i sobliudenii zakondatel'stva o religioznikh kultakh," *Sovetskoe gosudarstvo i pravo,* no. 1, January, 1965, p. 39.
64. Joshua Rothenberg, *The Jewish Religion in the Soviet Union* (New York, 1971), pp. 52–66.
65. Joshua Rothenberg, "Judaism in the Soviet Union: A 'Second-Class' Religion?" mimeo (B'nai B'rith International Council, 1970), p. 14.
66. William C. Fletcher and Anthony J. Strover, eds., *Religion and the Search for New Ideals in the USSR* (New York, 1967), p. 104.
67. Mordechai Altshuler, ed., *Russian Publications on Jews and Judaism in the Soviet Union 1917–67* (Jerusalem, 1970), p. xii. The bibliography was compiled by B. Pinkus and A. A. Greenbaum.
68. For the citations see Rothenberg, "Judaism in the Soviet Union: A 'Second-Class' Religion?" *op. cit.,* pp. 9–10.
69. Schechtman, *op. cit.,* p. 146.
70. *Conference Room Paper,* no. 35, p. 11.
71. *New York Herald Tribune,* July 17, 1963.
72. Abraham Ravich, "Circumcision, A Partial Breakthrough Against Cancer?" *National Jewish Monthly,* December, 1964. For a detailed discussion, see Rothenberg, *The Jewish Religion in the Soviet Union, op. cit.,* pp. 141–69.

CHAPTER 3

1. *Sbornik ukazov i postanovlenii Vremennogo Pravitel'stva* (Petrograd, 1917), pp. 8, 46. A Soviet work produced for UNESCO details some of the Tsarist restrictions upon Jews. See I. P. Tsamerian and S. L. Ronin, *Equality of Rights Between Races and Nationalities in the USSR* (Nijmegen, 1962), pp. 17–21.

2. *Istoriia sovetskoi konstitutsii v dokumentakh, 1917–56* (Moscow, 1956), pp. 57–58.

3. *Ugolovnyi kodeks RSFSR* (Moscow, 1964), p. 39. The Ukrainian Criminal Code provides for imprisonment from six months to three years. The codes of the other union republics specify similar penalties.

4. *Narodnoe khoziaistvo S.S.S.R.* (Moscow, 1967), pp. 803, 811; J. A. Newth, "Jews in the Soviet Intelligentsia," *Bulletin on Soviet Jewish Affairs*, no. 2 (July, 1968), pp. 1–12; and Zev Katz, "After the Six-Day War," in Lionel Kochan, ed., *The Jews in Soviet Russia since 1917* (London, 1970), pp. 330–31.

5. *Sovetskoe zdravookhranenie*, no. 3 (1970), p. 12. The decline was in absolute numbers as well, from 25,000 to 24,034.

6. The *samizdat* document is by Roy A. Medvedev. Entitled "Blizhnevostochnyi knoflict iyevreiskii vopros v SSSR," it was produced in May, 1970. An English translation of a small portion of the document appeared in *Survey*, vol. 17, no. 2 (Spring, 1971), pp. 185–201. (This work is hereafter referred to as Medvedev, *samizdat* document.)

7. *XV s'ezd vsesoiuznoi kommunisticheskoi partii (b)* (Moscow, 1928), pp. 400–401.

8. *Réalités*, no. 136 (May, 1957), p. 104.

9. *National Guardian*, June 25, 1956.

10. J. B. Salsberg, "Anti-Semitism in the USSR?" *Jewish Life*, February, 1957, p. 38. His discussions were initially published in a series of articles in *Vochenblatt* and the *Morning Freiheit* from October 25 to December 20, 1956.

11. *Observer* (London), January 13, 1963.

12. *Pravda*, March 8, 1962. The stenographic report of the meeting indicated that after Skriabin made this remark, a voice called out "Correct," and applause followed.

13. P. Rogachev and M. Sverdlin, "Sovetskii narod-novaia istoricheskaia obshchnost' liudei," *Kommunist*, June, 1963, p. 13.

14. Salo W. Baron, *The Russian Jew under Tsars and Soviets* (New York, 1964), p. 242.

15. Solomon M. Schwarz, *The Jews in the Soviet Union* (Syracuse, 1951), pp. 354–55, 364.

16. Alec Nove and J. A. Newth, "The Jewish Population: Demographic Trends and Occupation Patterns," in Kochan, *op. cit.*, p. 152.

17. *Ibid.*, p. 153. See also William Korey, "The Legal Position of Soviet Jewry: A Historical Enquiry," in Kochan, *op. cit.*, p. 93.

18. "Jews in the Soviet Union" (Novosti Press Agency, 1963); the figures

on total elected deputies to local Soviets are in UN Commission on Human Rights, *Periodic Reports on Human Rights,* Doc. E/CN. 4/860 (December 20, 1963), p. 181.

19. The percentage is reported in Medvedev's *samizdat* document.
20. S. Bialer, "How Russians Rule Russia," *Problems of Communism,* September–October, 1964, pp. 46, 48.
21. *Ibid.* The total number of Central Committee members is 241. Another 155 are candidate members. Of these, one—A. Chakovsky, editor of *Literaturnaia gazeta*—is also Jewish.
22. John Armstrong, *The Soviet Bureaucratic Elite: A Case Study of the Ukrainian Apparatus* (New York, 1959), p. 18.
23. Nove and Newth, *op. cit.,* p. 151.
24. *Pravda,* July 25, 1970.
25. T. H. Rigby, *Communist Party Membership in the U.S.S.R., 1917–67* (Princeton, 1968), p. 386.
26. John Fisher, *Why They Behave Like Russians* (New York, 1947), p. 108.
27. Harrison Salisbury, *Russia on the Way* (New York, 1946), p. 293.
28. William Korey, "The Legal Position of the Jewish Community of the Soviet Union," in Erich Goldhagen, ed., *Ethnic Minorities in the Soviet Union* (New York, 1968), p. 339.
29. Andrei D. Sakharov, *Progress, Coexistence, and Intellectual Freedom* (New York, 1970), pp. 65–66.
30. Medvedev, *samizdat* document.
31. Moshe Decter, ed., *Redemption! Jewish Freedom Letters from Russia* (New York, 1970), pp. 11–12.
32. *New York Times,* September 29, 1959.
33. The Convention is in the UN document *Study of Discrimination in Education,* Doc. E/CN. 4/Sub. 2/210.
34. Rogachev and Sverdlin, *op. cit.,* p. 13; and V. Komarov and V. Artamoshkina, "Takova ikh nauchnaia ob'ektivnost'!" *Vestnik vysshei shkoly,* December, 1963, p. 78.
35. N. DeWitt, *Education and Professional Employment in the USSR* (Washington, D.C., 1961), pp. 358–60.
36. Maurice Hindus, *House Without a Roof* (Garden City, 1961), p. 315.
37. *Vysshee obrazovanie v SSSR* (Moscow, 1961), p. 85.
38. Katz, *op. cit.,* p. 331. According to an article in *Soviet Life* in 1971 ("How Jews Live in the Soviet Union"), the number of Jewish students in the 1968–69 academic year was 111,900.
39. N. DeWitt, "The Status of Jews in Soviet Education," mimeographed (American Jewish Congress, 1964), p. 11.
40. See Nove and Newth, *op. cit.,* p. 157; and Katz, *op. cit.,* p. 331.
41. Katz, *op. cit.,* pp. 330–31.
42. See John A. Armstrong, "Soviet Foreign Policy and Anti-Semitism," in *Perspectives on Soviet Jewry* (New York, 1971), p. 70.
43. *Pravda,* July 16, 1971.

44. *New York Times,* July 19, 1971.
45. The appeal was published in *Survey,* Summer, 1970, p. 167.
46. Armstrong, "Soviet Foreign Policy and Anti-Semitism," *op. cit.,* pp. 70–71. Professor Zand, on his trip to the United States in September, 1971, told audiences: "I had everything in the Soviet Union, but I was a privileged slave among slaves. I was deprived of my human freedom and my Jewish identity."
47. The document is entitled *Yevreiskii vopros v SSSR* (Tezisy). It appeared in the West in May, 1970. A translation appears in *Bulletin on Soviet and East European Jewish Affairs,* no. 6 (December, 1970), pp. 49–50. The reference to "state organization" obviously means Israel.
48. Medvedev, *samizdat* document.

CHAPTER 4

1. Lenin, *Sochineniia,* 3rd ed. (Moscow, 1937), vol. XIX, pp. 354–55.
2. Boris Souvarine, "Gorky, Censorship and the Jews," *Dissent,* Winter, 1965, p. 83.
3. The episode is related in Isaac Deutscher, *The Prophet Armed: Trotsky: 1879–1921* (New York, 1954), pp. 325–26. Only at Yakov Sverdlov's insistence did Lenin give way on this appointment. But he had no hesitancy in appointing Trotsky as commissar of foreign affairs.
4. *Izvestiia,* July 27, 1918.
5. *Ugolovnyi kodeks RSFSR* (Moscow, 1922), p. 18.
6. *Ugolovnyi kodeks RSFSR* (Moscow, 1953), p. 23.
7. Solomon M. Schwarz, *The Jews in the Soviet Union* (Syracuse, 1951), pp. 274–89.
8. The various works are listed in Mordechai Altshuler, ed., *Russian Publications on Jews and Judaism in the Soviet Union 1917–67* (Jerusalem, 1970), pp. 51–66.
9. *Pravda,* February 19, 1929.
10. The episode is discussed in Isaac Deutscher, *The Prophet Unarmed: Trotsky, 1921–1929* (London, 1959), pp. 257–58. Medvedev relates that Lev Kamenev, following Lenin's death in 1924, was not made chairman of the Council of Commissars "on the pretext of his Jewish origins." Stalin is supposed to have said, "We must consider the peasant character of Russia." See Roy A. Medvedev, *Let History Judge* (New York, 1971), p. 44.
11. Quoted in the *New York Times,* January 15, 1931.
12. *Pravda,* November 30, 1936.
13. Isaac Deutscher, *The Prophet Outcast: Trotsky, 1929–1940* (New York, 1965), p. 369. The archives of the "old Bolshevik" E. P. Frolov disclose that Stalin made repeated statements to the effect that there were too many Jews in the opposition groups. See Medvedev, *Let History Judge, op. cit.,* p. 495.
14. See John A. Armstrong, *The Politics of Totalitarianism* (New York, 1961), p. 71.

15. Svetlana Alliluyeva, *Only One Year* (New York, 1969), pp. 152–53.
16. Yakov Kantor, "Aynike Bamerkungen un Oisfiren tsu di Fareffentlichte Sachhakalen fun der Folks-tselung in Ratenverband dem 15 Yanuar, 1959," *Bleter far Geshichte* (Warsaw, 1962–63), vol. 15, pp. 146–47. This work appeared in early 1964.
17. Details of this meeting were orally furnished to the author by J. B. Salsberg, a former Canadian Communist who was deeply involved in the problem at the time.
18. Sakharov, *Progress, Coexistence, and Intellectual Freedom* (New York, 1970), pp. 65–66.
19. Alliluyeva, *op. cit.*, p. 153.
20. H. Picker, *Hitlers Gespräche in Fuehrerhauptquartier, 1914–42*, 2nd ed., P. E. Schramm, A. Hillgruber, and M. Vogt (Stuttgart, 1965), p. 472.
21. John A. Armstrong, "The Jewish Predicament in the Soviet Union," *Midstream*, January, 1971, p. 27; and Armstrong, *The Politics of Totalitarianism, op. cit.*, p. 154.
22. Ilya Ehrenburg, *The War: 1941–45* (Cleveland, 1964), p. 121. The instructions were initially delivered by Shcherbakov's assistant, Kondakov. Shcherbakov told Ehrenburg, "The soldiers want to hear about Suvorov while you quote Heine."
23. Igor Gouzenko, *The Iron Curtain* (New York, 1948), pp. 157–58. At the beginning of the war, Stalin rejected a list of proposed editors for front-line newspapers on the ground that they were Jewish. See Medvedev, *Let History Judge, op. cit.*, p. 495.
24. Milovan Djilas, *Conversations with Stalin* (New York, 1962), p. 154.
25. Alliluyeva, *op. cit.*, p. 153.
26. Armstrong, *The Politics of Totalitarianism, op. cit.*, p. 406.
27. *Izvestiia*, May 25, 1945.
28. Stalin, *Sochineniia* (Moscow, 1951), vol. 2, p. 50.
29. Comments by Stalin on Jews are strewn throughout Svetlana Alliluyeva, *Twenty Letters to a Friend* (New York, 1967). See especially p. 159.
30. *Réalités*, no. 136 (May, 1957). The entire stenographic report of the meeting with the French Socialists is to be found on pp. 64–67, 101–4.
31. *Observer* (London), January 13, 1963.
32. Hannah Arendt, *The Origins of Totalitarianism*, 2nd ed. (New York, 1962), pp. 423–24.
33. See Paul Lendvai, *Anti-Semitism Without Jews* (New York, 1971), pp. 3–20.
34. Alliluyeva, *Only One Year, op. cit.*, p. 152.
35. George Fischer, *The Soviet System and Modern Society* (New York, 1968), pp. 65–117. I have drawn heavily upon Fischer's data for this section.
36. For a discussion of this type of personality, see Theodore Adorno *et al., The Authoritarian Personality* (New York, 1950). Konstantin Paustovsky, in a speech to the Moscow Writers' Union, characterized the

typical Stalinist bureaucrats as "cynics and obscurantists" who "without fear or embarrassment, carried on anti-Semitic conversations worthy of true Nazis." See Medvedev, *Let History Judge, op. cit.,* p. 543; and Patricia Blake and Max Hayward, eds., *Half-way to the Moon: New Writing from Russia* (Garden City, 1964), p. xxx.

37. Salzberg, *op. cit.;* see, also, Joel Cang, *The Silent Millions* (New York, 1969), pp. 134–35.
38. *Réalités,* no. 136 (May, 1957), p. 104.
39. *Le Figaro,* April 9, 1958.
40. J. B. Salsberg, "Anti-Semitism in the USSR?" *Jewish Life,* February, 1957; Cang, *op. cit.,* pp. 135–36.
41. See Ilya Ehrenburg, *Post-War Years: 1945–54* (Cleveland, 1967), p. 125; and Alliluyeva, *Only One Year, op. cit.,* p. 154.
42. The article appeared in *Pravda,* September 21, 1948. The role of the editor is mentioned in Ehrenburg, *Post-War Years: 1945–54, op. cit.,* p. 125.
43. *Ibid.,* p. 132.
44. Earl Raab, "The Black Revolution and the Jewish Question," *Commentary,* January, 1969, p. 23.
45. See Lendvai, *op. cit.,* pp. 3–10; and Yehoshua Gilboa, *The Black Years of Soviet Jewry* (Boston, 1971), pp. 146–87.
46. *Pravda,* January 13, 1953.
47. Yevgeny Yevtushenko, *A Precocious Autobiography,* trans. Andrew R. MacAndrew (New York, 1963), pp. 89–90.
48. *Krokodil,* January 30, 1953.
49. *Krokodil,* February 20, 1953. The article was written by Nikolai Gribachev, still prominent in literary circles.
50. Medvedev, *samizdat* document.
51. *Pravda,* April 6, 1953.
52. *Pravda,* February 28, 1963.
53. Cang, *op. cit.,* pp. 156–67.
54. "Economic Crimes in the Soviet Union," *Journal of the International Commission of Jurists,* Summer, 1964, pp. 3–47.
55. *Sovietskaia Litva,* April 4, 1962.
56. *Lvovskaia Pravda,* March 16, 1962.
57. *Izvestiia,* October 20, 1963.
58. *Pravda,* February 28, 1963.
59. *Manifestations,* Doc. A/5473, August 9, 1963, p. 59.
60. *Minskaia Pravda,* April 4, 1961.
61. H. Lumer, *Soviet Anti-Semitism—A Cold War Myth* (New York, 1964), p. 9.
62. *Pravda,* April 4, 1964.
63. A. Osipov, *Katikhizis bez prikras* (Moscow, 1963), pp. 276, 281.
64. Joshua Rothenberg, "Judaism in the Soviet Union: A 'Second Class' Religion?" mimeographed (B'nai B'rith International Council, 1970), pp. 8–9.
65. M. I. Iakubovich and V. A. Vladimirov, eds., *Gosudarstvennye pre-*

stuplenie: uchebnoe posobie sovetskomu ugolovnomu pravu (Moscow, 1960), p. 99.

66. *Kommunist* (Buinaksk), August 11, 1960.

CHAPTER 5

1. *Folksshtimme* (Warsaw), November 3, 1956.

2. Moshe Decter, ed., *Redemption! Jewish Freedom Letters from Russia* (New York, 1970), pp. 53–55.

3. *Ibid.,* pp. 46–49. American Ambassador Rita Hauser read a part of the letter to the General Assembly. Repeated interruptions by Soviet delegates prevented her from finishing it.

4. Mordechai Altshuler, ed., *Russian Publications on Jews and Judaism in the Soviet Union 1917–67* (Jerusalem, 1970), pp. 83–96.

5. Arthur Miller, "In Russia," *Harper's,* September, 1969, pp. 37–38. According to a leading authority on Soviet literature, "in the years since Stalin's death there appears to be a conscious attempt on the part of Soviet literary, publishing and censorship authorities to discourage any type of interest in Jewish subject matter on the part of Soviet writers and thus to prevent any discussion of it among Soviet readers." Maurice Friedberg, *The Jew in Post-Stalin Soviet Literature* (Washington, D.C., 1970), p. 59. Especially intriguing are the extraordinary lengths to which the authorities appear to have gone in order to suppress research by a Soviet historian, Marietta Shaginian, which suggested the possibility that Lenin's mother was of Jewish origin. See Marcin Wyzeimblo, "Was Lenin's Mother Jewish?" *Dissent,* April, 1971, pp. 141–44.

6. Professor Ina Schlesinger of the State University of New York assisted in the preparation of this study. An earlier study of the following works produced the same results: S. P. Alexeev and V. G. Kartsov, *Istoriia SSSR* (Moscow, 1960); F. P. Korovkin, *Istoriia drevnego mira* (Moscow, 1959); L. P. Bushchik, *Istoriia SSSR* (Moscow, 1958); K. V. Bazilevich, S. V. Bakhrushin, and A. V. Fokht, *Istoriia SSSR,* part II (Moscow, 1958); and K. V. Bazilevich, S. V. Bakhrushin, A. M. Pankratova, and A. V. Fokht, *Istoriia SSSR,* part III (Moscow, 1959).

   For a summary of the study, see William Korey, "The Legal Position of the Jewish Community of the Soviet Union," in Erich Goldhagen, ed., *Ethnic Minorities in the Soviet Union* (New York, 1968), p. 327.

7. *Rasskazy po istorii SSSR,* 4th ed. (Moscow, 1967).

8. *Istoriia drevnego mira* (Moscow, 1967).

9. *Istoriia srednikh vekov,* 7th ed. (Moscow, 1968).

10. *Istoriia srednikh vekov,* 5th ed. (Moscow, 1966).

11. *Istoriia SSSR,* 2nd ed. (Moscow, 1967).

12. *Istoriia SSSR* (Moscow, 1966).

13. *Istoriia SSSR,* 2nd ed. (Moscow, 1967).

14. *Istoriia SSSR* (Moscow, 1968).

15. *Istoriia SSSR—period imperializma* (Moscow, 1967). The manual is *Istoriia SSSR* (Moscow, 1968).

16. *Novaia istoriia,* part I, 25th ed. (Moscow, 1967).

17. *Novaia istoriia,* part II, 5th ed. (Moscow, 1967).
18. *Noveishaia istoriia,* 6th ed. (Moscow, 1967).
19. *Noveishaia istoriia,* 5th ed. (Moscow, 1967).
20. S. D. Skazkin, Y. V. Gutnovaia, A. I. Danilov and I. A. Levitskii, eds., *Istoriia srednikh vekov* (Moscow, 1966), 2 vols.
21. *History of the Ukrainian SSSR* (in Ukrainian) (Kiev, 1968).
22. *History of the Ukrainian SSSR* (in Ukrainian) (Kiev, 1968). This is a manual.
23. *History of the Latvian SSR* (in Latvian) (Riga, 1967).
24. *History of the Estonian SSR* (in Estonian) (Tallinn, 1967).
25. *History of the Lithuanian SSR* (in Lithuanian) (Kaunas, 1967).
26. *Literaturnaia gazeta,* March 2, 1949.
27. See Yehoshua Gilboa, *The Black Years of Soviet Jewry* (Boston, 1971), pp. 211–14. The *Small Soviet Encyclopedia,* published in Moscow in 1959, has the same bias as the *Large Soviet Encyclopedia.* It carries but a single paragraph of twenty-two lines dealing with Jews, as compared with the 1929 edition, which had four pages on Jews.
28. B. Z. Goldberg, *The Jewish Problem in the Soviet Union* (New York, 1961), pp. 65–66; Gilboa, *op. cit.,* pp. 72–77.
29. Altshuler, *op. cit.,* p. xiii.
30. *Izvestiia,* April 19, 1963.
31. A portion of the study is in William Korey, "Reporting the Eichmann Case," *Survey,* December, 1961, pp. 17–28.
32. *Ibid.* The Poland of 1960–61 was, of course, a far cry from that of 1968, when a massive anti-Semitic campaign was unleashed. However, as early as 1956 high Soviet officials were urging Poland to remove Jews from key political and administrative positions, and from the press and radio. See "USSR and the Politics of Polish Anti-Semitism 1956–68," *Soviet Jewish Affairs,* no. 1 (June, 1971), p. 19.

CHAPTER 6

1. The *Darmstädter Echo* gave the trial extensive coverage, which was drawn upon in this chapter. The Swiss newspaper, *Der Zürcher Zeitung,* provided excellent reportage. See especially its issues of October 3 and 4, 1967; November 7 and 9, 1967; and December 2, 1968. The *Israel-itische Wochenblatt* of Zurich also was useful, especially in articles on October 13, 1967; November 24, 1967; May 10, 1968; and November 10, 1968. The *Washington Post* of December 13, 1967, and the *New York Times* of February 14, 1968, offered fine background reports. See also *Der Spiegel,* no. 41 (1967). Newspapers on November 30, 1968, summarized the convictions which took place the previous day.
2. Much of the material in this chapter dealing with the Einsatzgruppen and their activity at Babi Yar is taken from *Trials of War Criminals Before the Nuernberg Military Tribunals Under Control Council Law No. 10* (Green Series) (Washington, D.C., 1950), vol. IV. See especially pp. 147–49, 211–13, 526–30. See also Gerald Reitlinger, *The Final Solution* (London, 1961), pp. 233–35.

3. Anatoly Kuznetsov, *Babi Yar, A Documentary Novel,* trans. Jacob Guralsky (New York, 1967), p. 58. Since this version was based upon the *Yunost'* serialization, I have used it here.

4. Ilya Ehrenburg, *People and Life: 1891–1921* (New York, 1962), p. 307.

5. Cited in Joseph B. Schechtman, *Star in Eclipse: Russian Jewry Revisited* (New York, 1961), pp. 91–92.

6. *Ibid.,* p. 92.

7. *Ibid.,* p. 88.

8. Solomon M. Schwarz, *The Jews in the Soviet Union* (Syracuse, 1951), p. 335.

9. A. Sutzkever, "Ilya Ehrenburg," *Di Goldene Keit,* no. 61 (1967), p. 30.

10. I have discussed these plans in "What Monument to Babi Yar?" *Saturday Review,* February 3, 1968, p. 19.

11. *Literaturnaia gazeta,* March 9, 1949.

12. *Sputnik,* April, 1967.

13. It was published later as *A Precocious Autobiography,* trans. Andrew R. MacAndrew (New York, 1963), pp. 116–22.

14. See Patricia Blake, "New Voices in Russian Writing: Introduction," *Encounter,* no. 115 (April, 1963), p. 33. See also Patricia Blake and Max Hayward, eds., *Half-way to the Moon: New Writing from Russia* (New York, 1964), pp. 24–25.

15. *Pravda,* March 8, 1963.

16. "Russian Art and Anti-Semitism: Two Documents," *Commentary,* December, 1963, p. 434.

17. *Pravda,* March 8, 1963.

18. The monthly newsletter was entitled *Politicheskii dnevnik.* Excerpts were published in the *New York Times,* August 22, 1971.

19. William Korey, "Babi Yar Remembered," *Midstream,* March, 1969, p. 37.

20. *Ibid.*

21. The revised edition of the Kuznetsov work carries this episode. See A. Anatoli, *Babi Yar* (New York, 1970), p. 475.

22. Vyacheslav Chornovil, *The Chornovil Papers* (New York, n.d. [1968]), pp. 222–26.

23. *Samizdat* material reporting on his arrest and trial is in Moshe Decter, ed., *A Hero for Our Time: The Trial and Fate of Boris Kochubiyevsky* (New York, 1970). Kochubiyevsky was released and allowed to leave for Israel in late 1971.

24. *Ibid.,* pp. 22–23. See also *New York Times,* June 5, 1969.

CHAPTER 7

1. Alexander Werth, *Russia: Hopes and Fears* (New York, 1970), pp. 218–19.

2. *Jews in Eastern Europe,* vol. 3, no. 7 (November, 1967), pp. 70–111.

3. *Ibid.,* p. 125.

4. *American Jewish Year Book, 1968* (New York, 1969), vol. 69, p. 190. The cartoons are from *Krokodil,* nos. 18 and 19 (1967).

5. *Jews in Eastern Europe,* vol. 3, no. 7 (November, 1967), pp. 119–32.
6. *United Nations Security Council Official Records, 22nd Year,* S/PV. 1352 and S/PV. 1353 (9 June 1967).
7. This was stated to the UN correspondent of the *London Jewish Chronicle.* See *Jews in Eastern Europe,* vol. 3, no. 7 (November, 1967), p. 120.
8. For Kosygin's speech and other citations from the General Assembly debate, see *United Nations General Assembly Official Records, Fifth Emergency Special Session,* June–July 1967.
9. See *Jews in Eastern Europe,* vol. 3, no. 9 (May, 1968); and *Eastern Europe and the Middle East Crisis,* Institute of Jewish Affairs Background Paper no. 6 (London, 1967).

   The Jewish Communist press carried extensive reportage of the disagreements within the Communist world. I have drawn upon these press accounts in the preparation of this chapter. On Hungary, see the Yiddish Communist newspaper of Warsaw, Poland, *Folks-Shtimme,* July 15, 1967, and the New York Yiddish left-wing newspaper *Morning Freiheit,* July 16, 1967. On Czechoslovakia, see the Israeli Communist newspaper *Kol Ha-am,* July 24, 1967. Mniachko's statement is in *Kol Ha-am,* August 17, 1967. On Yugoslavia, see *Morning Freiheit,* July 18 and 25, 1967. On the Netherlands, see *Kol Ha-am,* August 11, 1967. The same issue carries the official statement of MAKI, the Israeli Communist Party. The attitudes of the Scandinavian left are reported in *Kol Ha-am,* July 20, 1967. On Austria, see *Kol Ha-am,* July 7, August 10, and November 22, 1967. On Italy, see the Israeli left-wing Socialist newspaper *Al-Hamishmar,* July 11, 1967, and *The World and the Middle East,* nos. 3/4/5 (July 17, 1967), p. 10. The poll of the French Communists is in *Kol Ha-am,* July 23, 1967, as is Leroy's statement. The attitudes of the French intellectual left are reported in the leftist New York journal *Jewish Currents,* July–August, 1967.
10. K. S. Karol, "A Marathon Talk with Castro," *New Statesman,* September 22, 1967, p. 34.
11. An exception was the East German Communist regime. At a press conference in Vienna on September 6, 1968, the well-known research investigator of Nazis Simon Wiesenthal stated that the East German press, in its treatment of the Six-Day War, displayed a "blatant difference" in its terminology as compared with that employed by other Communist states. The "expressions" and "terms" used in the East German press, he said, were "strongly reminiscent" of the Nazi press.
12. Sakharov, *Progress, Coexistence, and Intellectual Freedom* (New York, 1970), p. 39.
13. Medvedev's *samizdat* document.

CHAPTER 8

1. Norman Cohn, *Warrant for Genocide* (New York, 1966).
2. See Artur London, *The Confession* (New York, 1971), pp. 231–52; and

Paul Lendvai, *Anti-Semitism Without Jews* (New York, 1971), pp. 243–59.

3. It was written by Yury Ivanov, who, according to *Khronika* of August 31, 1969, is "the only specialist on Israel in the Central Committee." Formerly, he had worked in the African section of the Central Committee's apparatus but, after a reprimand for drunkenness, was "transferred to the exit section in which only KGB workers are employed."

4. The date of the article's appearance is October 4, 1967. It was written by Yevgeny Yevseev, who, along with Ivanov, is a principal author of anti-Jewish tracts.

5. As reported in *Pravda Ukrainy,* January 20, 1968.

6. According to *Khronika,* no. 9 (August 31, 1969), K. Ivanov is a pseudonym for V. Semenov, deputy minister of foreign affairs.

7. Lendvai, *op. cit.,* p. 10.

8. October 16, 1968.

9. *Times* (London), December 2, 1968.

10. *Jews in Eastern Europe,* vol. 4, no. 5 (August, 1970), p. 77. Also see the United Press International dispatch from Moscow, April 27, 1970.

11. *Pravda,* May 15, 1971.

12. United Nations Security Council, *Provisional Verbatim Record,* A/PV. 1582 (25 September 1971), pp. 128–30. Malik repeated the argument in the General Assembly on October 21, 1971. See United Nations General Assembly, *Provisional Verbatim Record,* A/PV. 1972 (21 October 1971), p. 52.

13. One exception is an article in *Pravda Ukrainy,* September 6, 1967. A certain Professor V. Tanchev wrote that "the Zionist conception of God-chosenness of the Jewish people . . . promises the Jews that they will rule over the world. . . ."

Besides Kichko, a certain N. A. Reshetnikov, in a book published in Moscow at the end of 1968, *The Bible and Modern Times,* also wrote on the "chosen people" concept as a source of racism. See *Jews in Eastern Europe,* vol. 4, no. 3 (January, 1970) p. 72.

CHAPTER 9

1. *Pravda,* March 5, 1970.

2. The Medvedev criticism is in his *samizdat* document on the Jewish question.

3. Soviet authorities were only too anxious to show that Soviet Jews are assimilating. Moreover, there may very well have been anxiety in official circles that the census data might show that the Russians constituted a minority of the total population. The birth-rate of non-Russian nationalities in Central Asia was increasing at a faster rate than the Russian nationality. In terms of the policy of encouraging assimilation to Russian culture generally, it would have been unseemly should the census data show a minority of Russians in the Soviet state. As it was, the data

indicated that only 53 per cent of the total population considered themselves Russians.

4. *Izvestiia,* April 17, 1971. The other nationalities which declined in numbers were Poles, Mordvinians, Finns, Karelians, Czechs, and Slovaks.
5. L. N. Terenteva, "Opredelenie svoiei natsional'noi prinadlezhnosti," *Sovetskaia etnografia,* no. 3 (1969), pp. 20–30.
6. M. V. Kurman and I. V. Lebedinskii, *Naselenie bol'shogo sotsialisticheskogo goroda* (Moscow, 1968). As cited by John Armstrong, "Soviet Foreign Policy and Anti-Semitism," *op. cit.,* p. 64.
7. *Vestnik statistiki,* no. 12 (December, 1968), p. 49.
8. Nove and Newth, "The Jewish Population: Demographic Trends and Occupation Patterns," in Lionel Kochan, ed., *The Jews in Soviet Russia since 1917* (London, 1970), pp. 130, 143–44.
9. Armstrong, "Soviet Foreign Policy and Anti-Semitism," in *Perspectives on Soviet Jewry* (New York, 1971), p. 65.
10. Nove and Newth, *op. cit.,* pp. 143–44. According to a demographer writing in *Izvestiia* (May 9, 1971), male Jews in the Ukraine during 1969 married Jewish females only in 63 per cent of the cases.
11. This is hypothesized by Nove and Newth, *op. cit.,* p. 144. They estimate that there were more than 2.5 million Soviet Jewish losses during World War II, four times greater than the losses suffered by the Soviet population as a whole (p. 142).
12. Ivor J. Millman, *Soviet Jewry in the Census of 1970,* Institute of Jewish Affairs Background Paper no. 21 (London, 1971).
13. *Atlas narodov mira* (Moscow, 1964), p. 158.
14. *New York Times,* April 17, 1971. It quotes "a recently-published" Novosti pamphlet as saying that "by now there are about three million" Jews in the USSR. More significant, the leading Soviet Jewish apologist, Aron Vergelis, wrote an article for *Druzhba narodov,* no. 4 (April, 1971), pp. 204–21, the same month as the census figures appeared, in which he said, "I am one of the three million Jews who live in the Soviet Union." The article was entitled "Dvadtsat' dnei v Amerike."
15. See Aron Boyarsky's article in *Izvestiia,* May 7, 1971, and Lev Volodarsky's article in *Pravda,* May 7, 1971.
16. Maurice Friedberg, "Why Some Soviet Jews Are Getting Out," *National Jewish Monthly,* November, 1971, pp. 40–45.
17. Medvedev takes note of this phenomenon in his *samizdat* document.
18. Yakov Kantor, "Aynike Bamerkungen un Oisfiren tsu di Fareffentlichte Sachhakalen fun der Folks-tselung in Ratenverband dem 15 Yanuar, 1959," *Bleter far Geshichte* (Warsaw, 1962–63), vol. 15, pp. 146–47.
19. I. Kon, "Dialektika razvitiia natsii," *Novyi mir,* no. 13 (1970), p. 145.
20. Elie Wiesel, *The Jews of Silence* (New York, 1966).
21. This was noted especially in the Kishinev trial of June, 1971.
22. I have dealt with this subject in the *New York Times,* January 22, 1971. During 1971, the number of signers of a petition would approach or exceed one thousand.

UN Secretary-General U Thant revealed that he had received petitions from some eight hundred Soviet Jews. He did all within his power "to help" the signers and was, therefore, "gratified" that more than four hundred of the signers eventually reached Israel. See United Nations *Press Release* SG/SM/1539 (24 September 1971).

23. I have dealt with this subject in "Soviet Dissent Goes Abroad," *Progressive,* February, 1970, pp. 31–35.
24. A. I. Kholmogorov, *Internatsional'nye cherty sovetskikh natsii* (Moscow, 1970), pp. 68, 175.
25. Moshe Decter, *Redemption! Jewish Freedom Letters from Russia* (New York, 1970), p. 11.
26. See *ibid.,* p. 31. According to the 1970 census, there are fifty-five thousand Jews in Georgia, an increase of three thousand over 1959. The proportion of the nearly thirteen thousand Jews who emigrated from the USSR to Israel during 1971 is more than one-third.
27. *Ibid.,* pp. 34–35.
28. Moshe Decter, ed., *A Hero for Our Time: The Trial and Fate of Boris Kochubiyevsky,* p. 33. The title of Kochubiyevsky's essay was "Why I Am a Zionist." A year earlier, in June, 1967, he told a factory meeting: "And who has made me into a Zionist? *Pravda, Izvestiia* and *Komsomolskaya Pravda.* The Soviet press, with its unrestrained anti-Semitic campaign, has educated me to be a Zionist. . . ." See *Jewish Chronicle* (London), October 30, 1970.
29. From Medvedev's *samizdat* document.
30. *Ibid.* What Medvedev bases his estimates upon is not made clear.
31. This figure was suggested by a prominent and knowledgeable Moscow activist, Vitaly Svechinsky.
32. A copy of this memorandum is in my possession.

CHAPTER 10

1. José D. Inglés, *Study of Discrimination in Respect of the Right of Everyone to Leave Any Country, Including His Own, and to Return to His Country* (United Nations, 1963).
2. *Ibid.,* p. 59.
3. *Ibid.,* p. 15.
4. *Ibid.,* p. 17.
5. *Ibid.,* pp. 64–73.
6. *Montreal Statement.* Adopted by the Assembly on Human Rights, Montreal, March, 1968. However, within the USSR, copies of the Universal Declaration of Human Rights are rarely found, according to information provided me in January, 1972, by Boris Tsukerman, who had been legal adviser to the unofficial Committee on Human Rights of the Soviet Union (the Sakharov-Chalidze group). A letter from prominent dissenter Pyotr Grigorenko to Procurator Rudenko on December 4, 1968, relates that his copy of the Universal Declaration was confiscated by the KGB when they searched his home. He stated that the number of

copies published was "tiny" and "only for the use of jurists." See Abraham Brumberg, ed., *In Quest of Justice* (New York, 1970), p. 366.

7. See William Korey, "The Key to Human Rights—Implementation," *International Conciliation,* November, 1968, pp. 7–8.

8. *Economic and Social Council Official Records,* 34th Sess., 1962, Suppl. no. 8 (E/3616/Rev. 1), para. 105.

9. United Nations Sub-Commission on Prevention of Discrimination and Protection of Minorities, Conference Room Paper no. 85/Rev. 1 (7 February 1963).

10. Inglés, *op. cit.,* p. 85.

11. *Ibid.*

12. *Ibid.,* p. 87.

13. *Pravda,* July 9, 1960.

14. The exchange is carried in Co-ordinating Board of Jewish Organizations, *Memorandum on Discrimination in the Matter of the Right of Everyone to Leave Any Country, Including His Own, and to Return to His Country,* pp. 5–6. Submitted to the United Nations Sub-Commission on Prevention of Discrimination and Protection of Minorities, October, 1960.

15. *Ibid.,* p. 17.

16. *Literaturnaia gazeta,* April 29, 1958.

17. Discussed in the memorandum of the Co-ordinating Board of Jewish Organizations, *op. cit.,* p. 10.

18. *Réalités,* no. 136 (May, 1957), p. 67.

19. *Promoting Enduring Peace* (West Haven, Conn., n.d. [1957]); and *The Churchman,* April, 1960. The first source also went by the title *Report of the American-European Seminar on the U.S.S.R.*

20. Eleanor Roosevelt's biographer Joseph Lash reported the conversation in a letter to the *New York Times,* December 17, 1970.

21. *Pravda,* July 9, 1960.

22. *New York Times,* August 9, 1960.

23. See *Iskhod,* no. 1; and Richard Cohen, ed., *Let My People Go!* (New York, 1971), pp. 212–17.

24. See the document entitled "Is the Desire for National Identity a Crime? The Meaning of Soviet Anti-Zionism," prepared for the Commission of Inquiry on the Rights of Soviet Jews on June 22, 1971. Pp. 15–17 discuss the subject.

25. *Pravda,* March 5, 1970.

26. As reported by the UN correspondent of the *Jewish Chronicle* (London).

27. Quoted in the *Jerusalem Post,* March 21, 1971.

28. *Ibid.* In December, 1971, the Lebanese premier again expressed concern to a visiting Soviet delegation, saying that "every new Jew who arrives in Israel is more dangerous than a tank, cannon, or fighter plane." The head of the Soviet delegation assured the Arab leader that the number of Soviet Jews expressing a desire to go to Israel is not large, and that, besides, they "are unfit to carry weapons." The Soviet ambassador to

Lebanon went on to comment that his government "has been careful that [Jewish] emigration did not bring any harm to our friends the Arab states." See *New York Times,* December 18, 1971.

29. *Khrushchev Remembers,* introduction, commentary, and notes by Edward Crankshaw, translated and edited by Strobe Talbott (Boston, 1970), pp. 522–25.

30. For a detailed, though not fully accurate, breakdown of figures on emigration from the USSR during 1971, see the report of an American foreign correspondent in Moscow in the *Los Angeles Times,* January 6, 1972.

The Washington correspondent of the Israeli newspaper *Haaretz,* following an interview with an unnamed Soviet diplomat in the U.S., cabled his newspaper on January 12, 1972, that the diplomat said: "We are going to let go all those wishing to emigrate except for those who may add to Israel military potential and those who are in sensitive positions in USSR." The diplomat even surmised that the thirty-six thousand figure might turn out to be "too low."

That Jewish scientists in the USSR were having difficulty in obtaining exit visas was evidenced by an appeal signed in January, 1972, by nine of them and sent to leading international scientific bodies. Noting that they had been fired from their jobs after they applied for exit visas, they wrote that "the Soviet authorities particularly tried to oppose the departure of professional people," and that this is "amoral and contrary to the letter and spirit of international agreements and declarations." See *Jewish Telegraphic Agency,* January 14, 1972.

CHAPTER 11

1. An English translation of this transcript was prepared as a supplement to the journal *Soviet Jewish Affairs,* no. 1 (June, 1971). Unfortunately, no such detailed transcript is available for the second Leningrad trial. An English summary of the unofficial account can be found in *Jews in Eastern Europe,* vol. 4, no. 7 (November, 1971), pp. 51–68. The English translation of an extensive Riga trial transcript is in the same journal, pp. 93–159.

Aside from the regular, extremely spotty Soviet press reportage of the trials, *Literaturnaia gazeta,* July 7, 1971, carried selected quotations from the defendants in the second Leningrad trial. The selections were carefully chosen with the obvious intent of offsetting the negative world reaction to the various legal proceedings.

A useful legal analysis of the trials was prepared by René Beermann, a specialist on Soviet law, for *Soviet Jewish Affairs,* no. 2 (November, 1971), pp. 3–25.

An interview with the former editor of *Iskhod,* Viktor Fedoseyev, reveals how the transcript of the first trial was prepared. It was drawn from four separate courtroom reports based on surreptitious recordings, shorthand notes, and memorized portions of the proceedings committed to paper immediately afterward. See the *Jerusalem Post,* March 28, 1972.

2. Dr. Pinkhas Khnokh, the brother of defendant Leib Khnokh, contended that KGB provocation was an essential feature of the hijacking plan. He had arrived in Israel in April, 1971. At a press conference in Israel in December, Dr. Khnokh said that Tolstikov, the Leningrad Party boss, had told Party activists six months before the arrests: "A Zionist organization exists in our country. But do not worry: at a suitable time and place we will strike and destroy them." In Dr. Khnokh's view, the KGB had "well prepared" the "ground" for the hijacking attempt. See *Jerusalem Post,* December 15, 1971.

   At a Commission of Inquiry on the Rights of Soviet Jews, held in New York on June 22, 1971, a witness, Aleksander Gittelson, who had been at Leningrad State University during 1970 working on his doctorate, testified that he had been apprised of a statement made by Tolstikov similar to the one which Dr. Khnokh attributed to him.

3. This was related to me by Professor Mikhail Zand in September, 1971.

4. A "strict regime" is particularly harsh in such matters as receiving food parcels, letters and visits, nature of work, right to buy necessities in the camp shop, and degree of confinement. An "intensified regime" is less severe, while a "special regime" is more severe.

5. *Jews in Eastern Europe,* vol. 4, no. 6 (April, 1971), p. 24.

6. *Khronika,* no. 17 (December 31, 1970).

7. *Ibid.*

CHAPTER 12

1. These can be found in *Iskhod,* no. 4.

2. *Iskhod,* no. 2.

3. *Jews in Eastern Europe,* vol. 4, no. 7 (November, 1971) p. 5.

4. A *samizdat* document on the proceedings of the later Riga trial indicates that 1966 was the year of the creation of the Leningrad group as a formal group.

5. *New York Times,* May 16, 1971 (part E).

6. *Iskhod,* no. 2.

7. The Leningrad petition is in *Iskhod,* no. 2.

8. It is summarized in Richard Cohen, ed., *Let My People Go!* (New York, 1971), pp. 245–71.

9. *New York Times,* May 23, 1971. The letter was dated May 17.

10. Later, the *New York Times* correspondent in Moscow stated: "Evidence at the trials, as reported by Tass earlier, indicated that the machine, a photocopier, had never been put into operation." See *New York Times,* July 1, 1971.

11. According to the *Jewish Chronicle* (London), July 23, 1971, the defendants were "tricked by the prosecution into pleading guilty at their trial." The prosecutor was said to have promised them "light, purely symbolic prison sentences" if "they would admit their guilt." The *Chronicle's* story was said to have been based upon "unimpeachable sources."

12. Moreover, his parents wrote a letter to *Leningradskaia pravda* (May 14, 1971), which blamed "the vile role of foreign Zionist provocateurs" for the plight of their son.
13. See *Jews in Eastern Europe,* vol. 4, no. 7 (November, 1971), pp. 160–84.
14. A letter written by Hillel Shur to the Presidium of the Supreme Soviet of the USSR on October 25, 1971 disclosed that the alleged "slanderous" literature was a critical element in the pre-trial investigation. He quotes from a KGB document which referred to materials in the possession of Voloshin. They included three volumes of the pre-revolutionary *Yevreiskaia entsiklopedia,* Shimon Dubnov's *History of the Jews in Europe* (vol. 1), published in Riga in 1936, and three Hebrew grammar books published in Israel. The KGB investigator was quoted as saying that this material is "nationalistic and Zionist in content" and that it therefore would be held as "material evidence" in the case. Shur notes that both the encyclopedia and the history book were purchased in a Soviet bookstore selling used books and, therefore, could hardly be regarded as "slanderous," let alone subversive, material.
15. *Sovietskaia Moldavia,* June 24, 1971.

CHAPTER 13

1. The eyewitness was her mother, Rivka, who wrote the description for the *New York Times,* May 20, 1971.
2. *Jewish Observer and Middle East Review,* June 4, 1971, p. 9.
3. The episode is recounted by Rivka Aleksandrovich in the *New York Times,* May 20, 1971.
4. An English translation appears in *Jews in Eastern Europe,* vol. 4, no. 7 (November, 1971), pp. 93–159.
5. A copy of *Iton Bet* reached here in December, 1971.
6. Zhores A. Medvedev and Roy A. Medvedev, *A Question of Madness* (New York, 1971), pp. 214–15. This section of the book was written by Roy Medvedev. One "legal commentary" which he cited is M. P. Mikhailov and V. V. Nazarov, *Ideological Sabotage—A Weapon of Imperialism* (Moscow, 1969). It is not clear whether this source was drawn upon by Roy Medvedev as the "legal commentary" specifically with reference to Article 70.

CHAPTER 14

1. The translation is in the *Saturday Review,* September 18, 1971, p. 31.
2. Its bylaws were published in the *Saturday Review,* January 16, 1971, p. 24.
3. *Iskhod,* no. 4, carries their statements.
4. *New York Times,* October 7, 1971.
5. Svetlana Alliluyeva, *Only One Year* (New York, 1969), p. 153.
6. For a vivid illustration of this Judophilia, especially involving Yevtushenko and his colleagues, see Patricia Blake, "New Voices in

Russian Writing: Introduction," *Encounter,* no. 115 (April, 1963), pp. 34–35.

7. Salo W. Baron, *The Russian Jew under Tsars and Soviets* (New York, 1964), p. 164.

8. *Ibid.,* p. 61.

9. *Ibid.,* p. 70.

10. *Ibid.*

11. Boris Souvarine, "Gorky, Censorship, and the Jews," *Dissent,* Winter, 1965, pp. 81–83.

12. Maurice Samuel, *Blood Accusation: The Strange History of the Beiliss Case* (New York, 1966), p. 242.

13. *Ibid.,* p. 243.

14. Some of the *samizdat* material on the Kukuy case is in *Jews in Eastern Europe,* vol. 4, no. 7 (November, 1971), pp. 196–205.

15. *Khronika,* no. 21.

16. On the Palatnik case, see *Jews in Eastern Europe,* vol. 4, no. 7 (November, 1971), pp. 185–96.

17. Chukovskaya's protest is covered in the *New York Times,* October 11, 1971.

18. The episode is discussed in William Korey, "Soviet Dissent Goes Abroad," *Progressive,* February, 1970, pp. 31–35.

19. I am indebted to Professor Zand for this typology. He adds a fourth, the neo-Christians, in which group he includes Aleksander Solzhenitsyn. See the text of his lecture at Columbia University on October 6, 1971, in *Soviet Jewry Today,* vol. 1, no. 1 (November, 1971).

20. The reference here and the subsequent quotes are from his *samizdat* document.

21. Its Russian title is *Yevreiskii vopros v SSSR* (Tezisy). Zand told me that he was the author when he was in the U.S. in September, 1971.

22. Zhores A. Medvedev and Roy A. Medvedev, *A Question of Madness* (New York, 1971), p. 195. Sometimes ethnic origin has to be made clear in order to produce the necessary "trouble." Thus, when Soviet playwright Aleksander Galich, in late December, 1971, was severely censured by the Moscow branch of the Union of Writers, prior to his being excluded from that body, he was repeatedly addressed as "Comrade Ginzburg," his real name. See the *New York Times,* February 12, 1972.

23. The author has a copy in his possession.

24. *Jewish Chronicle* (London), October 22, 1971.

25. What transpired at the meeting is partly recorded by the *Jewish Telegraphic Agency,* October 22, 1971. A fuller report was obtained in Paris from participants. The Soviet Embassy in France made available an official stenographic account of the questions and answers.

CHAPTER 15

1. My view is supported by interviews with Soviet Jewish emigrants conducted by Dr. Zev Katz of the Center for International Studies at the Massachusetts Institute of Technology. See his *The New Nationalism in the USSR: Its Impact on the Jews.* Mimeo. (Cambridge, Mass., November, 1972).
2. Gershovich was allowed to leave in November, 1972.
3. The Markishes were permitted exit visas in November, 1972.
4. Rutman, Branover, and Yakhot were among those permitted to leave the USSR in the late fall of 1972.
5. Indeed, Deputy Minister of Interior Boris Shumilin, on December 29, 1972, announced in Novosti a major concession. Men who have reached the age of sixty and women who have reached the age of fifty-five are to be exempt from payment of the "diploma taxes." In addition, a sliding scale of payments corresponding with the amount of work performed for the state was introduced. Men who have worked 25, 15, and 8 years (and women who have worked 20, 12, and 6 years) will receive, respectively, percentage reductions totaling 75, 50, and 25. A principle advocated by Soviet activists was thus accorded official recognition. As put by Shumilin: "In repaying the costs for education, strict account is taken of one's length of work." Finally, the Soviet official said that those who have studied at night are to receive a 50 per cent reduction, and those who have taken correspondence courses are to pay 25 per cent less.

   Still, Shumilin emphasized that "restrictions" will continue to be applied "to those who have certain military training or by the nature of their work are connected with jobs affecting state interests." At a meeting on October 26, 1972, which he and other top officials of the Ministry of Interior and of OVIR had with approximately a hundred Jews headed by the scientist A. Voronel and several activists, Shumilin insisted upon maintaining restrictions in matters involving "the protection of state interests." A transcript of the one-hour-long discussion indicates that the Jewish spokesmen demanded that the Soviet Government publish the specifics on restrictions so that the applicants for exit visas will know what are the obstacles in their path. Disclosure would also permit them to appeal against arbitrary decisions. The Soviet officials adamantly rejected the demand.

   Soviet authorities finally published the text of the August 3 decree in the Bulletin of the Supreme Soviet, dated December 27, 1972, which appeared on January 20, 1973. In a footnote, the Bulletin explained that the specific schedule of new fees (which Shumilin had already disclosed through Novosti) would be published in 1973 in the Collection of Decrees of the Government of the USSR.

   For Jews, both in and out of the Soviet Union, the concessions provided by the graduated scale which took partial account of the years of work given by applicants for exit visas were declared to be unacceptable. A statement circulated by Jews in Moscow in January emphasized that the new schedule of exit taxes was still far beyond the financial capacity of most educated Soviet citizens. A young engineer or physician who had worked 12 to 14 years would still be required to pay 6,000 rubles, an amount that represents his total earnings for 5 to 6 years "assuming he does not use a kopeck for food, for his apartment or for living expenses." The author of the statement, retired journalist Grigory I. Teitelbaum, estimated that an engineer or doctor would be required to work more than 25 years in order to accumulate the funds necessary to pay for an exit visa.

Arbitrariness continued, accompanied by stepped-up harassment of militants. On December 27, seven prominent Jewish activists held a press conference in Moscow in which they described the sudden arrests of 63 Jews from Moscow, Leningrad, Kiev, Kharkov, Riga, and Novosibirsk during the week before Christmas. Besides arrests they also noted the application of other forms of "repressions." In a written statement, the activists observed that the authorities are striving "to scare other Jews from the struggle for emigration" even as they offer concessions "to calm down gullible Western trading partners."

6. In this connection, *Khronika*, no. 27 (October 15, 1972), notes that Professor Mikhail Zand, Dr. Meir Gelfond, and one Meniker had sent on May 26, 1972, a notarized statement to USSR Procurator-General Rudenko calling into question the judicial decision rendered in the first Leningrad trial. Their statement recalled that Mendelevich had been charged with writing the "incriminating" articles "About Assimilation" and "The Jews Break Their Silence," and that Khnokh had been identified in the trial as having in his possession the proclamation "Your Native Tongue" with allegedly "anti-Soviet contents." The sworn affidavit emphasized that Zand was the author of the first article; that he was the author of the first part of the second article, and that the author of the second part of this article wasn't Mendelevich but rather an unnamed person known to the three signers; and that Zand was the author of the third article which did "not have an anti-Soviet character." The sworn statement contended that these disclosures placed "under doubt the objectivity of the [first Leningrad] trial."

7. While Chalidze was in the United States in December, 1972, Soviet authorities deprived him of his passport, thereby making him stateless.

Index